TILL TAUGHT BY PAIN

Susan Coventry

Regal House Publishing

Published by
Regal House Publishing, LLC
Raleigh, NC 27605

ISBN -13 (paperback): 9781646036325
ISBN -13 (epub): 9781646036332
Library of Congress Control Number: 2024951372
Cover images and design by © studiochi.art

Printed in the United States of America

Regal House Publishing, LLC
https://regalhousepublishing.com

Praise for *Till Taught by Pain*

"A true-to-life love story that illuminates an intriguing woman's life, the life of her brilliant physician husband, and the wretched secret they share. The author brings deft insights and personal knowledge of medicine to this tale of talent, ambition, obsession, and powerlessness. Meticulously researched and rendered in compelling dual narratives, *Till Taught by Pain* is the style of historical novel I most admire: one that holds true to the history and the real characters underpinning it while pulling the reader magically into their world. Susan Coventry is a master of the form."

—Rilla Askew, author of *Prize for the Fire*

"A fascinating novel about one of America's greatest and most inventive surgeons and his lifelong struggle with drug dependency. Told through his point of view and his wife's, it's a moving testament to love, patience and the overwhelming grip of addiction."

—Jennie Fields, author of *Atomic Love* and *The Age of Desire*

"Susan Coventry's compelling novel *Till Taught by Pain* plunges us into the world of medicine in New York City and Baltimore's new Johns Hopkins Hospital in the 1880s and the emergence of a brilliant young doctor who, while researching cocaine as a local anesthetic, becomes addicted first to it and then morphine. Based on history and drawing from diaries and letters long locked away, Dr. William Halsted is an unforgettable character, marching through the shadows of early operating and research rooms, alternatingly making brilliant strides, and then once again locked in his own agonizing darkness. Even the support of his physician friends and the love of Halsted's clear-minded and devoted head nurse who becomes his wife, cannot entirely defeat the call of his secret syringes. An utterly engrossing story of a small group of people in medicine well over a hundred years ago. I was so sorry when the story ended, not wanting to leave the company of this difficult doctor who achieved the near perfection he sought in the operating room but never in himself."

—Stephanie Cowell, author of *The Boy in the Rain*, *Claude & Camille,* and *The Physician of London*. Winner of an American Book Award.

"With the skill of a surgeon, Susan Coventry stitches together an in-depth historical fiction novel about Dr. William Halsted, a brilliant physician whose many contributions to modern medicine were remarkable. Coventry infuses the complicated characters of Halsted and his wife Caroline with authentic love and heart-rending frustration. Anyone who's dealt with addiction or who's loved someone struggling with addiction will find an honest, yet compassionate portrait of a gifted man, who though he soared so high, might have achieved even more."

—Tracey D. Buchanan, author of *Toward the Corner of Mercy and Peace*

"This elegant double-biography, in the form of a novel, evokes the world of the unsung heroes who pioneered modern surgery. Along the way, *Till Taught by Pain* intelligently and fascinatingly explores the complexities of drug addiction in the context of ambition and a challenging but ultimately redemptive marriage."

—Mitchell James Kaplan, author of *By Fire, By Water*, *Rhapsody: A Novel*, and *Into the Unbounded Night*

To Mom and Dad

Prologue

1922, October

Baltimore, Maryland

1201 Eutaw Place, Baltimore, MD
October 16, 1922

Dear Dr. Welch,
Thank you for your letter and for the trouble you have taken trying to satisfy Dr. Halsted's sisters. As you say, the memories that I have are what stay with me and the hours between seven and half past eight when we would sit together are the most lonesome of the whole 24 hours…

—Caroline Hampton Halsted to Dr. W. H. Welch, October 1922

My vision blurred. Why was I doing this? No one had ever accused me of being a hysterical woman. I was never outwardly emotional; yet, here I was, tapping my private pain onto the keys of William's typewriter to burden his most steadfast friend with my grief. Hadn't Dr. Welch done enough for William over the years? Must he now also console the widow? An impossible task.

The letter would have to wait until I was more self-composed. I shouldn't be dwelling on how empty the hours were when I had tasks to fill them. If William were here, he would give me one of those wry looks. I could see him doing it.

"Oh, William."

Swiping the back of my hand over my eyes, I cleared away both tears and my late husband's image and, instead, regarded his study. *Off limits.* It had always been off limits. I never bothered him here. This was where he lost himself in his work—that fiction we'd told one another, not with words but with the lack of them. The neat chaos supported the story: journals bearing snips of blue paper as markers, stacked into orderly piles; one basket of correspondence to answer and one for his secretary to file; a draft of the paper he'd been struggling with, more crossed out on the page than remained; scattered books. And downstairs in his library, there were case files, laboratory notes, and more shelves and shelves and shelves of books and journals.

I moved to the window to pull back the drapes. Drawing in a breath, I could still smell tobacco, a distinctly William smell. It was twined down into the antique furnishings, the drapes, and the oriental carpet, too deep to ever dissipate. How sad I could not relish it, but it stank.

It was quiet enough to hear the soft tick of his Gustav Becker wall clock, a gift from a German colleague. The beats sounded slow, as though minutes must now crawl by to rebalance time itself after the hours had slipped away from us so quickly.

Over the past year, William had determined more than once to sort through the accumulation of a busy, productive lifetime, but he was distracted from so desolate a task by the more urgent call to complete what he had started, to move on to more. He'd been so purposeful. All his life, he had been purposeful. That's what people would remember. Wouldn't they?

Perhaps not his sisters. Ridiculous creatures. With their *Billy would want such-and-such* and *oh, we have to do this-and-that.* Billy? In the end, I'd thrown up my hands. I was only a wife; I wasn't about to argue with sisters. But neither would I trek up to New York to put him into a grave in the city he'd left all those years ago. I refused to see him buried under some hideously sentimental headstone with claptrap about angels. Thank God for Dr. Welch.

Dr. Halsted always said his sisters knew nothing about science and cared less. Mrs. Halsted, with your permission, I'll order the headstone.

He'd done it too:

William Stewart Halsted, M.D.
September 23, 1852-September 7, 1922
Professor of Surgery in the Johns Hopkins Hospital

Elegantly simple. William would have approved. And his sisters would not argue with the imposing Dr. Welch.

I would have to ask him what should be preserved for the university and the medical library. William's friend Dr. Crowe said the books and journals were worth quite a bit and I should sell them. But William left me ridiculously well provided for. Surely, he expected me to *give* the books to the school.

More worrisome was what to do with all the accumulated paper.

Someone—one of William's acolytes—would start nosing about, intent upon memorializing him. Would William prefer that only his published work survive to represent him? All this unfinished business, correspondence, notes for speeches—would it embarrass him to have people pawing through it? Would collected bits from William's life—not only journal articles but private letters, personal recollections, half-remembered anecdotes—be pieced together like a jigsaw puzzle to summate the man he'd been? William would hate that. Ill-fitting pieces ruined a puzzle, and not all William's pieces fit tidily.

He had to trust me to sift through the leavings, tidying them for posterity, before someone from the university arrived to cart all his precious papers away.

Precious papers—I had my own boxful back at High Hampton. My heart thudded painfully and heat rose to my face; William could write a pretty letter. I'd always intended to put a flame to them. One day. To keep them from a would-be biographer's hands.

Lucy would have to do it. I couldn't travel anywhere now. There was too much to do. Other things more damning to William's dignity than love letters might still be locked away in drawers and cabinets. I had to be the one to find them.

William would want his secrets, his untidy pieces, buried with his ashes.

PART ONE

Addict: (a-dikt') v.t. 1. To devote or give up, as to a habit or occupation; apply habitually or sedulously.

—*The Century Dictionary*: an encyclopedic lexicon of the English Language, Century Company, 1889-1891

1

1884, October

New York City, New York

THE OPHTHALMOLOGICAL CONGRESS IN HEIDELBERG

The usual Ophthalinological Congress in Heidelberg has just closed its session and a few cursory notes at this early date may interest some readers… Perhaps the most notable thing presented was the exhibition to the Congress upon one of the patients of the Heidelberg Eye Clinic of the extraordinary anaesthetic power which a two percent solution of muriate of cocaine has upon the cornea and conjunctiva when it is dropped into the eye—the discovery by Dr. Koller.

It remains however to investigate all the characteristics of this substance, and we may yet find that there is a shadow side as well as a brilliant side in the discovery.

—Dr. Henry Noyes, *The Medical Record,* Vol 26, No. 15, October 11, 1884

❧

Dr. William Stewart Halsted plucked the top hat from his head and unbuttoned his coat as he slipped inside Oskaar's, a seedy little tavern a short walk from Roosevelt Hospital. His friends and fellow surgeons, Dr. Frank Hartley and Dr. Richard Hall, favored the place because the food was cheap and the beer decent. Halsted settled for its convenience. The faculty of his teaching clinic for medical students needed a quick organizational discussion of schedules—supposedly—but mostly they were getting together for luncheon and fellowship. After last night's Surgical Society meeting, Halsted thought he could do without the fellowship. He'd stirred up a hornet's nest with his observations on Markoe's case presentation and wasn't in the mood for Hall's mockery.

The proprietor nodded a greeting and jerked his head toward the back where the doctors generally met. Their table was open. Hidden in the corner, two of its sides were cramped by walls. Usually the last to arrive, he'd be stuck between table and wall. Not today.

"A bowl of soup?" he said, then made his way to the roomiest seat, where he pulled off his gloves and propped his pearl-handled cane. He carried a medical journal and a newspaper tucked under his arm. He was early and prepared to wait.

Early, because he had canceled the surgery scheduled for him that morning. A forty-two-year-old man had a tumor beneath his cheekbone, less than a centimeter, that was reportedly excruciatingly painful. It looked vascular. Halsted didn't think it would take twenty minutes to remove it if he could sedate him. But the man had to weigh four hundred pounds; the risk of asphyxiation under anesthesia was too great.

He skimmed the newspaper but saw nothing about the family's company, so he set it aside. He didn't know why he kept looking for something he didn't want to see. Damn it. He couldn't stop seeing the headline that had been splashed across *The Brooklyn Daily Eagle* back in July:

Halsted, Haines and Co. Go Under For Two Millions.
The Effect on the New York Dry Goods Trade—A List of Preferred Creditors. The Crash Expected by the Dealers.

The Halsted name—dragged through the mud.

In its heyday, the family business, importers and jobbers of dry goods, had been lucrative enough to raise the Halsteds to the pinnacle of New York society. That was with grandfather at the helm. Father's mismanagement, his shenanigans, had run the company into the ground.

Halsted wanted no part of the tarnishing of the family reputation, but he was in it up to the neck. A Yale education, the College of Physicians and Surgeons, a study tour of Europe—he'd spent his father's money readily enough. Worse, he had recently accepted a ten-thousand-dollar loan from his younger brother Dick to build a dispensary at Bellevue Hospital. He could not abide the filthy condition of the surgical theater, but when he asked the administration to build a separate structure where asepsis could be maintained, they pled poverty, as if cleanliness was a luxury. They did, however, permit him to construct his own. So, he tapped his Wall Street connection, his financial genius brother, without realizing how deep in their father's mire Dick was.

Ten grand of filthy money to build a clean surgical suite. Ha! He hoped the newspapers wouldn't get wind of that.

Oskaar put a bowl of soup in front of him along with a stein of beer he hadn't ordered.

"Thank you."

The soup was generally edible. The meat platters looked like something he might have found in Welch's pathology lab. Which had never stopped Welch from ordering them. If only the man had not sailed for Germany a month ago for a refresher course in true medical scholarship before starting his new position. Halsted would have loved to hear what he thought of Markoe's presentation last night. If Welch had done the autopsy, they might have learned something from the case. It was a tough blow, losing him to Baltimore. Baltimore! There was nothing for a man of science in Baltimore. Little enough in New York.

"Your friends are coming?" Oskaar sounded impatient, as usual, even though the room was half-empty. Or perhaps it was just that German efficiency.

"Yes. They'll be here soon."

Oskaar would notice when they arrived. They could not be missed or mistaken. Hall was short, dark, and had the affectation of wearing bright-colored socks and trousers hemmed an eighth of an inch too short. Hartley had red hair—no more needed be said.

Halsted opened the journal and turned to the brief reports. He read the one from Noyes. Then he read it again. He didn't notice his colleagues approaching until they sat in their chairs.

"I'm sorry I missed it last night," Hartley greeted him, laughing. "I heard it was quite a performance." He mimicked Halsted's lecturing voice. "'Given that the arm is on the table, unconnected to the patient, I don't consider it a well-chosen example of an acceptably healed wound.'"

"I didn't say that out loud."

"Loud enough," Hall said, nudging his arm. "Better order more than that. You're a bear when you're hungry. You should've eaten something before the meeting."

"I meant to."

He didn't divulge that when he had gone home to change clothes beforehand, he came across his housemate on the floor, surrounded by vomit. He cleaned him up, put him to bed, and said he would sit with him. McBride bit his head off, said he'd be damned if he needed coddling. It wasn't coddling to care for a sick man.

Welch had been to the house just before leaving New York. He took one look at Tom McBride and ordered him back to Carlsbad to take the waters again. But McBride laughed and said he was not yet at the point of needing a pathologist's diagnosis. He insisted it was nothing. A touch of enteritis. A touch of gout. The man had always excoriated physicians who self-diagnosed. God! He'd raged at Halsted for recklessness when he operated on his own mother for gallstones, laying her out on her kitchen table at two o'clock in the morning.

It wasn't enteritis. It was Bright's disease—inflammation of the kidney. That was Halsted's diagnosis. Welch's too. McBride refused to hear it.

He cleared his throat. "I apologized to Markoe. I wasn't criticizing his use of catgut."

"You were." Hall signaled to the proprietor. "I'll have the soup. And a mug of that beer." Hartley ordered the same. When Oskaar walked away, Hall continued. "You were. But that presentation was tripe. What were you reading when we came in? Your eyes were like saucers."

"Oh!" His excitement flooded back in a rush. He pushed the journal toward his friend. "Look at Noyes' report. What do you see?"

Hall read it through.

"I see that I should have been an ophthalmologist. Everyone will now want their cataracts operated upon. Unless there is a…" He glanced at the report. "A shadow side."

"Let me see," Hartley said, reaching for the journal.

"It could revolutionize surgery," Halsted said. "Think. What if we didn't have to use ether or chloroform for routine surgery? If we could numb only the body part we need to cut? Just this morning, I had to cancel surgery on a man I didn't dare put under."

"What'll you do?" Hartley asked. "Rub some of this two percent cocaine on the skin?"

"Skin isn't permeable. The conjunctiva is a comparable sieve. Maybe injections?"

Hall shook his head. "If you plan to inject this stuff into a patient, you'd better make sure the effect is strong enough and lasts long enough to complete the job or you'll be back to where we were before ether. Strap down and slash."

"I wouldn't cut a patient before testing it." He made his plan as he spoke. "I think Parke, Davis, and Company synthesizes cocaine. I'll order a couple of grams and see what it does."

"To whom?" Hartley asked.

"I'll try it on myself. Don't be shy. This man, Koller, put it in patients' eyes! Now that took guts. I'll put it in my arm."

"Your foot would be better," Hartley said. "You don't need two feet to operate."

"I suppose we can try it at one of the students' clinics." Hall started to sound excited. "They'll be keen to experiment. *I'm* keen to give it a try. We can—" He stopped, colored slightly, and said, "I'm sorry, Halsted. It's your idea. If you don't want collaborators…"

Halsted's mouth dried. If this worked, the collapse of the family business would be nothing but a trivial annoyance. This would make his name.

Surgery had always been limited by three things: hemorrhage, infection, and pain. Proper technique could control hemorrhage. They were making enormous strides in preventing infection. But although general anesthesia allowed for surgery without pain, it was risky and too operator dependent. The rewards of true local anesthesia were limitless. Hall saw it too.

Oskaar interrupted, laying down bowls and mugs. "Anything else?"

"Not just now. Thank you, Oskaar." Halsted waited until he retreated. "Of course, I want collaborators." He looked at Hartley, who had been skimming the report. "Are you in?"

There would be credit enough to go around.

2

1884, November

New York City, New York

The first time I took 0.5 cg of cocainum muriaticum in a 1% water solution was when I was feeling slightly out of sorts from fatigue… A few minutes after taking cocaine, one experiences a sudden exhilaration and a feeling of lightness. One feels a certain furriness on the lips and palate, followed by a feeling of warmth in the same areas… The psychic effects of cocainum muriaticum in doses of 0.05-0.10g consists of exhilaration and lasting euphoria, which does not differ in any way from the normal euphoria of a healthy person… One senses an increase in self-control and feels more vigorous and more capable of work…

—*Über Coca*, Sigmund Freud, 1884

Twelve students would arrive at the McBride/Halsted residence in a little over an hour. McBride, recuperated from his acute illness, or so he claimed, was spending the evening at the University Club. In his absence, Hall helped himself to a vintage bottle of wine.

The house Halsted leased with McBride was more than adequate for the needs of two bachelor physicians. McBride occupied the third floor, Halsted the second. He had for himself a bedroom with a large dressing room, a spare bedroom for occasional out-of-town guests, a bath, and a study. The first floor comprised a medical office, a surgical one, a drawing room-parlor, a dining room, and a kitchen with a sizeable pantry.

The invitation to share McBride's lease had been a stroke of sheer good fortune. The man knew everyone worth knowing and, when he was in health, entertained lavishly: dinners, musicales, friends over for drinks, women over for late night amusement. Halsted embraced the lifestyle, minus the floozies—when he wasn't working.

He had been a mere medical student when he'd met the slightly older physician. McBride was one of the better lecturers in medicine. He lived on Madison Avenue a short distance from Halsted and his parents. If that wasn't awkward enough, he was Halsted's mother's physician. The man had seen her half-dressed. Halsted used to pass him from time to time on the street, which felt so uncomfortable that he had started greeting him, jokingly, as "Professor."

The professor was now more friend than mentor, but that didn't mean Halsted wasn't still learning from him. Although he liked to think he now taught McBride a few things in return.

In his office, Halsted arranged the specimens he intended to show to the students: a tumorous kidney and a gangrenous leg. There wasn't much to say about the kidney. The pathology was self-evident. The technique of removal could be described but not shown. The leg was more interesting. The students could take part in the dissection and discover for themselves the neurovascular bundles, the musculotendinous attachments, the numerous foot bones. He was most interested in the nerves. What would happen if one anesthetized a nerve?

"Are you certain you don't want a glass of this? It's quite good," Hall called from the kitchen.

"I'm certain." Red wine gave him migraines. He didn't admit this; it seemed a womanly affliction. He'd rather be thought abstemious.

Hall wandered into the office, wineglass in one hand, cigarette in the other, pink socks.

"McBride doesn't mind you bringing home bits and pieces? Doesn't it scare away his patients?"

If the professor could entertain females till all hours in the common parlor, Halsted could give clinics in his surgery.

"I don't leave them lying about."

"They rather smell though."

"Do they?" Halsted took a sniff. Then he hastily lit a cigarette. "That leg does. I'll take it back to the pathological laboratory after clinic." It would be late but he could use a walk, carrying a leg in a bucket across town; there was a joke in there somewhere.

Hall set down his glass. "Is Frank coming?"

They did not generally attend one another's clinics. They were too busy for that. But Halsted had asked them both to come to this one. The cocaine had arrived in the morning mail.

"He sent a message around that his case is running late. He might miss tonight. But he said we shouldn't wait on him to start our experiments. I made up the dilution."

"Two percent or four?"

"I went with four." If the effect was too strong, they could titer it down. "Should we wait until after the clinic? I don't think we should engage any students yet. It could be a colossal waste of effort."

"Why don't we try it before they get here? You can inject me. I'm not afraid of needles."

Halsted smiled. "I'll inject myself. We don't know what this will do. I'd rather not kill a rival surgeon in my own office."

"Rival?" Hall snorted. "Thank you for the compliment. Where are you hiding it?"

"I'll get it. It's upstairs."

He went up to his study, to the desk where he had left the solution he had so carefully prepared. He nudged open the drawer, spied Welch's telegram, and was compelled to scan it again. The coincidence of that telegram and the cocaine arriving the same morning made him uncharacteristically anxious.

Halsted shook his head, smiling in spite of the message. The price of telegrams infuriated Welch. He'd spend an hour planning his missives to save twenty cents. Because he couldn't countenance Halsted being overcharged either, he devised a code whereby McBride's condition could be precisely communicated for ten dollars or less.

Amused, Halsted had obliged by learning the code and letting Welch know that their mutual friend was doing surprisingly well. Then he added an aside, one in which he attempted to mimic the scholar's frugality.

TRIALING LOCAL ANAEST A LA KOLLER WITH HALL-HARTLEY STOP NEEDLES STOP WHAT THINK YOU?

Having a guaranteed salary must have made Welch giddy. That or true German lager.

GLAD TO HEAR MB DOING BETTER MAYBE DIAGNOSIS WRONG STOP I THINK SURGEONS RUSH IN WHERE ANGELS FEAR TO TREAD STOP

The man who threw aside a promising medical career in New York for a not-yet-constructed university office in Baltimore was urging caution? Ha! He would have to think of a suitably pithy response.

He plucked the cocaine and supplies from the drawer.

Returning to the office, he was assaulted by the rotten-meat odor of the leg. First things first, he threw open the window. Then he set the vial and needle on the examination table before Hall, next to a beaker of rubbing alcohol.

"I'm going to try infiltrating the skin first. If that doesn't work—"

"And our definition of 'work'?" Hall asked.

"Loss of sensation. Great enough to allow sharp dissection without pain. Long-lasting enough to complete a procedure. Let's say draining an abscess. We'll start small." He hoped that would satisfy Welch.

"And if infiltrating the skin doesn't work?"

"We take the needle deeper. Muscle. Nerve."

Hall nodded, rolled up his sleeve, and said, "Load up the hypodermic. No, wait." He gulped down the rest of the wine in his glass. "All right. I'm ready."

Halsted grinned. *Not afraid of needles?*

He drew ten minims into the syringe, then chose a spot on the back of Hall's arm, a third of the way between elbow and wrist. He inserted the needle obliquely to the skin. "Ah!" Hall's arm jerked. "It stings."

"Hold still." Halsted checked his pocket watch, then the syringe. "That was only about six minims. Deeper than I meant to go—uncooperative patient. No, don't rub it. Tell me what you feel."

"Stinging. Was that a needle or a curette?"

"Baby," Halsted mocked. He rolled up his own sleeve, rinsed the needle in the alcohol, then drew up another ten minims.

"Do you want me to do it?" Hall asked.

"Why? Revenge?" He checked his watch, then began injecting himself in roughly the same spot.

Hall stiffened with a sharp gasp and slunk to the floor. Aghast, Halsted dropped beside him and felt for a pulse. Hall was shaking. Seizing?

No. Laughing. Halsted dropped the man's wrist with disgust. "Not funny."

Hall sat up, wiping a tear from his eye. "Yes, it was. You should have seen your face."

"Look at my arm." He'd merely scraped the skin with the needle. The cocaine solution was nothing but a drip on the floor.

"What a good friend you are. If our positions were reversed, I wouldn't have gone to your aid. I would have grabbed a blade to excise the injection site from my arm."

"Idiot," Halsted said, affectionately. He checked his watch again. "Three minutes. What do you feel?"

"Nothing."

Halsted's face fell. "Too bad. Let me try another injection. I'll double the dose."

"No." Hall got to his feet. "I mean I feel nothing. From here"—he pointed to the injection site—"to here." He drew a line on his skin down to the end of the ulna, with thumb and forefinger spread nearly an inch apart, then narrowing.

"Cutaneous ulnar nerve," Halsted said, a little awed. "What about here?" He pinched Hall's elbow above the injection site.

"Hurts," Hall said, smiling. "By God, this will work. Try another spot."

"I want to time how long it lasts."

"We can time two places at once. This is going to work!" He pinched the side of his own arm. "I don't feel it. Maybe a little pressure. Cut me."

"I'm not going to cut you."

Hall laughed. "I'll cut you then."

"Why don't we wait for Hartley? You may have tasted too much of McBride's wine."

"No. This is the giddiness of success. Try my left elbow."

Halsted obliged him. Eight minims into the subcutis at the left elbow. By three minutes there had been no effect.

"Try the right."

"Hall, I already injected the right. Is the sensation back?"

"Coming back. Fuzzily."

"Let me record this before we forget." He jotted down notes, then asked, "Still feel your left arm?"

Hall nodded gloomily. "Maybe the skin is a little tingly. That's all."

Halsted rolled up his trouser leg. "I'll try a few minims in the skin where there is no major nerve. Then I'll go deep and get the nerve where it enters fascia."

The solution did sting. He wrote down the time. Within two minutes, he felt anesthesia below the injection for a distance of about two inches. Enough loss of sensation to remove a nevus, he suspected. Or a superficial vascular tumor.

The doorbell rang.

"Students. Let's stop for now. I don't want a free-for-all. We have to plan what to do next. This will work, Hall."

Hall's face was flushed with excitement. "Yes. I know."

⁂

Hartley joined them halfway through the clinic. When the students finally left, he ran his hands through his shock of red hair and said, "I thought you'd never shut up about that kidney, Halsted. Who knew there was so much to know?"

He handed Hartley a pencil and paper. "Write down the times, injection sites, and results."

Hartley nodded. "What have you found out so far?"

"Injections cause anesthesia along the distribution of cutaneous nerves. We think."

Hall added, "Except for my left elbow. That is immune to effect."

Hartley looked from one to the other, then shook his head. "Lads, I'm tired. I've had a long day. Can we be serious?"

"We are," Halsted said. "Write it down. We're trying Hall's right elbow next."

Hall was already rolling up his sleeves. "Fire when ready. Double the dose. No, quadruple the dose. I want this to work."

Halsted pulled the vial and hypodermic from the supply cabinet where he had stashed them. Hartley touched his arm.

"Were there any toxic effects? Constitutional symptoms?"

Halsted hesitated. Nothing he couldn't explain away as excitement. Except his head had, for a short period, felt unpleasantly hot. "None."

"Proceed," Hartley said, grinning.

Hall clambered onto the examination table. Halsted drew up thirty-two minims and injected them into Hall's right ulnar nerve at the olecranon. Then they waited.

At two minutes, Hall said, "I feel something. Tingling. Maybe numbness. Down the arm to my little finger." Hartley jotted it down. "Yes, definite numbness."

Halsted handed him an empty jar. "Squeeze this. Don't let go."

He squeezed while Halsted tried to pull it from him.

"Write down 'no loss of function or power.'"

Hall started to laugh. "I wasn't even half trying to hold on."

"Look at his pupils," Hartley said.

Widely dilated. "Write it down," Halsted said. He touched Hall's forehead. "And cold perspiration. Five minutes. How are you feeling? That was maybe too large a dose."

"Fine. Fine." Hall tried to push himself to standing, but his legs buckled. "A little dizzy." He sat down. Then he said, "Shit. I feel like shit. Get me a pan."

The pan was under the sink. Before Halsted could fetch it, Hall vomited on the floor.

"Six minutes," Hartley said, rather more calmly than Halsted felt.

"Are you going to be sick again?" Halsted asked Hall, wetting a compress with cool water and handing it to him.

"Maybe." Hall groaned. "I'd like to. But I didn't eat supper. All I've had since luncheon was McBride's wine. My head is pounding. Take my pulse."

Halsted grasped his wrist and counted. "One hundred-eight and bounding."

Hartley scribbled it down, then found a towel to clean the mess.

"Let me see you try to walk again," Halsted said. "Your skin is drenched. I should've used less."

"I told you to go strong."

"Yes, but I don't usually listen to you."

Hall laughed weakly. "Patients won't like this."

"We'll use less." Halsted turned to Hartley. "I'll try ten minims into the fascia in my leg."

Hartley raised an eyebrow, then nodded and picked up his pencil. "Sit down first."

"I wasn't going to hop on one foot. Hall, how are you doing?"

"Numb from elbow to wrist. Nauseous as hell. Dizzy."

Halsted sat, pulled up his trouser leg and pushed down his sock. He injected the full ten minims deep, through the muscle to the fascia. The needle hurt. For patients, it might make sense to inject subcutaneously first, numb the skin, and then go deeper.

Then they waited, Hartley tapping the pencil against the paper, Hall sweating, Halsted biting his lip, feeling a tingling down to his toes.

Hall's breathing evened out. "The nausea is easing."

"Twenty minutes," Hartley said. "How is sensation?"

"Coming back. How about you, Halsted?"

"My leg is numb. I can't feel my toes."

"Nausea?" Hartley asked, writing furiously.

"No." His head felt hot. "I'm warm though. Am I sweating?"

"Not visibly." Hartley took his pulse. "One hundred. What do you usually run?"

"I don't know. Sixty back at Yale. But I was lighter then."

Hall said, "I feel better. Significantly. Maybe a little dizzy. But really, quite good."

Halsted felt grand. "Lower dose is better."

"Can you walk?" Hartley asked.

Halsted stood. Then he laughed aloud. "This is the strangest sensation." He took a few careful steps. "The muscles work but I can't feel a thing. Good Lord! You could take off a toe and I wouldn't miss it."

"Let's not test that theory," Hartley advised.

"We should cut something," Hall said. "We should. To be a fair test. Not Halsted's toes. Let's take that hideous cyst off of Frank."

Hartley put a hand to his brow. "Oh, come now. I've had this since I was a baby. I'll miss it if it's gone."

"It's like a third eye. Or a devil's horn. It scares away the ladies," Hall said. "Let's take it off. Come on, Frank. For science."

Hartley looked past them for a moment, then set down his paper and pencil.

"If Halsted does it," he said. "Twenty minutes ago, I was cleaning up your vomit. You still look clammy. I'm not letting you near my eye with a knife." He turned to Halsted. "Welch said he thought it must be a meningocele. Sequestered."

Halsted palpated the cyst. It was small but tracked over the ridge of his friend's brow. It wasn't noticeable unless one knew to look for it. The sensible thing was to leave it alone.

"Hall is right. You're a monster. I can cure you."

Hartley laughed. "I give up. Inject me. Take the thing off. Just don't send me a bill."

"Climb on the table while I wash my hands. This will be grand."

He was absurdly glad to have such game friends, such partners. He felt…not inebriated, just…grand. The doors they were opening…

Hall said it: this was what success felt like—the giddiness of success.

3

1884, December

New York City, New York

THE NEW LOCAL ANAESTHETIC

For several weeks past, the medical press, including this journal, has teemed with testimony to the wonderful anaesthetic effects of the hydrochlorate of cocaine…the newly discovered fact that the parts supplied by a sensory nerve may be made insensitive by an injection of cocaine in the immediate neighborhood of the trunk of that nerve is of an importance that cannot be overestimated. That discovery seems to have been well established by the experiments performed by Dr. Halsted and Dr. Hall, recounted in the latter gentleman's letter, which we publish in another column…

—*The New York Medical Journal,* editorial by Frank P. Foster, M.D., December 6, 1884

"You are quite certain of this?" McBride asked, bearding Halsted in the corridor between the dining room and parlor. "I told Mrs. Parker it was a brief procedure and she would be home by evening."

"And that it would be painless," Halsted added. "Yes, I'm sure. If you doubted me—"

"I don't doubt you. Or your choice of procedure. I'm less sanguine about the cocaine."

"Ha! Doubting Thomas."

"I don't need to remind you of Mr. Parker's influence."

"No, you don't. Not for a fifth time," he snapped, then regretted it.

The professor did not look well. His weight was down and his carousing had ceased. There was a significant amount of gray in his hair and mustache. He was starting to lose patients, perhaps a greater blow than losing his health. If the Parkers went elsewhere, it could start an exodus of the elite.

Likely McBride would not have pursued this particular surgical referral, but Mrs. Parker's trigeminal neuralgia had him stymied. The woman was near suicidal from the constant facial pain. A Paravicini operation to excise the nerve would cure her. This was the type of procedure for which cocaine anesthesia had been invented. Invented by himself.

"Don't worry. This will be quick and easy, especially with the new clamp," he said, moving into the parlor. He'd designed a special clamp to allow a firmer grip on the nerve.

"The one you've never used before?"

"Stop. She will have the best possible team. Hartley has a particular interest in trigeminal neuralgia. And Hall—"

"Has a particular interest in cocaine."

Halsted laughed, but stopped when McBride reached out and pressed his fingers to his cheek, pulling his lower eyelid down.

"And how much have you had today?" McBride scrutinized his pupils.

"Stop that." He batted away his friend's hand. McBride awaited an answer. "Very little. I was out late and we were out of coffee."

McBride made a pained sound of disapproval, but the doorbell stopped any further grilling. Hartley and Hall entered the parlor: Hartley looking sober and Hall flushed and buoyant.

"Is she here?" Hall asked. "The lovely, wan Mrs. Parker?"

"Not yet," McBride said. "And you can keep your comments about her appearance to yourself."

"Yes, Doctor," Hall said with mock meekness.

Hartley sighed and pulled his hand through his hair. "Which office? The surgery? She should be lying down."

Halsted nodded. "The table is clean. The instruments are soaking in carbolic."

"All right. We'll make up the solutions. Hall?"

"I'm ready." He bounced on his toes. "Did your clamp arrive?"

"It's soaking," Halsted said.

"I smell another presentation to the Society."

"Not with Mrs. Parker's nerve," McBride warned. "She wants privacy."

Hall made a face; Hartley dragged him off toward the surgery.

"I hear her carriage," McBride said. He looked nervous, almost alarmed.

"I'll let her in. Why don't you go hide?" Halsted sneered. This was simple surgery. Yet McBride was treating them like medical students.

He opened the door just as the bell rang. The woman was pretty. And she was wan. Her brow had the knotted appearance of a chronic sufferer. She wore a dress of quality silk and her hat would cost a day laborer a month's pay.

"Come in, Mrs. Parker. Right this way. I'm so sorry you—"

McBride had followed him. "Good afternoon, Mrs. Parker. As I said, you are in very good hands. Dr. Halsted is the best surgeon in New York."

Only New York? How lowering.

She nodded and said in a tired voice, "I just want this done."

Halsted led her into his surgery. She barely looked at the furnishings: a fine oak table, cabinets, and two chairs—one with an angled back to allow a semi-reclined position, polished floor, shaded windows, a gold-framed mirror, and a fine painting of the Hudson, all designed to inspire confidence from the paying clientele. She lowered herself gingerly into the angled chair that McBride indicated and clutched the side of her face. "What do you need me to do?" she asked.

"Remove your hat," Hall said.

She obliged, with shaking fingers, and handed it to McBride.

"Just lie back," Halsted said. "I will administer the anesthesia and that should be the last you will feel of your pain."

She nodded, settled back, and closed her eyes. Hall spread a clean sheet over her neck and chest while Halsted removed his frock coat, rolled up his sleeves, and scrubbed his arms and hands. Hall squatted beside the chair, murmuring to the woman, trying to calm her. Halsted dunked his hands into the carbolic acid solution for a soak. Then he approached the patient. Hartley handed him the hypodermic needle.

"If you will open your mouth." He slipped his finger along the inside of her jaw and felt for the notch. "You needn't open quite so wide. That's better."

He inserted the needle and injected the cocaine.

"Ah! Ah!" she complained. McBride winced audibly.

Hall held her shoulder. "Almost done. Count to thirty." He counted aloud, slowly. Mrs. Parker's breathing slowed.

Halsted waited another minute, then flicked his finger against her cheek. "Do you feel any pain?"

"No. Just, I don't know. Vibration?"

"All right. Now, Mrs. Parker, I am going to put this gauze into your mouth to help keep it open. It will make it difficult for you to talk, but should you need to communicate discomfort, just make a noise, and I will pause to determine the difficulty. You should feel nothing, except the discomfort of too many hands in your mouth." The last was an attempt at mild humor, but she looked too frightened to respond.

He packed the left side of her mouth with gauze, then thoroughly wiped the operative side with alcohol. One could not sterilize the mouth, but it gave him time to be sure the anesthetic was working. She made no complaint, so he said, "Hartley, you can retract now."

Hartley retracted the tongue to the left and widened the opening by pulling back the right cheek. Halsted put his fingers into her mouth and felt for landmarks: the ramus of the jaw and the internal pterygoid.

"Scalpel."

Hall put the blade in his hand.

"Focus that light."

Hall lifted the lamp higher. Halsted cut through the mucous membrane down to bone.

"Spatula."

Hall handed it to him. He spread the incision wider, blotting the blood with gauze sponges. He probed with his finger down to the foramen and felt for the nerve.

"There it is." He blunt dissected until he could see the nerve clearly. "Clamp."

"This lovely new one?" Hall said, placing it into Halsted's palm.

He inserted it and clamped the nerve. It was a well-made instrument, holding fast with a satisfying click, but the woman's mouth was smaller than he had anticipated, leaving a tighter space for maneuvering than he would have liked.

"Scissors." He snipped one end of the nerve. "Almost finished, Mrs. Parker."

He pressed his finger in deeper, alongside the clamp to locate the further end of the nerve. Then he snipped at the far edge of the clamp.

Blood flooded Mrs. Parker's mouth in a great gush. He immediately tamped the vessel against the bone.

"Artery," Hartley said. Unnecessarily. Halsted recognized arterial blood.

She coughed, spraying blood and nearly biting off his finger, while Hall pushed her back down, gently but firmly.

"Damn it," Hartley muttered. "That must be the internal maxillary."

"Please hold that retraction," Halsted said. "Gauze."

Hall shoved a handful of gauze into his free hand, and Halsted began packing the wound. The gauze continued to redden.

He heard McBride mutter, "Good God," then, from the corner of his eye, saw the man stumble out of the room.

"More gauze." It was a tenet of his that if a surgeon prayed during surgery, it was only in order to have somewhere else to lay blame. Nevertheless, before he moved his finger away, he said a quick, silent prayer. "More gauze."

Hall kept handing; Halsted kept packing. Hartley removed the retractor, and Halsted kept packing.

"I think it's controlled," Hall said.

Halsted nodded. Unfortunately, that was likely because he had packed the wound forcibly enough to risk necrosis and sloughing of the soft tissue.

The woman's eyes were wide with fear. She would have felt nothing except the momentary sensation of suffocation, but she must have realized this was not normal procedure. And now, her mouth was so full she could not possibly close it.

"Hartley, prepare a dose of morphine, if you would." Halsted raised a couple fingers to indicate the dose. It would be best if the woman slept for a couple of hours. He leaned down and said quietly, "Mrs. Parker, it was a more difficult excision than I anticipated. You should rest awhile before we send you home."

She made a muffled protest.

"We will send word to Mr. Parker. Please, try to rest. I know you're uncomfortable but we're giving you some medicine that will help."

Hartley gave her the injection. She cringed. Halsted realized his palms were sweating. And he could hear his heartbeat in his ears. They stood in silence, watching until her eyes closed and her breathing evened out. Then they stepped from the bedside.

"Throw that clamp away," Halsted said, gesturing to the instrument table with disgust.

"You have the steadiest hands and coolest head—" Hartley began.

"Shut up. I bungled it."

"You're not the first surgeon to snip an internal maxillary. It's a well-documented complication."

"It's basic anatomy! Artery runs alongside nerve. The only weapon with which the unconscious patient can immediately retaliate upon the incompetent surgeon is hemorrhage." He had never botched something so simple before.

Hall threw the clamp into a metal basin with a clang. "What now?"

"I can't send her home packed to the gills with gauze. I'll put her upstairs in my spare room and hire a couple of nurses to tend her."

"That packing shouldn't stay—"

"I know. She'll slough. If her condition still seems tenuous in the morning, I'll transfer her to a private room at Presbyterian."

"Well," Hartley said, "when you are ready to remove it, let me know and I'll be here."

"I will, too," Hall said. "We'll finish what we started."

Halsted grunted. They were good men. "I guess we'd better go face the professor."

Hall grinned weakly. "No, I'm slipping out the back. Frank?"

Hartley said, "I'll watch her until the nurses get here. There is another dose of morphine loaded into the syringe that can be given in about four hours. But," he nodded to Halsted, ignoring Hall's attempt at levity, "you're on your own with McBride. You know what his first question will be."

"He already asked it. And that has nothing to do with anything. The clamp was too big."

4

1884, December

Brooklyn, New York

DRAMATIC AND MUSICAL AMUSEMENTS TO-NIGHT
BROOKLYN THEATER—Captain Mishler.
PARK THEATER—Wages of Sin.
GRAND OPERA HOUSE—Pique.
PLYMOUTH CHURCH—The Messiah.
HYDE AND BEHMAN'S THEATER—Specialty and Comedy.
ZIPP'S CASINO—Vocal and Orchestral Concert.
—*The Brooklyn Daily Eagle*, Tuesday Evening, December 30, 1884

I was restless. For different reasons, we all were: me, my sister Lucy, our bosom friend from Edge Hill School, Sally Carter, and even my brother Frank. We were restless enough to leave the familiar comforts of Columbia, South Carolina, at Christmastime for the bustle and excitement of New York, lured there, or perhaps coaxed was the better term, by my aunt Lu. In her letters, promises of festive activities—shopping and parties—warred with vaguely threatening references to Grandmother Baxter's ill health and advancing age. At any rate, it had been too long since we'd visited our maternal relatives up North.

Frank teased we were going so that we might be introduced to "New York gentlemen," but Lucy's horror at the mere suggestion that she would consider a Yankee spoiled the joke.

It was a horrible thing to make light of in any case. Lucy was charming, poised, and beautiful, but she was twenty-five, and suitable gentlemen in the South were rare as hens' teeth. I had recently turned twenty-three, which seemed disturbingly older than twenty-two; yet I resolved to remain unworried so as to not panic Lucy further.

Besides, my restlessness was not the result of the dearth of suitors. It was something worse, a general dissatisfaction with what life had to offer. Columbia was stultifying for a young, female Hampton. There were so many rules, so many expectations, and so many eyes following us wherever we went. We were General Wade Hampton's nieces! We could not think for ourselves and had to behave just so. The only girl more hemmed in by societal niceties was Cousin Daisy, the general's daughter.

If it were summer, I might have escaped to the Lodge, the family property in the North Carolina mountains. It was merely a hunting cabin in the woods, but I fantasized about making it into a farm. Or breeding horses up there. Managing it all on my own. I knew I was capable. Women had done such things during the war. But such perverse distortion of God's order had been wrought by necessity then. Not because a young lady was bored and restless.

And so, I accompanied my siblings to New York. We were "enjoying" what the city had to offer.

Haverly's Brooklyn Theater, for example. It was a staggering place. Grandmother Baxter said it seated fifteen hundred, and that night, every seat was full. We were in Cousin George's box; even so, I felt crushed. Or perhaps squeezed. My stays were so tight I could not breathe. Grandmother had not approved of my original choice of dress. It was too dowdy for her granddaughter to appear in publicly, though it had been fashionable enough in South Carolina. I'd been obliged to fit my unwilling body into a pink ruffled thing with a bustle borrowed from Sally Carter, whose waist was a good three inches smaller than mine. So it wasn't my fault that I was having a hard time appreciating the play.

Mr. Gus Williams, playing the title role, was said to be a brilliant comic actor. Unfortunately, *Captain Mishler* was not a comedy. The lead was miscast. The music was so-so. And there was a crowd of young men in the next box laughing loudly and so inappropriately, they could not have been watching the play. I suspected they were inebriated.

The stage darkened abruptly and the houselights came back up.

"Is it over?" I asked, surprised, a bit hopeful, turning around in my seat.

Cousin George laughed. I did enjoy my cousin. He laughed easily. "Silly kitten. It's only intermission. Shall we go downstairs for some refreshment?"

Frank said, "I could use a whiskey. Or a little of what those lads are having over there."

"You will do no such thing," Grandmother said. "There is lemonade if you're thirsty. That kind of boorish behavior at the theater—"

"I'm sure Frank was teasing, Mother," George interrupted. He turned to my brother. "After we escort the ladies home, I'll be happy to introduce you around at my club."

"You're supposed to be introducing Lucy around," Frank said slyly.

Lucy dug an elbow into his ribs.

"Lucy and Caroline," Grandmother said, then nodded to Sally. "And Miss Carter. I think you will all enjoy the New Year's ball at the Van der Poels' tomorrow."

I groaned inwardly. I'd been to a small Christmas party that had been grueling enough. I was convinced Northern men had wool between their ears. One ignoramus told me that I spoke like a Georgia peach. My reply—that where I came from, in *South Carolina*, fruit did not talk—had sent the man scuttling away. Lucy claimed I was impossible. But later, I heard her telling Frank, and the two of them laughed.

Grandmother grumbled, "Mrs. Sullivan had better deliver those new dresses tomorrow. Caroline, you look peaked. I believe you are right that pink is not your color."

"That and I haven't taken a good deep breath in over two hours."

Lucy shot me dagger-looks, but Aunt Lu smiled. "Dear, I haven't had a deep breath in thirty-five years."

"Let's go downstairs," George said again, taking Lucy's arm.

Frank offered one elbow to Grandmother Baxter and the other to Sally. I was left to lock arms with Aunt Lu.

The lobby, all polished dark wood and gilt adornments, was a worse crush than the mezzanine. George maneuvered us toward the doors, wide open to the chill December air, thank goodness, but we couldn't get very close. Everyone had the same idea.

"Well, now, Lucy," George said, sounding either delighted or amused. "I believe I *can* introduce you to a prize fish. Do you see that blond man over there near the wall? No, there," he said, touching her chin and turning it. "That is Dick Halsted. He's a broker at the Stock Exchange. I know him through the Van der Poels. His sister married Sam."

"Halsted of Halsted and Haines?" Lucy asked.

"Good Lord, Lucy! Have you been studying your New York Debrett's?"

Lucy tapped his arm with her fan—an affected gesture; she did it well. "Do stop teasing," she drawled. "I've heard of the company, that's all. They import quality dress stuff."

"They import more than that. Although, there was some talk back over the summer…"

"Talk?"

"George, we don't gossip," Grandmother said, and George's mouth stayed closed.

Aunt Lu said, "I don't think you would be pleased to make his acquaintance tonight regardless. He's with those roustabouts."

Now I looked closer. They were the men from the loud box. This was how New York gentlemen behaved? I understood why Lucy always said that she could never marry a Yankee.

The man was comely enough. Dressed to the teeth. He looked to be in his mid-twenties. His expression appeared a bit lost, and he was not as boisterous as his fellows. He looked a little embarrassed, truth be told.

There were six other men in the group. All men, no ladies. Four of them seemed to be about Mr. Halsted's age but acted younger, laughing and pushing at one another like schoolboys. Two were older, perhaps thirty, give or take a couple of years. One resembled Mr. Halsted, same color hair but thinning, and his ears stuck out dreadfully. He had thick shoulders and long arms that bowed out as though he were going to throw a steer to the ground. The sixth man, with a handlebar mustache, shifted foot to foot, almost twitching. His constant movement drew one's attention to his dancing feet where a half-inch of bright yellow stocking shocked the eye.

"Who are the others?" Frank asked, his nose wrinkled.

George shrugged. "Not in my circle. Oh, the other blond may be Dick's brother. A medical man if memory serves, but I can't think of his name. You will probably meet them tomorrow. I believe the brother is a good friend of Sam's." He swung his gaze back and forth between his female guests. "Any of you interested in physicians?"

"No," we all chimed at once.

"Not drunken ones at any rate," Sally added, a little gauchely.

Grandmother Baxter's lips pursed, but George rescued her with a laugh. "I guess that rules the whole profession out."

Half the Southern planters as well, I thought, but did not say it.

At that moment a bell rang, summoning us back to our box. Those young men let out whoops. One did something that sounded like an atrocious attempt to mimic a rebel yell.

Lucy's jaw tightened. "I hope they behave better in the ballroom than the theater."

I didn't care how they behaved. After all, I had not come to New York to meet men.

5

1884, December

Brooklyn, New York

DRAMATIC AND MUSICAL AMUSEMENTS TO-NIGHT
BROOKLYN THEATER—Captain Mishler.
PARK THEATER—Wages of Sin.
GRAND OPERA HOUSE—Pique.
PLYMOUTH CHURCH—The Messiah.
HYDE AND BEHMAN'S THEATER—Specialty and Comedy.
ZIPP'S CASINO—Vocal and Orchestral Concert.
—*The Brooklyn Daily Eagle*, Tuesday Evening, December 30, 1884

The cool air outside the theater felt magnificent; it had been hot inside. Halsted gathered the medical students about him like a hen with her chicks. How young they seemed. The play had been fine, and he was pleased they all enjoyed it, but he was a little nervous he would lose one and read about it in the newspaper the next morning.

New York Surgeon Misplaces Senior P&S Students. Examinations Postponed.

Hall hovered behind the boys, shooting irritated looks at Dick. The two had grated on one another all evening. He couldn't be bothered with why.

"I told you the Brooklyn Theater was a better choice than Hyde and Behman's," Halsted said to no one in particular. He laughed. "That Gus Williams knows the German type." For a moment, he was tempted to do his own impersonation, but the crowd on the street discouraged him. Where had all these people come from?

He waved down a horsecab, muscling past a clown who tried to steal it from him. Time to send the boys home. Even without Dick's snide comments, he recognized that the students' exuberance had annoyed some of the other patrons. Still, they'd earned a revel, having helped with the experiments after their clinics for a fortnight. And he had earned one, having discharged Mrs. Parker, fully recuperated and no longer in pain, just this morning.

"Good night. Good night." He packed them in and paid the fare, relieved to be rid of them. As the horsecab pulled away, he turned to Dick and Hall. "Well, the evening is still young. What next?" The brisk air energized him. The street lamps were overly bright, making it seem like mid-day.

Hall chuckled, but Dick looked perturbed.

"No early surgery tomorrow?"

"Oh yes," Halsted assured him. That was the excuse he always used to avoid frequenting taverns with his brother, who drank to excess. But it was also the truth. A large hernia awaited him. And a rectal abscess. "A long day planned. And then the ball tomorrow night at the Van der Poels'."

A New Year's Ball. Hosted by their sister Minnie's in-laws. It promised to be quite the crush.

"A full, full day. Not for Hall." He chortled. "He wasn't invited." He pulled a cigarette from his pocket, then wondered if he'd been clear in his meaning. "To the ball. He may attend my surgery if he wants to learn something." He laughed and lit his smoke.

Dick made a noise of disgust. "I'm going to the White Horse."

He turned to walk away.

"You aren't including us?" Halsted asked, surprised and a little irked.

"You're welcome to come." He made a half-hearted gesture. "Your friend too."

There was something sad in his little brother's tone. For a moment, Halsted was tempted to follow him. But Hall coughed and said, "Thank you, but no. I'm going to swing around to Bellevue and have a look at that amputee from this morning."

"The hospital?" Dick said, eyes widening. "In evening clothes at this time of night?"

"The patient won't care." Hall waggled his eyebrows. "But the nurses might. What say you, Dr. Halsted?"

Neither the White Horse nor a bevy of night nurses appealed to him. Nor did he wish to choose one over the other and offend brother or friend.

"No, I'm heading home."

"To sleep?" Dick asked. Aggressively, Halsted thought.

"To read and then sleep."

He wondered what McBride had been telling his brother. That he never slept anymore? McBride was one to talk. The professor's health had improved and he was taking advantage of it while he could. Halsted waved a goodbye and started to walk, anxious to get home. He'd ease his sinus congestion with a little cocaine, read *The New York Medical Journal* while his head was good and clear, and then catch forty winks before surgery tomorrow.

He stuck his cigarette in his mouth and let it dangle while he tucked his hands back into his gloves, then buttoned his coat across his chest. Damn, it was cold in the wind. December cold.

Tomorrow was New Year's Eve. That meant drunks and drunks meant trauma. He paused to blow out a cloud of smoke and watched it swirl away in the glare of the street lamps. It was doubtful he'd make the Van der Poels' ball. Likely he'd be in surgery straight through to Thursday. Thirty-six hours on his feet. He should go home and sleep. Then he'd tuck a packet of cocaine into his pocket and take it with him in the morning. They'd found it worked as well intra-nasally as injected.

He tossed his cigarette into the gutter and picked up his pace. Jittering. *Worked as well.* Cocaine was supposed to be for local anesthesia. For *surgery*. On *patients*. By what justification was he sniffing this stuff up his nose before an evening at the theater?

Welch said fools rushed in…

A fresh gust of icy wind blew away his disquiet. Halsted snorted and shoved his hands in his pockets. *Get hold of yourself, man. Welch doesn't know everything.* That was why these experiments were important. If cocaine caused any harm, they would have discovered it by now.

6

1885, December

New York City, New York

Personal Items—Dr. William S. Halsted, of New York, sailed for Europe in the *Werra* on Wednesday.

—*New York Medical Journal*, October 3, 1885

FUNERAL OF PROF. DRAPER

The funeral of Prof. John C. Draper occurred yesterday morning from the Church of the Transfiguration. The Rev. Dr. Houghton and his assistant, the Rev. Mr. Underhill, conducted the services. The church was crowded with friends of the dead man, including 300 students of the medical department of Columbia College and 150 of the College of the City of New York....

—*The New York Times*, Thursday, December 24, 1885

Dr. William H. Welch caught the first train to New York as soon as he heard: Dr. John Draper, surgeon, chemist, teacher, physician to the physicians, dead at fifty from pneumonia.

He was surprised to see that Draper's funeral was being held in the Church of the Transfiguration. A pretty little Neo-Gothic church, set back from the street and fronted by a garden, its congregants were known for espousing a liberal brand of Episcopalianism. He would have placed Draper elsewhere, somewhere older and more conventional.

Entering the crowded building, Welch spied numerous physicians he knew, but was glad to see Tom McBride alone near the back. McBride would not shun him for abandoning New York for Baltimore, and he wasn't sure he could say the same of some of the others. Life was too short for such nonsense.

McBride stood to shake his hand. Welch had a hard time hiding his dismay. Tom's once-bushy black hair was thinning and gray. His skin had a dry papery texture and his fingernails were white proximally with pink tips. His kidneys were failing.

"I thought you might come," McBride said.

"Of course. I owe him a great debt. We all do."

Draper had been an example to them all. Welch looked around at the mourners. Draper's reach had been long. He'd been a surgeon in the army and those colleagues, too, were out in full force. Such a powerful display of respect; it was a shame the man was not there to see it.

"Where is Halsted? Still abroad?" He would have expected the two to attend together.

"No. He got back a few days ago." McBride frowned. He gazed past Welch a moment as if thinking of something else, then said, "Do you have plans after this or would you have lunch with me?"

"No plans."

The man's expression worried him. He had heard rumors. The elite medical world was small. But he had been so busy getting established at Johns Hopkins, he'd only half-listened to conflicting stories from New York. And then he'd heard Halsted was going to a conference in Vienna, so he'd assumed everything had been sorted out.

The low hum of somber conversation began to still, and Welch quieted to center his thoughts on their deceased colleague. The organist played Chopin's "Funeral March," and the procession entered. The pallbearers were mostly medical men: Noyes, Van der Poel, Delancey, Delafield. It made his eyes ache. Then the choir sang an ode, with a marvelous tenor soloing. Rev. Houghton led them in prayer.

The eulogy passed in something of a blur. Welch found it hard to concentrate. McBride looked so ill. And Halsted was…where? If he were in surgery, McBride would have said so.

The funeral was simple and short. Welch followed McBride from the church, pausing to speak with other friends and acquaintances, reminiscing about Draper. His old friend Fred Dennis avoided him, but many others seemed to have called a truce. At least, no one alluded to his desertion.

The coffin was whisked away by the pallbearers to a special train that would take the body to Woodlawn for burial. So final. So sad.

As the crowd dispersed, McBride turned to him.

"Let's not go to the University Club. How about Pinards?"

"Fine." He wondered what kept McBride from the club. Too much pity from fellows who saw his health was declining? He took a couple of steps. "Shall we walk?" The day was crisp but sunny. "I can use a breath of air."

McBride grimaced. "I think I'll need a hansom. I tire easily."

"Oh, Tom." It must be bad for him to admit it.

"It is Bright's, of course. Chronic and relapsing. I plan to go back to Carlsbad in the spring to take the waters, but I need to see some things settled first. If you hadn't come for this, I was going to send you a telegram." His eyes gave off a hint of their old humor. "I changed my will. Left you my kidneys so you can say you were right."

"I'd rather be wrong." He waited a moment, then said, rubbing his chin thoughtfully, "But I would love to get my hands on your kidneys."

McBride laughed, buttoning his coat against the chill. "Flag down a ride, will you?"

Welch stepped to the side of the road. There were several carriages waiting. He engaged one then beckoned to his friend, who was digging around in his pockets.

"I've got it," Welch said. "The university actually pays me decently."

McBride shook his head. "I wasn't looking for my wallet."

He stepped up to the hansom and hoisted himself into it. Welch followed. New York horses had a smell of their own—not worse than Baltimore's nags, not better, just different.

"Draper could have said what it is," he mused. "That scent. The horse scent."

"Manure." McBride lit a cigarette and fanned the smoke with his hand.

"I know it's manure. But what's in it? What do New York horses eat that gives it that smell? What's the chemistry? Draper would know."

"Draper would say: 'That Welch is cracked. I don't sit around sniffing horseshit.'"

Welch smiled.

"So where is Halsted?" he ventured, once they were settled in and on their way. "Urgent surgery?"

"Halsted hasn't operated since May." Scowling, he added in a mutter, "Which is probably good."

"May?" If a man as driven as William Halsted had not worked in seven months, something was very wrong. "Why?"

"He's been 'experimenting.' Evangelizing. That's why he went to

Vienna. That and to get away from New York." McBride pulled a copy of the *New York Medical Journal* from his coat pocket. "I don't suppose you saw this? From September?"

"No. I'm a little behind. Something important?"

"Page 294." He put the journal in Welch's hand. "Read it."

Welch tried. After a time, he looked up to see McBride's grim jaw and worried eyes.

"Is he at the house?"

"Probably."

He called up to the driver. "Forget Pinards. Take us to Madison and Twenty-Fifth."

7

1885, December

New York City, New York

PRACTICAL COMMENTS ON THE USE AND ABUSE OF COCAINE; SUGGESTED BY ITS INVARIABLY SUCCESSFUL EMPLOYMENT IN MORE THAN A THOUSAND MINOR SURGICAL OPERATIONS.

Neither indifferent as to which of how many possibilities may best explain, nor yet at a loss to comprehend, why surgeons have, and that so many, quite without discredit, could have exhibited scarcely any interest in what, as a local anaesthetic, had been supposed, if not declared, by most so very sure to prove, especially to them, attractive, still I do not think that this circumstance, or some sense of obligation to rescue fragmentary reputation for surgeons rather than the belief that an opportunity existed for assisting others to an appreciable extent, induced me, several months ago, to write on the subject in hand the greater part of a somewhat comprehensive paper, which poor health disinclined me to complete…

—Dr. W. H. Halsted, *New York Medical Journal,* September 12, 1885, xlii, 294.

❧

Halsted shuffled through a pile of folders laid out on his desk, his mind racing erratically. This was a gold mine! He couldn't believe they hadn't presented this work—he and Sam. His brother-in-law, Sam Van der Poel, was a good doctor even if he could be a bit of a dunce.

Years ago, when Halsted had finally convinced his father that he needed to go to Europe to study surgery, he met up with his schoolmate Sam in Paris, who had been there for six months doing God only knew what. He'd fallen in with some Gullivers from Boston. Halsted's first night in the city, he followed Sam and his boys to Montmartre. They drank at least a magnum of champagne. When in Rome… The champagne was poison enough. But it was the mademoiselles that nearly finished him off.

Halsted was no monk. He had been to prostitutes while at Yale. Not often, but there were times...well, they all did. He hadn't made a habit of it. However, in New York, after a few months flushing gonococci out of sailors' urethras with corrosive sublimate, he'd sworn off the fancies for good. Until Montmartre. Ha!

The next morning, he grabbed Sam by the scruff of the neck and dragged him off to the train for Vienna. Sam didn't speak to him the entire train ride, but his huff didn't last long. When Halsted's family came abroad for a tour, he introduced Sam to his sister Minnie.

Sam had done a fair share of the corrosive sublimate work. They should collaborate on a paper. It would do Sam's career good. All this material...

He heard a knock and looked up as the door opened.

"Welch!" This was exactly the man he wanted to see. "You're back! Came up for Draper's funeral, did you?"

He rose from behind his desk, bumped his leg against the corner, and stopped. He started again, making a wider circle around the desk. McBride, standing in the doorway behind their visitor, watched every movement.

"I meant to go to the church, but I had—" He gestured to the pile of papers on his desk. "I'm working on a presentation. I'd love to have your thoughts. It's work Sam and I did back—"

Welch held up one hand to interrupt. Then he slapped something onto the desk.

"What is this?"

Halsted focused. "It looks like the *New York Medical Journal*."

"From September," Welch said roughly. "With your incomprehensible gibberish masquerading as an editorial!"

Halsted turned away, annoyed. He had never heard the man raise his voice before, hadn't thought him capable of anger. He glanced around his surgery. He'd put away the syringe and vial, thank goodness. The counters gleamed. The floor had been mopped. The instruments were all in their cabinets. Only the desk appeared disordered.

"Gibberish is overstating the case. It was hurriedly done, but I'm tired of imbeciles saying cocaine doesn't work. We've performed thousands—"

He heard McBride sniff, but it was Welch who pressed.

"Yet reported none of your work."

"I think Hall wrote up some little thing."

"Halsted. Stop." He lifted the journal and held it out, open. "Read it aloud."

He pushed it away. "I know what it says. Read it more carefully if you can't grasp it."

"A more careful read will not fix poor grammar."

Halsted flushed. Welch knew where to stick the knife.

"The meaning comes across," he argued weakly.

"Halsted! Listen to yourself. And you've stopped operating?"

"I operated in Vienna." He started to pace. Welch was one of *them*. Naysayers. Backward thinkers. Like McBride. And Hartley. Hartley had walked away from the experiments, from the clinics too—chased away the students. "I taught Woelfler how to do neurocutaneous injections. He was another skeptic. Now he's a convert. You should try it before condemning it."

"How much are you taking?"

"Me?" Damn McBride. He glared at the man, who was wasting away before his eyes and should be looking to mind his own health, not sticking his nose where it didn't belong. Then he answered Welch. "Not much. You should see what I'm working on. All those cases of urethritis. Sam and I have notebooks full of data that we never bothered to collate."

"Don't change the subject. How much weight have you lost?" Welch pointed toward Halsted's middle. "Or have you started patronizing an inferior tailor?"

Another slap. Halsted's tailoring was meticulous. Generally.

"I just got back from abroad. I was seasick. Or maybe some of the food had turned." He circled his desk again to find his cigarettes. "Did you come for something in particular?"

Welch's shoulders slumped. He didn't leave but took a step closer.

"What should we do about this?"

"We?" Halsted asked. Then felt his neck grow hot. "About what?"

"Cocaine is consuming you."

"That's absurd."

Welsh picked up the journal and began to read. "Neither indifferent as to which of how many possibilities may best explain, nor yet at a loss to comprehend, why surgeons have, and that so many, quite without discredit, could have exhibited scarcely any interest in what, as a local anesthetic, had been supposed, if not declared—"

"That isn't what it says." He pulled the journal from Welch's hand and reread his own words. He couldn't recall writing them, though he remembered the furious excitement that had driven him to write. Blood began pounding in his temples and the words blurred. His *name* was affixed to the bottom of that unintelligible diatribe. He sat down before his knees gave way.

"McBride, will you leave us?" Welch said, very quietly.

Halsted heard the door to the office close. He looked up. The concern on Welch's face almost broke him.

"Can you stop?"

"I have." He shook his head. "I've stopped, but then I start again."

"Why?" Welch sat in the chair opposite the desk. Settled in. He would not leave on his own and it would be impossible to physically eject him. Halsted's skin prickled.

"It's hard to explain." He fumbled to light a cigarette. He was not a fool; he recognized the drug had its downsides. It made him frenetic and impatient. His colleagues avoided him as assiduously as he avoided them. He had even fallen out with Hall—they were competing for the position of Chairman of Surgery at the College of Physicians and Surgeons. Competing! As if bright socks, juvenile witticisms, and clumsy fingers qualified a man for a department chair.

Welch waited, silent, while he smoked. Then he snuffed the stub. "I don't understand its mechanism. It deadens sensation where it is injected, but it heightens every other sense. It is…" He could not think of the words. "I'm no poet, but it's like being more alive. Alive to everything. I understand everything when I take a dose."

"I can see the allure. Knowing. You've always been determined to know."

Halsted nodded; that was it.

"But what about discernment?" Welch pulled a cigar and cutter from his breast pocket.

"Discernment?"

Welch tended to his cigar. "Want one?"

"No, thank you. I'll stick to mine."

Welch puffed and settled back. "Discernment. Understanding clearly. Discrimination. Good judgment. Perception of what is important and what is—"

"I know what the word means."

"Discernment is as important to scientific discovery as knowing. Does this cocaine help you to discern?"

Halsted frowned. He tried to sort what Welch was saying. "Probably not."

"What do you think of McBride?"

The switch disoriented him and he laughed. "McBride? I think he is an interfering cuss."

"I meant his health."

His laughter died. The next words came out choked. "Bright's. Getting worse."

Welch blew a smoke ring. "He should go back to Carlsbad."

"So I've told him a hundred times—"

"I wonder what is keeping him here."

Silence fell. Heavily.

"The professor is not my keeper," he said finally.

"That is not true. We're all our brothers' keepers. We buried Draper this morning. Before too long, we'll lose McBride. Do you feel no obligation to men who had such faith in you?"

He couldn't answer. He fiddled with the papers on his desk, reached for a cigarette, but then did not take it. He wished they would leave him alone.

"All right," he said, irked to be put on the spot. "I'll stop the experiments. Then will McBride go to Carlsbad?"

"He says he plans to. In the spring."

Halsted blew out a breath. Relieved. With McBride gone…

"So I will come back," Welch continued. "After I tie up a few loose ends in Baltimore."

"That's not necessary. I don't need a warden."

"For McBride's peace of mind."

He wouldn't argue. Welch was not likely to be as intrusive as McBride, who had once confiscated all the cocaine in the surgery office and thrown it away.

"Do what you think you have to," he said.

Welch rose, pinched out his cigar, and set it in Halsted's ashtray. "I will."

8

1886, March

West Indies, Caribbean Sea

The schooner *Vega*, Mr. E. M. Ferguson, Eastern Yacht Club, is about ready for sea, having been put in complete order for a cruise to the Windward Islands, at the foot of Twenty-Sixth Street, South Brooklyn. Her sailing master, Captain Bibber of Boston, Mass, has made 130 voyages to the West Indies, it is said, and, unlike some yacht-sailing masters, knows enough to heave his vessel to when in the night his latitude has been "run down." The *Vega* will sail next Monday.

—*The Boston Globe*, Boston, Mass., February 8, 1886

❧

Abducted. Kidnapped. Pirated. Seized.

"Shanghaied," Welch said.

"Impressed," Halsted added, seated on the deck of the schooner, staring out an expanse of blue-green sea, smooth as a tabletop. Welch had turned his captive's complaints into a word game.

Welch shook his head. "Only for naval ships. This is for pleasure."

"Pleasure," Halsted scoffed. Mind-deadening boredom more like. After weeks at sea, the novelty had worn off and anxiety set in.

He didn't know how Welch had done it. The man's powers of persuasion should be bottled and sold. Welch had returned to New York in early February and announced he had hired a schooner for a jaunt to the Windward Islands. Two months at sea. And Halsted would be jaunting with him. Three crewman and a seasoned captain would cater to their every need.

"Leisure, then. I don't suppose you've had a vacation in years." Welch sipped his Bordeaux. "Listen. Feel that ocean breeze. 'Till taught by pain, men really know not what good water's worth.'"

"Byron!" Halsted laughed, surprised yet not surprised. "You read Byron?"

"I read everything," Welch said with a smile. "I suppose I'll have to dig deeper to stump you."

"I wish you luck."

He stood and paced to the rail, stifling the urge to check his watch. Welch would let him know when it was time, then ask him to wait another hour. Sometimes he did. This evening, he could not. No game of chess, no cards, no word games or puzzles could stem the dread he felt building inside. He had to reduce the dose again tonight by another ten minims. He needed more, not less, and he feared he would give in to the need—and then what?

He had said he could give up cocaine readily. He'd been lying even to himself.

Welch did not administer the injection or measure it out. He said he trusted him not to cheat. That would have been a touching sentiment if not for the threat that lay behind Welch's method. The cocaine would run out two weeks before the journey's end. If he cheated, it would run out sooner.

The first leg of the trip had been strangely enjoyable. They had excellent weather. The food was superb. The island beaches were beautiful and the natives intriguing. He had always liked Welch but considered him more of a colleague than a friend. He'd never spent this much time with him before. He'd never spent this much time in such close quarters with anyone before. Welch made it easy. He was not only personable but genuine. The man conversed knowledgeably on any topic but never came across as overbearing. Mostly, they talked medicine, but they had moved on to literature, history, Yale, their families, and Baltimore. Welch liked the city well enough, but it was the university that he loved—the idea of it, the way Director Billings and President Gilman cooperated to bring Mr. Hopkins' ideal to fruition: a true university, a research-oriented medical college, based on the European model. It sounded too perfect to be real.

"Come sit down," Welch said. "You're making me nervous lolling next to the rail."

"Afraid I'll jump overboard?"

"Have you considered it?"

"Yes." But not yet. He reserved it as an option. The dark blue emptiness was strangely compelling.

"Then yes. Come sit down."

It sounded like an order, so Halsted obeyed. Anyway, it was hopeless: he excelled at swimming and had no doubt Welch would manage to fish him out.

Off the cuff, he said, "Tell me about the Southern belles you've encountered."

"The what?"

"McBride said you went to Baltimore for the belles."

"Oh, he did not." Welch laughed. "But I will tell you an amusing story."

"Go on." There was a blanket draped over the deck chair, so he wrapped it around his shoulders. He was sweating and yet he felt chilled. *Talk, Welch, talk.* He desperately needed distraction.

"The Southern hospitality is something to behold. I'm invited everywhere. There is, I'm afraid, no small notice of my unmarried state, so dinner engagements often include daughters."

"Ah." Welch had grown stout and was nearly bald. He was the kind of man that fathers would take to, but not daughters. "McBride's belles."

"I was prevailed upon to call at the home, the mansion, of Mr. Henry James, an acquaintance only, but we had mutual friends."

"Henry?" Halsted said, dredging up a smile. "A Yale man. Rowed crew with me."

"Hmm. I suspect you refer to the son. I called upon the elder Mr. James. A butler sat me in the front parlor and said Mr. James would be down momentarily. Then the butler went into the next room and made my presence known. I heard the occupants speaking amongst themselves. Four daughters. Hearing my name caused them some dismay. I had to listen to them decide whose duty it was to come entertain me. The argument became quite heated."

Halsted laughed but felt guilty for doing so. He wondered if Welch had been hurt or merely embarrassed. "What did you do?"

"I waited. Eventually one of them was pushed through the door by her sisters. I mean that literally. The surprising thing was the way she smiled. She apologized for keeping me waiting and giggled girlishly. Very charming."

"Yes, I know that pretty female laughter, like tinkling bells. They must practice it in front of their mirrors for hours at a time."

"Well, it quite took me aback. I'm sure she would have been horrified to learn I'd heard them and knew she was the sacrificial lamb. Ladies can be very false, I suppose."

"And rather stupid."

"Oh no. Just young. It was the father's fault, really, for foisting me upon them."

"Did he ever appear?"

"I don't know. I didn't stay long enough to find out." After a pause, Welch bellowed with laughter, which made it all right to join in. "The argument was really very amusing. Like something out of Austen. They were afraid to *talk* to me, Halsted. I don't know what they think pathologists do—"

"I expect they have some idea if they were afraid of you."

"I'd hardly describe an autopsy over dinner."

Halsted raised a brow. "No?"

Welch's jaw dropped. Then he smiled. "Point taken." He pulled his watch from his vest pocket, tapped it, and said in a gentle voice, "It's time. I don't suppose you can wait an hour?"

"Is it that obvious?"

"You don't look well." He stretched out his hand and squeezed Halsted's arm. "You'll get through this."

Halsted slipped his arm away and stood. "I'll be right back," he said, voice shaking. He headed for the ladder to go below, his relief outstripped only by his fear. Three more days of a dwindling supply. Then what? He couldn't conjure more out of sea air.

He made it to his room before he vomited from sheer panic.

❧

"Oh, for pity's sake! Let him go," Welch commanded, exasperated, responding to the commotion outside his door.

Captain Bibber gave the nod and Jake let go of Halsted's arms, which had been held tightly behind his back—as though he were a criminal, which, now, he supposed he was. They stood crowded in the galley below deck. A single lamp gave little light to aid the dim rays from the moon leaching down the ladder. All rather theatrical.

"Eight days, Halsted," Welch said, "we'll be in New York in eight days."

He looked angry. Or maybe disgusted. And a little ridiculous in a coat thrown over his nightshirt.

"I know," Halsted said.

He should be mortified, furious at himself, at Welch for subjecting him to this, and at the crewman, Jake, who had tracked him down in his cabin, caught him red-handed as the saying went. But he was oddly complacent.

"The lock is broken," the captain said. "The contents of the medical locker are in complete disarray and the morphine is gone."

Halsted hadn't known what comprised the schooner's emergency medical supplies. All he knew was that throwing himself overboard was preferable to eight more days of desperation. So after a supper he could not eat, after Welch had retired, after the captain took to his cabin and a single crewman had taken watch for the night, Halsted broke into the medical locker. He had to make do with what was there.

He should be ashamed, but the morphine prevented so intense an emotion. He felt only a numbness. Not quite the oblivion he'd sought, but a very welcome numbness.

Welch took a deep breath. For a long moment, he gazed, unfocused, at the bulkhead. Then he asked Halsted, "How much morphia is there? Enough to get you home?"

"I don't know."

"You will have to make it last. Or we will tie you to your bed. I will not have you—" He choked, then turned his head and wiped something from his eyes. "This is my fault. I didn't realize it would be this bad for you."

Halsted shrugged. He didn't want pity. He wanted to be cured. He could picture himself tied to his bed, like Odysseus lashed to the mast to keep from answering the sirens' call.

"I'll make it last," he said, exhausted by the struggle and resigned to it.

If he threw himself overboard, Welch would blame himself. Halsted hadn't sunk low enough to saddle the man with that.

9

1886, April

New York City, New York

EDITORIAL

To some persons, nothing is more fascinating than indulgence in cocaine. It relieves the sense of exhaustion, dispels mental depression, and produces a delicious sense of exhilaration and well-being. The after-effects are at first slight, almost imperceptible, but continual indulgence finally creates a craving which must be satisfied; the individual then becomes nervous, tremulous, sleepless, without appetite, and he is at last reduced to a condition of pitiable neurasthenia.

—Dr. George F. Shrady, *The Medical Record*, Nov. 28, 1885, p. 604

"Why don't we wait inside?" Dick Halsted asked Welch, shifting impatiently from foot to foot on the brick walk outside the townhome his brother shared with Tom McBride. "Why stand out here in the rain?"

Welch said wryly, "Open your umbrella." He didn't understand the affectation of carrying umbrellas yet refusing to use them. "I want to wait for Dr. Mattison. An ambush requires a coordinated attack."

Dick shook his head. "I still think bringing in an alienist is a mistake."

"Dr. Mattison is a neurologist, not an alienist. He's the nearest thing to an expert in this sort of case."

Dick winced. "Don't refer to Bill as a 'case.'"

Sheltering from the drizzle beneath his own umbrella, Welch puffed his cigar and nodded an apology. He was used to talking medicine frankly with other physicians, not talking about physicians, euphemistically, to their families. But if Halsted was not a 'case' of cocainomania, then no one fit the description. He had not told Dick about his brother's larceny on board the *Vega.* He'd said only that a two-month sailing voyage had failed to break William's habit. Something more drastic was required.

"There," he said, gesturing with his cigar, then dropping it to the walk.

A slender man in gray-striped trousers and a dark coat approached from the west, head ducked into the wet wind. Welch waved and called, "Dr. Mattison?"

"Yes," the man said, drawing closer and extending his hand. "You are Dr. Welch?"

"I am." He shook the physician's hand. "And this is Dr. Halsted's brother, Richard."

"Dick," Richard said, then shook hands also.

Dr. Mattison peered at Dick closely. "Does he listen to you?"

Dick gave half a laugh. "Never."

Welsh sniffed. The Halsted brothers were peas in a pod.

"Hmm," Mattison said. "I understand there is no wife or fiancée to make an appeal to the gentler emotions. So, you will have to be the lightning rod for his anger. Whatever he says to rile you, do not take the bait. Are you comfortable with this?"

Welch saw worry flicker in Dick's eyes, then they hardened.

"Whatever it takes," Dick said.

Welch believed he meant it. He was here, after all. And he had fronted a rather large deposit for the treatment without hesitation. Halsted shouldn't underestimate him the way he did, but then, Welch was no authority on relationships between brothers. Yet surely a rational man like Halsted would respond better to reason than emotional manipulation.

Mattison nodded. He turned to Welch. "You've spoken with Dr. Goldsmith?"

"Yes, thank you. He was very helpful." Dr. Goldsmith was the newly appointed superintendent at Butler Hospital, a very well-respected private facility in Providence, Rhode Island, discreetly distant from New York. His predecessor, Dr. Sawyer, was one of the foremost experts on alcoholism and morphiomania. Goldsmith was following in his footsteps. "I appreciate you arranging this—"

Dick interrupted. "You're assuming he will agree to go."

Mattison said, "I assume nothing. There is a very good chance he'll refuse."

"I'm not leaving this house until he agrees to it," Welch said.

The others looked at him a moment, Mattison impassively and Dick with a smirk that fell from his face as he recognized Welch's resolve.

"Let's go in then," Mattison said.

They knocked. McBride opened the door. If his skin did not look so sallow, Welch would say he was white as a ghost.

"He's in his surgery," McBride said, stepping aside to let them in. "Worse than ever."

"This is Dr. Mattison," Welch said, taking off his damp overcoat and hanging it on the coatrack. The others followed suit. He gestured to his friend. "Tom McBride."

"I've heard your name often," Mattison said. "All praise."

"Thank you. I've been following your recent work. Yours and Shrady's. I hope to God you can help."

Dick spoke up. "What do you mean worse?"

Frowning, McBride answered, "For the last two weeks, he has scarcely left the surgery except to replenish his supply. He was furious to find I eliminated his stores while he was gone. He hasn't touched any real sustenance in days."

"How often is he taking it? What route?" asked Mattison.

"Injections." McBride drew a deep breath, voice cracking, and said, "I suspect he is injecting himself every few hours, if not more."

"Good God!" Dick shouted. "Why haven't you—"

"Well, he knows we're here now," Welch said, putting a hand on Dick's arm. "Let's confront him before he gets his guard up."

Seeing their reluctance, Welch led the way down the paneled hallway, Mattison at his side. He pushed open the door to the surgery. The once-immaculate office was as messy as its occupant. Halsted slouched in his examination chair. He looked slovenly. Emaciated. Unwashed.

Dick gasped. He went to his brother's side and clasped his arm. "Bill."

Halsted yanked it away. "What the hell? What is Welch doing here? Who is that?"

Mattison had moved to the cabinets. Two vials and a syringe lay on the countertop. He examined them, shook his head, and said, "Check his pulse."

Welch did, surprised Halsted allowed it. The surgeon's hands were sweaty and tremulous. "One thirty-eight." That couldn't be right. Going on this way would kill him.

Now Halsted did pull back, glaring. "You didn't answer me. Who is in my office?"

"I am Dr. Mattison."

Halsted's eyes narrowed. "Ah. Hunting your subjects down, are you?"

He rose with effort and ambled to his desk, littered with loose paper and journals. He leaned on it heavily, removed his glasses to rub his eyes, put them back on, and began rustling through the debris. With a triumphant grunt, he plucked up one of the journals, *Alienist and Neurologist*, and opened it to a page marked by a slip of paper.

"'Correspondence. To the editor: If any reader of your journal has met with a case of cocaine addiction and will send me the fullest details at his command, I'll thank him for the courtesy, reimburse him for any expense incurred, and give him full credit in a coming paper. J.B. Mattison, M.D. Brooklyn. 314 State Street.'" He raised his head. "That's you."

Mattison nodded.

Welch could not help but be impressed. Halsted looked like the worst inebriate living on the street, yet he had not only been reading the literature but studying his own condition.

Halsted dropped the journal back on the desk.

"Who gets the honor of acknowledgment in this 'coming paper,' Welch or McBride?"

"Neither. They asked for discretion." Mattison regarded Halsted steadily. "Interesting that you marked the request. Perhaps you were thinking of contacting me yourself?"

"For what purpose?" Halsted sneered. "Confession?"

"Public service?" Mattison suggested. "You've been an enthusiastic proponent of the drug. And now, how can the genie be put back in the bottle?"

Halsted seemed, all at once, to shrink into himself. "It can't. Ask Welch. Ask Hall."

"That was my hubris," Welch said, worrying now about Hall. If he were suffering too, the scope of this tragedy was appalling. "I had no concept of the power of the drug. But you can overcome this, Halsted."

McBride joined the plea. "You can. Not alone, obviously, you need help."

"You're one to talk."

"I know. Denial is a strong deterrent. But I am going into treatment. You must also."

Welch tried an appeal to the scientist. "Dr. Goldsmith has an interest in studying the treatment of chemical cravings. Butler Hospital treats such conditions—"

"Butler Hospital for the Insane?" Halsted laughed bitterly. "No thank you. I won't shame my family. An insane asylum?" He turned to his brother, who had not moved from his side. "Dick? For the love of God! How can you be party to this?"

Dick said, "Don't hide behind the tired excuse of the Halsted name. It is your name that will be shamed if you give in to this without a fight. Bill, you're better than that."

"Then why don't you go to this asylum? You've been a drunkard longer than I've been taking cocaine."

Dick colored. He glanced at Mattison, still standing by the cabinets, then focused back on his brother. He forced a lopsided smile.

"You first."

Halsted froze. He stared at his brother a moment and then teared up and abruptly turned his head. Welch didn't know what the words meant to them, but obviously, that river ran deep. Still, he had his doubts that an appeal to the heart would work on a man like Halsted.

10

1886, May

Columbia, South Carolina

WADE HAMPTON'S BROTHER DYING IN COLUMBIA

Columbia, S.C. May 7 1886 [Special]

Colonel Christopher Hampton is lying at his home in this city dangerously ill. His brother, Senator Wade Hampton, is here, watching over his sick bed.

—*The Atlanta Constitution*, Atlanta, GA, May 7, 1886

❧

This. This was why God had made me. My purpose. Not marriage. Not children. Not respectable spinsterhood under my aunts' roof, then under my brother's, but this.

"Don't worry, Uncle Kit. It's all right," I murmured. "It doesn't matter."

"Kitten, I'm so sorry," he rasped, tears in his eyes. I wasn't quick enough with the pot and he messed the bed.

"Nothing to be sorry for."

I set the empty pot on the floor, then rolled my uncle onto his side, carefully peeled off his nightshirt, and used it to sop the flux. I managed to strip the far side of the sheet, then slipped it from underneath him. Newspapers had been layered beneath to keep the mattress dry. This was not the first time his bowels had loosened and I had learned, from past missteps, the best way to proceed. I wadded it to the floor, slid a towel under his hip, and grabbed the cloth and basin of warm water from the bedside table to wipe him clean.

"If this water is too chilly, tell me." Necessary but wasted words. He wouldn't complain if it were ice.

Uncle Kit was skin and bones, except for a belly so swollen that he looked with child. His skin was scaly; his tongue was furred; the whites of his eyes were yellow. And he smelled terrible, no matter how carefully I washed him. Dr. Taylor said it was his liver gone bad.

After blotting Kit dry with a towel, I reversed the process: layers of newspaper, new sheet, clean nightshirt. He had a sheen of sweat on his brow by the time I finished.

"Kitten…"

"Shhh. Don't upset yourself. Uncle Wade will be in shortly to tell you the day's news."

Uncle Kit nodded, closing his eyes as I gathered up the linens for the laundress. I ought to take away the soup bowl, too, since the broth had grown cold. Vera, our cook, one of the few of our people who hadn't scattered during the war, would fuss at me because he'd eaten nothing again. It peeved me that she expected me to force food down his throat.

"I'll be right back," I whispered.

I found Uncle Wade just outside the door. His gray-streaked mustache and beard were untidy and his shoulders sagged. He had suffered so much, fought so hard, lost so many loved ones; yet to me, he had never seemed old until these past few months, the toll of watching his younger brother's slow passing.

Had it been easier for him to witness my father's death—in an instant—on the battlefield?

"Is he sleeping?" my uncle asked. "Should I come back later?"

"No. I think he's waiting for you."

He gritted his teeth and went into the room.

I trudged down the creaky back staircase to deliver the dirty linens and dishes to the pantry. Aunt Dodie intercepted me on the way and reached for the bundle.

"Honey, it's a beautiful day outside. Go sit on the porch. Rest awhile."

Aunt Dodie, the youngest of my three surviving aunties, had borne the brunt of raising me, Lucy, and Frank, though it had been a communal effort. We were far from being the only fatherless children of our generation, and mothers, of course, were lost with tragic frequency, but we were distinguished by having lost both.

"I'm not tired," I lied.

"You're pale and have dark ridges beneath your eyes. Kit doesn't want you getting sick."

"I won't." My voice quivered. "I'll go for a walk later, when he's sleeping."

Aunt Dodie looked too sorrowful to argue. "Then I'll sit with him a couple of hours so you can get some rest."

That was how it had been. The aunties fluttered in and out, sending me to sleep, to eat, to take care of my own toilet. They sent me out for walks. They did what they could to spare me, but it was clear that I had taken on the primary responsibility of caring for my uncle—and I would not relinquish the role.

Lucy had stopped visiting the sickroom a month ago. She could not bear it—so she said. Frank came for an hour each day, then left to attend to Uncle Kit's business—so he said. I understood why they found it so difficult to see him this way but I didn't share their reticence to be near him. Nursing suited me. It was a dreadful way to discover a calling.

Uncle Kit was the only one I had told of my wishes. He supported me unreservedly. He always did. Unfortunately, the rest of the family would not. Caring for loved ones was one thing, but nursing was not an acceptable path for a lady. To win this battle I would have to draw on my "Hampton inheritance." While Lucy and Frank had gotten grandfather's famous height, Uncle Kit always teased that I was four-foot-seven inches of infamous Hampton bullheadedness.

I gathered clean sheets and towels and returned to the sickroom to find Uncle Wade reading aloud from the Bible. Closing my eyes, I half-listened and half-prayed until he was done. Uncle Wade stood, laid his hand on his brother's shoulder for a few moments, then cleared his throat and turned away without speaking. I let him pass from the room before stepping to the bedside.

"Are you ready for your medicine?"

Laudanum was the only thing that soothed Uncle Kit. He hadn't had a cigar or glass of whiskey in months. He hadn't eaten more than a mouthful at a time in days.

Kit nodded.

"Oh." I scowled, annoyed at myself. I'd taken the medicine spoon from the room with his soup bowl. "I'm sorry. I have to go for another spoon."

I fussed a moment longer, straightening his sheets and wiping his brow, then exited to nearly trip over Uncle Wade who was kneeling on the floor in the hall, hands clasped, head bowed. He looked up. His face was wet with tears.

His grief embarrassed me. Interrupting him made me feel I'd done something wrong.

"I'm sorry."

He got slowly to his feet. "Kit says you want to go to New York for nurse training."

"Oh!" I didn't think Uncle Kit would pass on what I had confided. Dr. Taylor said the best nursing colleges in the country were those founded on the Florence Nightingale model, and the best of those were in New York.

Now that my secret was out, I ventured, "I thought I could stay with the Baxters."

My mother had been a Baxter. All my maternal relatives lived up North. It was hard to envision a time before "Yankees" and "Rebels," but my parents' romance proved such a past existed.

"Kit says you have a nurse's touch." He sniffed. "I don't know that's something you can learn at any school, darling. Seems to me you already know what you're doing. But Kit says we ought let you go." He pulled a handkerchief from his pocket, wiped his eyes, and blew his nose.

Of course I couldn't go to New York while there was breath in Uncle Kit's body, but afterward…

"Thank you, Uncle Wade."

How good of Uncle Kit to think of me even as he suffered. How like him to smooth my path. The aunties would still fuss at me and Lucy would be horrified, but with Uncle Wade's permission, they could not prevent my going. And nursing, devoting myself to others, would be a fitting tribute to Uncle Kit's example.

Uncle Wade's gaze was distant. I wasn't sure he even heard my reply.

"Excuse me. I must bring something from the kitchen."

He stepped aside and I hurried past.

Outside the kitchen, I had to pause and lean against the wall to let a wave of grief pass over me. How could I bear losing Uncle Kit? How could any of us bear the loss?

While Uncle Wade led armies, Kit took responsibility for the whole Hampton brood. While Wade Hampton campaigned for office, stumped for candidates, and traveled back and forth to Baltimore, New York, Chicago, Washington—Kit Hampton stayed at home to look after us.

Uncle Wade might be the man the world would remember, but surely, it would be a better place if more men were like Uncle Kit.

11

1886, October

Providence, Rhode Island

THOMAS ALEXANDER MCBRIDE, M.D.; AN ACCOUNT OF HIS LAST ILLNESS

By D. B. St. John Roosa, M.D.

Mr. President and Gentlemen: Circumstances which I had no share in arranging made me one of the last professional advisors of the late Dr. Thomas Alexander McBride, and one of the witnesses of his ocean burial...The president of this society has requested me to communicate...such facts of his last illness as may be of sufficient interest and importance for a public recital.

...In the early morning of the 30th, I found that Dr. McBride was much changed for the worse. There was considerable ocular edema; there were numerous small hemorrhages in the conjunctiva with exophthalmos...Dr. Norr and myself consulted very earnestly together and we reluctantly decided there was nothing to be done...at about 12:15 on the morning of August 31, he quietly died from heart failure.

—Address read at a meeting of the Medical Society of the County of New York, Sept 27, 1886, published in the *New York Medical Journal,* vol. 44, October 2, 1886.

Pages torn from the *New York Medical Journal* fell out of the envelope addressed to William Stewart—the alias Halsted had been hiding behind. To call it a letter was a stretch. A note was clipped to the article.

"Debated whether to send this. May he rest in peace. I have a place waiting for you in my laboratory, should you choose, when you are ready. Best regards, W. H. W."

Halsted sat on the edge of his bed, lit a cigarette, and set it in an ashtray on his bedside table while he read through the entire article. Twice. Then he tore it in half and tossed it into the wastebasket. He stared at the wall a long while, drained of emotion, brain empty of thought. He reached absently for his cigarette only to find it burned out.

The professor was dead.

They had not parted on the best of terms. His fault. Everything was his fault.

He knew what would ease the pain leeching its way through the morphine-induced apathy: a dose of cocaine. His eyes moistened. Whether it was grief for his friend or the craving that he could not satisfy didn't matter. There was no bottom to this pit.

The program at Butler was benign on the face of it. Nourishing food—supervised, dining-hall style, three times a day; regular exercise—tennis was a ridiculous sport but he was getting the hang of it; scheduled activities—he chose gardening of all things, flower gardening; and meeting with his alienist, Dr. Lloyd, at first every day, then every other, now twice a week. He was allowed to read, which he did, voraciously, and to write letters, which he did rarely. It was all so humiliatingly mundane.

And then there was the morphine.

Early in his stay, he had been seized by the conviction he had been lobotomized. And he believed cocaine would restore his brain to its pristine state. Apparently, he trusted no one in the institution but a red-haired janitor, certain he was a lightly disguised Frank Hartley coming to his aid. What was true was that he bribed the man with two hundred dollars to bring him the drug from outside.

He should not have trusted him. The janitor reported the bribe to Dr. Lloyd. That was when the alienist suggested using morphine to calm his agitation. Or so he now understood. He recalled none of this. He could scarcely remember anything of those early weeks, so great was his misery and confusion. The agitation had been unbearable. Morphine was his only hope.

He hated the dullness it induced, a complacent sort of bliss, the exact opposite of the euphoria of cocaine. But the morphine pushed away despair.

It pushed away despair, but not grief.

We, some of us faculty, lay a few bets at commencement. My dollar is on you. Don't let me down.

Those had been McBride's words. Halsted graduated in the top tenth percent of his class and had been awarded first place in the Examination

Prizes—a coup for a budding surgeon. Surgeons were thought to be all hands and no brains, but he had once meant to change that perception. He would chase that elusive immortality of attaching his name to some great discovery.

How conceited he had been. How ambitious. How reckless. And how weak.

He had required escalating doses of morphine to drag him up from the depths, more than ten grains a day, divided and administered every few hours. Dr. Lloyd was now trying to wean him from it, but decreasing the dose made him sick. Very sick. He had no specific hunger for morphine, only the fear of another bout of cramping gut, loose bowels, constant nausea, and wracking pain. The symptoms were physical, unlike the intense mental anguish he felt when deprived of cocaine.

He had been pronounced "a challenging case" by his doctor. How was that for irony? Challenging cases had been his bread and butter. He never wanted to be one.

Halsted stood, kicked off his slippers and stepped into his shoes. Then he took his coat from the ladder-back chair and slipped it on.

His two-room suite—bedroom and sitting room—was comfortable, if smaller than he was accustomed to. Located in the Sawyer House, a new building with "luxury accommodations for private patients," it had its own bath, thank God. The closet was roomy and he was allowed to wear his own clothes. He even had a small bookshelf and desk. The carpet was shabby, but he wasn't in any position to complain. Compared to most of the patients at Butler Hospital, he was fortunate. At least he was not insane.

However, it was nearly time to meet with his alienist.

He left the room. There was no lock on the door. There was no such thing as privacy in an insane asylum. He walked the long hallway, exited the ward, and turned toward Center House.

The leaves had turned and many had fallen, blanketing the grounds with a kaleidoscope of yellows, oranges, and reds. The sun was out and the air was crisp and cold. So different from the soot-clogged air of New York.

The main building, Center House, was a three-story brick Tudor-Gothic structure with brownstone trim. He mounted the steps and entered—all on his own. They kept tabs on his whereabouts, but he no longer required an escort as he moved about. He was a functioning person. Welch and McBride would be proud. So long as they didn't see him rolling up his sleeve for another injection. So long as they didn't witness him writhing, twitching, and vomiting after his doctor adjusted down the dose.

He knocked on the door.

"Come in." Dr. Lloyd, seated behind his desk, glanced up. "Oh, it's you, Mr. Stewart."

Of course, his doctor knew his true identity, but politely maintained the fiction. Halsted money bought this pretense of anonymity.

"I believe I'm early."

The man smiled. "Better that than having to send someone to chase you down."

The joke was not funny. Halsted shrugged. "Not this time."

"Is something bothering you this afternoon? Something particular?"

"No." He paced a few steps, then sat in his accustomed chair, another uncomfortable ladder-back, but at least this one had arms. "Well, yes. I had word that a good friend died a few weeks ago."

"I'm sorry to hear that."

The doctor waited to see what else he would offer. It made Halsted tired, all the talking he was required to do. Sometimes he waited Dr. Lloyd out, saying nothing until he was asked a question. But he was not in the mood for games.

"I want to leave. I think I'm ready."

"Do you?"

Halsted nodded.

"Because of the death of your friend?" The doctor had very mobile bushy eyebrows that he used to good effect. The eyebrows did not think it a good idea to make so momentous a decision so rashly.

"Only partly," Halsted said. "It was a jolt, certainly, but I've been thinking this way for a while. I feel my progress here is stalled. I need to get back to work. My mind is shriveling. Things are happening out there."

"Things?"

"Surgical things."

"You feel you are ready to perform surgery." He made it more of a question than a statement. "You would put yourself back into the same environment with its temptations?"

Halsted hesitated, then answered truthfully, "No." He shifted in his chair. "I won't go back to New York. There's nothing for me there. But I've been extended an invitation to do some experimental anatomy work in Baltimore."

The eyebrows rose. "Have you now?"

"It's been a standing invitation."

"Yet you choose to go now? Just after hearing about your friend?"

"Are you afraid I am so sunk in grief I will relapse?"

"Are you?"

Halsted rolled his eyes. "You are exasperating."

"And you play your cards close to the chest. It's a reasonable question. Are you afraid of relapsing?"

"Yes." He balled his hands into fists. "But I'm more afraid of rotting away here. I have to leave sometime. I think I should leave now."

The doctor did not respond for several moments. He sat back in his chair and steepled his fingers. Finally, he spoke. "You came here voluntarily. You aren't being held against your will. In the past couple of months, you've worked diligently, cooperated in your treatment. You're obviously motivated."

Halsted nodded, teeth clenched. He heard a "but."

The doctor leaned forward and sifted through a short pile of folders on his desk. He pulled out one and thumbed it open.

"You are still taking six grains of morphine daily." The eyebrows registered disapproval.

"I know that is an enormous dose. But it's significantly lessened." He kept his voice even. "I believe I can continue to reduce on my own."

"Hmmm." His eyes moved over his notes. Halsted wished he could see what the man had written. "You have a place to go. Gainful work. Have you support in Baltimore? Family?"

He thought of Welch. "I have support."

The doctor set the folder down. "Let me suggest this. You are due for another dosage adjustment in two days. Let's advance that to tomorrow and escalate reductions over the next two to three weeks. I think you should switch to pills, rather than injections. It will be rough on you, no doubt, but I'd like to see you down to four grains before you leave us."

He wouldn't argue. He would like to see that too. Only he dreaded the next two to three weeks, getting *there* from *here*. But he would do it.

In the meantime, he would write to Welch accepting the invitation. It was time.

12

1886, November

New York City, New York

Candidate Name and Address: Caroline Hampton, 852 Lexington Ave, N.Y.C.
Condition in Life, single or a widow: Single
Present Occupation or Employment: [left blank]
Place and Date of Birth: Columbia, So. Ca., Nov. 20, 1861
Height: 4 ft 7 in
Weight: 130 lbs
Where educated: Edgehill, Albermarle Co, Va
Are you strong and healthy and have you always been so? Yes
Where if any was your last situation? How long were you in it? [left blank]
Names and Addresses of two persons to be referred to. State how long each as known you: Mr. C. L. Strong, 16 5th Ave, New York, has known me 15 years
If previously employed, one of these must be the last employer: Dr. N. W. Taylor, Columbia, SC, has known me 25 years
Have you read and do you clearly understand the regulations: Yes
Date: Oct 19, 1886
Signed: Caroline Hampton
—Nurse Training School Application Form

❧

New York City was just as I remembered from our occasional visits over the years: crowded, malodorous, loud, filthy. How strange to think that my mother had been born and raised in this place. I'd never known her, she died before my first birthday, but by all accounts, she'd been a lovely, merry, vivacious, charming, sought-after woman. I feared there was very little of Sally Baxter in me.

I was not to stay with my Baxter family after all. The school required its students to live in a dormitory annexed to the New York Hospital.

The days would be long and we could be called upon to work in the wards at any time, day or night. As much as I loved my cousins and Aunt Lu, I was glad I'd be on my own. My nursing ambition displeased the Baxters as much as it did the Hamptons. There was a plot afoot to divert me with introductions to New York gentlemen and that, more than the anticipated rigors of nursing school, had the power to send me racing back to Columbia.

We were housed three to a room. The rooms were small, chilly, and sparsely furnished: one bookcase, one table to share for use as a desk, three narrow beds, one closet, and three small lockers for our personal effects.

I was assigned Alma Kline and Kate Vanwie as dormmates. Our first step was to draw straws for the beds. Then we set to unpacking and learning with whom we would be sharing our lives for the next two years.

Alma started. Plump and pretty, she had an air of—not of command, exactly, but certainly she had no qualms about taking charge.

"My father is Benjamin Kline of Kline Brothers Importers of Coffee, Tea, and Spices," she announced, putting first things first—establishing her pedigree. "He thinks I'm mad, naturally, going about it this way."

"Going about what?" Kate asked.

"Why, meeting doctors! But I told him that hospitals simply teem with them."

"You're at school to meet men?" I agreed with her father; she was mad.

Alma blinked at me. "Not men, dear. Physicians."

Kate snorted. A very unladylike sound to emerge from the nose of such a classic, fawn-haired, delicate beauty. "Physicians are men. So, by definition, selfish, untrustworthy devils. I'm done with the lot of them. The only men I want to see are those laid out, sick and suffering."

"My, my," Alma said, grinning. "You have a story." She tapped her chin. "Vanwie? Are you—"

"Not a Schenectady Vanwie." Kate's mouth tightened for a moment before she finished the thought. "Cousins of a sort. A junior branch as it were."

Social pecking order in general, I understood. But as I had never heard of Schenectady, let alone the Vanwies, the admission meant little to me.

"And what about you, Caroline?" Alma asked, turning her attention.

Stating the obvious, that I wished to be a nurse, would make me appear the outlandish one. But I had no other excuse.

"I cared for my uncle while he was dying. And discovered nursing is my calling."

They granted that the respectful moment it required, then Alma said, "Where are you from? I can't guess."

"South Carolina."

"Oh!" Kate exclaimed, her brow knotting with interest. "Hampton? Is your father the senator?"

"My uncle. Wade Hampton is my uncle."

"Who?" Alma asked.

The question took me aback. Kate answered for me. "That Confederate politician. The one that is still spatting with General Sherman. Alma, you must read newspapers."

"Only the Society pages. I'm sorry, dear." She smiled at me, then in something of a whisper, she said, "Did he fight in the war? Or shouldn't I ask?"

My breath was clear taken away. There were people who didn't know of General Wade Hampton? It turned my world upside down.

"He fought," I said, chin up, voice vibrating with pride. "He was South Carolina's brigadier general." He was General Lee's right hand. President Davis trusted no man more. I wanted to say the words aloud, but…didn't.

"Two of my mother's brothers died at Gettysburg," Kate said. Then she reached out and pressed my hand. "It's hard to imagine, isn't it? It seems so far in the past."

No. It seemed like yesterday. Our wounds were fresh, reopened every day.

Alma put in brightly, "Well, we'll have to make you feel right at home. What on earth brought you to New York?"

"Our nursing schools are not as advanced." I didn't want to admit that, but it was true. "And I have family here. My mother's family. The Baxters."

"George Baxter?"

Hmph. But George Baxter, a mere banker, she knew?

"He's my cousin."

"Oh! Well!" Alma's smile grew. "You're half-Yankee then."

She said it teasingly, but the tension around her eyes lessened, and Kate, too, let out a little breath. It was only my gut that tightened. Half-Yankee? I felt the insult down to my bones.

"No, never," I said, trying to match her light tone while still setting her straight. "I am a dyed-in-the-wool Johnny Reb."

"Southern belle," Kate corrected me. "No one would mistake you for a soldier. Though Alma may find her territory invaded. I'll wager all the unattached physicians will be conquered by your voice alone."

"I don't need them all, darling," Alma said. "Just leave me one or two of the tall, handsome ones. Preferably one in Dr. Van der Poel's circle."

Even I had heard of the Van der Poels. Alma aimed high.

"You may have your pick of the lot," I drawled. "I was serious when I said I want to be a nurse, not someone's wife."

Miss Weeks, a senior nurse with a stern mouth but seemingly infinite patience, supervised my first dressing change on the surgical ward. Rows of iron-framed beds lined each wall, with space between for a chair. The beds were not curtained off. Each patient was subjected to the misery of his neighbor. Thankfully, the room was only three-quarters full of unfortunates who were either awaiting surgery or recovering from it. The remaining beds, with taut white sheets and smooth pillows, served as a rather ominous reminder that there would be more.

The supervising nurse of the surgical ward, Nurse Phelps, walked about inspecting for cleanliness, adding to my general unease. It had been my turn to wipe everything down, and Nurse Phelps was known to pounce on a speck of dust.

With careful concentration, I removed layer upon layer of gauze, moistening the deepest piece before peeling it from the wound. The patient, a man the age of my brother Frank, had suffered deep burns over his left arm and chest. He was heavily medicated, but groaned and whimpered nevertheless.

I flinched at the patient's pain—pain I was causing. This was hard.

The morning's lesson in anatomy had been fascinating. The hygiene lecture had been well-organized and interesting, though largely common sense. I felt perfectly at home in the classroom. I was a fish out of water on the wards.

"Very good," Miss Weeks said. "Now take note, because Dr. Davis will ask. Is there drainage? Odor? What is the color of the wound edge? The base? And then a new dressing needs be placed over the wound."

A commotion at the door interrupted the lesson. I tried not to succumb to the distraction, but could not help glancing away from my patient's bed. Two orderlies dragged a disheveled, screaming man into the ward. He was flailing, legs and one arm akimbo. The other arm swung limply at his side.

"No! No! Snakes! Help!"

His high-pitched terror made my skin crawl.

A conservatively dressed youngish man followed, his serious demeanor contrasting with his bright red hair. "Nurse!" he said, raising a hand to beckon to us. "Sedative."

Miss Weeks tapped my shoulder. "I'll finish here. Fetch the sedative tray for Dr. Hartley."

"Yes, Miss Weeks."

I hurried to the supply room. The sedative tray held bottles of chloral hydrate, chloroform, morphine, rubbing alcohol, gauzes, scissors, and a hypodermic needle. I grabbed the tray and brought it to the bedside.

The orderlies had strapped the man down, oblivious to his blood-curdling screams. The physician watched impassively. Then he glanced at me.

"Student?" he asked. I nodded. "Delirium tremens. Fell into the street and was run over by a carriage. That arm is broken, obviously. Scissors?"

I handed him the scissors, and he cut the patient's shirt near the shoulder then tore it down to the cuff.

He made a tsking sound and continued to speak over the man's moans. "Sometimes they complain of bugs. In this case, bugs would not qualify as delusions. He will need to be deloused."

"Yes, doctor," I squeaked.

"Wet some gauze for me with that chloroform." He took it and held it under the writhing patient's nose. The man slowly settled. "Now alcohol." I gave him another soaked bit of gauze. He wiped a spot clean on the filthy shoulder. He looked at me questioningly, then, without a word, took the needle and bottle and drew up a dose of the morphine rather than asking me to do it. His lack of confidence in my ability relieved rather than offended me. He injected the morphine, then bent down and began manipulating the arm, tsked again, and stood.

"That will have to be set in the operating room. He needs a splint for now. A thorough delousing. Shave the head. Face, too. He must be kept as quiet as possible. I'll take him to surgery tomorrow. Did you get all that, Miss…?"

"Hampton. Yes, doctor."

He smiled. He had a pleasant smile. "Good. I'm Dr. Hartley. Where are you from?"

"From?" My voice hitched. I didn't want to narrate my circumstances every time I met someone new. "South Carolina."

"I thought something like that. Welcome to New York."

"Thank you," I replied, uncomfortably aware that Nurse Phelps, the crone, was paying close attention to the exchange. Lesson one was that nursing students were forbidden to flirt with doctors or medical students. I hadn't thought that would pose a problem, but now wondered how I was supposed to respond to a doctor's pleasantries. I kept my expression neutral. He winked.

"All right, then, Nurse Carolina. Go fetch me splints and bandages."

After the first month, students were required to work in twelve-hour shifts with little supervision. Much of the work was repetitive, done by rote, so as I became more efficient, I was able to spend more time talking with patients, reassuring them, easing their pain rather than causing it. My primary duties were to provide sufficient fresh air, warm blankets, baths, massage of limbs, help with feeding, bed pans, and cleanliness, cleanliness, cleanliness.

Lectures, unfortunately, were often cancelled because there was too much practical learning to be done. Nursing students were cheap labor for the hospital, but I couldn't complain. After all, I was gaining skill, not to mention strength. On my last evening shift, I transferred a two-hundred-pound man from bed to stretcher unaided. I felt very accomplished, though I would not like to do it again.

This was exactly why the aunties had said it was not fit work for ladies; yet I preferred this to the challenges available to Hampton females: supporting the men's politics, fundraising for war memorials and church windows, making sure Southern society didn't run off the rails.

Today, I was attending my first autopsy, and I was rapt. Perhaps it was ghoulish, but I could not look away.

The corpse was laid out on the dissecting table. The pathologist, a rather ugly man, short, bent, and clean-shaven—I was not used to seeing so much face on a man—was assisted by an energetic diener. Physicians involved in the deceased's care sat in the first row of the amphitheater. Medical students lined the next two benches. Nursing students filled in behind. It was difficult to see, but the odor, a mix of chemicals and death, reached us readily enough.

When the pathologist lifted the lungs from the body to demonstrate the cancer, Kate fled the room to be sick, but I leaned forward, straining to see. Those were *lungs*. Diseased, of course, but actual lungs. They resembled the drawings in books more than the preserved specimens in jars in the anatomical laboratory. What did they feel like? How heavy were they? Surely lungs should float like clouds if they were filled with air.

The pathologist removed other organs one by one and set them on the table for display. There was less blood than I expected. When he removed and opened the bowels, a different yet unmistakable stench filled the air. I put my hand over my mouth and tried to breathe through my fingers, and was reassured to see medical students doing the same.

"No visceral metastases," the pathologist announced, slicing through the liver with a butcher knife. "The abdominal organs are unremarkable."

The liver was a solid brown mound of tissue. Had Uncle Kit's liver looked like that? The question had no sooner formed then I flushed with mortification at my morbid curiosity. The aunties would think me unnatural.

"The cause of death is suffocation due to tumor burden and pulmonary hemorrhage. The tumor here, at the carina," he pointed, "eroded through the pulmonary vein."

Cancer of the lung—I tried to remember my notes from the reading we had been assigned. Lung cancer spread to lymph nodes, liver, adrenal glands, bones, and to the brain. Would they examine the brain also? I felt a twinge of revulsion at the prospect.

Lung cancer was a disease of men of middle age. Why would that be so? I understood why women got breast cancer or ovarian cancer. But women had lungs. Why were theirs spared?

Alma, next to me on the bench, leaned closer and whispered, "Are you coming to our Christmas party? My sister-in-law invited simply everyone who counts."

How could Alma be thinking about a party now?

I shook my head and whispered back, "My aunt and cousins have claimed me for the duration of the holidays."

I'd seen very little of my Baxter family. The classroom and ward hours were long, and evenings not in the wards were taken up with studying. I did have time off, and tried to spend some of it visiting with Aunt Lu, but my fellow students were a social bunch, and the sights of the city beckoned. I had to give in and buy a few clothes. My South Carolina wardrobe seemed hopelessly unfashionable after seeing what ladies in New York were wearing. Skirts were narrower and bustles, thank goodness, were gone. I avoided the brighter colors and frillier costumes after Kate pointed out, not unkindly, that I was too short for excess, that it made me look childish.

I enjoyed myself well enough, but even so, I preferred the purpose-filled hospital and classroom to frivolous theaters, museums, and tea rooms. New York City gaiety made me uncomfortable.

Alma pouted. "There will be eligible men at our party. Men who are not doctors."

Her tune had certainly changed. We were taught to give total, unquestioning obedience to the physicians, no matter how unreasonable the request might seem. Some of the girls had started to complain they were being treated like charwomen. Perhaps things were different here in the North, but I saw no difference between this and what young ladies were told they would owe their husbands. Nurses had more freedom than wives.

"I'm sorry to miss that," I said, then turned my attention back to the demonstration. "Oh, hush, Alma." The diener had fetched a saw and chisel. "He is going to examine the brain."

13

1886, November

Baltimore, Maryland

JOHNS HOPKINS UNIVERSITY
Academic Year Begins October 1, 1886
Announcements will be sent upon application.
—*The Baltimore Sun*, Baltimore, Maryland, September 18, 1886

A couple of weeks late for the start of classes, Halsted was now a post-graduate student, along with sixteen other physicians enrolled in Welch's pathology course: Micro-Organisms in Disease. When he left Butler Hospital for the position Welch had promised him, he hadn't known what to expect. He might have been frustrated to find himself sent back to school if not for the fact that, looking around the lecture hall at his classmates, he saw he was in formidable company.

Naturally, the course was phenomenally well taught. But more important was access to the laboratory. This was what Halsted had been itching for, a place to study the questions that had arisen during the years he had performed surgery and those he had mulled over during the months he could not.

The bequest left by Johns Hopkins, a Quaker tycoon who believed that the United States should have a university and medical education on par with that of its European counterparts, rather miraculously provided Welch with the means to satisfy his vision for experimental medicine. That included the construction of the Pathological Building. A brand-new edifice, opened the previous month, the Pathological had originally been slated as the Dead House and autopsy theater, but Welch tinkered with the plans, transforming it into a place of instruction and scientific discovery. An unimposing rectangular brick building with a mansard roof, the Pathological was to be separate from the hospital itself, which was not yet built. It had two floors and a basement morgue. There was an autopsy theater, of course, with a newfangled dissecting table and a second-floor gallery so the audience could watch the proceedings from above. There were offices on the ground floor. But the majority of the second story was given over to laboratories.

The laboratory space was superb. Each room was lined on three sides by black wood-and-metal cabinets and shelves. The central portion contained long laboratory benches with sinks and gas faucets. The outer wall had large windows for natural light. Between the windows, cupboards hung over another countertop which stretched the length of the wall. Each of Welch's graduate students was allotted a cupboard and the associated counter space. As Halsted quickly learned, the spirit of cooperation was so great under Welch's benign eye that no one quibbled over space.

Welch was in charge, but not expected to undertake the whole enterprise alone. He had an associate, William Councilman, and a Fellow, Franklin P. Mall. Welch introduced Halsted to Mall, who held the adjoining cupboard, within a week of his arrival. "You two will get along well," Welch predicted, or perhaps commanded.

So they went to lunch and discussed their interests.

Mall was a good ten years younger than Halsted but had a mental focus and ability to synthesize observations that Halsted could only envy. He was impatient with foolishness, an impatience Halsted shared. His sense of humor was sharp, almost cruel. And he worshiped Welch as a superior being.

They didn't simply get along, they jumped into a collaboration.

Halsted wanted to know why intestinal anastomoses invariably failed. Cancers, diverticuli, perforations—these could, conceivably, be cured if the diseased portion of intestine could be excised, simple enough, and the un-diseased ends sewn back together, simple in theory. In practice, the connections broke down, spilling fecal material. Patients died.

Mall had, through a process of vascular injection and maceration of surrounding tissues, identified the arcuate network of vessels throughout the bowel, from those grossly visible to those seen only under the microscope. He had defined the various layers of the intestines from inside to outside: mucosa, submucosa, muscle coat, and serosa. He listened to Halsted's query and offered what he thought was the solution: the dense connective tissue of the submucosa. Sew that, not the muscle. The theory was intriguing.

What Mall could not do was operate. He didn't like moving parts.

But with Halsted's hands and Mall's eyes—Halsted was certain the puzzle could be solved.

Welch listened, over supper at their landlady's dining table, to Halsted's account of the day's progress. The first step was simply opening the peritoneum, gently handling the bowels, then closing the wound, to prove that their subjects, dogs, could withstand surgery. He insisted upon scrupulous asepsis and pain control. If they intended to extrapolate results to humans, they had to treat the dogs as they would patients.

"The dog was anesthetized, shaved, cleaned. Mall stood beside the table, his typical goggling self. The hardest part of the surgery was reminding him not to touch anything."

"You didn't require him to scrub his hands?" Welch asked, fork poised over a large slab of pot roast.

"Of course, I did. But he scratched his nose as soon as I made the first incision. Surgery goes a lot more quickly if he doesn't help."

Welch chuckled, then took a bite and chewed. Halsted talked more than he ate. His appetite was still poor.

"I made the incision. Mall leaned in. An enormous E*ustrongylus gigas e*merged. I heard a shriek and turned to see Mall had leaped onto the table behind us. He was white as a sheet and whimpered, 'Snake.'"

Welch laughed so hard he nearly choked. After a gulp of wine, he said, "Well, that should teach him to stand back."

"We'll see." He took a bite of his bread. Mrs. Simmons baked her own, and although Welch praised it to the skies, Halsted tasted sawdust. He swallowed and said, "I doubt it. His enthusiasm is hard to curb."

"And your own?" Welch asked. "You're...satisfied with how things are going?"

"I could not ask for anything more."

Nothing but a cure, which remained elusive. Worse than elusive. He had informed Welch that the treatment involved the use of morphine and that he was in the process of tapering. He didn't want to admit his lack of progress. He had not reduced his dose. Rather it had crept back up to eight grains a day and he felt a strong desire for more. Pills were not as effective as injections. However, they were easier to take. And to hide.

He dropped his napkin onto his plate and pushed back his chair.

"I'm going to read for a while before bed." He grimaced. "Time for my 'medicine.'"

Welch looked at him with sympathy and nodded. "I won't disturb you, but let me know if you need anything."

He couldn't hide much from the man. He had tried to lease a small house near the hospital grounds, but Welch arranged for him to let a couple of rooms alongside his own in a tidy boarding house run by Mrs. Simmons and her daughter. It was impossible to say no thank you to Welch, no matter how much he would have preferred privacy. Welch was keeping a wary eye on him. He was humbled and grateful and annoyed.

❧

Mall sat nearly immobile in front of the lab's window, peering into his microscope, fiddling with focus with one hand while drawing with the other. "What's that you're working on?" Halsted asked, hanging up his hat. He hadn't been to the laboratory in three days and wasn't sure how to respond when Mall asked why.

"Wait a minute," Mall said without turning around. He scribbled a few more lines, then sat up straight and turned. "My embryos."

"Ah."

Mall had myriad interests, one of which was embryology. He had a remarkable ability to peer at hundreds of microscopic slides representing serial two-dimensional views of a specimen and then reconstruct the three-dimensional object in his head. He had taken embryos of varying ages from different species and mapped out the development of organs from small cell clusters to identifiable structures. He was now engaged in comparing human embryos, exceptionally rare specimens, with other mammals. It was all very fascinating in theory but tedious in practice. Mall had a high degree of tolerance for tedium.

Mall looked him up and down. "You still don't look well. Welch said you were in bed with enteritis. Stay back if it's cholera."

"It isn't cholera." Enteritis was as good a term as any for morphine sickness, though it didn't do justice to the symptomatology. "Something I ate, I suppose."

Unfortunately, the cure was the poison. He had tried halving his dose. That was a mistake. He could not expect Welch, or Mrs. Simmons, or the woman's daughter, to nurse him. He was helpless to clean up after himself. At some point, the knowledge that he could simply end his agony overcame his resolve. The thought that cocaine would not only stop the sickness but make him feel well—truly well—frustrated him. If there had been cocaine in the house, he would have taken it.

It might have eased him through the worst. Now was not the time to attempt something as foolish as dropping his dose so significantly. He was functioning on morphine. Maybe that was the best he could hope for.

"Horace found a suitable a dog," Mall said. "Are you ready to start?"

"Now?"

"I'm sorry. Was the dog supposed to schedule an appointment with your secretary?"

Halsted grimaced. "Don't be cute."

"I'll have Horace bring it up. I took the liberty of blunting the needle to be sure you don't accidentally poke it through the submucosa."

"Accidentally?" He laughed. "You said the connective tissue is too tough to penetrate without force."

"I said I suspected it would be difficult to penetrate without force. I'm not disparaging your technique but you haven't done this before."

He had certainly sutured with care before, though not with a dull needle. That would be a challenge of a different sort.

"I will humor you since you went to the trouble of blunting it."

Mall pulled a face, then went to find Horace, the technician in charge of procuring and caring for the lab animals. Halsted set up the table for surgery, gathering the ether and cone for administering anesthesia, morphine to prevent pain, alcohol and carbolic acid for cleansing the skin and instruments, and corrosive sublimate to irrigate the peritoneum. And he located Mall's blunted needles.

This dog was to be their control. Halsted would operate in the usual manner, resecting a segment of intestine, then sewing the edges together with two rows of stitches in the muscle coat only. Their hypothesis was that an anastomosis without the inclusion of submucosa would break down. He was obligated to take every precaution to make sure it would not. No sloppy surgery.

Halsted removed his coat and rolled up his sleeves, then began scrubbing. There was something soothing in the rote process, as long as he kept his thoughts on the experiment ahead. He couldn't think of the hundreds, perhaps thousands of times he had performed the handwashing ritual. He couldn't dwell on the thriving career he once had in New York, the future that had slipped through his hands. Rather, he had to concentrate on this: experimental surgery, a better way to satisfy his need to know.

14

1887, April

New York City, New York

STUDIES OF CONGRESSMEN

The Faces of Some of Our Great Men and the Legs of Some

If you sit in the gallery of The House of Representatives and carefully study the faces and figures of these three hundred men, you will see that the commonly accepted notions about the Yankee type, the Western type, the Southern type, are all wrong… Now let us take a Southern State, South Carolina, for instance…Wade Hampton…with his veins full of the choicest and richest South Carolina blood…is the picture of a prosperous Connecticut capitalist… Yet Wade Hampton's physiognomy belies his character… He is the true ideal Southerner despite his banker's face. He loves the hunt… He casts the fly with the joy of the piscatorial artist, and he coaxes trout from coy hiding places, and if there are no trout, senators say he creates them that he may hook them. The fields, the open air, the saddle, the rod, the gun, are his delights. He has sat in the Senate many years almost dumb. His State sends him there because he is her hero, and an idol. He votes. That is all.

—*The Sun*, New York, N.Y., April 3, 1887

❧

I sat at the long table in the students' dining hall, choking down a breakfast of buttered toast and tasteless applesauce. I was homesick for Vera's cooking: ham and grits and fried eggs, but too tired to eat much of anything anyway. I'd worked twelve hours, studied, slept fitfully, and was due back on the ward in an hour.

A shadow fell across my plate, and I looked up to see Alma, dragging herself to the table carrying a tray with a folded newspaper tucked under her arm. She sat down heavily.

"Are you all right?" I asked. Alma had been on nightshift. She should be in bed.

"Just exhausted. And starving. There was no time to eat last night. Some street brawl ended with three stabbings and a gunshot. Thank goodness we change services today. Maternity will be restful after surgery."

"Ha." I had not been on maternity yet, but restful was not the word used by our classmates who had. I was glad to be switching services too. I'd been on the medical ward: pneumonia, cancer, advanced syphilis, and the omnipresent tuberculosis—the disease that had taken my mother. I preferred the excitement of the surgical ward, even though the patient mortality was high. There was something nevertheless heroic in the attempt to cure.

Alma handed over the newspaper. "Kate asked if you'd seen this about your uncle. She said it was cute. You'll like it."

I avoided reading Northern newspapers lest I stumble across a reference to Uncle Wade. The gossip was silly—he was retiring from the Senate; he was engaged to the actress Rhea—but the politics were worse. The Republican newspapers scorned him, accusing him of pandering to the veterans, of lying to the Negroes. That was patently false. As I'd argued to Kate, Uncle Wade was a friend to the freedmen. She asked how I could square that with the knowledge he had once owned so many of them. When I informed her there was no contradiction, she tossed her head and said there was no reasoning with me.

I didn't want to read anything Kate shoved under my nose; nevertheless, since Alma was waiting, I skimmed until I found the Wade Hampton name. The piece implied Senator Hampton was no more than a folksy Southern sportsman. And that South Carolinians stupidly returned him to office out of misguided adulation of an old war hero.

"Well, wasn't that a waste of ink?"

Alma appeared startled. She flushed slightly. "I thought it was sweet. He sounds darling."

I folded the newspaper and handed it back. Uncle Wade would be delighted to think pretty young Alma found him darling. But he probably wished he could shoot the reporter who made him out to be so.

"He can be. But most of the time he's a bear. I don't want to be late." I stood and pushed back my chair. The nurse in charge would assign duties for the day, but it didn't hurt to be forewarned. "Is there anything I should know? I'm going to the surgery floor. Who operated last night?" I hoped it was not Dr. Dennis. They would all come down with post-operative infections and he would blame the nurses.

"Dr. Hall."

"Oh." Dr. Hall was understood to be a skillful surgeon, but he breezed in and out of the hospital, usually working nights, and had a reputation for being short with the staff.

"When I went off duty, he was still in the operating theater with the patient who'd been shot. I doubt the poor fellow will make it. He was *old*." Alma's gaze dropped to the table. It was not our place to pronounce upon such things.

"I guess we'll see." Then in a conciliatory way, I added, "Tell Kate thank you for sharing her newspaper. But it was my uncle Kit who used to say Uncle Wade could create trout out of thin air."

Alma nodded, but her attention had shifted to her cold toast and wet-looking eggs.

After a quick stop in the dormitory to brush my teeth and affix my nursing cap, I hustled to the surgical ward. Nurse Phelps greeted me with an impatient scowl.

"We're busy, Miss Hampton. A bit of fuss last night. Will you chart vital signs until Dr. Hall's patient is returned from surgery? Trauma. He will be yours."

"Yes, ma'am." Good. I preferred charting vitals to changing bandages.

Before I'd finished, two burly orderlies carried in a stretcher bearing a reed-thin old fellow with the worst pallor I had ever seen. The anesthetic must be wearing off, because he was moaning in a way that churned my stomach.

"Miss Hampton?" Nurse Phelps was administering a purge. She gestured to the new patient with her head.

I directed the orderlies. "You may set him over here. What is his name?"

"Mr. Monkton." One of the orderlies handed me a chart and a paper with orders scribbled on it. Dr. Hall's handwriting was close to illegible, but it looked like standard post-operative instructions: a rather large dose of stimulant, warm blankets, and a schedule for morphine.

I tucked Mr. Monkton in, murmuring assurances, and told him I was leaving to fetch his medication and would return. He was in no condition to respond, but his eyes opened to stare blankly at the ceiling.

Alma's assessment was right. How on earth had such a frail old man gotten mixed up in a street fight? I wished there was time to read the notes on the chart, but they wouldn't tell his story, just the extent of his wounds and how much blood he had lost. There was a large bandage over his flank which did not bode well.

I gave him the stimulant and elevated his legs. After a few moments, I rechecked his pulse. Thready. His skin still looked waxen. The morphine had put him right back to sleep, making it harder to tell if he was worsening.

"Miss Hampton?" Nurse Phelps voice was like a crow's caw. "Have you finished charting? Or do you think Mr. Monkton has the luxury of a private nurse?"

Excuses would bring down more censure, so I said only, "No, I'm sorry," and left Mr. Monkton's bedside to finish my tasks.

After charting, I was given charge of bedpans, and discovered the necessity of bathing Mr. Porter right away. He was awaiting surgery for an oozing fistula but was so anemic that Dr. Hartley wanted him to have a week of iron-rich feeding first.

It was a while before I returned to Mr. Monkton. His color was better, but not much. His pulse was weak but no worse. He must be a tough old coot; maybe Alma was wrong.

At that moment, Dr. Hall appeared, swooping into the ward, bringing with him a strong odor of tobacco and two trailing medical students. Although he was likely considered a handsome man, he looked haggard. Surely, he should not be so thin. He glanced absently around the room, then his gaze fell upon Mr. Monkton. He approached the bed.

"Good morning, Dr. Hall."

He nodded, picked up the chart, and flipped it open, then shut.

"Nicked mesentery." He frowned at the man, then lifted his arm and felt for the pulse. "He should have a dose of strychnine."

"He—"

"A tenth of a grain." He scrunched his eyes tight, then opened them. "One of the residents will be along shortly." He waved a hand over his patient like an irreverent blessing. "Keep him warm. Not much else for it."

He didn't bother to check on the other patients, but strode, heavy-footed, from the room, the medical students following, looking overwhelmed.

I tucked Mr. Monkton's arm back under the blanket, took his temperature and recorded it, then moved onto the next bed. A stout man with white whiskers and a flushed face grinned at me. He reminded me in a vague way of Uncle Wade. Maybe it was the amputated leg.

"Good morning, missy. Is it time for my morning whiskey?"

I pretended to check his chart. "Not yet."

He chuckled. "Worth the ask."

I helped him to sit up, handed him his newspaper, promised breakfast would be served soon, and tended to two more patients before Nurse Phelps joined me at the next bedside.

"Miss Hampton, aren't you forgetting something?"

"Am I?" Frantic, I tried to think what it might be.

Nurse Phelps harumphed. "Dr. Hall ordered a stimulant for Mr. Monkton."

"Oh." I breathed easier. "Yes, but I had already given it."

With a lift of one eyebrow, the nurse-in-charge said, "Before it was ordered?"

"Dr. Hall wrote the order with the post-op instructions."

"And then gave a verbal after examining the patient."

Two doses? That didn't seem right. What if that put too much strain on his heart?

"I just assumed—"

"Miss Hampton! I hope you are not about to tell me you assumed you knew better than the doctor."

"Certainly not." I assumed Dr. Hall had forgotten what he'd written. But it wouldn't help my case to say that.

"Give it now."

"But—perhaps I could send a message to Dr. Hall to request clarification?"

"Miss Hampton, that is a demerit. It is evident you did not forget but intended to ignore the order."

I couldn't defend myself without digging in deeper. I gritted my teeth and did as I'd been told.

While helping to serve morning meals, wiping down trays, changing bandages, I kept one eye on Mr. Monkton. The second dose of strychnine had done nothing to improve his pulse or his color, but thank goodness, it hadn't seemed to hurt him.

About three hours into my shift, the man suddenly vomited. I raced to the bedside. He was lying supine, so, naturally, he choked. I turned him and tried to swipe the vomitus from his mouth with a washcloth, but he continued to cough and grunt for several minutes. Finally, he settled. I'd have to change his sheet but was afraid to jostle him.

Nurse Phelps came to my side. "Bring clean linen. I'll help you. Then I'll send word to the surgical resident. He may want to examine him again. That bandage looks wet."

I went to the supply closet and returned with sheets. Mr. Monkton's lips had a blueish cast. Before we could strip the soiled sheet, he seized. It was horrible. He bit his tongue; his mouth filled with blood. The bandage slipped from his flank, and the wound gaped as his stitches tore. Nurse Phelps and I together were able to keep him from falling to the floor, but little else.

Nurse Phelps checked for a pulse, then said in a matter-of-fact tone, "I'll call for the resident to pronounce him."

I stared at the corpse, knees shaking.

"Is this the first patient you've lost?" Nurse Phelps asked.

"Yes." Other people I'd nursed had died, but not while I watched.

"You aren't going to faint, are you?"

"No, ma'am."

"Good. You know, Miss Hampton, this is our calling too. To be there when they go."

Was that supposed to be encouragement? I lifted my head and met her steady gaze.

"Is it our calling to *send* them?"

Nurse Phelps' expression did not change. Nor did her tone of voice when she said, "If you hadn't discharged your duty, how do you think you'd feel now? We are not doctors, Miss Hampton. It would behoove you to remember that."

15

1887, April

Boston, Massachusetts

CIRCULAR SUTURE OF THE INTESTINE

In the hope that an experimental investigation of the subject of intestinal suture might contribute somewhat to our knowledge of the causes of failure as well as of the conditions of success of enterorrhaphy, I have undertaken during the past winter a series of experiments in the Pathological Laboratory of The Johns Hopkins University in Baltimore. I wish on this occasion to express my thanks to Dr. Wm. H. Welch, the Directory of the Laboratory, for his kindness and advice, and also to acknowledge my indebtedness to Dr. F. P. Mall, Fellow in Pathology of the Johns Hopkins University, for his kind assistance in the operations and especially for calling my attention to many points concerning the minute anatomy of the intestine.

—Presented by Dr. W. S. Halsted on April 5, 1887 in a lecture at the Harvard Medical School, Boston, Massachusetts.

The lecture hall was nearly full. It had impressive acoustics; while Halsted had been speaking, one could hear the proverbial pin drop. He felt a hundred eyes upon him: several tiers of physicians, surgeons, medical students, even a few nurses. And somewhere amongst all those eyeballs were those of his old Yale roommate, Rev. Sam Bushnell, invitation courtesy of Welch.

The presentation of the results of sixty-nine circular intestinal anastomoses was well received. Very well received. Thank God. He made the right decision.

He had come *this close* to canceling, this close to failing despite the success of their experiments and the importance of their discovery. But for Mall's sake, Halsted realized he couldn't simply quit. So, he made the damn promise to Welch.

Aside from a couple mishaps with anesthesia and the few lethal cases of post-surgical adhesions with obstruction, they found that intestinal anastomoses which brought together the submucosal layers succeeded so long as the mucosa was not violated. If the suture lines did not incorporate the submucosa, the anastomoses failed.

He had quickly perfected a tiny stitch that picked up a thread of the tough connective tissue without breaching the whole—using a sharp needle, thank you very much.

Soon, within a few years perhaps, safe intra-abdominal surgery should be routine rather than miraculous.

Mall had been pleased with their joint success, rightly so, but had declined Halsted's invitation to attend the lecture and present the pathology. He'd drawn some very nice pictures, he pointed out, for Halsted to show. Well, Welch had warned Halsted the fellow was shy.

Welch had also told Halsted that Mall would be a phenomenal scientist because he was observant and detached.

Observant.

Three weeks earlier, they were compiling their data and decided they needed one more example. Mall set up the table while Halsted scrubbed. Alongside the instruments were drug vials, which now included cocaine for local anesthesia as well as morphine and ether. Under the glare of the desk lamp, Mall opened the notebook he had been using to record results and impressions. He picked up the vials, peered at them, and jotted something down.

"Where is Horace?" Halsted asked.

"Coming," Mall answered with a grunt.

He joined Halsted at the cast-iron sink and lathered his hands. Then, without warning, he grasped Halsted's wrists and rather forcibly studied his arms before releasing them with a sniff. "What the hell, Halsted?"

"What?" he asked, growing chilled.

"Your pupils are the size of dinner plates, your arms are pockmarked, and there is only half the amount of cocaine in that vial than there should be."

Halsted walked away from the sink, wiped his hands dry, and rolled his sleeves down. He was too furious to deny anything. It was no one's business but his own.

"Welch sent you to spy on me? Is that it?"

How was he supposed to have resisted? Every time he entered the lab, he had to stare at the vial. When he was not in the lab, he pictured the drug there, waiting for him.

Mall's jaw dropped. "Welch knows?"

His shock convinced Halsted that Welch had said nothing to Mall.

Shame overwhelmed him. His voice shook as he answered, "He knows I have been using morphine to break a cocaine habit."

"Morphine? Morphine, too?" Mall glanced back at the vials, then at Halsted. He looked stunned. Pale. Almost sick.

Halsted laughed hoarsely. "I have my own morphine. I haven't stolen the dogs'."

Mall continued to regard him as though he were a stranger. Then he said, "I thought my measurements were faulty."

"*What?*"

Mall swiped a soapy hand across his forehead. "If I was recording the wrong dosages, we'd have to start over. Shit, Halsted."

Halsted stared at him a long moment, then broke into laughter. How meticulous Mall was. The dogs' anesthetic doses were immaterial to the study. His laughter trailed off when Mall didn't join in.

Mall grabbed a towel to rub his hands and face. "I'll start looking for another surgeon. It's not my job to monitor the drug supply. Our collaboration is over."

He tossed the towel into the laundry bin.

Detached.

The abruptness of Mall's reaction took Halsted aback.

"I wouldn't want to hinder your career," he said, sneering.

"It's not my career that concerns me." Mall pulled a cigarette from his pocket. "I watched my mother die from rum fits. I'm not going to watch you destroy yourself."

Maybe not so detached.

Halsted drew in a deep breath and let it out slowly. He should have obtained his own cocaine. Then Mall would never have noticed.

"I'm going to stop."

"I don't believe you."

They stared at one another. Angry. Both of them. And Halsted was scared. He didn't know what Mall might do. He could lose his position and then he didn't know what would be left to him.

"I'll tell Welch. Help me finish these experiments, put together this lecture, and I will do whatever he says."

After a long pause, Mall nodded and finally lit the cigarette he'd been caressing. "All right." He took a hard drag. "I suppose someone has to present the work. It's good. But if you don't tell Welch, I will."

Likely the two had discussed him behind his back afterward. But at least he'd been the one to confess his relapse to Welch, who'd seemed more saddened than surprised.

Thank God the lecture had been well received. His very best effort—Mall and Welch deserved that much from him.

There were a few questions afterward, which he answered as succinctly as he could. He'd run over his allotted time and men were anxious to go to dinner. He was anxious to get to the station. After much internal debate, he'd packed a vial of cocaine; another dose couldn't hurt at this point, but there was no private place here to take it.

As he gathered his notes together, a familiar face topped by bright red hair approached him at the podium: Frank Hartley.

"Well, well, Halsted. You've landed on your feet after all." He smiled. "That was a splendid presentation. Impressive."

"Thank you. Are things well with you? I wasn't expecting anyone from New York." He wouldn't have come if he was. Bad enough having to face Sam.

"I saw the notice. It sounded interesting and the train ride isn't so far. Besides, I wanted to see you." He sounded sincere. "I'm glad you're well."

He didn't disabuse him. Instead, he asked, "How is Hall?"

Hartley shook his head. "Poor. I don't see him much anymore. How is Welch?"

"Thriving."

"Good. No one deserves it more. Have you supper plans? I don't know this Harvard crew. We could catch up—"

"I would like to." He would. Anything would be better than where he was headed. "But I have a train to catch."

"You're heading back immediately? Baltimore is that compelling?"

He forced a smile. "I'm visiting some family. New England family. Since I'm here."

Hartley nodded. "Well, it was good to see you."

The man drifted away. Halsted packed his papers into his case, thanked his hosts, answered the last few questions, deflected another dinner invitation, then located Sam, who had been waiting patiently by the nearest exit. Sam would take him to the train. See him off. Report back to Welch.

"Hello, Bill. That was nice work." Sam shook his hand. He was heavier. His hair was thinner but mustache bushier. His eyes looked sad. "Except for the poor dogs. I guess you can't work on rats with those paddle-thumbs of yours."

Halsted managed the requisite smile. Back in school, he'd first confided his interest in surgery to Sam, who'd laughed and drew his attention to his short, flat thumbs. Well, it hadn't been his hands that had failed him.

"That's a challenge for another day. I suppose I ought to thank you for coming."

"No. It's awkward. I don't believe it's necessary, but, well, there you have it."

"You never knew Welch at Yale, did you?"

"Oh, we met. We had a class together. Greek theater. Brilliant man. Knew more than the professor did."

A long pause followed.

"I have a carriage waiting. Are you ready?" Sam asked, not quite meeting Halsted's eyes.

"A carriage? We can walk, surely. I sent my trunk ahead. The station isn't far."

Sam shook his head. "Not to the train. I'm…well, I'm escorting you to Providence. Give us a chance to talk."

Halsted let out a long, low whistle. Evidently, Welch was taking no chances. The promise Halsted had made was to commit himself back into the insane asylum.

It seemed his word wasn't worth all that much.

16

1887, August

Baltimore, Maryland

Please feel at liberty to publish, in any way you wish, your work on intestinal suture. I only regret that circumstances prevent me from keeping my part of the contract. If you still feel as kindly disposed as when you offered to make me a diagrammatic drawing of the coats of the intestine, be assured that I would appreciate the service... It would please me very much to hear from you now and then... I would like to write more but I am not very well.

—William Stewart to Franklin P. Mall, May, 1887, from Providence, R.I.

Please do not think me unappreciative of your kindness... Dr. Welch tells me that you have made some beautiful sections of the intestinal specimens. I hope that you will think it worthwhile and may find time to write them up. I have about finished my article and expect to have it copied and ready to send to Baltimore for Dr. Welch's inspection and yours in about one week... Hoping to hear from you soon again, and to see you again before you become too well known and fly too high.

—William Stewart to Franklin P. Mall, June, 1887

❧

Welch was in his office in the Pathological, reading, when a light tap on the doorjamb disturbed him. He glanced up to see Franklin Mall fidgeting nervously in the doorway.

"Come in, Mall. Sit down. I was going to come find you after luncheon."

Mall came in but did not sit.

Anyone walking by would think them an odd pair, Welch reflected: Mall—thin, nervous, delicate-featured with prominent ears and a reputation for misanthropy, and Welch—placid, running to fat, bald, genial. Yet they had much in common and one thing in particular.

"Did they let you in? Did you see him?"

Welch nodded. "Please sit." He opened a box on his desk. "Would you like a cigar?"

"No," he said brusquely, taking a chair, then correcting himself. "No, thank you."

Welch took one. He clipped it, lit it, then puffed. He laid it in his tray. It wasn't fair to keep Mall waiting like this, but he was having trouble finding the words.

"He'll likely stay through the fall. Maybe longer."

Mall gaped, then snapped his jaw closed. "Bad, then?"

Welch nodded.

"I don't understand," Mall said, twisting his hands together. "The paper he wrote, his last letter—"

"Written over a month ago."

"Yes, but he was improving."

"I thought so too." Welch rubbed his eyes, then picked up his cigar. His chest ached. He sifted through a pile of journals on his desk then pulled out a year-old copy of *The Quarterly Journal of Inebriety*. "Have you seen this? By Dr. De Montyel? The abstract is enough."

He flipped it open to a bookmarked page and handed it to Mall, who read silently. Welch had memorized the words:

> Injections of morphia have as a result a double action: a benign and a special action upon the nervous system by which its natural function becomes impossible after a certain term without the assistance of the poison. These two effects are separate and distinct from each other: the second is manifested when the first is no longer exhibited. There are, then, two forms of morphiomania; the one resulting in a temporary good effect, the other a vital necessity; and, after a variable period, the cases of the first pass over into the second.

After a few moments, Welch said, "It was ridiculous to think morphine could cure cocaine hunger, just as it was foolish to tout cocaine as a cure for morphiomania."

He located a more recent journal.

"And this is in *The Lancet*. Dr. Mattison's work. It's lengthy. But here is the crux. 'To the man who has gone down under opium, and who thinks of taking to cocaine in the hope of being lifted out of the mire, I would say "Don't," lest he sink deeper. I have yet to learn of a single instance in which such an effort reached success, but know of many cases where failure followed, or worse—cocaine or coca morphia addiction.' That is where our friend now stands: coca morphia addiction. He needs both."

"It's been four months! Surely they're not still plying him with morphine and cocaine."

"No. He is weaned from the drugs. But it seems that weaned from and cured of are not the same thing."

Mall scowled. "Like alcohol then. Abstinence will only be temporary."

Welch quieted. It was not fair to Halsted to say more. He had seen him only briefly. Halsted had lost weight and looked ill. Not only physically ill, he had the dull expression of one sunk in melancholy. Halsted had always been a man of curbed emotion, but Welch had learned to read him: the pink ears of embarrassment, the reddening neck of anger, the twitch of the lips that suppressed laughter, and always the light in his eyes. They burned with curiosity; they flared with irritation; they glinted with humor. Seated on a cheaply constructed ladder-back chair, wrapped in a thin blanket, Halsted had given one-word answers to Welch's attempts at conversation. In the depths of the man's eyes, there was nothing but dark.

They had taken away his braces and shoelaces and allowed no sharp objects in the room.

Welch's voice was hollow as he answered. "Worse than alcohol, I fear." He cleared his throat. "But there is always hope. Are you a praying man, Mall?"

The question flustered him. Mall stood up and looked at both far corners of the room before shrugging. "I think I come from Lutheran stock."

"Ha-Humph!" Welch laughed in spite of himself. How very *Mall*. To answer embryologically. "Fortunately, I am an ardent Congregationalist. I will do the praying. As for you, keep writing to him. He reads the letters, I am told, even if he does not answer them. Send him more of your drawings. Appeal to that mind of his. That beautiful mind."

Mall gave him a long look, then turned his gaze toward the ground. "I told him I would replace him with another surgeon. I wish I had not said that. I didn't mean it. He's quite irreplaceable."

Welch smiled. "And he knows it. That's why I have faith he'll return."

PART TWO

Enable: (e-nā'-bl) v.: 1. To make able; furnish with adequate power, ability, means, or authority; render competent.

— *The Century Dictionary*: an encyclopedic lexicon of the English Language, Century Company, 1889-1891

17

1888, April

New York City, New York

TEN TRAINED NURSES GRADUATED

MANY COMPLIMENTS FOR THE NEW-YORK HOSPITAL SCHOOL

Ten young women fully equipped with the knowledge and skill requisite for the care of the sick and wounded, said goodbye last night to the New-York Training School for Nurses. The graduating exercises, which were pronounced the most successful in the history of the school, were held in the reception rooms at No. 8 West Sixteenth St., which were well filled with friends of the school and of the pupils… Professional nurses of the modern type are as distinguished for blooming health and beauty as were those of an earlier day for the opposite characteristics and the class of last night was certainly no exception to the rule…

The names of the graduates are as follows:

De la Z. Hughes, Kate M. Reid, Sarah J. Neff, Mary Hustler, Kate Vanwie, Caroline Hampton, Alma S. Kline, Haitie E. Macdonald, Isabella Ross, Delia A. Falieu

—*New York Tribune*, New York, N.Y., April 4, 1888

The reception rooms of New York Hospital had been transformed: festooned with streamers and filled with pots of flowers. We freshly minted nurses wore light blue dresses with starched white aprons and caps. We tried to contain our exuberance behind serious expressions, pretending newly acquired gravitas, but our guests were uninhibitedly gay. Noisy well-wishers clustered around their particular graduates.

I was encircled by a select few of my loved ones. Aunt Dodie and Aunt Lu took turns hugging me while Lucy and Sally Carter awaited their chance. My brother Frank and my remaining Hampton aunts and cousins had not been able to make the journey. Of course, Uncle Wade was too busy; I hadn't expected him, but Frank's absence hurt.

Aunt Lu fussed. "We are all so very proud. I wish Mother had been alive to see this."

That was sweet to say, though I knew Grandmother Baxter would not have approved.

Cousin George pushed himself forward, dragging his wife, Emmelin, who embraced me, smiling shyly. Emmelin always seemed a little colorless next to George.

"We're bowled over!" George said. "Look at you, cuz, in that nursing costume and cap, with those curls around your face." He whistled through his teeth.

I couldn't help blushing. I was a bit vain about my new hairstyle. Two nights ago, I'd given in to the importuning of one of my classmates and allowed her to cut my hair for the ceremony. The result pleased me: the shorter curls tucked nicely into my cap.

"What is next for my clever, beautiful sister?" Lucy asked, taking her turn to hug me and kiss both my cheeks. "You'll come home now, won't you?"

"Of course, she will. She needs to spend time at the Lodge," Aunt Dodie said. "Look how thin and pale she is. You must come home and let *us* take care of *you*."

Aunt Lu protested, "We'll take care of her! We won't let her start work right away no matter how they clamor for her."

"Clamor is a gross exaggeration." I laughed. Miss Duggan, the head nurse, had asked me to stay and work in the wards at New York Hospital. The superintendent of nurses at Charity Hospital had also offered me a position. It was nice to be wanted, but I turned them both down. I'd had more than enough of the city. Aunt Dodie was right; I needed to spend time in the North Carolina mountains. "I want to look down south. Somewhere near to Cashiers."

"Nonsense! No opportunities down south can compare to what you'll find here."

Opportunities. By that, Aunt Lu meant a wealthy, well-connected husband.

George put up a hand. "Enough. This is Caroline's day. Don't spoil it squabbling over her. If she still insists on going to the Carolinas, then she must go." He grinned. "New York will still be here when she decides to come back. Now, I have reservations at Delmonico's. And my carriage is just outside."

It wasn't a mile from the New York Hospital on West Sixteenth Street to the garish restaurant with the largest, tenderest beefsteaks in New York City. But I knew better than to suggest to George that we walk. He insisted on doing everything in style.

"The numbers are a little uneven, so I had to invite a few people to meet us there," he said, sweeping his hand to demonstrate: one man to six ladies. My breath caught. What had he done? Was he conspiring with Aunt Lu?

"Who?"

"Emmelin's brothers, of course. And Charlie and Edward wanted to come." Charlie and Edward Strong were cousins-once-removed. That made five men. "And," he winked, "I thought to ask Joe Peabody from the bank."

"You didn't." My heart sank. Was it permissible to strike one's cousin at one's graduation?

"No, I didn't." He chuckled. "He keeps asking about you though."

"Mr. Peabody?" Lucy asked. "Of the Irvington-on-Hudson Peabodys? Well, Caroline!"

"He has hairy knuckles." I didn't take much notice of men, generally, but when I did, I noticed their hands. Mr. Peabody's were revolting. Everyone was staring, so I added quickly, "And he hasn't much conversation."

"Honey, that's true of all bankers," Sally said.

George gasped, then put a hand over his heart.

"Who did you invite then?" Lucy asked, laughing as though she knew the answer.

George smiled broadly. "There he is." He waved his arm high over his head.

I turned, braced for someone awful. Instead, I saw a tall, lean, dark-haired man whose face was as familiar as my own.

"Frank!"

He squeezed his way through the throng of guests, then caught me up and twirled me.

"Caroline! Ah! The best of us, proving it once again. Congratulations."

"You did come!"

"Did you honestly believe I wouldn't? Honey, I spent last night hiding in a hotel, just to surprise you."

"You did?" I laughed, delighted. How clever he'd been, saying he couldn't leave Woodlands just now; his letter had been so convincing. And then he'd sent that congratulatory telegram yesterday. The liar!

My heart felt full. How I'd missed them! I'd missed home so dreadfully. It had been a true test of my endurance.

Oh no. Something else to endure—Nurse Phelps was approaching.

The surgical ward head nurse stopped several feet away and beckoned to me. The woman was dour, decked out in dark gray with her hair pulled back in a severe knot, while all the other staff were nearly as festive as the guests.

"Excuse me," I said with an inward groan. I left Frank's side to speak with her.

"Miss Hampton," Nurse Phelps said. "Congratulations."

"Thank you."

"I heard from Miss Duggan that you turned down a position. She said you wished to return to the South."

"Yes. It's my home."

She made a small harumphing noise. "I have not heard much about the hospitals in the Carolinas. Have you accepted a place?"

Shaking my head, I avoided admitting I had not yet begun to look. I needed to spend time at the Lodge first. I wanted to ride my horse and walk through the woods, dip my feet in the streams. But I was not about to confess that to Nurse Phelps.

"Hmm," the nurse said. "Would Baltimore suit you? A new hospital will be opening there, one associated with the Johns Hopkins University. Have you heard of this?"

"No. I'm afraid not." Why on earth would I have? But it was intriguing. A hospital in Baltimore? Maryland had not been part of the Confederacy, but its heart, at least, had been with the South. Uncle Wade had even lived there for a while after the war.

"They'll be opening a nursing school as well. They'll be needing staff, particularly a head nurse to help get things started. I have a long acquaintance with the director of the project, Dr. Billings. He says they are only interested in 'the cream of the crop.' I would be pleased to give him your name."

"Mine?"

"Why, yes. You have a natural talent. You learn quickly. You're helpful to your fellow students. Most importantly, you put your patients' needs ahead of your own." She paused. "With experience, you'll learn to better navigate your way around the various quirks of the physicians."

"Oh." I didn't know how to respond. Was Dr. Hall's forgetfulness considered a quirk? "But I don't have any experience. If Dr. Billings wants a head nurse, I'm not qualified."

"He wants a good nurse. There are, unfortunately, very few trained nurses for hospital duty with significant experience. Not many stay with it for more than a few years, except, of course, for those in the religious orders. The hospital is still under construction. It won't open for another six months or more. I can't guarantee anything, but if you're interested, let me know."

"Thank you. I may be."

How disorienting. I had misjudged Nurse Phelps entirely.

"Now go and enjoy your family time. You've earned it."

18

1888, November

Baltimore, Maryland

October 3,1888
Dear Pepper,
I have received a definite offer from the J.H. authorities and have determined to accept it. I shall leave you with deep regret. You have been like a good, kind, brother. There need be no hurry about any official action, I only write this so that you may be the first to know of it.

Yours sincerely,
Wm. Osler

—Dr. William Osler to Dr. William Pepper, University of Pennsylvania, Department of Medicine

Welch said there was no better man than Willie Osler to head the Medical Department. Dr. Osler was European-trained, although, being Canadian, he favored British medical universities to German ones. Until September, he was a revered Professor of Clinical Medicine at the University of Pennsylvania. He knew everyone and everything. The Board offered him the appointment of Physician-in-Chief.

Well, that was fine. Halsted knew the university, and eventually the hospital and medical school, wanted only the best. If Welch said Osler was the best, it must be so.

Then he met him.

The man was charismatic. Halsted felt the pull of his outsized personality. When in a small group, he found the doctor personable, warm, and engaging. He had a way of listening that Halsted could see made people feel heard. Halsted liked him and felt liked in return. That was the man's power.

It was only in large gatherings that Halsted discovered Osler was, in fact, irritating. There was such a thing as too lovable. Osler played to the crowd. And his sense of humor was juvenile.

Or, perhaps Halsted was simply an old crotchet. Welch found Osler amusing. Of course, Welch liked a low prank too. Halsted would happily leave them to their backslapping bonhomie. He had work to do.

He'd returned to Baltimore last December after nearly nine months at Butler. Mall welcomed him with open arms and a hundred waiting projects. They talked surgery, anatomy, and science. That was all, thank God.

Welch's conversation was more promiscuous. In the course of a supper, he would flow seamlessly from the description of a remarkable autopsy specimen that Councilman had carried across town from the Bay View Asylum in a bucket hanging from his bicycle handlebars to Fontane's *L'Adultera*, which was not, in his opinion, racy enough to warrant its banning, to a gentle question of what Halsted had read at Butler and if reading had helped, followed by a reminder that Halsted was free to peruse the bookshelves in his office. Recently, Welch had begun to mention this or that person of his acquaintance who questioned him about a boil, a painful cyst, a tumorous growth, a fluctuant gland—mightn't Halsted pop around to such-and-such an address and have a look? Bring his bag.

And so, in preparation for rejoining the world of practicing surgeons, he had begun performing some rather minor operations in and around Baltimore. Oddly enough, his New York reputation, the good one, still clung to him, and he carried with him the anticipated prestige of Johns Hopkins Hospital when he shuffled up to the door of these few anxious, generally well-heeled sufferers. Surgery did not provide the rush of excitement it once had, nothing could, but working felt good. He had not lost his touch.

Welch not only superintended his surgical rehabilitation. Like McBride before him, Welch made sure he was not "a dull boy." New York had its University Club. Baltimore had the Maryland Club. A convivial atmosphere with good food, stimulating conversation, an eminent membership, and strong political underpinnings, the conveniently located if somewhat dilapidated clubhouse was Welch's second home. Halsted allowed himself to be swept along. He ran into his old chum Henry James who, thankfully, did not seem inclined to match-make for his sisters. He dined frequently with a local lawyer, community benefactor, and classical scholar, Major Richard Venable. "Major'" was the rank he had obtained in the army—the Confederate Army. He was a Virginian by birth. One had to be careful talking recent history or politics with Marylanders. Halsted learned to listen to the accent before venturing any non-medical opinions, not that he had many. Conversely, Osler had an opinion about everything. And was probably right.

Dining at the Maryland Club could be diverting. He played his own part well enough to satisfy Welch. But in truth, he had a difficult time shaking his apathy.

If he were honest, the closest thing he felt to excitement was talking with Osler one on one. Osler's knowledge of medicine was encyclopedic, and his curiosity was unquenchable. His enthusiasm was enough for two men, and it spilled over. The medical man had some thoughts already about collaborative efforts: how physicians could most efficiently refer patients for surgery, how surgeons could and should utilize medical consultants. He was a born leader and organizer. Halsted admired him, in small doses.

Small doses. Fraught words. He had been nearly fifteen months without.

The hospital construction, after dragging interminably, had finally been completed in June, save for minor fixes that were ongoing. Welch anticipated the hospital would not open until spring of next year. But things were now moving quickly. He could feel the change.

Welch would allow him to fiddle around in the laboratory as long as he continued to publish and present at meetings, but that was not the role either of them envisioned he would play. In Osler, Welch had found his ideal chief of medicine. He wanted Halsted for Osler's surgical counterpart. The old Halsted wanted it too. The current Halsted wanted it, but not as badly as he wanted twenty minims of cocaine.

19

1889, February

Baltimore, Maryland

The hospital trustees are about to appoint Dr. Halsted as surgeon to the hospital and dispensary...they are not prepared to give him the full title at present, but he will have all of the surgical work of the hospital. There is no doubt about his ability and qualifications for this very important position, in case he has no relapse to his former state. They realize of course that there is some risk...

—Dr. William H. Welch to his sister, Emeline Welch Walcott, February 12, 1889

Halsted strode along the open walkway, the bridge between the ward buildings, head tucked down, cigarette in hand. A week back from a surgical conference in Vienna, he was headed to lunch to give Councilman and Mall a report. He was supposed to meet them at the usual tavern across Jefferson Street. The place was even seedier than Oskaar's, with worse food but better beer. He wasn't hungry or thirsty and would rather have continued the dissection of the cadaver that Councilman had procured for him, but he had promised to meet the men at one o'clock sharp. Having failed to join them the last three days, he dared not skip another lunch.

He would not be good company. His mind was elsewhere: with parathyroids. Tiny organs. There should be four. Paired. Two superior and two inferior, lying in contact with the thyroid, sometimes partially embedded within it. But they were maddeningly inconsistent in location and sometimes even in number. He had seen corpses with three. With six. He found one once in the thymus. That could all be very amusing for anatomy professors bent on torturing students learning to dissect the neck. But for a surgeon desiring to remove a goitrous thyroid who wished to avoid inducing fatal tetany, those tricky parathyroids were not amusing at all.

Someone touched his shoulder and he jumped, then whirled around, heart pounding.

"Oh!" Welch huffed. "I didn't mean to startle you. I thought you heard me calling you."

"If I'd heard you, I would have waited so you wouldn't have to run your stubby legs," he grumbled, embarrassed to have jumped.

"Hmph. Not necessarily." Welch smiled, catching his breath. "I've seen you duck down hallways to avoid fellows."

"I do not."

"Osler."

"Well, Osler. Yes." He puffed his cigarette. "I was thinking."

"Ah. That explains it then. You think harder than any man alive. What about?"

"Parathyroids." Perhaps he could pick Welch's brain. The man had dissected more necks than anyone else in America. Where did those tiny organs get their blood?

Welch's smile grew. "Naturally. What else do young men's thoughts turn to on a lovely false spring day. Where are you going? Lunch?"

He nodded. "Mall and Councilman are waiting."

"Hmm. Mind if I join you?"

"Of course not."

Welch fell into step beside him. "Mall doing all right?"

"Mall? Of course, he is. What do you mean? Why?" Halsted stalled.

Their conversation had been confidential. If and when Welch needed to know, Mall would tell him. He'd been a Fellow in Pathology for three years. Above him, he saw Welch and Councilman, who were not going anywhere. He was beginning to question whether if to move up, he must move on.

Halsted already felt he was hanging onto his sanity by a thread. If Mall left…

Welch shrugged. "He's been antisocial."

"He's always antisocial."

"More so." Then Welch clapped a hand on his shoulder. "Or I'm oversensitive. I thought I saw *him* duck down a hallway. Maybe it's me!"

"Maybe you were with Osler."

Welch laughed. They left the hospital grounds, making small talk about the sewage smell and the muddy roads. Welch asked him if he'd read the reports of yellow fever spreading in Florida and moving north.

"Do you think it'll reach here?" Halsted said. He hadn't given it much thought.

"It's been a warm winter. There are cases in Kentucky already."

"Are you keeping track?" It wouldn't surprise him if Welch was drawing maps and graphs.

"Somewhat. It's a fascinating disease. I've dissected a few cases in the past. One in New York."

Welch launched into an explanation of how it might spread and what the autopsies had shown. Halsted only half-listened. His friend could certainly talk. It almost sounded natural, as though he wasn't jabbering on only to avoid the topic he dared not touch.

The hospital was set to open in May. Without a surgeon.

Director Billings and President Gilman had been excited at the prospect of snaring Sir William Macewen from Glasgow. A student of Lister, Dr. Macewen was a rising star. Stealing the surgeon away from the Glasgow Royal Infirmary would have been quite a coup. Welch was less enthusiastic. He had interacted with Macewen some years ago and said the man was "difficult." Coming from Welch, who never spoke ill of anyone, that should have been taken as warning. However, the Board persevered. Macewen strung them along. He was immoveable in his requirements: an exorbitant salary and the prerogative to import his entire Scottish nursing staff and an assistant or two. That was a slap in the face to a fledgling institution that prided itself on being the cream of the American crop. The Board dropped its pursuit.

Welch, of course, saw an opening. Halsted suspected Welch was advocating for him but he didn't want to know. It was all rather sad to think about. He had been here all along—while they had been panting after Macewen.

They stepped up to the door of the tavern. Welch pulled it open and Halsted entered first. He spotted Councilman waving them over. Mall was with him. They were not at the usual table, but rather the largest one, the one with benches rather than chairs, and they had company: Herter, Booker, Sternberg, Johnson, nearly everyone from the lab. And Osler.

Osler sprang to his feet, held up his mug, and called out, "He's here!"

Who? Halsted turned to Welch, puzzled. Welch was smiling. He pulled an envelope from his pocket.

"This came for you this morning. You were already gone to the lab."

Halsted took it. He felt his ears burning. The envelope bore the Johns Hopkins' seal. He opened it, scanned it.

—head of the Dispensary, rendering surgical services as its Surgeon-in-Chief...*acting* Surgeon to the hospital, duties to be determined by the Executive Committee...*appointment for one year...*

A kick in the gut. Clipping in-grown toenails in the dispensary. "Acting" surgeon, under the supervision of the Board.

Welch took hold of his elbow and announced, "I introduce to you: Johns Hopkins Hospital's surgeon!"

A table full of colleagues shouted congratulations and raised their drinks to toast him. As if he deserved congratulations for having walked his career backwards nearly ten years.

He turned to Welch.

Welch said, under his breath, "Don't give me that look. It doesn't work on me."

The man had maneuvered this, set him up. Now he had no option other than to pick up a mug, graciously accept the good wishes of his colleagues, then hold his nose and accept the very temporary appointment.

Well, no. It was simpler than that. He had no option. It was only thanks to Welch he had this much.

20

1889, March

Baltimore, Maryland

February 28, 1889
Madame,
The Hospital Trustees are inclined to postpone, for several months, the organization of the nurses home and training school—but when the hospital is opened, in May next, a chief nurse and perhaps three other nurses will be required. If you would like to be considered as a candidate for one of these places, can you come to Baltimore and confer with the director of the hospital and the chief physician on Saturday, March 16? I have no doubt that the Trustees would meet your expenses in coming.
Yours respectfully,
D. C. Gilman
—D.C. Gilman to Caroline Hampton, February 28, 1889

Frank had intended to lease a carriage while in Baltimore, but Major Venable, with whom we were staying, had insisted we make use of his. I felt quite pampered, riding to my interview in the luxurious barouche, though I'd have enjoyed it even more if Frank had let me drive.

Major Venable was an old friend of Uncle Wade's, a friendship that had been renewed during his Baltimore days just after the war. He was as gracious as could be, showing me the pleasanter neighborhoods and taking me to Lexington Market to shop. This felt right. The city reminded me very little of Columbia and nothing at all of New York. Cousin Daisy, in Washington with her father, had enthused over the possibility of me moving to "such a charming place, only a skip away." Even my aunts grudgingly admitted Baltimore might not be so bad, though they did not see why I didn't stay in Columbia. How was I to explain that I could not abide going backwards?

In Columbia, all anyone talked about was poverty and politics. The only direction they ever faced was behind.

Fortunately, Frank supported me, probably because he'd learned it was easier than fighting me. When the letter arrived from Mr. Gilman, Frank immediately made arrangements to escort me.

However, I must take charge from here. We had arrived at the corner of North Howard and Little Ross streets, the university campus. How crowded together everything was. The buildings, three or four stories tall, nearly shut out the sun.

"We're here, Frank. Stop here and help me down."

Frank eased the carriage to the side of the road. "Wait a moment. I'll bring you right up to the door."

The university building was intimidating: four stories of brick with decorative tall windows on the top floor. There were two front doors, one with a portico. I guessed that was the door I should use. I squeezed my hands into tight fists, trying to control my nerves.

Frank lifted me down. "Do you want me to come in with you?"

"Heavens, no." How would that appear? "This shouldn't take more than an hour. You should ride around. Enjoy the barouche."

"What if you finish before I return?"

"I'll have a look around the campus. Don't worry about me. I'll be fine."

"No doubt." He grinned at me. "Go show them what Hamptons are made of."

I worried my expression was grim, but I marched off with determination, mounted the steps, and opened the door.

A sign indicated where I should find President Gilman's office. The corridor was narrow, its walls painted dull white with a few portraits of no one recognizable. A plaque on the door at the end of the hall let me know I had arrived.

I knocked and entered a small office. A neatly dressed, gray-haired woman sat behind a desk. She glanced up and smiled.

"Miss Hampton? Miss Caroline Hampton?"

"Yes." With clammy hands, I gripped my reticule tight.

"Please have a seat. They will be ready for you shortly. Would you like a cup of tea?"

"No, thank you."

I sank into the chair nearest the door. I'd had nothing but tea for breakfast, being too nervous to eat. Now, I wished for a biscuit. If my stomach rumbled during the interview, I would die of mortification.

A clock on the wall showed 10:50, confirming I was just early enough to be on time, but the hands moved with agonizing slowness. The secretary asked a few polite questions which I answered with equal politeness, though I could not have said later what the questions were or how I replied.

At 11:10, the door to the inner office finally opened. I stood. A statuesque woman exited, followed by a man of middle years with an untidy mustache and enormous mutton chops. The woman extended her hand and the man shook it. If he was surprised by such forwardness, he did not show it, but I was flabbergasted.

"Good day, Miss Hampton," the man said to the woman. "Thank you for coming. It was indeed a pleasure. We'll be making our decision very soon."

She smiled. "Thank you for your time."

The man glanced past her and nodded at me. "Welcome, welcome. If you wouldn't mind waiting a few more minutes, please? We will ask you in, in a moment."

I cleared my throat and said, "Yes, of course." I hoped he didn't notice my confusion. How was I to explain that *I* was Miss Hampton?

He ducked back inside and closed the door.

The secretary said, "Can I do anything for you, Miss Hampton?"

The woman said, "A hansom would be most welcome. I didn't know how long I would be so I didn't ask my driver to wait."

The secretary nodded and left the room.

Curiosity got the better of me. "Excuse me, but I could not help… is your name Hampton?"

The woman turned, smiling brightly. "It is indeed. Isabel Hampton." She had an unusual accent that I could not place. "And you are?"

"Caroline Hampton." My head swam. "Such a strange coincidence."

Isabel laughed. "It certainly is. And you have a meeting with Mr. Gilman also? How confusing for him!" In a conspiratorial tone, she added, "They're hiring a head nurse for their hospital and training school so I came down from Chicago—I'm superintendent of nurses at Cook County Hospital—to see if the position would suit me."

The woman's overconfidence put my back up.

"I've been invited to speak with Mr. Gilman also. About the nursing position."

Isabel swallowed her smile. "Oh? You must be older than you appear."

"I must be." I met her stare with one I learned from Uncle Wade. Isabel blinked first.

"Well, I will wish you luck. I didn't mean to unsettle you before your interview. What did you think of the hospital?" Her expression turned earnest, falsely earnest. "I have so many ideas I scarcely knew where to begin."

"The hospital?" I didn't think anything of it. It hadn't opened yet.

"Surely you went to see it. The grounds at least."

I shook my head. That had not been on Major Venable's list of places to show me. What would be the point in looking at empty buildings?

"Well." Isabel smoothed her hands down the front of her skirt. "You must tell them that you are adaptable." Butter wouldn't melt in her mouth.

"Thank you, I will."

The secretary returned, rescuing us. "Miss Hampton, there is a hansom outside."

"Thank you, Miss Culvert. You've been most helpful." She gave me a curt nod and swept out the door.

I took my seat again, feeling ill. The door to the inner office opened almost immediately and I jumped back to my feet.

"Come in, please," Mr. Gilman said. "Miss Hampton? Isn't that strange?" He smiled. "Miss Hampton just left."

"Yes. We met."

He held the door for me. Three men, who had been seated around an oval cherry table, rose and made little bows. This office, or conference room, was furnished with expensive-appearing chairs that matched the table. A rather pedestrian oil painting of the harbor dominated the long wall. There was one partly shaded window, casting dull light onto the floor.

"Miss Hampton, this is Mr. King, president of the Board of Trustees."

A bow-tied, older gentleman with a kindly face but squinty eyes made another small bow.

I murmured, "How do you do?"

"Mr. Billings, advisor to the Construction Committee—"

This man appeared younger, or at least fitter, with more hair and fewer wrinkles. He had a neatly trimmed but tobacco-stained mustache obscuring his mouth and wore too much pomade in his hair. He bowed also. His eyes looked strained. I nodded to him, wondering what Nurse Phelps had told him about me and if it would help.

"And Dr. Osler, physician-in-chief."

Dr. Osler twinkled. There was no other way to describe it. He appeared to be in his thirties with thinning brown hair and a mustache with short, tapered handlebars. His lips were full and smiling. He was of average height, thin but not scrawny, and carried himself as though he considered himself good-looking enough not to have to think about it as he worked his charm.

"My dear Miss Hampton, welcome to Baltimore. Please, sit." He pulled out a chair for me. "I hope you're enjoying your visit?"

"Very much." I sat, feeling very small facing them all.

"Which hotel are you patronizing?" Mr. King asked.

"No hotel," I answered, perhaps too quickly, shocked by the question. Unmarried ladies did not stay alone at hotels. "I'm staying with Major Venable, an old family friend."

"Major Venable?" Mr. Gilman repeated.

The others exchanged glances. Impressed. I had not meant to use his name like that.

"How delightful," said Dr. Osler. "I dine with him often at the Maryland Club. Brilliant man. Brilliant."

We made small talk for a quarter of an hour. If Southern women were trained for anything, it was for setting the men around them at ease, but I was not here to pass the time of day. I grew impatient and finally asked, "Is the hospital still on track to open in May?"

The conversation shifted. Mr. Gilman and Dr. Osler did most of the talking; the other two men stayed quiet. They reviewed my credentials, asked me what I found most rewarding and most challenging about nursing, questions I had prepared myself to answer.

Then Dr. Osler said, "You are single, is that correct? Never married or widowed?"

"Unmarried." I forced a smile. "And no intention to marry."

His eyebrows flickered. "I call that a shame. Some young man's grave loss."

I knew these questions, too, would be asked. I had no wish for a husband. None for children. I'd practiced until the words were rote and I could say them without blushing.

"You're too kind." I accentuated my drawl.

Mr. Gilman said, "Naturally, we do not dictate the personal lives of our employees. Our nurses are expected to be of the highest moral character and we have no doubt that you are. But consistency is important, particularly in a hospital that is just getting started. With so much new, we will rely heavily upon our nursing staff to lend a certain… stability to our patients. And, frankly, to our doctors. Who will have trouble enough getting their feet on solid ground without reliable nursing support."

"You don't wish to invest in nurses who will leave within a few months to start a family. I appreciate that. I fully intend to devote my life to nursing."

"You graduated in…" Dr. Osler shifted paper in a pile in front of him.

"In the spring of last year."

"And were offered positions at New York Hospital and at Charity?"

"Both in New York. A marvelous city, but my heart is too southern to make my home so far north. Baltimore would suit me better." I prayed that was the truth.

Dr. Osler chuckled. "You are speaking to a Canadian, Miss Hampton. New York *is* the south. Baltimore is the deep south."

Mr. Gilman said, "You say you intend to devote your life to nursing. Hypothetically, of course, would you be prepared to commit yourself to five years at Johns Hopkins Hospital? Ten years? Twenty?"

"Ten years, certainly." In ten years, I would be thirty-seven. How old would Aunt Dodie be? Aunt Anne? Aunt Kate? "I could not commit to more. I have maiden aunts who will be elderly. If they were to need me…"

"Oh, well, certainly," Mr. King said. "Family obligations must needs be considered."

I smiled at him, then noticed Dr. Osler sneaking a look at his watch.

"Have you any other questions for us?" Mr. Gilman asked.

I hesitated, my mind gone blank.

"If not—"

"I suppose I am curious how many candidates you are considering."

"Four. We will be completing our interviews today and will make our decision quickly."

He rose, signaling that we all should. He gestured to the door and saw me out. I could hear chairs shifting and scraping behind me as the others sat back down. No other candidate waited in the outer office. Perhaps the men planned to take lunch.

"Good day, Miss Hampton. I hope you enjoy the rest of your stay. Please give our regards to Major Venable."

It occurred to me then that I did have a question. The letter had mentioned that they might hire additional nurses, not just the head. Had they filled the other positions?

It was too late to ask now. Besides, that would be conceding defeat.

"Thank you for speaking with me." I did not extend my hand.

"It was our pleasure."

I nodded goodbye to Miss Culvert.

Frank was waiting in the barouche and hopped down as I approached.

"Did they hire you or are they fools?" he asked.

"They said they'll let me know soon."

He handed me up. On the ride back across town, I confided my impression of the men I had spoken to and of the hospital they were building.

"Frank, would you take me to the hospital grounds tomorrow? I'd like to walk around for an hour or so."

"Whatever you wish. Do you think you'd like to work here?"

"I believe so. It sounds like an extraordinary opportunity."

I didn't tell him that it sounded like a missed opportunity. I didn't mention Miss Isabel Hampton, who would no doubt be offered the position of chief nurse.

21

1889, March

Baltimore, Maryland

The traditional isolation of the life of the research worker is broken when a spirit akin to his comes near. Those are the days of greatest happiness when in the rivalry and the strife to understand Nature, now the one, then the other, opens up his heart. So it was when we two worked together, but not often comes such fortune into one's life.

—Carl Ludwig (Leipzig) to Franklin P. Mall (Baltimore), 1886

Halsted tramped down the path alongside the ward buildings from the Administration Building toward the Pathological Laboratory. The neat rows of brick buildings usually satisfied his sense of order, but today irked him. It was a beautiful day for the middle of March yet the warm sun on the back of his neck was no comfort. He felt low.

Mall confided yesterday that he would take the position in Worcester at Clark College. He was being offered a professorship and Halsted could not blame him for seizing the opportunity. But it was a blow. Mall would leave Baltimore by the end of May to return to Ludwig's laboratory for the summer before undertaking the challenge of setting up his own.

He would do groundbreaking work wherever he went. Mall was a scientist through and through. By God, he would miss him.

Possibly his own appointment last month had influenced Mall. He claimed Halsted would abandon research for clinical work. In truth, he dreaded just such a thing, especially if Mall left. But he had to do it to prove to himself that he could. He had to justify Welch's faith in him.

Halsted dug around in his pockets for a cigarette. He needed something to take the stink from his nose. Baltimore was an unhealthy swamp, drowning in its own sewage. Yet there was no better place to be. Surely Mall knew that. They'd been making such strides!

He continued walking briskly while he turned his coat pocket inside out, searching, irritated, trying to push his dissatisfaction from his head. Five, six years ago, he'd been attending surgeon at Roosevelt Hospital, surgeon-in-chief to Emigrant Hospital, and visiting surgeon at Bellevue, among others. Now the administration was hesitant to offer him anything more than "acting" surgeon. Little wonder he—

"Oh!"

He heard the gasp. His eyes flew wide to see a petite woman—a soft bundle of full skirts and long cloak—springing out of his way with surprising nimbleness. A piece of paper fluttered to the ground.

"I beg your pardon," he said, hurriedly scooping it up.

When he straightened, he towered above her, which gave him an oddly powerful feeling. Then an uncomfortable one as he thought he might have dashed her flat onto the ground. He glanced at the paper—a crudely scrawled map of the hospital grounds. "Are you lost?"

"Not precisely."

Her cheeks were a rather becoming shade of pink. She had dark hair with a few curls at her forehead, but mostly tucked into a bonnet. Her cloak was plain but of good material. He was not a Halsted for nothing; he recognized quality cloth. The skirts were a simple brown plaid. She would not shine at a ball, but this was no ballroom. He found her a rather splendid adornment for the hospital grounds.

She said, taking the map from him, "I'm on a tour."

"Generally, one observes one's surroundings when on a tour."

Her expression soured and he realized he'd been curt. And was in the wrong.

She said, "I suppose I was blinded by the glamor of all this rectangular red brick." She had an extraordinary accent. As though she were tasting her vowels before letting them go.

"I didn't see you," he said, thinking to make an apology, but sounding, even to himself, like a supercilious New Yorker.

She stared, eyes flashing, and he braced himself for a cut he felt he deserved.

Then, without warning, she laughed. Incongruously, her laughter was strident, coming from deep in her chest, a heartfelt expression of amusement. He smiled awkwardly. He hadn't gotten the joke.

"My brother," she said, "who is six feet tall, barrels into me with some regularity and gives the same excuse. I thought he was only teasing."

"It was my fault entirely," he said, at last finding his manners. "I was lost in thought. And I'm very nearsighted. Please—" He gestured to her map. "Let me help you find what you're looking for."

"I'm not looking for anything in particular. I'm only looking. I have an hour before my brother returns for me and—" She stopped, flushed, and took a step back. "I've taken up too much of your time. Good day, sir."

"I'm in no hurry." He was curious. Who was she? What was she doing here?

"We have not been introduced," she said, taking another step back and brushing at her skirts. "Good day." She turned away.

"I am Dr. William Halsted."

Looking over her shoulder, she said, exasperated, "That is not how it works."

He knew that. He said, "I know. New York Society is every bit as hidebound as…?"

"South Carolina." She bit her lip. "Columbia." She appeared at war with herself. Then she sighed and conceded, turning back to face him. She looked through him rather than at him, as if she were seeing something else. "Well, Dr. Halsted, I've heard of you, so perhaps that counts."

He felt his chest puff. How could she have heard of him?

"I am Miss Hampton."

"Oh!" Everything made sense now. "You've come about the nursing school. Congratulations. Everyone was very impressed."

She reddened and her brow creased skeptically, but her voice was hopeful as she said, "Indeed? You're too kind."

"Oh no." He felt almost jocular. "I heard the superintendent position is yours."

Yesterday, Gilman, King, Billings, and Osler interviewed three or four candidates for head nurse of the hospital and nurses' training school. Osler had asked him if he wanted any input, which was gracious enough he supposed, but it was only to read through the applications, not to attend the interviews. He was only acting surgeon, after all. He declined.

Miss Hampton's face lit, but only for a moment. Then her eyes narrowed. "From whom did you hear this?"

"Dr. Welch. Who heard it from Dr. Osler."

As the words left his mouth, he realized something was off. The men who interviewed Miss Hampton had, reportedly, been so taken with her appearance, they scarcely discussed her credentials. Welch said Osler called her a goddess. While Miss Hampton was very pretty, he couldn't quite see Osler going into raptures over her. Even more disturbing, he was certain she was supposed to be a Canadian. That's what Welch had told him. In reply, he'd scoffed that Osler would choose a Canadian over Florence Nightingale. Miss Hampton was not from Canada.

She hummed a little in the back of her throat. Then she smiled and said, "I believe your friends were talking about Miss Isabel Hampton. I am Miss Caroline Hampton."

"I didn't know there were two of you." What a horrible coincidence. And how maladroit he was. "I beg your pardon. I should not have spoken."

"Think nothing of it. Miss Isabel Hampton already informed me that she would be head nurse." Her smile tightened. "In the hallway before my interview began."

"She sounds horrid."

"Oh no." She shrugged and waggled her hand. "She's more deserving. She's had a great deal more hospital experience."

He didn't want her discouraged. She had spirit. And she'd been quite forgiving of his boorishness.

"You were invited to interview. Your credentials must be sound."

"I graduated only recently and have been caring for family members since. It isn't the same."

"Do you wish to return to hospital work?"

"I do." She did not elaborate.

"Here?" How absurd that he should feel invested in whether or not she came to Johns Hopkins. But the hospital needed more than one nurse.

"Perhaps. Baltimore is more to my liking than New York."

Was that a conversational gambit or just a factual reply? He had intimated to her that he was from New York. Was he now supposed to challenge her dislike for his home state? Was he contemplating flirting? His neck felt hot beneath his collar.

"I really must go meet my brother," she said. "He'll have his carriage and he'll be put out if he has to come searching for me. Thank you for your time, Dr. Halsted."

"It was my pleasure, Miss Hampton."

He stepped aside to let her pass. He kept his eyes wide open as he walked on. He passed the last of the ward buildings. The Pathological stood before him. He was struck, suddenly, by the utilitarian appearance of the structure and, glancing over his shoulder, of the entire campus.

Ha! The glamor of all this rectangular red brick. She'd gotten the better of him. That put her one up on Osler.

❧

He was still chuckling to himself over the odd encounter when he entered the laboratory. Mall was not there, but Booker was. An older physician—thick-waisted and generally found chomping, rather than smoking, a cigar—he'd cut back on his private practice and taken a fellowship with Welch just to get his foot in the door at Johns Hopkins. A smart man, he did not love laboratory work but he was good at it.

The dog carcass was already laid out on the gleaming dissecting table, instruments organized alongside in the order Halsted prescribed.

Halsted took off his coat and hung it on the stand. Booker was a Virginia man, had been in the army, in fact. He couldn't get over the number of ex-Confederates here in Baltimore.

Without meaning to speak of her, but unable to stop himself, he said, "I just ran into one of the nursing candidates having a look around. A Southern girl—lady."

"Eh?" Booker did not appear interested. "Mall says he'll be late. He asked me to help out here. He's meeting with Welch."

Telling Welch he was leaving? Did Booker know? A pall fell over the room.

"What did you think? Of the nurse?" Booker asked in a grunt, putting a bucket of formaldehyde at Halsted's feet.

"She was pleasant enough. I mistook her for the candidate Gilman and the others chose. They are both Miss Hamptons."

"Hampton?" Booker's jaw dropped. "Not one of Senator Wade Hampton's brood?"

There was a Senator Hampton. Halsted was not much interested in politics but he had heard of him. A war hero of some sort. From South Carolina.

"I think she must have been. She said she was from Columbia."

Booker let out a long whistle. "That is some blue, blue blood. But it couldn't be one of the general's daughters. He wouldn't let his daughter work. Did she tell you her given name?"

Halsted thought she did. "Yes, but I can't recall."

Counting on his fingers, Booker said, "Well, the nieces would be Anne—no, I think she died a few years back—there's Lucy and Caroline. A slew of cousins but they aren't Hamptons."

"Caroline. It was Caroline."

Booker considered this a moment, then gave a snort. He pushed up his sleeves and jerked his chin at Halsted as if to tell him to get started. Halsted picked up his scalpel.

"Did Mall tell you the history of this one?"

"Said you reversed the gut so he could see if peristalsis went both ways." Booker nodded at the dog with its swollen discolored abdomen. "It didn't."

"No. We thought it might at first."

"Hmph. Mall thought it might. You didn't, but he wanted proof."

"Well, he was right. I had no basis for stating an untested opinion as fact."

Booker looked amused. "That young man is a pistol. I'll bet he said it just like that to your face."

Halsted felt a pang. Mall had said it just like that.

Booker pointed. "And you want the whole thing? Or just the anastomoses?"

"The whole thing."

"Might need another bucket then."

Halsted waited until he retrieved another bucket from storage and set it beside the first. Then he made his incision. The smell was foul. Booker recoiled.

"Anastomoses broke down. Look at that dilation!" Halsted marveled. He should have waited for Mall.

Talking nasally, as though he'd stopped breathing, Booker said, "So they didn't hire this Miss Hampton, you say?" When Halsted shook his head, he went on. "That's probably for the best. It isn't her fault, mind, but if it is Wade Hampton's niece, she was reared by those aunts in the hills. We don't need any of that around here."

He laid the scalpel down. "Any of what?"

"Do you want me to slosh some water in there? Clean things out a bit?"

"Yes. But tell me first: any of what?"

Booker grunted. "It's a perverse story. Happened a long time ago. Before the war. I guess there's no reason you would have heard it up there, but folks in the South are pretty well versed in each other's business and everyone knows of the Hamptons."

He should tell Booker to shut up. Old plantation gossip did not interest him. He knew too much of New York's secrets to branch out into the South. But he held silent.

"The general had five sisters. All younger. He was still a young man himself at the time. His father was the head of the family. I don't think there was a wealthier planter in all of South Carolina. Mississippi too. Must've owned half the slaves in the south." Booker poured a pan of water over the entrails. "Well, his sister, the father's sister not the general's, was a plain little thing. Hard to unload even with a dowry that would make Old Johns Hopkins himself think twice. She had the misfortune to catch the worst type of fortune hunter. Man by the name of James Hammond."

Halsted mopped the water into the drain and picked up another scalpel.

"You are talking about who? Miss Hampton's great aunt?"

"Not so much the great aunt, poor lady. The scoundrel was the husband. It's common knowledge he bought a slave woman and her daughter and fathered children on both."

Halsted made a noise of disgust. "I hope this story has a point."

"I'm getting to it. This uncle also had his way with the elder four sisters. The fifth was just a baby or he would have taken her too. Even the fourth was only ten or twelve."

Halsted threw down the scalpel. "Good Lord!"

"The father didn't call the scoundrel out. The scandal would have been ruinous. But everyone noticed the break in the two families. They'd been close and now Hampton was doing everything he could to wreck Hammond's career. He was in politics at the time but didn't last long. The story leaked out, of course." He shook his head. "Old Wade should've shot him."

"What happened to the sisters?"

"Happened? Oh, none of them was, you know, in a family way. But the taint was there. The eldest died a few years later. And the others kept pretty quiet for a while. People still received them, naturally. They were

Hamptons. But there was some talk that they weren't all that innocent in the affair."

"You said one was a child!"

"Who might have been imitating her sisters. I'm not saying that, but some people did. It doesn't matter either way. No man was ever going to marry a Hampton girl. People have long memories for things like that."

Halsted didn't respond. He tied loops around the bowel proximally and distally, then eviscerated with practiced ease. A sharp blade along the mesentery and the small intestine spooled out in his hand; he teased out the large intestine with gentler traction. Then he dumped the entire mess into one bucket.

"Can you rinse that, divide it at the cecum, and let it fix in two buckets until Mall has a look? I'm going for a walk. I'm stifled."

He washed his hands, pulled his coat back on, and left the building.

Booker's clear implication was that Miss Caroline Hampton carried some sort of inter-generational taint. He believed she was unqualified to serve as a nurse because her aunts had been assaulted by a man whom they logically trusted.

What else had he said? That Miss Hampton must have been reared by those aunts? Where were her parents? The whole story was disgusting. Disgusting and sad. And he could not get the image of that thoroughly respectable, spirited lady out of his head.

He walked rapidly, retracing his steps across the yard and past the administration building. He was angry and felt a headache coming on. His apartment called to him. One advantage to his appointment, he no longer lived in Welch's pocket. He had been awarded convenient living quarters on hospital grounds—ghastly rooms, but he could fix that. He should go there and calm down. Drink a strong cup of coffee. Instead, he flagged down a hansom.

"North Howard Street. Johns Hopkins University."

The trip was not a long one. He jigged his feet the whole way, trying to burn off his anxiety. He was behaving irrationally. Likely foolishly. But Booker's story infuriated him.

At the university campus, he climbed from the carriage and handed the man his coin. He was beginning to calm. But he had come this far. And, once upon a time, he had been the type of man who acted boldly, who sometimes acted on impulse. He missed being that man.

He entered the office of the president. "Is Mr. Gilman in?"

Miss Culvert shook her head. "No, Dr. Halsted. He's gone for the day."

"Dr. Osler asked for my opinion of the nursing candidates. I'd like a look at the files."

"Of course, Doctor." She pulled four folders from a stack. "But I believe they've chosen the nurse superintendent."

"That's all right." He thumbed quickly through the files and pulled out Miss Caroline Hampton's. She trained at New York Hospital. He skimmed the recommendations. Efficient. Hard-working. Exceptionally bright. Always courteous. Ha!—glamorous red brick.

He set the file down and plucked up the secretary's fountain pen. In bold letters, across the front of the file, he wrote: *Hire for head of the surgical ward, per W. S. Halsted, M.D., acting surgeon.*

22

1889, May

Baltimore, Maryland

HOPKINS HOSPITAL WILL BE OPENED TODAY

Johns Hopkins Hospital will be formally opened this morning. The ceremonies will commence at 11. Addresses will be made by Mr. Francis T. King, president of the board of trustees; Dr. John S. Billings, U.S.A., and Dr. D.C. Gilman, president of Johns Hopkins University and director of the hospital. Governor Jackson will make the closing address and declare the hospital open. Invitations have been sent to the mayor, city council, to federal, State, and municipal officers, the judiciary, senators and members of Congress, and to heads of educational and philanthropic institutions, members of the bar, clergymen, and members of the medical profession. Over 1,200 invitations were sent to persons at a distance. A great crowd is expected…

—*The Baltimore Sun*, Baltimore, MD, May 7, 1889

Halsted stood at the mezzanine balcony in the Rotunda, the central hall of the Administration Building. Yesterday, empty, it had been an entirely different place. Now a great multitude stood cheek by jowl to ogle the lofty domed ceiling, the decorative crown molding, the marble floors.

They would begin admitting patients next week. The surgical load would be light at first, but it would grow. He wasn't sure he had the energy to start over. Setting bones, draining abscesses, debriding burns, plucking out bullets and God knew what else from tracts and body cavities, hour after hour, day after day—once he could not get enough of these things. Now the thought of it all made him tired. He needed to keep his mind occupied, not only his hands.

He would have help. Or hindrance. He'd written to McBurney in New York, who recommended a promising surgery-minded graduate named Brockway. He would be Johns Hopkins' first resident surgeon.

And, while Halsted had been in Vienna, Welch met with a candidate to assist in the dispensary, a Maryland native named Finney or some such thing. He was just finishing his training at Massachusetts General and was highly regarded there. Although in Halsted's opinion, Mass General was behind times so this Finney would likely need to be retrained.

The morning's addresses had been numbing. All the excitement had been like a droning of bees in his ears. He skipped the collation and went to his apartment for a rest—euphemism for an eighth of a grain of morphine. Again.

He could blame Mall for taking a position elsewhere; he would be gone by the end of the month. He could blame the Trustees for failing to acknowledge his worth. For that matter, he could blame dog number seventeen for dying of tetany even though he had carefully isolated the parathyroids and transplanted them into the well-vascularized spleen, failing to support the hypothesis he knew must be correct. But it wouldn't help, this trying to lay blame where it didn't belong.

He was thirty-six years old, too young to conclude life was nothing more than a series of disappointments, but there it was.

Mall had skipped the ceremonies. Lucky him, he could. He was working in the laboratory, trying to tie up loose ends. Halsted stubbed out his cigarette on the railing. Mall had said he could use a little help.

As he turned towards the stairs, he saw Welch approaching with a solid young man in tow, carefully but rather cheaply attired. As they came close, Halsted diagnosed the man's expression as nervous earnestness.

"There you are," Welch said. "This is Dr. John Finney." He nodded. "Dr. William Halsted. I'm supposed to meet with the governor so I'll leave you two to it."

To what? Halsted wondered.

As Welch wandered away, Halsted peered over the top of his glasses to get a good look at his new assistant. Ten to one he played football in college. Square-headed and scrubbed-looking, he had a luxuriant mustache and close-cut hair with a silly just off-center part. He should fix it or wear a hat.

Halsted focused his attention back out over the railing. "Big crowd, isn't it?"

"Yes, sir."

Was he a "sir" already? His mind went blank. Welch had enumerated the fellow's qualifications already, judged them satisfactory. Halsted didn't need them repeated. He glanced toward the windows, the sunlight streaming in.

"Nice day, isn't it?"

"Yes, sir."

Enough of this. They'd either rub along well enough or they wouldn't. Mall had likely given up on him coming around. He stole a glance at his watch.

"I'll have to ask you to excuse me. I have an appointment in the laboratory in a few minutes. What time can you report for duty?"

Finney looked as though he'd swallowed a wasp. "I beg your pardon, sir?"

He hoped the "sir" thing would not last long. "I want you to come down and work in the surgical dispensary. When can you start?"

His eyes got bigger. "I-I'm not finished at Mass General until July." He added frantically, "I suppose they might let me off a little earlier."

"Yes, I fancy they will. Just come down as soon as you can. I'll be expecting you."

The man was like a loopy Irish Setter, panting for a stick to chase.

Taking the back stairs to avoid the throng, Halsted left the Administration Building. Medical people and various functionaries littered the grounds in clusters, milling about. Head down, he plowed his way to the Pathological. He thought he saw a flash of brown plaid in the corner of his eye and paused. The pattern was different, of course, and the woman too tall. He counted that, momentarily, as another of life's disappointments before recognizing he was being absurd.

He entered the building and jogged up the stairs. He was feeling fitter than he had been. The small doses of morphine he allowed himself were doing no harm. It was silly, really, to imagine a few minims of cocaine would send him hurtling back into the abyss. This melancholy was worse.

Drawing near, he heard voices: Mall and Welch. So, the meeting with the governor was a ruse to escape. He poked his head inside. It was diverting, seeing the pair of them together: they were so disparately sized.

"Am I interrupting?"

Both men looked toward the door.

"No," Welch said. "In fact, we're waiting for you. That didn't take long. What did you think of him?"

Halsted shrugged. "Personable, I suppose."

Welch gave him a long look. "Will he be satisfactory or are you still looking?"

"Looking?"

"For an assistant in the dispensary."

"You hired Finney for that," Halsted said, confused.

Welch puffed up. "I did no such thing!" He sounded exasperated. "I would never step on your toes. *You* are the head of surgery."

"Temporarily."

Mall got to his feet. Noisily. "Excuse me, but if you two are going to spat—"

"We aren't."

"I dispute that," Welch said.

Mall scuttled out while Halsted held his breath. Welch turned to him, scowling.

"Stop pouting," he commanded.

Halsted sniffed. "Pouting?"

"I would not have thought it of you, but you are. You were one of the few who stood by me when I decided to leave New York. Now you are treating Mall the way Fred Dennis treated me, trying to make him feel guilty."

"I haven't cut him off! I'm encouraging him. I am—"

"Pouting. And you are peeved the Trustees do not yet have full confidence in your recovery. Yet can *you* say you are fully confident?"

Halsted blanched.

"I thought not." Welch sighed. His voice softened. "It's hard. I know it is hard. But you have been managing extraordinarily well off the drugs. I hope, I pray, that every day it will get easier for you."

Welch didn't know. Thank God. He didn't suspect.

"I hope so too," he said. "But I am wary that it will get harder, not easier. Working with Mall has kept me sane. Going back to the surgeon's life will be New York all over again. Productive but…" But empty.

Welch did not speak for a long moment. Then he said, "If all we achieve is another New York, then we have failed. Halsted! Where is your vision? What do you think I'm working for here?"

"Medical education on par with European schools. The German model—"

"Pah. Nothing so small. I don't want us to simply plant in German furrows. I want to break new ground. Look at this nation, Halsted. What we've done. What we have overcome. Johns Hopkins is not to be a copy of the German school, or the British school, or the French school. We will be the American school. The best and brightest of our young men will train in Baltimore." Welch was impassioned enough to pace and throw out his arms. "We will be the model for others. In twenty years, thirty, smart young men from abroad will come here to learn from us. That is my vision. Believe me, Halsted, I may love you like a brother, but if I didn't see you fitting into this vision, I would not be holding on so tight. I've seen the way you operate. I've listened to the way you reason. I know you are the right man for this."

Welch paused, then pulled out his handkerchief to wipe his brow. He smiled a bit sheepishly.

"All right. Stop gaping as if you're watching a mad man rant."

Halsted forced a snort. "As if?"

Welch stuffed the cloth back into his pocket. "The Board will come around. Keep on as you are. Mall is a brilliant young man, but he lets you be lazy. You know microscopy. You can see the same thing he sees. Of course, you can't draw to save your life…" Welch trailed off, waiting for the laugh Halsted could not give him. Gently, he said, "I'm here. When you want another set of eyes on your work, I'm here."

"Yes." He stared at the ground. "Yes, I know."

"When I corresponded with Sam Bushnell before…he wrote of the day you decided on surgery. He said he saw it in your face. You said, 'We're on the verge of something. Surgery is going to change.' *We're on the verge of something.* Not they are. We are. This is your vision too."

Halsted couldn't help smiling. The man was on a roll. "Please stop before you make me weep."

Welch laughed. "I'm making myself teary. But I mean it. Just do what you do. The Board will come around." Then he muttered, "Acting surgeon my foot."

23

1889, July

Baltimore, Maryland

Before beginning a surgical dressing it is important to have at hand everything likely to be needed: it is awkward for yourself and fatiguing for the patient when you have to leave in the midst of the process to find something that has been forgotten. Of course, when the doctor is to do the dressing you can not always tell just what he will call for, but the things you know will be wanting should always be ready; and after you have seen a dressing once you should certainly know how to prepare it again.

—*Textbook of Nursing* by Clara S. Weeks-Shaw, D. Appleton and Company, 1883

❧

The hospital grounds sprawled over four city blocks. The hospital pavilion comprised a collection of buildings forming an *L*. At the center of the *L*'s base was the Administration Building. On either side, a vaguely symmetrical row of buildings stretched along Broadway, from Monument Street to Jefferson Street. The pavilion right-angled at Broadway and Monument, extending all the way up to Wolfe Street. The Nurses' Home, on Jefferson Street at the bottom of the *L*, was where I now resided. The Pathological Laboratory, where Dr. Halsted seemed to spend the bulk of his time, was at the top, on the corner of Wolfe and Monument. They were at the two farthest extremes, though why I had taken note of this, I couldn't say.

He was a funny man. I couldn't quite make him out. The first time he walked into my ward, I thought he didn't remember me. His face registered no surprise to find that the woman he'd nearly barreled into was now in charge of his patients. Yet when he asked a question, he spoke to me by name, so he did remember. He'd known I'd been hired. For a moment, I imagined he might have had something to do with it, but that was ridiculous.

He was, I quickly discovered, the fussiest man God ever placed on the earth. Never a loose button—as Aunt Kate would say. That not only applied to his tiptop tailoring, but to everything he touched in the surgical ward. Of course, I kept his instruments clean, his scissors sharp, his favored suture material readily at hand, though he never had to replace a stitch that I ever saw. He expected meticulous care of his patients before and after surgery. I learned to anticipate his questions. I was able to report the color and volume of urine each patient produced—and he asked, every time, until I showed him where I had written it down. I thought his eyes smiled at me then, but probably not. His demeanor was always so serious.

He was particularly attentive to surgical dressings. They must be neither too dry nor too moist. Both those impregnated with bichloride of mercury and those soaked in carbolic acid must be readily available because he had specific purposes in mind for each, which I was still trying to figure out. And heaven help any nurse who did not trim loose threads from the dressings before handing them to him. A thread from a dressing prepared by one of the nurses in my charge wrapped around his fingertip once, and he looked so repulsed, shaking it off, that I wanted to crawl into a hole. I made sure my nurses would henceforth be more conscientious and double-checked their work myself.

I had full charge of the surgical wards, male and female, a single building cut in half by an open walkway, near the bend of the *L*. It was a tremendous responsibility, starting from nothing but rooms with beds and boxed supplies to a functioning, adequately staffed facility in which to care for patients. I worked twelve-hour shifts five days a week, and one six-hour day. Each week I had one afternoon and one full day off. I didn't quite know what to do with myself when not in the ward. I wrote letters, read novels, went for walks, all while thinking about my patients, until I strolled over to see for myself how they fared.

Once, in order to explore a little of the city, I attended the theater with Louisa Parsons, my counterpart on the indigent Men's Medical Ward. Louisa had trained at the Florence Nightingale School in London, so I stood a little in awe. To my delight, Louisa was also acting as nurse superintendent. Miss *Isabel* Hampton had been awarded the position, accepted it, and then informed the Board of Trustees she could not start until September. The woman had nerve. Or perhaps gall.

The Nurses' Home, a large square building made of the requisite red brick, had three stories and a basement. The top two floors were currently empty but would house students in the fall. The basement contained the kitchen, dining room, lecture hall, and a few rooms for storage and miscellaneous spaces. The ground floor had a parlor, the library, and rooms for the head nursing staff. My apartment comprised a tiny sitting room and a bedroom. It was no more than a glorified dormitory, but it was my own and I loved it, though I suspected I would enjoy it more when the students arrived. It was a bit lonely. The staff nurses, hired from Baltimore and its environs, returned after work to their homes.

The nurses' dining hall was not yet opened. Miss Parsons and I took our supper together in the hospital dining room.

Dr. Halsted, I noted, ate at a table with other physicians whom I was learning to recognize: Dr. Osler, of course, everyone knew, and Drs. Booker, Councilman, LaFleur, Finney, Kelly, Welch, and so many more. That was not to say all the physicians were always there, only that I noticed who was there and when. They seemed convivial, Dr. Osler especially so. Of course, I could not know this. The table was too far away to listen. But I watched. From the corner of my eye, I watched them. I wished I could listen. The atmosphere in the new hospital was electric. The doctors were poised on the edge of something, something phenomenal. Yet it did not occur to those smart, busily important men that they could not succeed without the contributions of their nurses.

Dr. Brockway appeared then, hurrying into the dining room, looking rather frantic. He sped toward the group of physicians. Dr. Halsted stood. He nodded when Dr. Brockway spoke. Then he abandoned his supper tray and left the table, his resident in tow.

He came straight to our table. "Miss Hampton, will you assist in the operating room? There is a gunshot. Brockway says it cannot wait till morning and Miss Porter has gone home."

"Yes, of course," I said, rising quickly.

The request terrified me. Although I'd assisted in several operations during my training, it was always under the surgical nurse's supervision. I had never even set foot in Dr. Halsted's operating room. And he was so very fussy. What if I made a mistake?

But he had come straight to me. He knew where I was without having to search. I'd believed he was largely unaware of my existence. No, I couldn't quite make him out.

24

1889, August

Baltimore, Maryland

Ford's—Opens Next Monday Night
BRISTOL'S GREAT HORSE SHOW
A Funny Play Acted by Equines!
The Comedy of Schools!
In many acts but no "waits."
BRISTOL'S EQUES-CURRICULUM
A Manege of Educated Horses.

The School, with Professor Bristol, will give a parade, with flambeaus, on Saturday evening, starting at 8 o'clock from the neighborhood of the Opera House. All the Horses will be in the turnout, with Bristol's Band and other music, colored lights, etc. The sale of seats commences Saturday.

—*The Baltimore Sun*, Baltimore, MD, Friday, August 16, 1889

Halsted checked the *Sun* four times on Friday, and the announcement didn't magically disappear, unfortunately. That would have made the decision for him. He sent a boy yesterday to purchase two tickets, which he expected he would throw away. He imagined the "Great Horse Show" would be as ridiculous as it sounded. In its favor, no one he knew was likely to attend.

The whole thing was rather agonizing. He wished he'd simply passed over the announcement but to ignore it after having fixated upon it was cowardly.

Miss Hampton was fond of horses. He'd overheard as much, though he hadn't intended to eavesdrop on her conversation with Finney. He was simply waiting to ask her about the tuberculous hip in bed two.

And now he had ended up with two tickets in hand for—he shuddered—a comedy enacted by equines.

The most likely outcome was she would make a polite excuse and that would be the end of it. Or, he could simply tell her someone had given him the tickets and he could give them to her. Perhaps she and Miss Parsons would enjoy an evening out.

Or he could stop acting like a schoolboy and go ask her.

He swallowed the last of his coffee, washed the cup and pot, then brushed his teeth and finished getting dressed. His collar looked a bit dingy as he tied his necktie, so he changed his shirt and tried again. At least he wasn't Finney—showing up in the Dispensary in the morning with a lipstick smear on his collar. The man was worse than McBride.

He would have to have a word with his launderer. They used too much starch and not enough bleach. Welch teased him he should send his shirts to London to be cleaned since he complained so often. He was beginning to consider it.

He picked up his hat and cane and made his way out to the yard. He trod the walkway to the surgical ward and mounted the stairs.

Miss Hampton was hard at work, sponging the amputee in bed seven. She glanced up when he came in and gave him the look that meant: *just a moment, please.* She would not, he knew, expose a patient to a chill. Rather even the head surgeon should cool his heels.

"When you are finished," he said, "I'd like to speak with you in the hall."

Her eyebrows rose, then she nodded. His voice had sounded brusque. He hoped he hadn't worried her. This was every bit as awkward as he'd feared. He stepped back into the hallway and lit a cigarette, then paced back and forth until she appeared. She shut the door behind her. The click echoed along the empty hall.

"Yes, Dr. Halsted?"

"Um"—he paused, but could think of no suave way to lead into it so he pushed on ahead— "would you consider…have you heard of the Bristol Horse Show?"

She nodded. "I have."

"Would you like to see it? I have two tickets. For tomorrow night." Her half day, he had already confirmed. "The opening."

She blushed. Surely he was blushing also. His neck was terribly hot.

"That sounds lovely," she said, so quietly he barely heard her. Then she looked up at him and smiled. "Thank you. I've heard the show is entertaining. And I am not working Monday night."

"I hoped not. Hoped you were not working, not that you would not like to go."

Her eyes crinkled as though she would laugh. Thank goodness she didn't. Hurriedly, he pressed on.

"It's at the Opera House. I'll hire a carriage—"

"Oh, do let us take the trolley. It runs by the Opera House, I believe, and I've wanted a chance to try it."

She was better at this than he was. He'd thought a carriage would be less public, which it would be, but perhaps a little too private for her comfort.

"The trolley it is," he agreed. "Shall I come for you around 7:15? I wouldn't want you to miss the parade."

"Why don't we meet at the trolley stop? That would be convenient for us both."

Much better than he was. Two acquaintances meeting at the trolley could be coincidental.

"Very well." The difficulty then would be escorting her from the trolley stop back to the Nurses' Home. It would be dark. The walk was short, but he couldn't let her walk it alone.

It occurred to him that he had wasted his youth, if escorting a lady to an evening's entertainment was so daunting.

"I should…" She pointed to the door and edged toward it.

"Oh yes, of course."

"Will you still be operating on Mr. Farraday tomorrow? Or may I allow him his breakfast?"

"Mr. Farraday?"

"With the inguinal hernia?"

"Ah." A remarkable case. One of the largest hernias he'd ever seen, but without ever any sign of incarceration so the surgery was not urgent. "Is there a reason I shouldn't?"

"It's his wedding anniversary. His wife wants to bring him a cake."

Miss Hampton had mentioned something about this before, but he'd forgotten. Or not paid attention.

"Oh, I don't think he'll be in any mood to eat cake. Post-operative pain and ether in his system?"

"Yes, well," she said, with the merest hint of exasperation, "that is why I thought perhaps Tuesday. I believe your morning is free."

Postpone surgery for an anniversary cake? He had a dog who would be seven days post-op that he needed to sacrifice for necropsy. He would have to rearrange the entire day.

"Certainly, Miss Hampton. Let Miss Porter know it will be Tuesday."

"I will, thank you. We'll have a little ward party. It will cheer Mr. Bickers as well."

The amputee. A man with a hundred complaints. He didn't envy Miss Hampton having to attend that so-called party.

"I am all for cheering Mr. Bickers."

She smiled. "Wonderful! We'll make sure there is a piece of cake for you."

25

1889, August

Baltimore, Maryland

Ford's—Opens Next Monday Night
BRISTOL'S GREAT HORSE SHOW
A Funny Play Acted by Equines!
The Comedy of Schools!
In many acts but no "waits."
BRISTOL'S EQUES-CURRICULUM
A Manege of Educated Horses.

The School, with Professor Bristol, will give a parade, with flambeaus, on Saturday evening, starting at 8 o'clock from the neighborhood of the Opera House. All the Horses will be in the turnout, with Bristol's Band and other music, colored lights, etc. The sale of seats commences Saturday.

—*The Baltimore Sun*, Baltimore, MD, Friday, August 16, 1889

What on earth did one wear to a horse play? I settled on my brown plaid walking dress. It suited most purposes and I refused to throw myself into a tizzy over a dress. However, I did take special care with my hair. It wouldn't be tucked into a nurse's cap and it was trickier to pin it under a bonnet. If he weren't so particular, I could be less so.

Nothing could have surprised me more than to learn that Dr. Halsted was going to Bristol's Horse Show, unless it could be that he invited me to it. Surely it was not his cup of tea. Perhaps I should be miffed he thought it was mine—except that I was looking forward to it.

I laughed to myself. I would be happy to go to a cockfight if it would get me out on an evening. I may not be a social person, but neither was I used to hibernating in a cave, which was how I was beginning to feel.

Yet how strange to go with Dr. Halsted to a show. I could tell myself he simply wanted company and none of his fellows was willing to attend such lowbrow entertainment; I could tell myself that but not make myself believe it.

Oh, I was making too much of this. From what I'd heard, Dr. Halsted sprang from New York high society. Likely he was desperate for entertainment and this was the best he could find in Baltimore. I was what he must make do with. For now.

I powdered my nose, put on my wrap, and walked to the trolley stop.

I was early. So was he.

"Good evening, Dr. Halsted. It's a perfect evening for this, is it not?"

He smiled. "Hello, Miss Hampton. It's humid for a native New Yorker, but I imagine you consider it balmy, compared to Columbia?"

Weather. The last resort of the conversationally inept.

"If I were home, I would be in Cashiers. The mountains."

"You sound wistful."

"I am." I peered at him, curious. He sounded different. Relaxed. He didn't carry the usual tension in his shoulders. Perhaps he was a true aficionado of equine comedy. "I may be from Columbia, but I consider Cashiers Valley, in North Carolina, my real home. There is no place more beautiful. More peaceful."

"But you are in Baltimore?"

I smiled. "There is no place more interesting for a nurse than Johns Hopkins."

"Or for a surgeon. Here is the trolley. You say you've never been on one?" We waited as the horse pulled the car up in front of us. He took my elbow as we mounted the stairs, and said into my ear, "I fear it is less fun than you think."

I glanced away while he paid the fare, then he guided me to a bench. The car was an open one. He slid in first, to be nearer the street. The trolley started with a bit of a lurch.

The street noise made conversation difficult, but after a few minutes I noted, "It's slow."

"You sound disappointed." Was he grinning?

"I am a little." I smiled back. "I'm yearning for my horse." For the breeze in my hair. "Nellie."

"An original name for a horse."

I laughed outright at his teasing, and his smile broadened. Oh, for heaven's sake. I'd forgotten myself and brayed like a mule. I hated my laugh. Frank and Lucy used to tease me unmercifully, mimicking it. I schooled my face to more refined amusement. "She is Nellie the third, if you please. I was a child when I named my first Nellie."

He might be amused to learn that most Hampton horses were named for Confederates with whom they shared personality traits. Or he might not. He couldn't have been more than a schoolboy during the war. Why would I imagine the names of Uncle Wade's colorful brothers-in-arms would make any impression upon him at all?

Maybe it was better that it didn't. His impressions would likely run counter to mine.

With a twinge of discomfort, I changed the subject, calling upon all my genteel lady skills. My throat began to feel dry, trying to talk above the noise. He carried his part of the conversation; yet I could not help but feel we were boring each other. It was easier to talk in the hospital, when we had something real to talk about. It was a relief to reach the Opera House.

He didn't offer his arm, only touched my elbow briefly to indicate the way. He had purchased tickets, good ones, so rather than wait in a line we moved right down to seats in the front, actual seats, with cushions and padded arms. We were close enough to smell horse. Dr. Halsted did not sprawl, but sat very straight, hands on his knees, elbows tucked in. There was too much noise to talk comfortably, so aside from a few comments about our relative comfort, we didn't try to speak. It was all rather awkward, as I'd feared.

Then the music started, with the parade of horses and accompanying flambeaux men. It was an amazing spectacle. One act flowed into the next, and I remained entranced. My favorite was the horse classroom.

Mattie, the equine "mathematician," did sums while at horse school. I couldn't see how it was done and, delighted, I could not stop laughing. There were nearly thirty lovely horses and one ridiculous mule. The mule rang the school bell and swung on a swing. Professor Bristol was a consummate showman, but his skill in horse training was not debatable.

At intermission, Dr. Halsted excused himself for a short time and returned with a box of popped corn to share while we compared our impressions. He looked tired but pleased. No, not pleased—happy. Almost boyish. I found myself wondering if he was handsome. He had close-cut dark blonde hair with a high, sloping forehead, very aristocratic. He had the proverbial jug-handle ears but his mouth was quite nice, a little shadowed by a neat mustache. He was not South Carolina handsome but I suspected he was New York handsome. Not that it mattered in any way. But in that same way that it didn't matter, I wondered if he thought I was pretty.

"Thank you, Dr. Halsted," I said, as he shook the last few kernels into my hand. "I am enjoying myself more than I imagined I would."

He chuckled. "I'm not sure how to take that."

"Oh!" I laughed too. "I meant the Bristol Horse Show. It really is very entertaining. I thought I would find it silly. Didn't you?"

He gave me such a wry look, I put a hand over my mouth and laughed again.

"You do find it silly."

"I am enjoying myself more than I imagined." He sounded almost languid. It was pleasant, but a little strange. He was usually so intense.

The second half started. Again, everything else melted away as I lost myself in the magic of Professor Bristol's marvelous horses. He had them skipping a rope! Let Dr. Halsted laugh at me. I had not had so much fun since the circus at home.

Afterward, we joined a large crowd moving back to the trolley. He scowled at the line.

"If it is all the same to you, Miss Hampton, I will flag us a hansom."

"That's fine." It was quite late. And we both had to work early in the morning.

He had a flair for summoning cabs. We were soon on our way. He did not attempt to sit closer than he should. He looked very tired, but I supposed I did also. We talked of the soot in the sky, blacking out the stars. Nighttime weather.

The hansom brought us to the entrance walk to the Nurses' Home. Dr. Halsted jumped out and handed me down. He accompanied me to the steps but not up them.

"Thank you, Miss Hampton, for your delightful company."

"I enjoyed it very much."

"As did I." He stood there a moment, as if perplexed about the proper way to take leave.

It was embarrassing. So, I said, "Good night." I took a few steps backward.

He looked relieved, said "Good night," and walked away.

26

1889, September

Baltimore, Maryland

VIII. SUPERINTENDENT OF NURSES AND PRINCIPAL OF THE TRAINING SCHOOL.

1. The oversight of the Head Nurses, Assistant Nurses, Probationers and Orderlies is committed to the Superintendent of Nurses.

2. She is charged with the responsibility of the Nurses' Home, and the instruction of Nurses in the Training School, and is authorized to prescribe courses of study, to select and accept Probationers, to keep their accounts, and to make contracts with them for their respective terms of service. She is empowered to make, with the approval of the Superintendent, all necessary rules for the government of Nurses.

3. She shall constantly supervise all nursing work, and shall observe carefully the manner in which Nurses and Orderlies care for the sick.

4. It shall be her duty to approve of requisitions for ward supplies. She shall see that proper economy is exercised in the distribution of the food, in the use of all materials for surgical operations and dressings, and in all ward supplies and furnishings.

5. She shall have charge of the surgical storeroom, and give notice to the Superintendent when further supplies are required.

—*By-Laws, Rules and Regulations of The Johns Hopkins Hospital,* Adopted November 6, 1889

ꟹ

As Halsted had predicted, the hospital had gotten busy quickly. He was now operating six mornings a week—Osler called him "Jack the Ripper" behind his back. The dispensary ran well enough with Finney handling most of the procedures, but Halsted did pop around to help in the afternoons. He couldn't spend much time in the dog lab, though he had not abandoned it. Welch rode him hard about writing up his work and presenting it, frowning at his excuses. And he still had not received a permanent hospital appointment. No surprise he was restless.

Miss Hampton was busy also. The new superintendent of nurses, the other Miss Hampton, had taken charge earlier in the month and was shaking things up. His Miss Hampton seemed to scowl a lot more. He knew she had been friendly with Miss Parsons, who had resigned, driven off, he supposed, to Maryland Hospital when Miss Isabel arrived. He hoped Miss Caroline would not leave too.

He had called upon her services thrice to assist in surgery when Miss Porter absented herself. The first time was emergent. He made allowances for her unfamiliarity with the O.R., but had been more impressed by her self-possession than by her skill. The second time, Miss Porter was ill. The schedule was too backed up to skip a day. Miss Hampton was off duty but came in when asked. She was a different nurse altogether: organized, efficient, prompt. He made some comment to Brockway afterward and the young man laughed.

"That is because you frightened her to death during that bullet wound."

"Frightened? I did no such thing."

"Maybe not. But Miss Hampton cornered me a few days later and made me walk her through every instrument in the storeroom. Asked how you referred to them. She laid them out on a tray and made a diagram to memorize."

"Good Lord. I must have frightened her." He drew on his cigarette, perturbed. Then added, "I wish I could scare you. You still don't know the difference between when to use a mosquito clamp versus a needle-nose."

Brockway's responding laugh sounded nervous, which was Halsted's intention. But he hadn't meant to frighten Miss Hampton. Not in surgery and not after the entertainment he'd taken her to. Yet she'd bolted from him when he walked her to her door. As if she feared he would press her for another engagement.

He hadn't. He wanted to wait a proper amount of time. Then they had grown so busy and now he worried too much time had passed.

Well, it wasn't important. Fortunately, there had been no resulting awkwardness on the wards. Passing her out walking the grounds, yes. He never knew whether to stop and chat or not. But in the wards, there was no difficulty at all.

He was headed there now. Brockway said the scalp wound he'd sutured was febrile. Halsted had let the resident handle the whole case by himself; it was only a laceration, not a deep stab. He suspected Brockway was just being hypervigilant, but he'd have a look.

A lone nurse—not Miss Hampton—was wiping down bedframes with disinfectant. She stood to attention when he walked in, but he waved her to continue. He started toward the scalp wound, then paused, hearing voices from the storeroom. Not raised voices, but firm ones.

"...should have gone through *me*."

"They were ordered before you arrived. Miss Parsons approved the order."

"She should not have. I've never seen anything so wasteful. Two dozen. Two dozen! There are a half-dozen brand-new arterial clamps in the surgical closet. Unused!"

"They were too large."

"Oh, for heaven's sake. Send these back. The others will do well enough."

He poked his head into the room. "Is there a problem?"

The nurse superintendent started, then said, "No. Nothing, Dr. Halsted."

He looked to Miss Caroline. Her lips were compressed and her eyes angry, but she shook her head and said, "No."

He glanced at the box in Miss Isabel's hands. "Are those my instruments?"

She looked down. "No. There was a mistake. Miss Parsons requested two dozen clamps!" She made wide eyes and laughed a little.

"I requested them." He turned to Caroline. "Please have them unboxed and sent down to surgery. Then let Miss Porter know to schedule that new rectal ulcer the first morning the operating room is free." He nodded to the superintendent. "I'm glad those clamps finally arrived. The others were tissue crushers, not clamps. They should be discarded."

He exited the storeroom. The ladies were silent. Then he heard the sound of things being shifted about. He wondered, vaguely amused, if Miss Caroline would shift everything back after Miss Isabel left to rearrange another ward. He didn't envy Caroline.

He hoped she wouldn't leave.

The scalp wound looked good. He checked the temperature chart. The patient had been up two degrees that morning, but after that, normal. He set the chart down and cocked his ear toward the storeroom. They were being very quiet. He made a quick round to check his other post-op patients, though Brockway had visited them all that morning. Then he nodded to the nurse who was now wiping windowsills and left.

He returned to his apartments and brewed himself a strong cup of Turkish coffee before his afternoon in the morgue. He had another neck to work on. He would solve this parathyroid dilemma one way or another.

As for the other dilemma…he sifted through the folders on his desk until he found the draft of the bylaws sent to him by Hurd, the new superintendent of the hospital. Gilman had been doing a fine job, but he was president of the university and couldn't do double duty forever. Halsted liked Dr. Hurd. Welch liked him.

He flipped pages until he found what he was looking for: superintendent of nurses. He read the job description. Good Lord. They were looking for a tyrant. And apparently got one.

He drummed his fingers on his desk. It would be a severe disappointment if Miss Caroline left. He should probably talk to her first, but, remembering her thin-lipped disavowal of any problem, he suspected she was one to fight her own battles. She would refuse his interference.

On the other hand, Miss Porter was an adequate operating nurse at best, and tended toward the sickly. Whereas Miss Hampton showed admirable initiative. And good health.

Bite the bullet, man—he scolded himself. Just go have a talk with Dr. Hurd.

27

1889, September

Baltimore, Maryland

THE CLAMP TWIST IN THE CONTROL OF THE HAEMORRHAGE
A vessel or bleeding point inaccurately caught by the artery clamps and requiring immediate ligation for any reason may, as is undoubtably well known, often be controlled by a half-twist or slight rotation of the clamp. The precise situation of the vessel may then be determined by cautiously untwisting the instrument to the degree necessary to permit the escape of a fraction of a drop of blood and then retwisting. Now, instead of removing the clamp…

—The Employment of Fine Silk in Preference to Cat-Gut and the Advantages of Transfixing Tissues and Vessels in Controlling Haemorrhage. Also, an account of the introduction of gloves, gutta-percha tissue and silver foil by Dr. William S. Halsted, J. Am. M. Ass. Chicago, 1913 lx:1119-1126

I would keep my full salary and my rooms in the Nurses' Home. I was not—Dr. Hurd assured me, in the frightening confines of his office where I had been unceremoniously summoned—being punished or demoted. In fact, it had not been the nurse superintendent who made the reassignment, but rather the head of surgery had asked for the change.

"You see, he is not entirely satisfied with Miss Porter, but said he was impressed with the surgical ward nurse who has substituted during Miss Porter's absence."

Dr. Halsted had asked for me? Oh! I could not make the man out. He had ignored me for over a month after the horse show. Except, of course, for the necessary communication over patients, but even then, he glued his eyes to the charts. If he was impressed by my work in his operating room, he'd done nothing to show it. *And he ignored me for over a month!*

Worse than ignored, he actively avoided me. I would see him approaching down a path in the courtyard, then he would catch sight of me and abruptly change course. Once might have been a coincidence, but it did not only occur once. It was quite uncivil.

"So," said the hospital superintendent, "if you are amenable…"

"Yes. Thank you, Dr. Hurd. I'm excited by the opportunity."

That much was true. I found surgery fascinating.

I was not to start immediately. I had a week to train my replacement on the wards and to learn the ropes from Miss Porter, who was to be reassigned to the dispensary. I would still be under Isabel's charge, but after that encounter with Dr. Halsted, the nurse superintendent was already less heavy-handed. She had clearly not reckoned upon Dr. Halsted's "quirks."

I didn't understand him either, but I would. I would. A Canadian Hampton might be cowed, but a South Carolina Hampton never shied from a challenge.

❧

Dr. Halsted limited his operating hours to the mornings, in theory. That did not mean shorter workdays for me. I had to prepare the operating room beforehand and see to its cleaning afterward. I had to keep the storage room stocked and organized. Sometimes, I visited the wards afterwards to make sure the patients were comfortable though that was not required of me. And I was called upon after hours for emergencies. After all, I lived on hospital grounds.

There were not many cases requiring evening surgery. But this evening, an important citizen of Baltimore arrived with severe abdominal pain, vomiting, and bleeding per rectum.

"Acute onset," Dr. Brockway related breathlessly. "Distension. No bowel sounds."

I watched Dr. Halsted, cigarette dangling from his mouth, feel the man's abdomen then put his ear to it. He frowned.

"What is your impression, Brockway?"

The resident said, "Diverticulitis, I think."

"Hmm. You might think it, but not for long." He asked the patient loudly, "When did you last eat, Mr. Frank?"

"Hours ago," the patient groaned. "But I retched it all out."

Dr. Halsted took his pulse. "Miss Hampton, can you prepare the room?"

"Yes, Dr. Halsted." I hurried off to change clothes. I could have everything ready in an hour.

Dr. Brockway prepared the patient: shaving, washing, administering morphine and then ether. Dr. Halsted donned his white clothes, his rubber boots, and hooked up the irrigation for the table. Then we all scrubbed our hands with strong soap and plunged them into mercuric chloride until Dr. Halsted deemed enough time had passed. Then he began.

I never tired of watching him. He was so very intent. He gave direction in a quiet voice and never grew flustered. Sometimes he paused, studying the field, before the next cut or clamp or tie. I pitied Dr. Brockway then, seeing his curiosity and frustration as he tried to guess what Dr. Halsted was thinking. I tried reading the man's mind too, but that was unproductive. It was more efficient to watch his hands. To anticipate where they would move.

He did not have "surgeon's hands." His fingers were short and indelicate. His thumbs, I could only describe as bizarre. They were short even relative to his fingers and appeared flattened. They were not pretty, but watching those hands mesmerized me.

I was tired tonight. If I weren't here, I would already be in bed. I found the silence and Dr. Halsted's slow, careful movements to be lulling. He incised the skin, the subcutaneous fat, the peritoneum, meticulously, bloodlessly, clamping or tying off tiny vessels as he cut.

Then he was in the abdominal cavity. The sigmoid colon was distended, dusky, and twisted about the mesentery.

"Hmmm." He felt behind it. "No fecal contamination. Brockway, what do you think?"

"Untwist it?"

Dr. Halsted nodded. "I think so too."

I watched him unwind the tangled bowel. So carefully. Then he paused to see what would happen. We all waited. The congestion lessened. It still looked dusky compared to the small intestine but it definitely pinkened.

"Would you pex it?" Dr. Halsted asked.

Dr. Brockway chewed his lip. "Yes?"

"Yes, I would too." His eyes rose to mine. "This tends to recur."

He moved the bowel about, then sutured a part along the lateral wall, while Dr. Brockway retracted, occasionally applying thin-nosed clamps.

A red stain appeared. Dr. Halsted flicked Dr. Brockway's hand away and gave one of the clamps a twist. Dr. Brockway sucked in a breath, but Dr. Halsted merely checked the clamp, then held up his fingers and I passed him more suture. He placed two more ties, nodded at Dr. Brockway, and they proceeded.

Finally, Dr. Halsted began closing. So slowly, so very gently, I found my eyelids growing heavy.

"Why don't you finish, Brockway," he said, stepping back.

The young surgeon took over eagerly. Dr. Halsted watched a while, then went to the scrub sink to wash his hands. He stepped outside.

"Cigarette break," Dr. Brockway whispered.

I was wide awake now. The resident finished. I helped him dress the incision. We slid the patient back onto the stretcher. Dr. Halsted returned.

"Take him to the ward. Make sure his pain is well controlled. Keep an eye on him."

Dr. Brockway nodded. "Yes, sir." He wheeled the stretcher out.

Dr. Halsted yawned. "Excuse me. I do beg your pardon."

"No need to apologize. It's quite late."

"Yes. These late cases are annoying. Fortunate there are so few." He looked around, squinting, then said, "Well, good night, Miss Hampton. Good rest of the night. We start early again tomorrow."

He left the room. I sniffed. He might have a good rest of the night. I had to clean and set up for tomorrow. I would be here another two hours.

Even so. Even so, I looked forward to early morning tomorrow.

28

1889, November

Baltimore, Maryland

THE RADICAL CURE OF THE HERNIA

Dr. William S. Halsted presented five patients upon whom he had performed his operation for the cure of inguinal hernia. He described the operation as follows:

1. The incision begins at the external abdominal ring and ends one inch or less (less than one inch in children) to the inner side of the anterior superior spine of the ilium on an imaginary line connecting the anterior superior spines of the ilia…

7. The skin is united over the cord by interrupted stitches of very fine silk. These stitches do not penetrate the skin, and when tied they become buried. They are taken from the underside of the skin and made to include only its deep layers…

—Presented at The Johns Hopkins Hospital Medical Society, Baltimore, November 4, 1889

❧

Halsted entered his apartment on the third floor of the hospital administration building, shut the door, and turned the key in the lock. He leaned against the door for a moment and sighed.

Surgery had gone long. The subclavian artery had taken an aberrant course and Brockway had not—no, he couldn't blame it on Brockway—the surgery had been bloodier than it should have been. Aneurysms were always tricky. There was a solution though. If Mall had not packed up and left, they would have solved this by now.

He opened his eyes to study his hands. Were they quivering? A surgeon's hands should never shake. They had not trembled during surgery. The day that happened, he would hang up his apron for good.

He stepped away from the door.

His apartment, furnished with fine mahogany cabinets, desk, and chair, with heavy damask drapes, a good Persian carpet, and the correct color wall—he'd had the painters back four times—used to give him satisfaction, but was so comfortable to him now as to be all but invisible. The realization saddened him. Was it true: familiarity breeds contempt?

He could not believe Chaucer's old adage held true. Not in every instance.

He wiped his mustache. His lip was sweating. How he hated this, feeling like this. Yet he'd done it to himself. Knowing. But knowing too that if it were not for morphine, it would be cocaine.

He removed his coat, hung it on the rack, and made himself walk slowly to his desk. He sat in his armchair, and slowly opened the drawer. Self-control was key.

A knock interrupted and he slammed the drawer shut.

"Who's there?"

"Welch."

He rose to unlock the door. The man filled the doorway like Gargantua.

"Come in. What brings you to my humble abode?"

"Humble?" Welch looked around pointedly, then put his fingers in his vest pocket. "I want to congratulate you on the paper you gave to the society last night. Brilliant work."

Halsted shrugged. "Five patients." They threw the word brilliant around too readily. If they were all brilliant, they needed a new word for Welch. "We'll see if it holds true."

"It will. Burying the sutures? Groundbreaking! The dog work has been time well spent. You'll get that appointment, see if you don't."

"If I do, I know whom to thank."

He was still only acting surgical chief. Neither he nor Welch counted the appointment he had received last month: professor of surgery to a medical school that did not yet exist.

"Pah. But listen, that isn't the only reason I've come."

Halsted lifted his eyebrows, questioning, then stepped back and gestured to a chair.

"Cigarette?" He raised the lid of his jeweled tin. Tobacco would help, briefly.

"No. I'm not staying long. This will be embarrassing." Welch sat but did not settle back. He leaned forward. Earnest. That was disconcerting. "Halsted, there has been some scuttlebutt."

Cigarette an inch from his mouth, match unlit, he froze. No, it couldn't be. He was careful. Who would say anything? Who could? The floor seemed to swirl beneath his feet. Yet Welch said the appointment would be forthcoming…

"About a distinguished—if crusty—old surgeon and an attractive young nurse."

"Oh, good Lord." He sank into his chair. The relief he felt was immediately replaced by guilt. People were talking? About Miss Hampton? He couldn't do that to her.

"There have been a few sly words here and there. Among the nurses, mostly, you know how hens are. But then Councilman said he was certain he saw the two of you coming out of the theater on Saturday. The matinee! Good God, man. Nobody goes to the theater for the matinee. He said he would have approached you but feared his body would end up in the harbor."

Halsted managed to light the cigarette and gave himself a moment before coming up with, "This is unfortunate." He meant that literally. He was not trying to be flippant.

"Halsted." Welch's voice took on a hard edge. "I've never known you to be indiscreet with women. And Miss Hampton is a *lady*."

"I know that." His neck and ears burned. He knew Caroline deserved better than skulking around as they had been.

"I have no business asking what your intentions are. But the precedent is a bad one unless you are serious." Welch paused, embarrassed, to grunt, "Which, frankly, seems as farfetched as the thought of you being indiscreet with your nurse."

"I am serious."

The words were stated flatly. It *was* none of Welch's business. And yet, it was a strange relief to confess. Welch stared, studying him with the same fixed look he'd give a new pathological specimen. Then dawned the satisfied smile—and his diagnosis.

"Halsted, you are. You're smitten."

Halsted stubbed out his cigarette, unsmoked. "Laugh if you want to. It is rather comic."

"It isn't comic."

"Tragic then."

"Don't." Welch reached out a hand and laid it on his shoulder. "Halsted, don't. How does she feel?"

"How should I know?" He only knew how he felt: eager when he awoke, eager to go to the operating room where he would see her. He wanted all of this—all of this opportunity—and Caroline. He wanted it all. But more than simply having it, he wanted to deserve it. He could not convince himself that he did.

"Hmph. I imagine there are ways." Welch leaned back in his chair. "Ask Finney."

He tried to chuckle but shook his head instead. "I don't know. She is rather strikingly straight-forward. If I dared ask her, I've no doubt she would tell me without mincing words."

"You asked her to the matinee."

He nodded.

"Anything else?"

He wouldn't admit to Bristol's Horse Show. "We've been to dinner."

Welch didn't need details. Asking her to dine with him after letting so much time pass had taken all his courage. She was gracious to accept. And an amusing dinner companion. The very next day he invited her to the matinee, which was gauche, he knew. He careened from one extreme to the other.

"And you enjoyed yourselves?"

"Well, I did." He drummed his fingers on the desk. It was awkward to speak of this with another man. Maybe he should write to one of his sisters. Not Minnie. She would blather to Sam. No doubt Bertie would be thrilled if he asked her for advice. He'd certainly never gone to her for any before. "The thing is, I don't know her well enough to know if I should pursue this. But I won't have people talking about her." Good God, he could imagine what Booker would say.

"So the dilemma is how to get to know her without causing gossip."

"And to let her get to know me." His voice hitched. "She doesn't."

"Everyone has skeletons in the closet. Don't let that discourage you. Your future is more important than your past."

Welch was smiling broadly. How could he dismiss Halsted's skeletons so cavalierly?

"What if past is prologue?" That was as near to confession as he could bring himself.

"Then 'what to come, in yours and my discharge.'" Welch pushed himself to his feet. "I will have you to supper this weekend. You and Miss Hampton. We'll dine. Play some cards. I'll excuse myself to take my cigar onto the porch. A big fat one that will take a long time to smoke."

"Thank you. But I don't think one evening will suffice for me to judge how she feels."

"I will judge." He still smiled. "No more secrecy, Halsted. It's the hiding that can be ruinous. That and letting this go on for too long."

"No. That wouldn't be fair to her," he agreed, though perhaps Welch no longer referred to Miss Hampton.

"All right, then. Too much chitterchat." Welch stepped to the door. "I have a pile of papers to read as high as my ears."

"Last week the pile was only up to your neck."

"'Never put off till tomorrow what may be done the day after tomorrow just as well.'"

Halsted scratched around in his memory. Wilde? No, too American. "Twain."

Welch grinned and poked him with a finger as thick as a cigar. "Impressive. I was sure you'd guess Wilde."

"I don't guess."

Welch chortled at him. "I'll catch you out yet."

He let his friend out, then locked the door behind him and, wasting no time, returned to his desk drawer. He could feel his anxiety leeching away as he slid it open. Was it easing? Or worsening? What a blackguard he was. He didn't even deserve Welch.

29

1889, November

Baltimore, Maryland

Between doctor and nurse there should be the most perfect *entente cordiale*; let him find you always ready to second his efforts with an enthusiasm equal to his own.

—*Textbook of Nursing* by Clara S. Weeks-Shaw, D. Appleton and Company, 1883

ও

We had an audience in the operating room again. Sometimes Dr. Halsted was cordial with visiting surgeons anxious to observe his technique; other times he was quiet, as with Dr. Blumquist. The patient, a gouty Baltimore merchant, had developed a mass under his arm. Dr. Blumquist poked at it a week earlier in his office and caused it to bleed so profusely that the patient demanded a referral to "that surgeon at Johns Hopkins" at once. He had been cooling his heels in the paying ward for a week. I could not have said who was the more unpleasant, the patient or Dr. Blumquist.

The patient was prepared and anesthetized on the table. I stood in my place, between the two doctors, feeling squashed by Dr. Blumquist's encroachment. Across the table, Dr. Brockway tried to pretend the interloper was not there.

Dr. Halsted was marvelously calm. The moment I placed the scalpel in his hand, the room fell silent. He leaned over and incised the skin. I handed him a sponge. Whatever the mass, it was bloody. Or traumatized by the previous poke. Dr. Brockway engaged with his clamps, as he had learned so expertly to do. From time to time, Dr. Halsted paused to tie off a bleeder with the delicate silk thread he favored. He made it look simple; I knew it was not. I fitted my own movements to those of the men, handing this, taking away that. I didn't blot unless Dr. Halsted indicated, with that tiny flick of his finger, that he wished me to blot.

Dr. Blumquist grunted and muttered observations and suggestions without seeming to realize he was talking to himself.

"Ah! There!" the man exclaimed, as Dr. Halsted peeled back a mass of fat and clot, revealing a bulging feeder vessel.

Horrified, I watched Dr. Blumquist's fat finger extend toward the wound. I fell against him as heavily as I dared, stomping his foot as if I'd lost my balance.

"Oh! I do beg your pardon!" I drawled in my best Georgia peach voice. I pulled away from the hands enthusiastically steadying my waist.

"No, indeed!" Dr. Blumquist chortled. "You aren't the first little lady to feel faint seeing blood."

I would have stomped him again but caught Dr. Brockway's wink.

"Clamp?" Dr. Halsted said.

The question mark alone alerted me that I was too slow and he was peeved. Generally, his requests were declarations. I put a clamp in his hand. The wrong one. He merely held it away from the wound until I exchanged it for another. The surgery proceeded. He resected the tumor, a mass of fat and cysts and blood, then closed the wound meticulously. That surprised me. Satisfied with the trainee's progress, he now usually let Dr. Brockway close.

He wiped his hands on the towel that I gave him and stepped away from the table. "Brockway, will you escort Dr. Blumquist and his patient back to the ward? I'll take this specimen over to pathology."

"Yes, of course."

I helped Dr. Brockway transfer the patient to the stretcher and waited until they were gone before fixing my attention on Dr. Halsted. He had not carted off the specimen but was waiting to speak to me. He looked put out. "*Fainting*, Miss Hampton?"

It shouldn't need explaining. "He does not scrape under his fingernails."

He nodded. "That is the least of his transgressions."

He said nothing more but stepped out of the room. He hadn't taken his specimen, so I was not surprised when he returned, hands washed, cigarette poking from his lips. He didn't look me in the face, but said, sounding uncomfortable, "See here, is Brockway bothering you?"

"Dr. Brockway?" The question puzzled me until I recalled the wink. Surely Dr. Halsted had not noticed that. I could have sworn his eyes had not left the patient's armpit. "Not at all."

He grunted. "Well, if he does, I'll speak to him."

I wanted to laugh. Instead, I held my tongue and went about my business. I had to finish on time. I needed to tidy up and put on civilian clothes. I was expecting company.

Under Dr. Halsted's scrutiny, I gathered the clamps, needle holders, and scalpels and placed them in a pan to be washed and disinfected. Then I collected the sponges, counting them as I deposited them in the trash. I made a notation in my record book. Why on earth hadn't he left for pathology?

"Are you counting those?"

"Yes." A blush stole into my cheeks.

"Inventory?"

It would be simpler to say yes. "No. Not exactly." I faced him. "In New York one night, a patient was brought in, young man, very sad, he'd fallen from a delivery cart. His spleen ruptured. The surgeon on duty operated at once."

"That's a difficult surgery under the best of circumstances." He blew out a cloud of smoke and regarded me with the intent, interested look I so loved.

"The patient did not survive. He died two days later. At autopsy, they found a sponge."

"That is unacceptable." He tamped out the cigarette. "Even so, a retained sponge was not likely the cause of death. Shock, I suspect."

"Yes, well, that was the report. But how do we know? I was curious, I suppose, to see how often sponges might be left behind."

"Hmph." He looked a little unsettled. "And what have you discovered? How many have I left inside my patients?"

I made a show of looking through my notebook, tapping the bottom of a couple pages with my pen.

"None. But you are down six arterial clamps."

He started. Then a smile lit his face and his eyes glittered at me. "Ha! Well done. That'll get a laugh out of Booker."

With that, he finally moved to the table, picked up the pan holding his specimen, and laid a towel over it.

"Are you free this evening?" he asked, staring down, as if asking the question of the tumor. "There is a restaurant up by the university Welch says he likes very much."

I had already teased him once. I didn't dare ask him if Welch would be accompanying us. How very strange that evening had been; I'd felt like a third wheel. Until Dr. Welch, as if trying to draw me in, asked what it had been like to grow up in post-war Columbia. He was a man who regularly bit off more than most men could chew. I cast about for a suitable story and hit upon Uncle Wade's triumph at the Statehouse. The first time he'd been elected governor, the election was contested, or so the ex-governor claimed. There was a standoff between Federal troops and Uncle Wade's supporters. He made a short speech, averting catastrophe with a few inspired words. I supposed I was boasting a bit, but both Dr. Welch and Dr. Halsted looked more startled than impressed. Then Dr. Welch said: *Caesar at the Rubicon.* Dr. Halsted said, *Well, but he didn't cross.* And Dr. Welch said: *Hmm.* It was an uncomfortable moment. Then Dr. Halsted threw out a Latin phrase that made Dr. Welch laugh. A minute later, he excused himself to smoke a cigar. A very strange evening.

Well, I could not go to dinner.

"Thank you, but my sister and a friend are coming up from Washington this afternoon. I haven't seen them since leaving Columbia."

"Your sister Lucy?"

He remembered, though surely I hadn't mentioned my sister to him more than once or twice. I nodded.

"They wish to see where I work. To have a tour of the famous hospital. Then we are dining with Major Venable."

"Oh. Very nice. Well, please give him my regards."

He carted the specimen to the door. Then he paused and turned around.

"Would you care to bring your sister and friend to tea? I would like to meet her. Them. If they would care to be introduced."

He had one foot against the door as if to make a quick escape and seemed embarrassed such an invitation had come from his mouth.

"They would be delighted. I would be delighted," I assured him, though they would be more baffled than delighted, and I could not envision anything more awkward.

"What time do they arrive?"

"The train is due at two o'clock."

"Shall we say four o'clock then? I am on the third floor of Administration. Suite four."

"Oh." Good heavens. His suite? "Yes, that would be fine."

He left with his tumor. I shuddered to imagine what Lucy would report back to the family. His suite?

❧

Lucy and Sally appeared nonplussed when I said I was taking them to tea with the head of the department of surgery. I had mentioned him all of once in a letter to Lucy, when he helped me escape from under Isabel's thumb. I hadn't even given her his name.

Yet they gamely followed me up the stairs and down the hallway to suite four.

He opened the door. He was freshly shaved and looked very dapper. We stepped inside. I tried to hide my shock. His sitting room appeared transplanted from a Madison Avenue mansion.

An Oriental carpet with an intricate design covered the floor. The bulk of the furniture was of mahogany, dust-free, including bookcases, cabinets, and a desk, as well as a small table and matched chairs. The wall was the color of buttercream. The paintings on the wall showed city scenes, Paris and somewhere in Germany from the lettering in its shop windows. I could not guess the artist but felt I should be able to. Antique lamps were set about the room, lighting it softly. It was all tastefully expensive.

A door in the side wall was tightly shut. I envisioned a bedroom behind it and flushed.

"Please, come sit down," he said with a gesture.

"Miss Hampton, Miss Carter, permit me to make you acquainted with Dr. Halsted," I said, remembering myself.

They exchanged greetings and pleasantries and sat.

The table was covered with a blindingly white cloth, smooth as glass. A small serving tray containing dainty biscuits dusted with sugar was set on top. Not a crumb or speck of sugar dirtied the cloth.

"I hope you had a pleasant journey," Dr. Halsted said. "Miss Hampton told me you were arriving from Washington."

"Yes," Lucy said. "We were visiting my uncle and cousins."

"Senator Hampton," he said, proving he knew.

"How is Uncle Wade?" I asked. "I worry the strain of it all will take a toll."

"Oh." Lucy smiled. "You know how he is. He doesn't bend or break. He sends his love. Daisy too. Washington is very exciting." She turned to Dr. Halsted. "Have you been?"

"A few times," he answered genially.

Lucy blushed. She could do it at will. "How silly of me. Men are so well-traveled, aren't they? It's much more of an occasion for ladies to venture from home."

Lucy had been back and forth to New York, Mississippi, Charleston, Richmond…her little-old-me act drove me to distraction. But Dr. Halsted charmed and charmingly, said, "Well, I hope you venture to Baltimore more often. Miss Hampton," he tilted his chin to me, "would be pleased, I'm sure."

He spoke of a few of Baltimore's attractions: the market, the park, the old Fort. I suspected Major Venable would take us driving and said so.

"Would you like tea?" he asked, standing and moving to his mantelpiece.

I stifled a laugh. A gas laboratory burner was perched upon it, and above that, a copper pot. It looked terribly out of place, yet how resourceful. He poured water into the pot from a pitcher. Then he fetched a tray from a corner table that held a china teapot, delicately patterned, with matching cups and saucers, sugar pot and creamer, and small silver spoons.

"Why this is lovely," Sally exclaimed.

"My mother's. I haven't much occasion to use it." He looked a little embarrassed as he set the tray down. "I prefer coffee." He straightened. "Would anyone like coffee, rather? I would be happy to brew some."

"Tea is fine," Lucy said and Sally murmured agreement. I imagined Dr. Halsted would have liked an excuse to make the drink he preferred. Or a glass of whiskey. Perhaps he'd fortified himself before the tea party.

"I would like coffee, if it isn't too much trouble," I said.

Lucy appeared startled, but said, "Coffee would be equally lovely." Sally nodded.

"All right," Dr. Halsted said, looking pleased. "I'll fetch the coffee cups instead."

He went to a cabinet behind his desk. I rose and picked up the tea tray, thinking to make room by moving it back to the corner table, then realized I was acting the lady of the house. I halted, embarrassed, halfway between the two tables. Dr. Halsted rescued me.

"Nurse Hampton," he said, carrying a silver tray with four small white silver-rimmed porcelain cups and a lidded jar. Did he have formal service for twelve complete with oyster forks tucked away in his cabinets? "We're not in the operating room. You needn't anticipate my directions. But if you would set that tray aside it would help."

I did. Then rather than sit idly, I followed him to the mantel to watch. He opened the jar and scooped out a few mounds of powdery dark coffee to dump into the pot.

"Sugar?" he asked.

I nodded. "Please."

He smiled at me. "I meant—" He subtly changed the tone of his voice. "Sugar."

"Oh!" I laughed and fetched the sugar bowl from the tea tray.

He measured six spoonfuls and added them to the pot. He stirred the mix, lit the burner, and returned to his seat. Lucy engaged him in a discussion of the merits of coffee versus tea.

Too restless to sit, I remained at the mantel, studying the copper pot. It looked well-used but well-cared for. No surprise. I noted a miniature on the mantel and picked it up. A pretty woman. I put it back down. I turned to face the party and accidentally kicked a small trash basket. Glancing down, I saw a bakery box, crushed, with sugar spilling out. He'd run out to the bakery. Something inside my chest melted. How carefully he had prepared.

"Miss Hampton? Is that boiling?" Dr. Halsted asked, rising, looking a little worried.

"No. Not yet."

He came back, wrapped a handkerchief around the handle, and poured froth and coffee into the cups.

"Hmm. That looks about right," he said.

It looked rather awful. Perhaps we should have stuck with tea. How Lucy would laugh later. We sat down. He passed out the cups. I dared a sip. It was the most delicious coffee I had ever tasted. Of course, it would be.

We stayed a polite forty minutes, then thanked Dr. Halsted and took our leave, promising to give his regards to Major Venable. I lingered in the doorway as my visitors started down the hall. I turned back to see Dr. Halsted picking up the tray. He looked exhausted. Lucy could run a man in circles. His society rearing showed itself in his responses, but foolishness made him impatient, and, in Lucy's mind, men preferred women to be a bit stupid.

"I expect your friends will pity you the challenge of entertaining three Southern ladies for coffee."

"On the contrary. I will be the envy of the Maryland Club."

"Pish-tosh." I smiled. He sounded sarcastic, more like himself, and I was glad. "Thank you, Dr. Halsted. It was very generous of you to do."

I backed out of the doorway and let it close before he could protest any more. I wasn't flirting. His efforts had truly touched me.

I followed down the hall and caught the whispering between Lucy and Sally.

"Nonsense," Lucy said. "How could Caroline consider a doctor? Or anyone but a planter? One of our gentlemen. Could you imagine Dr. Halsted on a horse?"

Good heavens! I made my feet loud and came up behind them, exclaiming, "I wonder what Major Venable has planned. Do you think he'll let me drive his barouche if I ask?"

"Kitten!" Lucy exclaimed. "Don't you dare!" Then my elder sister fixed an eye upon me and repeated, "Don't you dare."

30

1890, January
Baltimore, Maryland

In the winter of 1889 and 1890—I cannot recall the month—the nurse in charge of my operating-room complained that the solutions of mercuric chloride produced a dermatitis of her arms and hands. As she was an unusually efficient woman, I gave the matter my consideration and one day in New York requested the Goodyear Company to make as an experiment two pairs of thin rubber gloves with gauntlets. On trial, these proved so satisfactory that additional gloves were ordered.

—"The Employment of Fine Silk in Preference to Cat-Gut and the Advantages of Transfixing Tissues and Vessels in Controlling Haemorrhage. Also, an account of the introduction of gloves, gutta-percha tissue and silver foil," by Dr. William S.Halsted, J. Am. M. Ass. Chicago, 1913 lx:1119-1126

❧

Dr. Halsted had gone to New York for the holidays to visit family. I was allotted three days off by the superintendent of nurses. I spent Christmas Day at the home of Major Venable with other displaced Confederates he had collected. We ate true country ham. It was all very jolly, I told myself.

Dr. Halsted was due back today and I was anxious. I wasn't sure I'd have a position when he returned.

His last case before leaving had been a lengthy wiring of a fractured patella. When he used wire, his compulsive cleanliness intensified. I could swear oath there was not a germ within miles.

The longer soak and repeated dipping of hands and instruments in the disinfectant had been agonizing, but I did my best to hide my discomfort. The chemicals were too harsh and the effects were cumulative. Every night I coated my hands and arms with Vaseline. In the morning I dabbed the cracks and fissures with glacial acetic acid. From elbows down, I looked like a field hand. I was managing, but that last surgery had nearly been too much.

When it was finally over, Dr. Halsted trailed Dr. Brockway to the wards. I cleaned the room. He returned before I was finished, carrying a small package. He was wearing his shy face—which always made me nervous. The last time he'd asked me to supper he cancelled at the last minute with no explanation. I wasn't sure, if he asked again, whether I should say yes. I hadn't yet figured him out.

"Miss Hampton?"

"Yes?" I set down the instrument tray.

"I wanted to wish you Merry Christmas before I head home. Not home, I mean to New York. I'm sorry you won't have opportunity to go to your family's lodge."

I smiled at him. "Thank you. I hope to be able to visit in the spring."

He nodded and held out the box. To my relief, it bore the stamp of a local confectioner. Well, of course, he knew the rules; even Yankees could be well-bred. A few sweets were within the bounds.

I hadn't gotten him anything. That would have been odd. I reached out to take it and he gasped, dropping the box onto the tray.

"Miss Hampton! Good Lord, what is wrong with your hands?"

That was rude. I tried to draw back but he caught hold of me.

"Is that from the mercuric chloride?" He bent over my hand as a suitor might, but tsked with disgust. "Have you had headaches? Has your urine turned green?"

"Oh, for heaven's sake!" Had he actually asked about my urine? "My skin is sensitive to corrosives. Is that so strange?"

I pulled away. He held out his own hands, which looked merely dry and rough, not damaged, as mine did. He seemed to be comparing what he had seen of my hands to his.

Then he pinched his lip and frowned.

"I fear you will pick up an infection, Miss Hampton."

"My hands are not in the wounds."

"You handle dirty bandages."

"And then wash my hands."

He looked pained. "I wish you had said something."

"What was I to say? I don't want to lose my position."

He looked even more pained. "No. No, but this won't do." He turned and took a few steps, then turned back. "Let me think."

He left the room, deep in thought. Presumably he'd spent Christmas thinking about my hands. Ha! I knew what New York was like during the holidays. Theater. Parties. Balls. Did he dance? I suspected there was little he couldn't do if he chose. Would he choose to? With whom? No, I couldn't even wallow in misery over it—it was too hard to picture.

The day was cold and overcast. The grounds were too muddy to go walking. The nursing students were either in the wards or shut in their rooms or each other's. Isabel and I did not socialize. I had been reading Dickens in the library without paying attention to what I read, feeling gloomy. I heard the ring of the front doorbell, then the matron's approach to the library. I looked up as the stern older woman appeared.

"Miss Hampton? Dr. Halsted is calling."

The woman was peeved. The rules against gentleman callers were rigidly enforced: fathers and brothers only. In the parlor. But that was for the nursing students. There was no guideline for the unexpected occurrence of the head surgeon calling upon the operating-room nurse. No doubt once Isabel learned of this, there would be a new rule prohibiting it.

I didn't want Mrs. Abbott to be troubled.

"Would you mind asking him to wait? I'll grab my coat and meet him outside."

The woman sighed her relief and said, "Certainly."

I took an extra moment to comb my hair. I put on my coat and kidskin gloves. My hands looked much better now, but that might sway him further. If he remembered.

I met him on the stoop. It was drizzling—cold, Baltimore drizzle. Droplets coalesced on his top hat. I shivered in my coat.

"I've been thinking about your hands," he said, dropping his cigarette and toeing it into the dirt.

"Good afternoon, Dr. Halsted. I hope you had a pleasant holiday. Is your family well?"

"Oh." His eyes laughed. "Very well. My sister, Minnie, decorated a tree. It was quite festive. I trust you enjoyed yourself as well? Welch says there was a party in the dining room? Finney indulged in too much punch?"

"He sang something in Irish."

"I didn't know he spoke Irish."

"He does not."

He nodded. "Now," he said, "may we discuss your hands?"

"All right," I said grudgingly. But he had been thinking of me—at least, of my hideous skin condition.

"May I see them?"

I removed my gloves and extended my hands. He took hold of them. He was wearing calfskin gloves, exquisite ones.

"Yes," he said, "I think these will fit."

"Excuse me?"

He let go, then pulled a paper sack from his pocket. From it, he extracted two long-gauntleted gloves. Made of rubber.

"Try them," he urged.

I put them on. They fit rather well.

"Will they work?" I held my hands up, examining the gift.

"Here." He handed me a fountain pen. "Pretend this is a forceps. Pass it from hand to hand. Try not to drop it."

It was simple enough. The grip was secure and my sense of touch was not too greatly diminished.

"Wherever did you ever find these?"

"I asked an acquaintance at Goodyear to make them when I was up in New York."

Because naturally he had an acquaintance at Goodyear. "I can hardly wait for someone to need surgery."

"I'm sure we can scrounge up a case in the next few days." He handed me the bag. "Merry Christmas. There is a second pair. They can be sterilized. If they work, I'll order more."

"Thank you." He had gone to no small effort. Over his holiday. While visiting family.

"Well." His gaze dipped to the ground. "I didn't wish to lose you."

I felt rather cherished. How was I to respond?

He continued, "I've never had a nurse so efficient."

Efficient? "Thank you, Dr. Halsted," I drawled. "I do try."

He smiled wryly, as though he realized the compliment had fallen short. "I suppose I should let you out of this rain."

"I'm glad you're back." I paused to let him hear that I had missed him, then said, "I'm anxious to get back to work."

31

1890, March

Baltimore, Maryland

And what delights can equal those
That stir the spirit's inner deeps,
When one that loves but knows not, reaps
A truth from one that loves and knows?
—Alfred, Lord Tennyson, *In Memoriam* A.H.H., XLII

❧

The day was clear and although winter's chill was not gone, it had softened enough that, wrapped in a warm cloak, I could pretend it was a refreshing summer breeze. Major Venable had offered to take me riding outside the city on my next day off, and I was tempted to accept. Unless Dr. Halsted invited me somewhere. But he hadn't sought my company the past fortnight, and I would not sit around pining. A ride in the country sounded lovely. I truly needed fresh air, a tangle of trees—proximity to a horse.

The grassy walk between the Nurses' Home and the wards was not enough.

It had been a frustrating morning. The operating room was hot and close, the surgery ran long, and Dr. Halsted was in a mood. Not that he was discourteous, but he was quieter than usual. A little slower. It made Dr. Brockway nervous. The silly man dropped a retractor on the floor and the clang caused me to jump. I thought that Dr. Halsted closed his eyes for a moment to pray for the strength to hide his exasperation with us both.

The surgery itself was a routine setting of a tibial fracture. Routine? A lesser injury had claimed Uncle Wade's leg, but it was routine enough now that I didn't see why Dr. Halsted had spent so long at it.

Enough. I was going to walk circles for twenty minutes and during that time I would ban the man from my thoughts.

Except…there he was. Immaculately attired, cane in hand, heading purposefully toward the Pathological. I had not walked this way hoping to see him. Or maybe I had. He was sure to think so. Before I could change my direction, he saw me, and altered his direction to approach.

"Miss Hampton," he said as he drew closer. He was smiling. Whatever had been bothering him earlier seemed to have resolved itself.

"Good afternoon, Dr. Halsted. It's a pleasant day for a walk."

He glanced around as if he hadn't noticed the weather until I mentioned it. Which was not unusual. He often seemed to inhabit some other world.

"Indeed, it is." Then he cleared his throat. "Were you walking anywhere in particular?"

I shook my head. "I just wanted to take some air."

His nose wrinkled. "Some of *this* air?"

"Beggars can't be choosers." To prolong the interaction, I said, "Major Venable has offered a buggy ride outside the city on Sunday—"

"The major did?" he interrupted, eyes narrowing. He looked miffed. "I suppose you will go?"

A flush of embarrassment swept over me. I knew the two were friends, just as he knew Major Venable was practically a part of the Hampton family. I was making conversation, not trying to spark a rivalry. Good heavens. The major was old enough to be my father.

"Perhaps you would like to come with us," I suggested.

"Oh no. No," he said, twisting the cane in his hand. "I wouldn't intrude."

"Pish-tosh. He'd prefer your conversation to mine. And then I would be able to enjoy the ride without having to entertain him."

I popped my hand over my mouth, realizing how rude the words sounded.

"Please don't repeat that."

He smiled. "I suppose it would be stealing a march to suggest that you and I go out to the countryside *without* Major Venable. I could hire a carriage and driver."

Did he say hire a *driver*? I could not bear for him to so humiliate himself.

"I had not accepted Major Venable's offer. I'm not sure this weather will hold. You were, I suspect, on your way somewhere? Not walking about aimlessly as I was?"

"To the Pathological. I wanted to look at—well, come with me. I'll show you."

I heard a rising excitement in his voice, as if he truly did wish to show me what drew him to the laboratory.

"All right."

I allowed him to lead me away from the Nurses' Home, even though, as Isabel would be quick to point out, I had no business following the surgeon around.

He said, "The operation this morning had me thinking about the leg tumor in bed three."

"Young Mr. Carter?" Perhaps whatever this was about would explain his mood that morning.

"If you say so." He ducked his head, chastened. No doubt somewhere in his training he had been told not to refer to patients by their affliction. "He'll need to be prepped tomorrow night for surgery in the morning. I don't want to amputate for such a small bump, but I suspect a cancer and it's better he loses his leg than his life."

We walked up the steps of the Pathological and Dr. Halsted opened the door, guiding me through it with a brief touch on my elbow. I felt a moment's lightheadedness. Which was ridiculous. Dr. Osler grabbed my elbow every time he had an enthusiastic point to make, which was every time he entered the room, and it didn't make me faint.

"Have you been in the Pathological before?" he asked, pointing the way to the stairwell.

"Only on tour before the hospital opened."

"I know I needn't ask if you're squeamish." He smiled at his joke. Or perhaps he smiled at me. He looked a little proud. "There are skeletons in the museum for teaching. Two articulated and few disarticulated. I want to look at the leg bones."

As we exited the stairwell, I heard voices coming from one of the rooms down the hall. I started toward them, but he touched my arm again and said, "No, this way."

We went toward the quieter, unoccupied part of the building. He paused before one of the doors, pulled a key from his vest pocket, and opened the door. The room was dark. I held back while he stepped into the room and lit the lights. What was he thinking? Did he not see the impropriety? I followed, leaving the door open. I tried to explain away my reticence in case he'd noticed it.

"I'm not squeamish, but I admit the thought of lurking skeletons gave me pause."

He laughed. "They're put away in the closet. Welch said he didn't want the janitors suffering coronaries."

The room was quite large, but not large enough to dispel the odor of bleach and formaldehyde. Windows along the outer wall were unshaded, with a view of distant red brick. Polished wooden shelves and cabinets lined the other three walls, leaving space only for two doors, the one I was standing beside and one leading to a closet. The floor was tiled and gleaming. Furniture included a desk, six small tables for students, twenty or so folding chairs stacked up against the windows, and, in the middle of the room, a large display table.

Dr. Halsted opened the closet and wheeled out an intact skeleton. Then, after disappearing into the closet for several moments, he emerged with a box. He set it on the large table, opened it, handled a few of the bones, and laid them out.

When I moved closer, he returned to the skeleton.

"See here? Tibia—shin bone. Fibula—calf bone." He squatted onto his haunches and ran his hand up and down the bones, frowning with the same intensity he'd shown during the morning's surgery. He rose, still lost in thought.

"And Mr. Carter's tumor is in his tibia?" I asked, to remind him I was there.

"Yes," he said quietly, still distracted. He came back to where I waited.

The table was for demonstrations. It was taller than for typical use, a little awkward for me, like peering onto a shelf. Dr. Halsted picked up two of the bones and examined them.

"See…" He turned to me, bones in hand, still frowning, as I stepped nearer. "I've been wondering if the fibula could replace the tibia. It is not made for weight-bearing, but under stresses, bones will remodel." He glanced down and his whole countenance changed, from pensive to embarrassed. He faced the table again and set the bones down hard. "I'm so sorry. I must be boring you to death."

"Not at all." *Not at all.* "If you could replace the tibia instead of amputating, Mr. Carter could keep his leg. Will you try it?"

"No. I couldn't…no. The idea only just occurred to me this morning. Mr. Carter's leg should come off sooner rather than later and I'd have to study…" He bent over the table as if operating. "Well, look here at the shape, these grooves. That would be where the tendons attach—oh, ah, can you see?"

I stretched on my tiptoes, trying to see around his shoulder.

"Yes. But if you moved them closer, I'd see more comfortably."

He looked down at me, bit his cheek, then looked away. He held the bone—not held, clenched—clenched it so tight his knuckles went white. Then he dropped it and said, quickly, as if hurrying the words out, "Or I could move you closer."

"Excuse me?"

"Will you permit me?" He put his hands toward my waist but did not touch me. The heat in his eyes and slight flush of his cheeks told me he wanted to.

"Oh." Of course, he wanted to, or he would not make such a ridiculous suggestion. My face burned. This was unprofessional. And a little thrilling. Shutting my eyes tight, I said, "Yes, go ahead."

He lifted me up and settled me on the table. He took his hands away, slowly, as I opened my eyes. He was standing much too close and looking at me even more intently than he had been studying the bones. He didn't step back when he should have. Warmth radiated from his body.

"Miss Hampton?" His voice was unbearably tender. I was terrified he meant to kiss me and equally terrified he did not. How curious this feeling was, wanting and fearing in equal measure.

No. This would not do. Not in a laboratory next to a pile of bones. How would I ever tell Lucy?

I put my hand on his chest and gently pushed him back, but the words of reproach I'd been taught to say if a man behaved inappropriately would not form. I twisted sideways toward the display and said, "How would you reattach the tendons?"

"Oh good Lord! I do beg pardon!" Dr. Osler exclaimed.

Dr. Halsted leaped away. Dr. Osler stood in the doorway, grinning ear to ear. He strode in and glanced about, taking in the skeleton, the bones strewn on the table, my dangling feet, Dr. Halsted's red face.

"Osteology?" Dr. Osler said. "Fine, fine. I'm sorry to interrupt. I have a patient I want you to come see. Finney said he thought you were heading here. Said you were muttering something about bones."

I slipped off the table, feeling less undignified standing on my own two feet. I hoped I didn't look as guilty as Dr. Halsted did. We'd done nothing wrong.

Dr. Halsted walked away from the table, to the desk. He took a cigarette from a case in his pocket, then lit a match. His movements were very precise. Controlled. Almost exaggerated. "What patient?"

Dr. Osler extracted a piece of paper and a fountain pen from his frock coat, scrawled something, folded the paper in half, and put it into Dr. Halsted's free hand. "Men's ward. Bed eight. Admitted as a scrofula. Let me know what you think."

Dr. Halsted took a deep drag from his cigarette, then dropped it into the ash tray on the desk. "I'll go see him this evening."

Dr. Osler turned to me. "It's a lovely day out. Enjoy your afternoon, Miss Hampton." He left the room whistling.

Mortified, I dared return my attention to Dr. Halsted, who was refolding the paper, his face white.

"Well, that was embarrassing," I said. Better to address it. Forthrightly.

He said nothing. He looked a little ill. He had not only folded the paper but wadded it. Dr. Osler evidently scribbled more than the patient's bed number.

"What is it?"

He came nearer and held out the paper for me to take, but then closed his hand over mine before I could read it. "Miss Hampton, would you consider…do me the honor…I mean to say, Miss Hampton…"

I pulled the paper from him, smoothed it over my palm, and read the lines.

"Tennyson? *In Memoriam*?" What an odd man Dr. Osler was. I said it aloud. "What an odd man Dr. Osler is."

It broke the tension as I'd hoped. His eyebrows rose. A little color washed back into his face.

I made myself shrug. "I suppose I should be peeved he thinks of me as someone who 'knows not.'"

"I'm sure he meant me. I'm really very stupid." He shook his head. "I'm making the most horrible muddle of this."

"This?"

"Courting you." He flung out an arm, gesturing to our surroundings. "You'd be forgiven for not recognizing the attempt. A bouquet of bones. A lecture on the tibia."

I pressed the paper back into his hand. "'And what delights can equal those…'"

"Miss Hampton, will you marry me?"

Now I was figuring him out rather quickly.

"Are you asking because Dr. Osler walked in on us alone together?"

"I'm asking you in this deuced awful way because he walked in on us. But I've been trying to ask you for the last fortnight."

"Now that is a lie! I've scarcely seen you except in surgery."

"I know." He shook his head. "I've been terrified. Terrified you'd say no."

We regarded one another in silence. Once again, I felt the strange mix of yearning and fear. He really was endearing. And I loved the way his mind worked: his curiosity, his cleverness, the way the excitement of a new problem blotted out his shyness. But was that reason enough to upend my life now that I had finally begun to settle into it?

Or had I settled into it precisely because it brought me close to him?

I loved that he did not flirt, or that when he tried, he did it so poorly. I loved that he shared what was most important to him: his work. Dr. Osler's little note was more apt than he could know.

"You mustn't feel pressured into this," he said, sighing heavily. "Osler's a terrible old gossip and loves an amusing tale, but he isn't malicious. He's more discreet than he seems."

"I'm not worried about Dr. Osler."

He tensed. And paled.

"No? Then…?"

"No. It's more that I promised ten years to the hospital and—"

"Ten years?" He blew out a breath. "You're not an indentured servant. Who demanded that?"

"Not demanded. It wasn't like that. But they hired me, at least partly, on the strength of my devotion to nursing. I can't possibly resign after so short a time."

It was very likely I'd have no choice after this, whichever way I answered.

"Resign? Why should you do that?" He looked genuinely aghast. "There are couples who practice together."

"I'm certain none of those couples are Hamptons. Or Halsteds. And not at Johns Hopkins."

Not only were the nurses unmarried, the men were all bachelors too.

"It seems I haven't thought this through." He grimaced. "I don't want to lose your contribution to the operating room. No doubt you'd like to escape from it, but spending *more* time with me rather than less cannot appeal."

"I love watching you work. I would miss it dreadfully if I left."

He walked away from me, back to the desk, and lit another cigarette. He smoked in silence, then said, "I don't mean to hound you. If your answer is no, then it is no."

"I didn't say no. It's just…sudden. I-I believe I would like to marry you, but I never wanted to marry anyone. I'm trying to figure myself out."

He laid down his cigarette and sniffed a laugh. "I never expected to marry either. I suppose we'd be a strange pair. Miss Hampton, please don't think I would push you out of the operating room for refusing me. I will promise not to moon over you if you stay."

"I haven't said no," I insisted. It would be easier to simply say yes. "I'm not being coy, truly, but may I have a little time to catch my breath?"

"Well, yes, of course." He stubbed out the cigarette, then took hold of the skeleton. "I'll put these away, then go see Osler's patient. Perhaps it would be better if we left separately."

"Of course." I started immediately for the door. He was hurt. Maybe he'd hoped I'd fling my arms around him shouting, yes, yes. But if that was what he wanted, he didn't want me.

"Miss Hampton?"

I looked over my shoulder.

"I-I don't think I said this. I should have…well. I hope you know that I…I'm quite…" He looked choked. "Fond of you."

So very, very endearing.

I should say yes.

My gaze drifted to the window. He wouldn't leave the university. I would have to live in Baltimore. I could run from a position but not from a husband. I would have to give up all hope of ever making my home in Cashiers.

"I'm fond of you too." I fled the room.

32

1890, March

Baltimore, Maryland

And what delights can equal those
That stir the spirit's inner deeps,
When one that loves but knows not, reaps
A truth from one that loves and knows?
—Alfred, Lord Tennyson, *In Memoriam* A.H.H., XLII

❧

"I'm sorry to disturb you, Welch." The man looked well settled in for the evening: dressing gown, cigar, glass of madeira at his elbow, the *Encyclopedia Britannica* open on his lap. "Mrs. Simmons told me to come up."

"Come in." Welch closed his book and set it on the side table. He gestured to the glass. "I don't suppose…"

Halsted started to refuse, then said, "All right."

One eyebrow rose as Welch got to his feet to retrieve an extra glass from his sideboard. He poured a drink. Halsted went to take it.

"What brings you?" Welch asked.

He took a sip before answering. "This is quite good, you know."

"Yes, I do." Welch waited.

"There is a patient Osler asked me to see." Good God, what a coward he was. "Admitted as a tuberculous lymphadenitis. A Mr. Townsend," he thought to add. "Young man. No skin changes. Some night fevers. A single, hard, non-tender lymph gland, perhaps four centimeters."

"Ill contacts?" Welch asked.

"An uncle with pthisis. Whom he sees frequently."

"Still not buying it. Where is the gland?"

"Supraclavicular."

"Not scrofula."

"No. I arranged to have him transferred to the surgical ward, pending Osler's approval."

"Hmph! Why do you think he consulted you? He's not likely to misdiagnose a lymph gland cancer as tuberculosis." Welch returned to his chair and sat with a slight groan. "Anything else I can do for you?"

Halsted realized his friend had seen through his flimsy excuse. But instead of confession, he digressed again. "Have you a copy of Tennyson's *In Memoriam*?"

The eyebrow flicked up once more and, with a louder groan, Welch pushed himself from his chair.

"Enough theater." Halsted laughed. "You act like an elderly arthritic."

"I just want to be sure you properly appreciate all my efforts to accommodate your strange requests."

"You know I do."

Welch moved to the shelves lining the wall.

The pathologist's study was something to behold. Books two or three rows deep filled the shelves. There was once a method to the arrangement but that had long since fallen victim to overcrowding. Welch relied now on his prodigious memory. As far as Halsted knew, nothing was ever mislaid for long. The desk, if one could see it, was fine quality cherry, but it was so buried in piles of correspondence sandwiched between layers of newspaper, there was no hope of ever digging it out. There were growing piles on the floor. In another few years, they would not be able to find Welch in the room.

The only tidy spot was the corner of the sideboard where he kept his cigars and madeira. Welch ran a fingertip along the spines of one row, then plucked out a slim leather-bound volume.

"This?" He threaded his way between two piles to hand the book to Halsted.

"I knew you would have it somewhere." He opened the book and scanned, flipping pages rapidly.

"That is not the way one reads poetry," Welch said in a mock appalled tone.

"This is an ode to a dead friend." She could not have been right about the reference. He felt vaguely disappointed with her and annoyed with himself for feeling so.

"What did you expect from a poem entitled *In Memoriam*?"

"Something a little more…romantic."

"Huh." Welch's face scrunched as he scrutinized Halsted's. "More specifically?"

"Along the lines of one who loves and doesn't know versus one who loves and knows."

Welch took the book from him and thumbed through it for a few seconds. "Like this?"

He felt a small thrill. "Yes, that's it, by God. Have you the whole thing memorized?"

Welch shrugged. "I know my Tennyson."

Halsted read it again and the verses above and below, trying to get the sense of it—though of course it really had nothing to do with the matter at hand. Then he noticed the page was dog-eared—only the one page. His heart sank. "He was here." He glared at Welch accusingly. "Wasn't he? Osler?"

"Why, yes. Earlier this evening. He wanted my opinion on a scrofulous patient of his."

Halsted whirled away, letting the book fall to the desk where it blew a few papers to the floor.

Welch laughed. "Now who is being theatrical?"

"He told you? I gave him too much credit. I said he could be discreet." He clenched his fists. "I will wring his neck."

"Be more gracious. A story like that? A secret like that? He thinks he discovered love itself. He had to tell someone." Welch took a sip of his drink. "And he knew *I* wouldn't spread the story around. Moreover, he had to check the reference. He was a little afraid he misquoted and we couldn't have that, could we?"

"So you don't have the poem memorized."

"Ha! Sentimental claptrap." Welch's smile lit the room. "So, what did she say?"

"What do you mean?"

"Don't toy with me. You are a coward, not a cad. When will you be reading the banns?"

"She has not answered yet. She wants time to consider."

The man's smile faltered. "Ouch."

He turned so Halsted could not see his face. He suspected Welch was annoyed with Caroline. But Welch surprised him by continuing evenly. "Well, that proves she is your match. Of course, she needs to consider. Marriage is not to be undertaken lightly. And there is your history to digest, though I'm sure it will, in the balance, weigh in your favor."

"I haven't told her."

Welch faced him. His expression spoke volumes. The weight of his silent disapproval wrung Halsted's heart. He swallowed a few painful dry gulps before daring to explain himself.

Welch spoke first. "You must. If she hears it elsewhere, she will be justifiably angry. It must come from you. Even if you believe it has no bearing—"

"Oh, come now. How could it have no bearing? Do you think I plan to attempt hiding it? From my *wife*?" Welch's condescension made him mad. "I've been trying to bring myself to confide in her. For two weeks, I have practiced the speech in my head."

"Is it so shameful for you?" His whole bearing gentled. "Still? Halsted, you have faced this manfully. She will understand. To fight and overcome—"

"It is not something one 'overcomes.'"

Welch's silence was different this time. Not disapproving. Fearful.

"You haven't still the cocaine habit?"

Halsted shook his head. "Not the habit. But the hunger. It's there. All the time. It is a fight with myself every day. A few minims won't hurt. One sniff. I hear a voice in my head saying it even now. Every night I go to bed and thank God I've made it through another day. Every morning I wake and worry it will be the day I succumb."

"But you don't. That is your strength."

"That is the morphine."

Welch sank into his chair. For a long moment, neither spoke. Finally, Welch sighed and said, "How much? How often?"

"More than I am willing to admit."

"You must tell her."

"I will. I would not have proposed without telling her but Osler forced my hand."

"Tomorrow. It is not fair to her to make her deliberate twice. I don't know what she thinks she must consider—"

"She doesn't want to give up her position."

"What?" He looked so comically surprised that in any other situation, Halsted would have laughed. "I thought that was why a woman became a nurse, in order to hook a doctor."

"Not Miss Hampton. Unless it is simply that she's disappointed by the fish she caught."

"That is unlikely. I've seen the two of you together. She hangs on your every word."

Halsted waved off the encouragement, saying, "And challenges every other word. Never publicly, fortunately, but I can sometimes see it in her eyes. She is extraordinary."

"You'd better tell her before she says yes and joy paralyzes your larynx. You are smitten beyond rational behavior. You propped her up on a pile of bones like a human sacrifice and stole a kiss? You?"

"Oh, now, you cannot listen to Osler."

"No? His observational skill is supposed to be unsurpassed. What did he get wrong?"

"I didn't steal a kiss." Then he admitted, "I was too slow."

Welch barked a laugh. "Overthinking it were you? Now that, my dear friend, sounds like you."

33

1890, March

Baltimore, Maryland

A lady refusing proposals:

SIR: Surely there must have been something in my behavior toward you, upon which you have set a misconstruction. Of what it consisted I am wholly unconscious; but that such has been the case, I feel convinced by an attentive perusal of your letter, which I have just received. I assure you that I feel much flattered by your preference of me, as well as by your proffer of our becoming mutually better acquainted; but with every feeling of regard toward you, I beg respectfully to decline your addresses. What my reasons may be for so doing, you will not, I trust, inflict upon me the pain of declaring; suffice it to say, that I cannot admit them, and I confidently hope that henceforward you will feel the propriety of not recurring to this subject.
—"The lady's guide to perfect gentility, in manners, dress, and conversation…also a useful instructor in letter writing…" By E. Thornwell, H.W. Derby & Co., 1857

❧

I hadn't slept. My morning toilet required extra care to hide my swollen eyes and red nose. I was too wretched to eat breakfast, which was just as well since I wanted to leave the Nurses' Home early enough to go walking before church. Maybe the exercise would help me think.

How much fun we had had at Edge Hill, Lucy, Sally, and I, composing exquisitely polite letters, rejecting a half-dozen nonexistent suitors for imagined egregious deficiencies. How cruel we were, laughing at hurt. And how much easier it would be to write a letter than to tell a dear kind man to his face: no, I cannot.

I'd practiced for hours, tossing and turning in bed. One could not say: *No. And do not press me for my reasons.* I owed him a why. But my reasons were ugly and selfish.

I never wanted to be a Mrs. Mr. Somebody. I couldn't abandon my calling after less than a year. I didn't wish to share my precious vacations with someone else's family. I could not envision a life that did not include Cashiers. I didn't want to have to defer, always, to the opinion of one man who would rule me. I didn't want children—that made me a terrible person but I didn't.

Never in my life had I felt so miserable. My head ached. My chest hurt. I couldn't breathe. My legs were leaden. I was so desperately sad. I would have to tell him this afternoon. It wasn't fair to make him wait.

Opening the front door took almost more effort than I was capable of exerting. How was I ever going to get through the day? Why not return to bed? Plead indisposition. Oh, Isabel would love that. I stepped outside.

And saw Dr. Halsted in the courtyard. Silk-hatted, black-gloved, dashing. Waiting. I felt the spark of delight, the little lift I always felt upon catching sight of him at unexpected moments—and every single time he walked into the operating room.

He threw his cigarette into the grass and came toward me.

"Good morning, Dr. Halsted," I called out, going to greet him.

Then I stopped short. His necktie was crooked. His face was pale.

"Miss Hampton, I hoped to catch you." He came forward, stumbling. "To apologize. I put you in a most awkward position yesterday. It was inexcusable. You mustn't feel obligated to answer a petition so inappropriate. I can only hope you are able to put the whole unfortunate—"

"Stop. Are you saying you withdraw your proposal?"

"I'm saying I shouldn't have made it. Should not have put you in—"

"In such an awkward position. Yes, I heard." His breathing was uneven and he had gone from pale to florid. I suspected his pulse was racing. He looked ill, but I felt more so. "I beg your pardon, but what is inexcusable is refusing me before I've had the opportunity to decline."

"No?" His expression flattened, stunned as if struck. Then his gaze fell to the ground. He murmured, "Of course. It would be no." His disappointment tore my heart. I couldn't fathom what was wrong, what had changed. Well, I wouldn't know unless I asked.

"I didn't say no. I said you owed me the opportunity to say it. Withdraw your withdrawal."

He nodded. Choked and confused, he said, "All right. It is withdrawn. Now you might refuse me."

"No, I don't think I will, Dr. Halsted. I am honored by your attentions, and would be very happy, I'm sure, to be your wife."

"Miss Hampton—"

"Now we are engaged to be married, sir, and if you desire to break the engagement you must state your reasons and they must be very good reasons, or, as I understand the way of it, my brother will likely call you out."

His eyes reproached me, but he nodded again, swallowed hard, and said, "I have not been forthcoming with you about...about difficulties in my past."

Difficulties? I ran the list through my head. Gambling debts? Illegitimate children? Dueling? Perhaps he had a wooden leg. I was so hurt, so mortified, that my mind ran to absurdities. If I was not careful, I would laugh. I might even cry.

"Shall we go sit down?" He glanced rather desperately down the walkway to one of the benches set along the paths. Wooden leg it must be.

I led, aware of him behind, lighting another cigarette as if his life depended upon sucking in the befouled air. Thank goodness it was so early in the day; no one else was out walking. The benches were all empty. Never in my life could I have envisioned so bizarre a courtship. This was not how things were done. We sat. I gritted my teeth to keep my chin from quivering.

"When I worked in New York," he said, quietly, with effort, "I experimented with cocaine anesthesia. On myself. I developed a habit of taking it."

"Oh." The breeze chilled. I had heard similar rumors about Dr. Hall. A fine surgeon once, people whispered, now... Now he left sponges in body cavities.

"Believe me, please, I intended to tell you this weeks ago. First. Certainly before I blurted that proposal. I would not have embarrassed you, would not have pursued you, if you had chosen to distance yourself from me."

"Because you used to take cocaine?" His situation was nothing like Dr. Hall's. I'd heard from Alma that the man had been asked to resign.

"That isn't all." His voice dropped lower. "I had to be hospitalized. Twice. For quite some time. My doctor attempted a morphine cure."

"Oh," I said again. So it was quite bad, his cocaine habit. The cure was "attempted." He said nothing for a while, so I prompted him. "And?"

"Welch lured me back to sanity, to sobriety, with a position in his laboratory. And now, my appointment in the hospital, I owe also to him. It was not something that could be hidden from the administration."

"Nor should it be." I looked at him. Hard. "Is there another 'and'?"

"And I am not cured. I no longer use cocaine. But I do occasionally resort to morphine." Then he stood up abruptly. "And I am still lying. It is more than occasional. It is often. And now, Miss Hampton, please, you must understand that you can't marry me. I mean, I understand that you will not."

I rose also and hooked my hand into the crook of his elbow.

"Please sit back down."

He did, head hung so low he looked like a hound dog. I sat beside him. I felt the warmth of his thigh pressing against mine. My earlier misery was gone. Replaced by purpose. This brilliant man…

"I want to be your wife. I do not, however, intend to spend my life nursing you. You must promise me that you will stop."

"I've tried. I cannot swear that—"

I pressed my fingertips to his lips, quieting him, then lightly caressed the line of his jaw.

"Promise me."

He caught my hand, kissed my fingertips, and whispered, "I promise."

34

1890, March

Baltimore, Maryland

Halsted told me some time ago that he intended writing…to tell you of the good luck he is in, but he is not in any condition to be relied on and I shall not wait any longer. The whole hospital is delighted over the announcement of Halsted's engagement to Miss Hampton and he is the happiest man you ever saw. Dr. Welch is pleased to death over it… I have seen him but twice in the last two weeks. His thyroid dogs die and lie around for days but he cannot spare the time to come to the laboratory.

—Dr. William D. Booker to Franklin P. Mall in Worcester, Massachusetts, March 22, 1890

My dear Mall:

I know that you will be amused to know that I am engaged to be married. A good joke for you I know. I wish that I could see your chuckles. Miss Hampton reminds Booker and me very much of you. I suppose that is the reason I proposed to her.

Yours,

Wm. S. Halsted

—Dr. William S. Halsted to Franklin P. Mall in Worcester, Massachusetts, March, 1890

❧

"This thing has quite run away from us," Halsted told Welch, seated in the back of the tavern for a late lunch, having waited until mid-afternoon when the place would be empty. He had never had so much trouble avoiding his colleagues. They hid in the woodwork, waiting to pounce.

"By 'thing,'" Welch said, salting his salted cod, "you mean your wedding?"

Halsted set his fork on the edge of his plate. He'd ordered the chicken, though he knew better. It was inedibly dry. He could not identify the green leaf on his plate.

"I've been to enough of them," he said. "I should have been prepared."

"Miss Hampton does not strike me as requiring elaborate ceremony. I would think, rather, to blame any excess on you." Welch washed down his fish with a quantity of beer.

"Oh, well, yes. I want to do it right. I'll be going to South Carolina next week to ask her brother for her hand." He ducked his head but still felt the heat of Welch's wide smile.

"I'd like to be there for that! What will you do if he says no?"

"Elope with her." He was serious.

"Good for you." Welch looked him long in the eye. Then blinked. "Brother? Not father?"

"Her father died at the Battle of Brandy Station. She was not even two."

"A martyr to 'the Glorious Cause.' Explains a few things, I suppose." Welch sighed and shifted his weight in his chair. "This is a good thing. I believe you owe Osler a favor for bringing you to the point."

"He seems to think so." The story was spreading. Fortunately, although it made him appear ridiculous, no discredit fell upon Caroline. Osler could spin a tale. "I have a favor to ask of you."

"Whatever it is, I'm inclined to grant it. But first…" Welch reached into his breast pocket and pulled out a cigar. He looked as perfectly at home in the dank tavern as in the finest New York restaurant. Or, for that matter, up to his elbows in eviscerated bowel. "I have some good news I am now permitted to share. Your cup is overflowing. Your appointment has been approved. Chief of surgery. I told you they—"

"Oh? Very good. I'm glad of it. Welch, I suspect this is an inconvenience—"

"I said they have approved your appointment," Welch repeated, setting down the cigar and leaning forward over the table as if to make himself better heard.

"Yes," Halsted nodded impatiently, "thank you. I know you had a hand in it."

"Your *work* is the reason. I thought you would be more—"

"Will you be my best man?"

Welch straightened, eyes widening, then put a hand on Halsted's wrist. "That is quite an honor. I will."

"You'll have to go to Columbia in June. *Hamptons*, you see. There is no choice in the matter. I don't know how we ever won that war."

"I've always wanted to see fair Columbia," he said, relaxing back into his chair.

"I would challenge that statement as absurd on its face, except that one never knows what will entertain you."

"I would go to the North Pole to see you say 'I do.'" Welch beamed at him. "I hope I may give the toast."

"Keep it short."

Welch lit his cigar and puffed it, eyes dancing.

"Mall thinks you and Booker are pulling his leg. I assured him it was true. You will be receiving a frantic letter shortly."

"A telegram, yesterday." Halsted gave up on his meal and pushed the plate aside. He put a hand to his pocket then remembered he'd forgotten his cigarettes. "Called me a lost cause for research. But added sincere congratulations."

"Ah, good."

"He misspelled sincere."

Welch laughed. "Don't read too much into that. In the paper he sent me to look at, he misspelled canine twice. I crossed it out and wrote in *dogg*. With two g's." He reached into his pocket again. "Here." He handed Halsted a cigar. "Aside from the spelling it was good work, naturally. Don't bolt. I am compelled to warn you about the small dinner we'll be attending tonight at Osler's."

"What about it?" He borrowed Welch's cutter and clipped the cigar. Osler said he'd gotten a couple of canvasbacks from a grateful patient out in the country and invited a few friends to share, Miss Hampton included. Halsted would have begged off, but she said if they didn't face him now, they never would.

"The entire faculty will be there. To celebrate you and Miss Hampton."

"Ah," he said around the cigar as he lit it. He wasn't entirely surprised. "Weren't we celebrated enough Sunday evening at Gilman's?"

"That was the university faculty. This is the hospital. I'm sorry. We're making you run the gauntlet for your prize."

He drew in a drag and let it out. "I'd run it ten times." He paused a moment. His euphoria was punctuated at odd moments by utter terror. "I keep thinking I will wake up. That it can't be real. That someone as beautiful and clever and…wonderful…would marry me. I told her everything. And she said yes."

Welch's eyes softened. "Of course, she did."

35

1890, March

Baltimore, Maryland

Johns Hopkins Hospital
March 19, 1890
Dear Aunt Lu,
I wanted to write you before but I have had to answer so many notes of congratulations that I am very tired of writing. This is my 7th tonight and it is long past 12:00 now. Your last letter is rather hard to answer as it is hard to express one's feeling about such things. Dr. Halsted and I have worked together most satisfactorily for nearly a year and during that whole time he has never spoken a cross word or ever been lacking in the greatest considerations…I do not think I shall regret it… It is very pleasant to be first with someone and be taken care of and anticipated in everything and tho, of course a good deal of that will wear off, I still I think we are enough alike in all of our tastes and ways to make each other happy… One thing I am sure of is that I will never find Dr. Halsted anything but considerate, kind, and respectful. We have made all our plans very nearly. I leave for home Monday and Dr. H. comes on to see my folks the end of the week. Sometime in April I am going to N.Y. for clothes and we will be married in June. We are going to take a furnished house for a year and take time to get some nice house that can be well fixed up before we go in. Dr. H. is the most fussy of men and nothing suits him unless it is a little bit better than someone else's which means considerable extravagance. Still, if he makes the money he might as well spend it and I luckily am very moderate in my tastes… Do you think that Mrs. Sullivan would do anything for me if you wrote to engage her for April? What do you advise as to clothes?

C.H.

—Caroline Hampton to Lucy Baxter, March 19, 1890

I pushed my writing desk from my lap to the bed and massaged my hands. Maybe that appeal for Mrs. Sullivan's services would mollify my aunt. Although a bit outdated, Mrs. Sullivan remained one of the most sought-after dressmakers in New York. Which would please William also. The dear, silly man. Although too serious and dignified to be a dandy, he certainly skirted the edge. Fortunately, Frank told me to buy absolutely everything I needed and have the bills sent to him. The cost would be staggering, but he was used to Lucy's requests, so he must know what he was in for.

I skimmed the unsatisfactory letter, then resolutely folded it and put it in an envelope. It didn't express what I meant to say—it sounded defensive, uncertain, and I was neither—but I was too tired to try again. Anyway, how was I supposed to answer such questions?

Had Dr. Halsted considered my wishes when asking me to give up nursing—the work I had trained so hard for, the profession I had pronounced to be my calling in life?

I could hardly explain that Dr. Halsted had very nearly rescinded his proposal when I told him I would be obliged to resign.

I knew he was telling the friends who teased him that he was the one making the sacrifice since he would be losing his "efficient" operating room nurse. Whereas I would be escaping the tedium of lengthy operations where everyone was afraid to breathe too loudly lest they annoy him.

He was not the ogre in the surgical theater that he believed himself to be. At least, I had never thought so. I'd told the truth when I said I would miss watching him operate.

Aunt Lu worried I was behaving out of character. Hadn't I always adamantly denied any intention of marrying? Most especially not a man from New York! Was I certain this was what I wanted?

I couldn't explain to my aunt, or to anyone, really, why I changed my mind. It was trite to say that when I swore that I would never marry I had not yet met William. Yet it was the only explanation that made sense.

Aunt Lu asked if I loved him. I could hardly tell her how I'd felt when Dr. Osler came across us in the laboratory. Well, mortified, of course, but before that. Reckless. Allowing him to lift me onto the table,

I had felt reckless and breathless and curious. *Desired.* And…desiring. One did not relate such things to one's maiden aunt.

Why him? Why not someone younger, or handsomer, someone with a Southern drawl who knew the proper way to sit on a horse?—as Lucy would, no doubt, demand to know.

Such men did not interest me. They never had. William, with all his virtues and all his faults, fascinated me.

Not one of my womenfolk would understand how I could have fallen in love watching a man perform surgery, that I had fallen in love with a pair of hands.

The picture I had painted for Aunt Lu: kind, considerate, respectful—did not do William justice. He was all of that, yet I would not marry him, or anyone, with such meager qualifications.

I wanted to spend my life with him because he was the most intelligent man I had ever met. He was curious. Methodical. Careful. Gentle. Sometimes caustic, but never with me. Humorous, though not everyone appreciated his humor. Maybe none of this was love. Maybe it was merely admiration. Even so, I believed what I had written to Aunt Lu: we would make each other happy. William was not perfect, but he had made me a promise.

And he was hurting; he needed to be loved.

36

1890, June

Columbia, South Carolina

Millwood
April 6, 1890
Dear Aunt Lu,
I am writing this P.M. all of my due letters and having done my duty I will give you the little I have left of my brains... Between letters and clothes I am swearing.

Dr. H. has so many jackets that I don't think I can do as usual and simply order a dress to cost so much... I must say that I wish the whole performance was over. Dr. Halsted left yesterday much to the relief of the family. I enjoyed his visit very much and I think he had a very pleasant time... Aunties did not take to him very kindly as he is very quiet, not at all "chatty to strangers" and not in any way their idea of a "gentleman." He neither rides, hunts or fishes—cares nothing about horses or dogs and is devoted to his profession. So on the whole they don't approve but say nothing...I never expected anything else however. Lucy and I leave Thursday for New York to get clothes... Cousin Louisa has been most kind but I am afraid that she is too extravagant for my purse as well as being very gay for my sedate tastes. She writes proposing a heliotrope street dress and Dr. H. and I nearly fainted...

—Caroline Hampton to Lucy Baxter, April, 1890

❧

I had wished the time away; there was no getting it back. For better or worse, as of this morning, June 4, 1890, I was now Mrs. William Stewart Halsted.

Everyone said the ceremony was beautiful. Lucy, Daisy, and Sally were bridesmaids. They were beautiful. William said I was, but he had to say that. I wore a pale lavender dress, the best of which could be said was that it wasn't heliotrope. Or white. I didn't wish to look as though I were in the operating room.

Naturally William outdid everyone in his dark gray morning coat, striped trousers, and cream-colored vest. Standing with him were Dr. Welch, his brother Dick, and my brother Frank. Trinity Church was filled with Hamptons, Prestons, Haskells, a few Baxters, and William's sisters with their husbands, including Dr. Sam Van der Poel, which seemed to please William very much—another gentleman who didn't know which end of a gun should face out. The aunties tiptoed around my new husband, and he, them. Uncle Wade blustered at him and slapped his back with a vigor bordering on assault, but William bore him with good humor. Frank was quite beside himself until he and William discovered they had both rowed crew in college. Then they got along well enough.

I had my own row to hoe with William's family. His father did not come; William predicted he would not. His sisters walked around with their noses in the air, complaining about the heat. And Dick was an odd duck. For a wedding gift, he'd sent forty-three separate silver pieces, nothing matching. William had just shrugged and said: *Well, that's Dick. Let's just hope he keeps out of the whiskey barrel at the reception.*

The reception was informal. A Southern barbecue. I told William it was my revenge for all those Johns Hopkins fancy dinner parties. He looked so pained I had to assure him that I was only teasing. It had been an awkward two months: too much family, far too much attention, adjusting to the fact that we were a couple, and William…

I now recognized the signs and was annoyed that I, a nurse, had not seen them before. In the mornings, he was most himself, though restless without work to do. In the mid-afternoon he would often grow testy. He'd have a "rest" and be most congenial in the evenings—when his pupils were tiny, his lids a little droopy, and the muscles in his neck and about his mouth relaxed. Lately, I suspected he was taking an extra dose in the morning, but I could scarcely blame him. For the last week, I'd had a headache from my scalp to my shoulders that was only now beginning to ease. The promise of Cashiers was my morphine, I supposed.

"I think, Mrs. Halsted, it is time for us to leave," he said quietly, returning from cigars with the men.

I rose, and he waited while I kissed everyone again.

Dr. Welch stood his post by the carriage in the drive. He opened the door for me, helped me up, then shook William's hand and said something I didn't hear. William climbed up beside me. The door shut. Dr. Welch signaled to the driver and sent us off to our hotel.

I turned to William and smiled. "It feels a little mean leaving him behind."

For the past two nights, William and Dr. Welch had been at the Columbia Hotel. Dr. Welch would surely be following us in a few minutes.

"He can find his own carriage," William said, twining his fingers in mine.

I settled against his shoulder and looked up into his eyes. His pinpoint-pupil eyes. He must have pills. He hadn't absented himself from company long enough to inject himself. Well, this was not a discussion for our wedding night. There would be time, secluded in the Lodge.

"Caroline? Do you think I might finally kiss you? I think I've been admirably patient."

"Patient? Or frightened of my shotgun-toting menfolk?"

"You overheard that?" His eyes widened. His pupils didn't.

"Frank did. You didn't see him, I suppose? Oh, don't look so embarrassed. He thought it was funny. He said you were muttering to that barrel-shaped man."

"They must be mystified why you married me."

"They are mystified by most things I do. Yes, you may kiss me."

He did. Very sweetly. Very tenderly. Very different from the brief brush of the lips he'd given me in church with everyone watching. He seemed to mean it more now and he continued to kiss me for quite some time. Pulling me close. Touching my lips with his tongue. It was all very new to me. A little embarrassing. I could see why ladies were not supposed to ride alone in closed carriages with their young men. I was getting a bit rumpled.

The carriage slowed. It was the shortest ride between Millwood and Columbia I'd ever spent. Surely my face had never been so pink. I felt almost like giggling, which would have been mortifying to both of us. He looked irritated. No, not irritated. I didn't know what he looked.

We emerged from the carriage into bright sunlight. He gestured across the street.

"Shall we have a walk in the park? I don't think either of us is used to so much sitting."

"That would be lovely." It was too early for supper. Far too early for anything else. Perhaps we should have tried to catch the train for

Walhalla today after all, and be over halfway to the Lodge. But it would have made things so rushed to shoot for the early one, and the next would put us into Walhalla very late. Too late.

I tucked my arm in his and we strolled. We didn't talk much at first, but I felt no need to fill the silence. It was nice, actually, after all the folderol, to be silent. We explored all the paths we came to before turning back toward the hotel. William didn't smoke a single cigarette. I breathed in the sultry Columbia air, thick with flowers. Oh, I missed home! I hoped, more than hoped, I prayed that William would fall in love with Cashiers.

"Are you hungry?" he asked.

"Ladies are never hungry."

"Is that so?" He smiled. "I suppose I will learn a few things about ladies. Would it please you to take some supper?"

"Very much." I hadn't been able to eat breakfast or anything at the barbeque. My stomach was finally starting to settle.

We made our way to the hotel. Most of our things had been sent on to Cashiers. We kept only a few small bags here. William had a key to the suite. Blood thudded in my ears as he took it from his pocket and opened the door. Then he swept me up and carried me over the threshold without any warning. I yelped, then laughed. He was laughing too. He kissed me on the nose.

"I'm going to change clothes," he said, setting me down.

There were two bedrooms, two baths, and a small sitting room in our suite. He went into the far room. My bag was waiting in the nearer. I changed from my wedding dress into something simpler. Cooler. I was still laced too tight. I blocked thoughts of the night from my mind. I wasn't nervous. Not afraid. It was natural, after all; I'd learned all about it in hygiene. Only I hoped I didn't get pregnant. Not yet.

He knocked on my door. We went down to supper. The dining room was elegant, papered in blue-and-yellow floral wallpaper, with dark wood trim, and widely spaced tables covered with white damask cloths.

"Oh, my word," I said, pulling back. "There is Dr. Welch." For some reason, that embarrassed me.

William snorted. "He won't bother us if we don't bother him."

We were given a secluded table in the corner. I ate without being aware of the food. We talked about work—a patient he'd left behind for Finney that he would have liked to operate on himself, a woman with an interesting thyroid, that carcinoma who'd died, Brockway's progress. He ordered a bottle of champagne, but neither of us finished even a glass. We did not ask for coffee. We weren't rushing, but neither did we linger.

William looked at the bottle of champagne. "Should I have this sent over to Welch?"

He was still there. Smoking his cigar, reading a newspaper. He looked perfectly at ease, though quite alone.

"Yes, do."

He spoke to the waiter, settled the bill, and escorted me back to our suite. Inside the door, he took me into his arms. I realized I'd been on edge all evening, waiting to be kissed again. I put my arms around his neck, returning his embraces, emboldened by the thought he belonged to me as much as I belonged to him. Then he stepped back, taking down my hands and pressing them in his. He had that same irritated look he'd had before.

"I suppose you are tired, Caroline. This has been a long day. A long week. And we have a long train ride tomorrow. I'll let you sleep."

I spent my wedding night alone.

37

1890, June

Columbia, South Carolina

THE SEXUAL ORGANS

The continued use of opium or morphine has a decided effect on the sexual apparatus… In man, the first indication of an effect on the sexual organs is increased desire; this, however, giving way sooner or later to partial or total impotence.

—"Drugs that Enslave. The Opium, Morphine, Chloral and Haschisch Habits," by H.H. Kane, M.D., Philadelphia: Presley Blakiston, 1881, p 45.

❧

William rose early, grumpily, and prepared for the day. He heard nothing from Caroline's room, so he read a paper that Mall had sent him, went down to the restaurant, ordered breakfast, and brought up a tray. He knocked and went in. The drapes were drawn. A valise with a few things spilling from it was propped in the corner. Caroline was awake, though still in bed, a wide four-poster with a light brown spread tangled about her. She looked well-rested, exactly the way a new bride should not appear in the morning after her wedding night.

"Good morning, Mrs. Halsted," he said with false cheer. He thought she grimaced at the greeting, but she followed quickly with a smile.

"Good morning, William. I suppose you think me dreadfully lazy."

"Not at all. I'm afraid I am still keeping surgeons' hours." He brought the tray to her. "I thought we might have a leisurely breakfast before catching the train."

She was so beautiful, tucked under the bedclothes. She wore a simple yellow nightdress and he suspected she would have none of the usual daytime buttressing women wore underneath. He wanted to sit beside her. To lie beside her. What an injustice he'd done, marrying her.

He set the tray on the bedside table, then pulled up a chair.

"Is your headache gone?" he asked. She'd been complaining of a nervous headache for a week. Not yesterday though. It was wrong of him to imply last night was her fault.

"It is. Having the ceremony over is a tremendous relief. Oh, and we will be in Cashiers tomorrow! You'll see. It's everything I told you."

He poured her a cup of coffee and added cream and sugar, the way she took it. "Thank you, William." She smiled again. "You spoil me."

"You're easy to please."

Those were the wrong words. At least, they sounded wrong to him. Still, she sipped, then set the cup down and buttered a biscuit and broke a piece to put into her mouth.

"Aren't you eating?" she asked, after finishing the biscuit.

He had no appetite. He'd taken no morphine last night or this morning. He was not nauseated yet, but feared the train ride. The less he ate the better. "I had a bite earlier."

She ate a little more, conversing easily about the wedding. Nothing that taxed his ability to respond. Then she pushed aside the bedclothes and said, "I should get ready. It always takes longer than it should to prepare oneself to travel."

He stood, eyes on her pretty bare feet. "I'll finish my packing too." He hurried from the room. He closed the door to his own, then leaned his head against it, eyes shut. Pained.

Yesterday, in the carriage, he had felt overwhelmed by how happy he was, how fortunate. He adored his beautiful wife, his *wife*, with everything that entailed, every liberty he was now permitted. She'd welcomed his kisses. His brain, his heart—those organs ran riot. But, unfortunately, the rather necessary organ remained unmoved.

He wanted to make love to her, yet he had known he would not be able to. After supper, after kissing her again and obtaining no inkling of physical arousal, he fled the field.

She had every right to divorce him. What he should do was go now and confess the problem, before she began imagining the difficulty lay with her, with how he felt about her.

She'd understand. She was a nurse. Nothing fazed her. He'd amputated that gigantic carcinoma of the breast, leaving a gaping cavity, and she behaved more professionally than Clarke, the assistant surgeon under Brockway—that boy was bright enough but he would never be a surgeon. He left the room ill.

His mind was racing. He knew he couldn't confess this; not because Caroline would be embarrassed but because he would. Of all morphine's afflictions…and cocaine had never done this. Too much the opposite, in fact. He had some, a very small amount, in his physician's bag, for patient emergencies, not his own. He wouldn't touch that. He would reduce the morphine. He'd taken none in almost twenty-four hours. He would have to take some on the train, but less. Less. Maybe a reduction in the dosage would ameliorate the problem. If not, he'd have to explain. Tonight. He couldn't run from her again.

38

1890, June

Walhalla, South Carolina

Coca as an aphrodisiac.
The natives of South America, who represented their goddess of love with coca leaves in her hand, did not doubt the stimulative effect of coca on the genitalia. Mantegazza confirms that the coqueros sustain a high degree of potency right into old age; he even reports cases of the restoration of potency and the disappearance of functional weaknesses following the use of coca…
—*Über Coca*, Dr. Sigmund Freud, 1885

I was not upset. How could I be? No, I was glad.

With the wedding behind us, William now meant to keep his promise. There was no mistaking the symptoms on the train. He looked ill. He ate nothing. He did not initiate conversation and, when I did, he grew increasingly peeved. For a short time, he slept. When he woke, I engaged him with a booklet of puzzles. He agreed to play along because—"Oh yes, word ladders. Welch is partial to those"—but he became impatient with the more difficult examples. They were not that hard. He started to fidget, then fidgeted more.

We changed trains in Greeneville. The next stretch was up into the mountains. I gently informed William we had more than two hours to go. He disappeared into the washroom and when he returned, he was calm.

I had seen cases of morphiomania in my training, but I couldn't imagine William in such a state. He was so…smart. So capable. He was Dr. Halsted, for goodness' sake, surgeon-in-chief at the Johns Hopkins Hospital. Part of me wanted to believe he merely took a little morphine every now and then, but he didn't need it. His behavior on the train proved that hopeful theory wrong.

And then he was so dear, afterward. He peered out the window with me and chuckled at my enthusiasm as I pointed out landmarks. He teased me, pointing out trees. He went to the dining car and brought back lemon ices. I shared my *Abbeville Press and Banner* and we laughed at the oddities in the news. He held my hand.

The train arrived at Walhalla. William hired a porter to take our bags to Biemann's Hotel. He had double the baggage I did, and I knew he'd sent triple the trunks on ahead. As long as he didn't fuss at me, I wouldn't fuss at him; but, honestly, did he need so many jackets for a couple of months in the woods?

We walked to stretch our legs after the train travel. That was something we did have in common, the preference for a brisk walk to a short carriage ride. We would have to learn, over the next few weeks, what other interests we shared now that I would no longer be his operating room nurse. I would no longer be a part of the main part of his life. That would take some getting used to.

"Not much of a town, Walhalla," William mused.

I decided no response was needed. We continued to stroll, my hand tucked comfortably in the crook of his elbow. The hotel at the end of the road, the best in the county, did not show to advantage if I tried to see it through his eyes.

"Biemann's is magical for me," I said, before he could disparage it. "It's where we often stop on the way to the Lodge so all of my memories here are precious."

"That is a high bar to set for me. Perhaps we should stay elsewhere."

I laughed. "There is nowhere else. As you noticed, it's not much of a town." We passed a tavern, a tiny general store, a carriage house, and a few two-story residences that had seen better days. "A lot of the commerce was lost during the war. The farms failed."

I didn't say anything more about it. He didn't press. I had been a baby during the war so had no memories to share. Which was probably a good thing. He was nine years older, so he would have had a different experience. We would have been on different sides. Strange how little difference it made to him. To us, I meant, of course.

We climbed the steps and entered the lobby. I'd been in grander places since, but this was still Biemann's.

"You are glowing," he whispered against my ear.

"I'm happy."

He made an odd noise, deep in his throat. Then he stepped up to the registrar and signed, took the key, and returned.

"Shall we?" He gestured to the stairs.

Would there be a repeat of the previous evening? We would dress, dine, then go to our separate beds? I'd ask tonight what I should expect. I told him I didn't want to spend my life nursing him, but I hadn't meant I would leave him to suffer alone.

He put the key in the lock and opened the door. This time, he let me enter on my own two feet. It was a small room: one bed, one closet, one bath. I felt a blush crawl up my neck as I turned to him.

He said, "The bridal suite wasn't available. I said this would do."

That answered my questions, I supposed.

❧

We spent a while unpacking what we needed. After I refreshed myself, William ducked into the washroom to shave. He must have done it hair by hair, he was so long at it. I was dressed and ready by the time he emerged. I waited while he fussily tied his tie and brushed nonexistent lint from his jacket. Then we went to supper.

The food was not particularly good, but it wasn't poor enough to explain his disinterest. He smoked cigarette after cigarette and talked so rapidly I could barely keep up. The waiter had a goiter, which led to a half-hour discourse on the thyroids of his dogs.

"I'm sorry," he said, abashed. "You're very patient with me. I don't miss being at work. Don't think that."

I wasn't sure what else to think, but I smiled and said, "I should hope not."

He was not fidgety, not restless. Rather, he was a strange sort of calm. Elated calm, if there could be such a thing. Even so, when he asked if I wanted dessert or tea, I said no. He'd spent enough time watching me eat. He took my arm and steered me from the dining room. We passed by the empty ballroom. The doors were open and we could see inside—the polished floor, the elaborate chandeliers, floor to ceiling windows leading to the terrace, some of which were open for air.

"That's lovely, isn't it?" he said, pointing with his cigarette. "Did you ever dance there? Do you like to dance?"

"Yes. No. And yes, I suppose." I laughed at his wry face. "I was too young to go to dances when they were held here more frequently. I did enjoy dancing at school with my girlfriends, but I haven't danced much since."

"Why not? Surely Hamptons attend balls."

"Oh, for heaven's sake. I don't know. I went, yes, but I always felt…" This was silly. "I felt the men who danced with me were disappointed. You've seen Lucy."

He halted, spun me to face him, and stared. "What can you mean by that?"

"They asked me when her card was full."

"She is not half as pretty as you are."

"I'm not fishing for compliments." I wished I hadn't told him that. I wasn't jealous of Lucy but facts were facts.

"It is not empty flattery. Lucy is ordinary. I can't even picture her now in my head. But I still remember how you looked when we first met. A brown plaid dress. A squashed-looking bonnet. A rather scorching glare. Yes, I think it was the glare that won me over."

"Ha! You have odd taste, Dr. Halsted."

"Come dance with me."

He pulled me into the ballroom and twirled me for effect, then guided me out to the terrace. It was a perfect night: breezy, star-filled skies, the scent of magnolias in the air.

He hummed softly and we danced a few moments on the terrace. I felt ridiculous and charmed. Then he pulled me closer and we swayed rather than danced. His lips brushed my ear, making me shiver with an ill-defined delight and horrified embarrassment. I put my hand on his chest to distance myself.

"I'm more accustomed to reels. We did not dance like this at school."

"Hmm?" He laughed softly then bent as though he would kiss me.

"This is too public, William," I protested, turning my face away. I half-expected Dr. Osler to poke his head onto the terrace.

William stepped back. "Then let's go to our room."

Given my orphaned state and the surfeit of maiden aunts, it had fallen to Emmelin, Cousin George's wife, to inform me what to expect. Rather than horrify the family, I'd thought it easier to go through with the charade. After an exhausting day of shopping in New York, my shy cousin-in-law had taken me aside. Emmelin said I needed only to follow my husband's lead. Men knew what to do instinctually. I almost laughed at that, but poor Emmelin was trying so hard. She warned I was likely to find it unpleasant. But it wasn't always. Emmelin blushed furiously. If I did find it unpleasant, I must bear it for my husband's sake.

I had not found the instruction helpful.

William gave me time to dress for bed. When I emerged from the washroom, he had already dressed, or rather undressed, as well. He wore a coffee-colored silk dressing gown. Seeing him made my knee bones feel mushy.

"I'll just clean my teeth," he said, scooting past me, shaving kit in hand.

He was thorough at that, too, taking as long as he did to scrub for surgery. But considering how many cigarettes he'd smoked, I was just as glad he was being thorough.

I climbed into bed, under the coverlet, and waited.

He finished, finally. He dimmed the light, discarded his dressing gown, and slipped in beside me.

"Caroline," he murmured, taking me into his arms.

His expression was very intent. More so than I'd ever seen him stare at a surgical field. Good heavens. What a horrible thought! I shouldn't make comparisons like that.

But soon enough, I couldn't think much at all. He was very busy.

Until, a fair time into the procedure, he paused, rolled off me, and reached to the ground for his dressing gown. My mind was all in confusion until I saw him pulling something onto himself that could only be a prophylactic. My relief was overwhelming.

He rolled back and resumed. Things happened fairly rapidly after that.

I would not say it had been unpleasant. He certainly had not found it so, and I liked that he was so pleased. After a few moments, after relieving himself of the sheath, he lay back beside me and made the obligatory inquiries. I didn't think I had bled, which worried me, but he made no comment on the matter. Well, I wouldn't have expected him to check. I murmured something noncommittal about being fine, then blurted my question.

"Are we taking precautions?"

He started, then sighed. "I'm sorry. That's something we should have discussed first."

"Yes." It was not his decision to make alone. "But I'm not angry. I'm not ready for children. I-I'm glad you thought of it, actually."

"I'm not ready for children either. I will be, though, Caroline. I promised you."

"I'm not in any hurry. Not for children."

He kissed me, then pulled up the coverlet and closed his eyes. I tried to sleep also. I was quite tired. Very happy. And very tired.

❧

I woke feeling chilled. The window was open. It was still dark outside. William was not in bed. His dressing gown was not on the floor. I waited a good while. Listening. He was in the washroom. Lamplight filtered under the door. He was being very quiet. Could he be reading? Maybe he was ill. I pitied him so intensely I felt ill myself. What sort of wife would leave her husband to suffer without offering what help she could? I rose from bed and crossed the floor. I knocked on the door but received no answer. Frightened, I opened the door.

He was using the closed toilet as a chair. Leaning back. Eyes closed. Face slack as though he were asleep but he wasn't. His breathing was fast and shallow. His shaving kit had fallen to the floor next to his surgical bag, which was open and, from the looks of it, had been rifled through. A hypodermic needle and vial lay in the sink. I stepped inside the small space and he did not stir. I picked up the vial. It was not morphine.

"William," I whispered. What had I done, marrying this man? I was bound to him now. For better or worse. I shook his shoulder and said loudly, "William! William!"

He opened his eyes slowly. His gaze darted around the room, confused. With difficulty, he focused on me.

"Miss Hampton?"

"For pity's sake, William!"

"Caroline!" His eyes widened and he blanched. "What are you doing in here?"

I walked out and slammed the door. I had to leave.

My bag was light. I threw it onto the bed and began tossing things into it willy-nilly. I was angry enough to cry, but wouldn't bother to do so. The washroom door opened.

"Caroline."

"You lied to me."

"Not at the time. I'm sorry. Please, I...please stop. Listen to me."

I paused. My bag was a mess. It would never close. And I could hardly storm onto the streets of Walhalla in the middle of the night.

"What? Talk then. Why on earth would you do this?" I waited. He said nothing. Then I got angry again. "I will go on to Cashiers in the morning. I hope you will return to Baltimore."

"I couldn't make love to you! I wanted to and I couldn't. That is morphine. Cocaine is this—tonight."

Lessons from school ran through my head. I hadn't applied them to him. I couldn't.

He said, "I wanted to be a *husband* to you. I owe you that much."

"Don't you dare!" I plucked up the closest thing at hand, my hairbrush, and flung it at him with all my might. It glanced his elbow. My aim was abysmal, so Frank had always said.

"I will not be your excuse," I said levelly. "You didn't take cocaine so that you could make love to me. You made love to me so that you could take cocaine. You ran from our bed to your next injection. Were you counting the minutes until you could get away?"

"No!" His face went ashen. "Caroline, no."

"Don't you care that I will think you have relapsed anytime you… we…"

"Are you leaving me?" There was no emotion in his voice. He was trying to give me that choice. A shiver ran through me.

"No." Pity and guilt warred with hurt and anger. "You're ill. I want you well." I needed him well. I cared for him too much to hurt him more than he was hurting. "Can you be well? Can you be honest with me?"

"I can…be honest."

"Well, then, we will start from there."

PART THREE

Succeed: (suk-sēd') v.: 1. To follow; come after; be subsequent or consequent to. 2. To take the place of; be heir or successor to. 4. To arrive at a happy issue; obtain the object desired; accomplish what is attempted or intended.

— *The Century Dictionary:* an encyclopedic lexicon of the English Language, Century Company, 1889-1891

39

1890, June

Cashiers Valley, North Carolina

WADE HAMPTON'S NIECE MARRIED

Columbia, S.C., June 4 — The first wedding in the Hampton family for many years was celebrated at Millwood, the Hampton country seat, five miles from Columbia to-day. The contracting parties were Dr. William S. Halsted, formerly of New York City, but now chief of the medical department of the Johns Hopkins University, Baltimore, and Miss Caroline Hampton, daughter of Gen. Frank Hampton, who was killed during the civil war, and niece of Senator Wade Hampton. Miss Hampton some years ago concluded to adopt the vocation of nurse. She entered Johns Hopkins in that capacity, and has risen to the control of the entire department devoted to that purpose. It was there that she met Dr. Halsted.

Miss Hampton has practically completed the study of medicine and as soon as the medical department for women is established at the Johns Hopkins, she will receive the degree of M.D., so that husband and wife will both be members of the profession.

—*The Sun*, New York City, New York, June 4, 1890

A hired coach took us as far as Rocky Bottom. We didn't speak much. I supposed we both had a lot to think about. I soothed myself by watching the countryside roll by. I loved the woods in June. Everything smelled of leaves and damp earth and flowers waiting to burst into bloom. William read journals he wanted to catch up on. I didn't see how he could read, jouncing along in a carriage, but I wouldn't force the scenery upon him. He would have to come to appreciate it on his own. Or not.

In Rocky Bottom, old Uncle Jeff met us at Colonel Beaker's house and transferred our bags to the wagon bed. William looked on, smoking tiredly.

Well, I'd wake him up. Uncle Jeff had hitched the wagon to Jeb and Jubal, my favorite pair.

William looked startled when the old groom handed me up into the driver's position.

"You are coming, aren't you?" I teased.

He tossed his cigarette to the ground. "You're joking." He looked at Uncle Jeff, who shook his head and snickered. William gamely climbed up beside me.

"Hold onto that silly hat," I warned. "GEE-ON!"

I eased the team into a trot. William did hold onto his hat, then onto the seat when I gave the horses their head. The wind caught my hair and chafed my cheeks. It felt wonderful. I couldn't wait to be home where I could truly ride.

When the road grew rougher, rutted, I slowed and stole a glance at William. He smiled at me and said, "Good Lord."

"I needed that." I gestured about to the loblolly and scrub pine, the Carolina hemlock, the hickory and oak. "I needed this."

I looked forward to the steeper climb, the narrow switchbacks, the sheer drop-offs, the wet-or-dry creek beds, the fallen branches blocking the road. The challenge never failed to stir me, though my city-bred husband might have a coronary.

"Isn't it beautiful?"

"You are beautiful, Caroline, when you're happy. I hope you always will be."

"No one is always happy." In my experience, people rarely were. Yet there were moments. "But I believe I will be happier with you than I was without."

We spent a quiet month alone but for Vera and Jeff. We went for long walks. A few sedate rides. William was learning his way. He never complained, though I knew there were days he was miserable. He was cutting back on his morphine incrementally. When he "rested" in the afternoons, I took Nellie out. We jumped fences. It helped.

William had given me the cocaine vial and told me to dispose of it. He said I should go through his bags and trunks to prove there was no more. I made a face at him. "Don't be silly. That would take months."

We shared a bedroom. It was Uncle Wade's, but he rarely came to the

Lodge anymore. The other bedrooms were tiny and cluttered; William would have been claustrophobic in one of those. We slept together but gave each other space in the bed, except that sometimes we ended up curled around one another. We hadn't made love again, but one night he...well, he kissed me and caressed me in a way that had made me feel...well, it had been very nice.

We gave each other space during the day also. Another thing we had in common: we both needed time alone.

William loved the flower gardens, particularly the dahlias. I often found him wandering among them, bending over to pull weeds or pick off a bug. One morning he confided that his father had gardened, growing exotic flowers in a hothouse in their Irvington summer home. It was the only time I'd ever heard of him speak of his rarely mentioned father without irritation. I resolved to fill the gardens with dahlias—make him believe it had been his idea.

Space was not always easy to find, especially on rainy days. The main house was quite small. Rustic, William called it. There was one front room to serve as parlor, library, salon, everything. The furniture was rough. A braided rag rug covered the plank floor. Calico curtains fluttered in the open windows. William was enamored of the large open fireplace. It was often cool enough in the evenings for a fire. In the mornings, we sat together on the porch in the aunties' rocking chairs, drinking coffee and watching the clouds, enjoying the view of the mountains spread out before us. And we talked. Filling in the gaps.

"So, you went to school here?" he asked one morning, his voice strained, polite, yet clearly working his tongue around a bad taste in his mouth.

For a moment, I considered teasing him, but it embarrassed me a little, what he'd evidently been thinking. On our ride the day before, I pointed out the schoolhouse. My aunts had had it built. One room. Gray clapboard walls. William pronounced it quaint and said nothing more. Now I understood why he'd looked like he swallowed a squirrel.

"Oh, good heavens, William." I laughed a little falsely. "The school is for the valley children. Lucy and I went to the Edge Hill School for Girls." For emphasis, I added, "The proprietress is Thomas Jefferson's great-granddaughter."

"Boarding school?" He hid his relief poorly.

"In Virginia. We learned mathematics, literature, the sciences, and fluency in French. And, of course, painting, music, flower arranging, and dance. You needn't worry. I was taught everything necessary to prepare me to be a fine Southern wife." A little peeved at my defensiveness, I added, "Or an acceptable Yankee doctor's wife."

"I wasn't worried. Only I've heard that many Southerners lost everything after the war…"

"We weren't poor, William."

"No, of course not."

"It was only that we had no money."

His brow creased. "That doesn't amount to the same thing?"

"Not at all. We're *Hamptons*."

"Yes, well," he said, as if agreeing that that settled it. But it hadn't. He hesitated then asked, "But you weren't…scarred by it all?"

"Of course, we were. Those were frightful years. Reconstruction was horrible. You can't imagine."

"Reconstruction was worse than the war itself? Wasn't that more frightening?"

"I was a baby," I reminded him. "I took security for granted."

He pressed. "Have you no memories of the war?"

"One," I admitted reluctantly. One I didn't like to recall. Security was *not* a given and I'd known that. "Just a fragment, a distorted fragment, but the kernel of it is real."

He regarded me patiently.

"Fire." Even to bring up the memory made me relive it. "I can still feel it. The heat. The smoke. I remember screaming: *Dodie, Dodie, Dodie.* My favorite aunt, you see."

"Oh, Caroline," he sighed.

"The aunties are distraught. Frank is sobbing. I'm barefoot in the street. The whole city is burning. I remember—" I shuddered. My voice grew faint. "I remember I felt chest-tightening, breath-robbing, black-visioned terror. I was three years old, but I remember how alone I felt."

I'd had no words for my fear. Fear of being forgotten. Left behind.

"I'm so sorry."

I tried to smile at my own absurdity as I said, "Whenever I see a fire I still think: *Yankees!*"

"That's dreadful. What-what happened?"

"Sherman happened. He burned Columbia."

William put a hand on my knee. I glanced at him. Then, embarrassed, looked away.

"But what happened to you?" he asked.

"My uncle Kit arrived. I don't know where he'd been, or how he'd known we needed him. He was suddenly just there." *He scooped me up, held me close.* "He put us all in a wagon and we left Columbia huddled in the bed, embers raining down. In my mind, we came here, but that seems doubtful. He couldn't have brought us so far."

"Kit? I don't recall meeting a Kit."

"He died." I took a deep breath. "Not in the war. Later."

And I was going to devote my life to service in his memory. Instead, I married a Yankee.

"How did he—"

"William, please. Let's talk about something else. And not your recollections of the war. I don't want to hear those just now." Or perhaps not ever. We had enough to get through.

❧

We'd been in Cashiers nearly five weeks when one of our near neighbors, Mrs. Sweeney, rode up in her wagon.

"Hello, Miss Caroline!" She pulled up to the porch, nodded suspiciously at William, and said, "I was down to the post office. I heard you would be here so I brought your mail."

"Thank you kindly. Mrs. Sweeney, this is Dr. Halsted." The woman had surely come to satisfy her curiosity. She would tell all the neighbors Miss Caroline's Yankee husband dressed like a fusspot. "We were married down in Columbia a couple weeks ago."

"Oh! Well, then." She looked him up and down. "You meet the general?"

"He did."

William added, "A formidable gentleman."

"A gentleman, all right. I suppose he approves or you wouldn't be here." She picked up the letters and newspapers. I stepped from the porch to take them.

"Thank you, Mrs. Sweeney. Would you stay for a glass of lemonade?"

"Oh no, thank'ee. I wouldn't intrude on your honeymoon. You take care now." She glanced up at William. "Good day, sir."

"Good day to you." He looked amused.

The woman rode off. I sorted the mail, handing William three letters—Welch, Mall, and one of his sisters—and kept three for myself—Lucy, Lucy, and Aunt Lu. We settled back in our rocking chairs to read. I started with the letter from Aunt Lu.

A clipping from a New York newspaper was enclosed. A wedding announcement. I sniffed with irritation. We had agreed not to post anything. We didn't want a big to-do. I read it and frowned.

"They got more wrong than right."

"What?" William asked.

I passed it to him. "Aunt Lu sent this from *The Sun.* Uncle Wade is right. Editors can't be bothered with details."

He read it through. His neck reddened and his mouth went tight. He looked at me and growled, "Osler."

"What?"

"Osler sent this in."

"Really?"

"He might as well have signed it. He thinks he's amusing," he fumed. "I'm sorry, Caroline. He—"

"He says I'll be a physician. We'll practice together!" I burst into laughter. That man. He knew exactly how to get under William's skin. "Oh, William. It *is* funny!" I did so like William's friends. "I bet Aunt Lu is having conniptions! And poor Cousin George! And your sisters!"

"Caroline."

I looked up, catching my breath, tears of mirth on my cheeks. How Uncle Kit would have loved the joke. "He promoted my father to general. That was good of him."

"You have the most wonderful laugh."

"William! Good heavens." I tried to hold it back but couldn't. He laughed with me. *He* had the wonderful laugh. I wished he would laugh more often.

He stood and held out his hand.

"Come lie down with me for a little while, will you? We'll read our letters later."

40

1890, December

Baltimore, Maryland

SENATOR HAMPTON WOUNDED
ACCIDENTALLY SHOT BY HIS SON WHILE HUNTING IN MISSISSIPPI
Columbia, S.C., Nov. 26—The startling news was received here to-night that United States Senator Wade Hampton had been shot by his son while hunting in Mississippi. Coming at a time when his defeat for re-election is being seriously considered by the new political regime, the news created no small sensation. The particulars of the unfortunate accident came through a telegram to the senator's son-in-law, Col. John C. Haskell…

—*The New York Times*, New York, N.Y., November 27, 1890

❧

Halsted identified four parathyoids and isolated the delicate vasculature for two of them before giving up. He felt awful. The corpse would have to wait. He pulled the skin flaps together, fixed them with a single thick black suture, laid a cloth over the face and neck, then a sheet over the body, and wheeled the stretcher back into storage.

While washing his hands, a wave of nausea swept over him. He vomited into the slop sink and washed away the evidence. He had to go home.

He pulled his sleeves down and put on his jacket and overcoat. He couldn't tell if he was hot or cold. Damn it!

Attempting the dissection had been stupid. He was weaning—again…still, it hardly mattered anymore—and missed a dose. Idiotically. He'd tried opening his pill case on his way to the Pathological and the thing flipped out of his hand and spilled. He spotted the case next to the walkway, but he was not about to crawl on hands and knees in the frost-dead brown grass, nose to the ground, looking for pills. He should have gone straight home. He would now.

He found his walking stick, popped his silk hat on his head, and started up the back stairs. As he neared the top, the door was flung open and Osler came jogging down, in a tweed overcoat, the picture of sartorial elegance, physician's bag in hand.

"Halsted! Oops." The doctor danced aside. "Excuse me. Is Booker down there? We're supposed to round."

"Haven't seen him." He tried to brush past. Osler caught his arm.

"Halsted?"

"I'm in a bit of a hurry."

"So I see." He let go of Halsted's arm, but stepped in front of him, blocking his escape. "Permit me?" He put the back of his hand to Halsted's forehead and scowled.

"Mrs. Halsted is waiting."

"I don't doubt it. Hold still." He looked at his watch, then at Halsted's chest. "I am counting your respirations. Breathe normally."

He couldn't breathe normally when he was panicking. "Stop this foolery."

"Hmm." Osler looked at him for what seemed a long time. Then he sighed. "I thought you were done with this."

He knew what Osler saw. Cold sweat. Fasciculations. The man was hand in glove with President Gilman and the rest of the Board; he would know the sordid history. This was it. Disgrace. The end of his tenure here.

"Will you let me pass?" Or would he have to throw the man down the stairs?

Osler said, "Who is your physician?"

Halsted had no answer for that. He liked to imagine his health was good.

"So, then," Osler went on, "I am. Whatever you may choose to tell me will not leave my"—he gestured about the stairwell—"office. You don't believe me—my little poem was out of line, Welch said, and I'm sorry. But the doctor-patient relationship is privileged and I would not betray that. How bad is this?"

Halsted gave up. "Bad."

"I cannot condone you treating patients—"

"I time my doses. It doesn't affect my work."

"How much are you using?"

"I don't wish to say." Eight grains. Eight! "But I am decreasing."

"You need help. It is very difficult to cure *oneself* of a morphine habit."

"I've done it before."

Osler pursed his lips. "Exactly my point. Halsted—"

"Thank you for your concern. But I really have to get home. I mislaid my pills and I'm not well."

Osler looked down at his bag, then sighed and opened it. He pulled an envelope out of an inner pocket and said, "Hold out your hand." Halsted did. Osler shook a pill into it. "That is sixteen milligrams."

He swallowed hard. "Better make it two."

Osler's face did not change. No censure, no pity—he shook out another.

Nothing was so sweet as the bitter sting on the back of Halsted's tongue. He swallowed spit and pills. And pride. He owed Osler now.

"My intention had been to be done with this by the time we returned from North Carolina."

Osler winced. "That was how you spent your honeymoon?"

"Part of it." This was awkward. If Osler ever breathed a word... "Not the first few weeks, obviously. But I had promised Mrs. Halsted and she... I'm having a cigarette." He pulled out his case. If only he'd reached for a smoke while crossing the yard instead of a pill. "Do you want one?"

"You smoke too much."

"That wasn't what I asked."

"No, thank you."

Osler waited while he lit up and pulled the smoke into his lungs. He breathed out, hoping the pills would take effect soon. He wished Osler had given him an injection. The image of that made him queasy. He started talking to distract himself.

"I promised Mrs. Halsted." He coughed. "If she had generaled South Carolina, I tell you the Confederate flag would be flying over our capitol now."

"So, what happened?"

"I halved what I was taking by the end of July. In August, the aunties descended. Mrs. Halsted's aunts. We were staying in their summer home in the mountains. Columbia was hot. They're old. They sent a telegram from Pickens. Caroline...Mrs. Halsted could not tell them they weren't welcome."

There was laughter in Osler's eyes. He said, "You would think they would've known."

Caroline was in a quandary. He'd been irritable, to put it charitably, and she'd borne it. Nursed him when he needed it. Borne it all. But she wanted her family to love him, at least to accept him, and he was a foreign creature in their eyes. A foreign creature in the throes of morphine withdrawal would be beyond the pale. He said he would pause the weaning. She reluctantly agreed. He didn't pause; he rebounded.

Even so, seeing her with her aunts—batty old women—made him love her all the more. He suspected they drove her crazy, but they would never know it. She was so good to them.

He was glad Booker had gossiped so he understood. Of course, they were batty. Caroline never said anything. He wasn't entirely sure she knew.

"One would think. But it put an end to the process. I had to start over upon our return. I am going to quit."

"I imagine so. Since you promised Mrs. Halsted." He stepped aside. "Go on home. But, Halsted, if you need help…"

"Yes, all right, Doctor. I don't have to say I know where to find you. I can't get rid of you."

He started to feel better, physically, on the trolley, but he was still irritated. With himself, mostly, but with everything in general. He hated feeling like he had dragged Caroline away from what she loved most in the world. He hated the house they leased. He hated that he and Caroline hadn't been getting along. His fault, but that didn't make him less irritated. Rather more.

He was working constantly, trying to make up for lost time. He shouldn't have called it that, making excuse to her for his repeated absences. Their honeymoon was not "lost time." But Welch had a vision and he was trying to fit himself into it. Johns Hopkins had formed a Medical Society. William presented at its first few bi-monthly meetings, four case series, before proposing to Caroline. He presented four more case series at the October meeting alone. Two more last month. One at the meeting last night—another evening Caroline spent without him.

He thought she was losing patience, but the truth was, he was. Operating nearly every morning, afternoons in the dispensary, rounding with the residents, the laboratory, writing, always writing late into the night.

He and Caroline hadn't shared a bed since returning to Baltimore. They hadn't been intimate since, well, since the aunties showed up.

And the worst…

The trolley reached his stop. Bolton Hill. He climbed down and turned his feet toward Madison Avenue. Rows of large Baltimore brick townhomes. Tiny patches of grass in front. White steps scrubbed clean. Not quite identical, but close. Their house was poorly laid out. He couldn't fix it without knocking down walls. Welch poked fun, pointing out it was one of the largest houses in a community of oversized houses. Caroline said it was fine. He found it stifling.

The worst was Caroline was unhappy. Of course, she was. After months of freedom, fresh air, her horses, and those sad-eyed hounds, he yanked her back to the city, stuffed her into that claustrophobic house, and abandoned her. He complained about work but he had work. He'd stolen hers from her.

Something was going on back in South Carolina that bothered her. She wrote and received mountains of mail. She took subscriptions to three or four newspapers. He had been feeling…irritable a week ago at supper and she started in with Uncle Wade and Mr. Tillman or some such and he'd blurted, "I don't care about politics."

It didn't matter that he'd apologized immediately. He hurt her.

She looked stunned for a moment, then said, "Of course, you aren't interested in South Carolina contests. How silly of me." Next, she asked him about his work, in piercing detail proving she listened to all his minutiae, and made insightful comments that would have delighted Welch but made him feel worse.

The next night, he tried to make it up to her by asking about her day. She laughed and said Betty—the new housekeeper—had taught her to make crab cakes. She changed the subject back to him. The next day, when he asked, she reported only that a trip to Lexington Market had been a bit chilly. That was, pointedly, all she had to say.

And then, God help him, when he pressed her the evening before last to tell him how she spent her day she said, "I shopped for a new bonnet. The brim is perhaps too wide, but it is a lovely shade of mauve and has the cutest floral spray. I hope you don't mind the expense, but I just couldn't say no to it."

She did that thing with her accent. The thing that made him snicker to himself when he heard her do it to others.

He didn't know how to fix this. Aside from buying her a new bonnet every night until she broke down and laughed. But he was afraid to try it. She might fling it at him. So he'd gone to his meeting last night and left her alone. He hadn't even seen her since yesterday morning.

He climbed the steps to his house. Unlocked the door. She usually came running down to greet him when the door opened, to take his coat and hat and give him a kiss. She wasn't there. This was ridiculous. He wasn't going to bellow for her.

He went upstairs to shed his hospital clothes, take a pill, and bathe before dinner. He took two. The hot water soothed him. He nearly fell asleep in the bath. He dragged himself from it and dressed. He considered going to the table in his shirt sleeves, but force of habit made him don his jacket.

The house was very quiet. He stopped outside Caroline's bedroom and knocked. There was no answer. He went down and poked his head into the kitchen. "Betty? Have you seen Mrs. Halsted?"

The housekeeper, an older colored woman who knew all the Baltimore recipes and cleaned fastidiously enough to suit him, shook her head. "No, Doctor. Not for a few hours. She was in the reading room last I saw."

"Thank you."

He headed for the library. One had to go through the parlor to get there. Ridiculous. The door was half-closed and there was no lamplight coming from inside. He pushed the door open. She was asleep on the settee. Sound asleep—she didn't stir when he came in. She was curled up and had a handkerchief crumpled in her hand. His heart dropped. He tiptoed closer.

A piece of paper had fallen to the floor beside the settee. He bent to pick it up. He wouldn't read her letters, except that the first words leaped out. *Don't be alarmed.* His eyes were pulled along the page. He sat on his haunches.

It was her sister's handwriting. Alarming news from home. Don't believe all the newspapers say. Uncle Wade will recover. *Recover?* McDuffy is beside himself. *Who the devil is McDuffy?* Uncle Wade has taken to calling him d'd Yankee or General Grant just to tease him out of his low spirits.

"William?" Caroline rose to her elbow.

He put the letter beside her. "I'm sorry. I didn't mean to keep reading."

Her brow furrowed. "I don't hide things from you."

"I know. Nevertheless. What is wrong?" He put a hand on her arm. "Please?"

"My cousin shot my uncle in the head."

"Good Lord!"

"It was an accident. They were hunting. Someone should tan McDuffy's hide; he knows better."

"Than to shoot his father in the head? I would hope so."

"It's not funny." She sat up, frowning.

"I'm sorry. Of course not. What happened?"

"Uncle Wade was sprayed with bird shot. He was hit in the eye. Dr. Taylor says he won't lose any sight. Lucy said his head is a mess of bandages."

"I'm sorry. Does this…" He took a deep breath. "Does this effect his election chances?"

She didn't answer.

"I understand this Tillman nuisance was elected governor. There is considerable concern the legislature will fail to stand by Senator Hampton."

"William, you don't have to study the newspapers." She gave him a soft look. "I appreciate it. I do. But you have enough on your plate. I shouldn't have been so peevish."

"You're worried about your loved ones. It was wrong of me to brush it off."

Her mouth pursed. "Well, yes. It was." Then she shifted on the settee, pulling her skirts to set them aright. "I'm just bored. And trapped. And you're right about this house."

"What can I do to help?" He took hold of her hand and kissed her knuckles. "I can resign from the dispensary. Let Finney—"

"No! Oh, that would make everything worse."

"Being trapped here with me?" he teased.

"Yes."

Then he had an idea. "Perhaps a runabout or a dogcart?"

"You'd need a horse for that."

"I wouldn't." He pretended to shudder. "You would."

She stared at him a moment. "Oh, we couldn't."

"Why not? We could empty the trash out of the carriage house. Hire a man."

"But the expense, William! A horse in the city just for me to—"

"Do you want me to write to Frank for advice on purchasing the horse? I think I can manage having a carriage built to order."

"A dogcart. I would love a dogcart. And, William?"

"Hmm?" Her eyes were glowing; it warmed his heart to see.

"I'll need a dog."

41

1891, April

Columbia, South Carolina

The morphine habit is difficult of eradication... The baneful drug has become a necessity; if withheld, every cell of the organism cries out in agony... There are two methods of leaving off: the sudden method and the gradual method. Levinstein is a conspicuous advocate of the sudden method...the practical difficulties in the way of sudden suppression are very great; dangerous collapse is likely to ensue, and wild and maniacal delirium... The gradual method advocated by Burkhart...is the one in use by most specialists... By this method, the acute accidents are avoided, but the patient is long kept in a state of irritation, teased and tantalized without being satisfied... It is needless to say that the gradual or "tapering off" method cannot be effectively carried out at home, or in a private boarding house. No patient was ever yet weaned from morphine in that way; at least, no inveterate case was ever so cured.

—"On the Treatment of the Morphine Habit," Erlenmeyer, Albrecht, 1889.

We have been much troubled over Halsted. He went to South Carolina a month ago for his health and will not be back until the middle of this month. He was looking dreadful when he left, but recent letters from him are very encouraging. He is gaining strength and weight and is playing lawn tennis, etc. It would be a calamity to lose him.

—Dr. William Booker to Franklin P. Mall, May 3, 1891

Will you kindly grant to me an extension of my leave of absence until July 15, 1891? For six months I have had what I suppose to be malaria, and I think that it would be inadvisable for me to return to Baltimore before the middle of July. I regret exceedingly that I am compelled to ask for a vacation at this time of the year.

—Dr. William S. Halsted to Dr. Henry Hurd, Superintendent of the Board of Trustees, Johns Hopkins Hospital, April 8, 1891

❧

Two telegrams arrived at the same time, one from Dr. Welch, one from Dr. Osler. I debated a moment, then tiptoed into William's room.

We were staying at the Columbia Hotel rather than at Millwood with the family. Naturally, the aunties concluded William was standoffish. Frank privately told me I'd married a wise man, yet I thought Frank was befuddled too—this was not how people behaved with family. But they were dealing with Uncle Wade's crisis. I was not about to introduce them to William's. Standoffish was the lesser of two evils.

In February, Dr. Clarke accidentally stuck William's finger during surgery. William brushed it off: such things happened. He developed an abscess. Finney had to debride it. William suggested he inject the tender site with cocaine first. Perhaps he was testing himself. Perhaps it was the excuse he'd been searching for. Things had gone downhill from there. I had never seen him so ill, or so defiantly insistent he was well. He sneaked cocaine and denied he was doing it. Rather nastily. I'd known, of course, that he could be acid-tongued, but it was not as amusing when he directed his venom at me.

So I manipulated him. Uncle Wade had been ousted from the Senate by the legislature's vote in mid-December. Young firebrands—croakers who had been mere tadpoles when General Hampton suffered his youngest brother's death in battle and held his own dying son in his arms—accused Uncle Wade of cozying up to Yankee senators and fraternizing with Negroes. In March, he left Washington for good. The whole Hampton family rallied around him and I *was* a Hampton, even if I'd traded my Confederate bona fides for marriage to a Yankee surgeon. I squeezed out a few tears and William agreed, petulantly, to accompany me home.

I hid him in the hotel, bringing in Dr. Taylor, who, according to William, was a worse quack than Osler. Nevertheless, after months of ricocheting between the two drugs, he was worn down enough to submit to my care.

He was terribly ill: vomiting, chills and tremors, sweats, nightmares if he slept at all, and pain. He said it was like being stretched on a rack and beaten. Last night he'd begged for a little extra morphine, just this once. Nights were worse. And I gave in. I regretted it immediately but he was so grateful that I suspected I would slip again. My choice was that or to sit in a chair at his bedside, watching him writhe and groan for hours on end.

He was sleeping now. Would it be worse to wake him or to risk his wrath by deciding two telegrams could wait?

"William?" I whispered. Then, louder: "William?"

He opened his eyes. His hair was mussed from sleeping. I wanted to smooth it but he didn't like, I had learned, to be touched while he was tapering.

"You have telegrams. From Baltimore. From Dr. Osler and Dr. Welch. Do you want me to leave them? Or…"

"Open them." He cleared his throat and tried to sit up, reaching for his glasses. "If you would. Osler's…no, Welch's first."

I opened Welch's.

MALARIA?

I handed it to him, confused.

Glasses perched on the edge of his nose, he focused, then cast it aside with a snort. "He doesn't waste words. Let me see Osler's. He'll tell me what's what."

I opened Osler's. "William, what in the world?"

MALARIA?

He read it and his lips twitched. He glanced up. "I requested extended leave until mid-July. I told the Board I had malaria."

"Oh." He lied to the Board? "Osler knows?"

"Nothing gets past Osler. He won't…he'll keep his mouth closed. At least, he won't offer anything." He chewed his lip. "I'm not sure he'll lie."

"I hope he wouldn't." Good heavens. Would they all lie to protect each other? How was that right? Guiltily, I realized I was doing the same. But it was different for a wife.

William looked at me sideways. "I think," he said heavily, "they are trusting me to keep my word to you. I'm trying, Caroline."

"I know you are." I ached for him. Three months? I couldn't bear going through this that long. How could he? "What if you were to stop all at once? You're suffering so much now. Can it be any worse?"

He paled. "Levinstein's method. No. No, I can't."

"Levinstein's?"

"Abrupt cessation." He wrung his hands. "They tried that, my second admission to Butler."

"You were sicker than this?"

"Bodily? I don't remember. Bodily misery reaches a threshold I suppose." He started to shiver. His voice dropped low. Confessional. "I have a horror. I suppose all men do. Of madness. Death is preferable."

"You aren't mad."

"But I was. A mind is a terrifyingly fragile thing. I—they say I broke a chair over an orderly's head. For stealing my medical bag."

"He stole from you?"

"No. No, of course not. I believed he'd stolen my bag. With the cocaine. Or morphine. I don't know. I didn't even know that I'd assaulted him. I woke up, if it could be called waking, in restraints. Think what it was like: being insane and unable to break free." He looked away, pressing his fingers to the bridge of his nose. "I wouldn't—I never would have believed myself capable of violence. I'm not risking that with you."

"Then we'll take it slowly." I wasn't afraid for myself. Only him. "If it takes three months—"

"I want to be done with this. For once and all." He lay back down with a groan. "We'll see what the Board says. Probably 'malaria' with a big question mark."

❧

We had the answer a week later. The Board "fully appreciated the reasons why a long vacation seemed necessary." Did they? "In spite of the serious crippling of the department in consequence of such a prolonged absence…" Serious crippling? As opposed to a trivial crippling, I supposed. They did have the good grace to hope for an improvement in his state of health. With that, and with Dr. Finney's agreement to act in his stead, the Board granted William an extension of leave until May 15th. One month from the date of their letter. Three weeks from now. Of course, if it proved "inadvisable" for William to return, a further leave could be granted.

William's jaw tightened. "I have to go back in May."

I rose from his side and picked up his empty soup bowl. He was eating. We had started taking walks in the park, short ones, to work off his twitchiness. He still had so far to go.

With a bleakness that chilled my bones, he said, "One more reduction, I think, is all I can manage. Cut me back to four grains and I will stay at that, just for now. I—"

"Don't." We would return to that house that he hated, the burden and challenge of the hospital, the eyes of his colleagues. He managed perfectly well on four grains of morphine. Until he needed four and a half. "Don't say you promise." I couldn't bear another lie.

42

1893, April

Baltimore, Maryland

Our first case is that of a tuberculous knee-joint which we exsected. The patient is a woman of 40 years of age, and her trouble commenced a year and a half ago. When she was admitted to the hospital she was suffering greatly and wished to have the knee operated upon. The disease was quite advanced…

—"Tuberculous knee-joint. Goitre. Operative treatment of old dislocations of elbow." *Exhibition of Surgical Cases at The Johns Hopkins Hospital Medical Society*, Baltimore, April 3, 1893

❧

Halsted was in good spirits. He had accompanied Caroline to church the previous morning, though he had no inclination to worship a God he was uncertain of, and he let her jolt him around the park in her dog-cart in the afternoon. It was a fine spring day. They would be leaving for Cashiers at the end of the month and she was all joy. After supper, she listened to him practice his presentation for tonight's Medical Society meeting and she told him where to shorten it.

You do run on. Well, he did. To soothe his ruffled feathers, she spent the night in his bed. He was in very good spirits.

The weather was so fine again this morning that Finney took the liberty of cancelling surgery and setting up another baseball game out in the yard: old men against the interns and residents. Welch kept score. Halsted took his Yale position at second. It felt good to run the bases. And they won.

Afterwards, he headed to the ward to round on his patients. He couldn't rely on the new surgical resident, Phippen, or the dullard assistant resident, to see to things the way he'd relied on Brockway. That promising young man had abruptly resigned two years ago to get married and go teach anatomy in New York. Phippen was an unfortunate stopgap.

He would get rid of Phippen when Joe Bloodgood returned from Europe. He could make something out of Bloodgood. Even though he came to Hopkins from the medical side and had no surgical training, he was a bulldog about work. And although he looked as mild-mannered as a shoe clerk, he didn't shake in his boots when Halsted asked him a question.

He still remembered the first time he'd taken Bloodgood, who was assistant resident at the time, to evaluate a patient of Osler's. The three of them stood at the bedside. It was a case of Peyronie's disease, or as Osler called it: "squint cock." Scarring with contractures of the penis made it impossible for the patient to aim his urinary stream, or anything else. Surgical options were limited. He asked Bloodgood, "How would you treat this?" With a straight face, the young man answered, "Massage?" Osler had to step away from the bedside. Halsted had managed not to laugh, but barely. Not even Hall would have dared a joke like that, back in the day.

Hall. That chapter was closed. He wrote to his old friend when he'd become engaged to Caroline, reaching out, but had never heard back. Still, maybe it was because of Hall that he'd sent Bloodgood to work with the Germans for a few months, and promised him the coveted resident surgeon spot upon his return.

In any case, he needed someone who could work. The medical school would be opening in the fall and he would have to devote time to teaching, which would mean less time in the laboratory. Of course, the medical school was part of the vision. The nuisance part.

He shouldn't complain. The medical school was at least three years behind schedule. The Board had run out of money. To finance the project, they had to accept the conditions of a women's charitable group that had raised hundreds of thousands for the purpose. They wanted women admitted to the medical school. This caused no small degree of consternation among the faculty. Halsted wasn't sure where he stood on the matter. All he knew was that if Mrs. Halsted was in the room, he had better give the plan his full-throated support.

Not only was Caroline insistent women should be doctors, she was equally adamant that more men should be trained as nurses. Specifically, she thought he should have a male surgical nurse. It tickled him that she could be jealous. It wasn't as though he proposed to all his nurses.

He detoured to the dining room. He'd round after lunch. He should find Finney and ask him to try to hire a male nurse over the summer while he was in Cashiers.

The usual men, five of them today, sat at the attendings' table along the back wall. He didn't see Finney, but he made his way over nevertheless. There was an open place next to Welch, between Welch and Osler.

As he approached, he heard Osler's voice, which, naturally, carried.

"Finney is a superior surgeon. Certainly he deserves an appointment in the school. Assistant professor of surgery, at least."

At least? Halsted's step hitched. Was Osler suggesting promoting Finney above him? He was down to four grains a day and managing splendidly. So splendidly he thought maybe he shouldn't disturb the equilibrium this summer by trying to taper more. His discomfort casted a shadow on Caroline's happiness and he'd like to spare her that this year. He walked closer.

"He's quick and handy. There is no better surgeon at getting himself out of a scrape."

Halsted pulled out the chair and sat. He gave Osler a cutting look.

"Is that the definition of excellent technique? The ability to get out of a scrape?"

Osler started. "Oh, hello, Halsted, didn't see you. But yes, of course. That's why I am unable to rank your skill above his."

The table quieted.

Osler continued, "You never get yourself into scrapes to get out of."

Halsted felt his ears redden. Who knew what the man had been going to say before he was caught? Osler was congenitally incapable of keeping his mouth shut.

Calmly, he retorted, "By the same token, your nattering skill is unsurpassed."

Osler led the laughter. Then Welch returned them to the subject.

"We are discussing faculty appointments for the medical school. And I have a present for you."

He pulled an envelope from his breast pocket and slid it along the table. The return was The University of Chicago, a school that had ambition to become the Johns Hopkins University of the Midwest. To that end, they lured Mall from Worcester a short while ago to head their anatomy department. They offered him a full professorship and threw money at him.

"Tickets to the Columbian Exposition, I suppose?"

Mall had invited him to come to Chicago in May for the World's Fair. He was as enthusiastic about the city as he was the school. Halsted knew Welch had broached the possibility of Mall returning to Baltimore as professor of anatomy. But the Board could come nowhere near the salary Chicago paid him. Although they had the money, Mall was just entering his thirties and despite the solid body of work he'd already published and his enormous potential, they wouldn't pay him more than men with more advanced careers.

Halsted had written him a rather syrupy nudge. Mall answered with the request that he visit Chicago for the Exposition.

Welch merely humphed and cut his cigar.

Halsted opened the letter. No tickets.

My Dear Welch…etc. etc. etc. I gave the offer due consideration etc. etc. etc. I am hard put to leave Chicago after less than a year of effort when they've invested so much etc. etc. etc.

And Mrs. Halsted said *he* ran on. He skimmed more quickly.

Nevertheless…

Halsted set the letter down.

"He's coming?" His voice was thick so he cleared his throat and said, "He's coming back."

Welch puffed a perfect ring of smoke and nodded. "I'm sure the deciding factor was you being here."

"No. You are his hero, Welch."

"In his last letter, he asked me if you had abandoned the dog lab for connubial bliss and surgery. I told him you had not."

Osler said, "Rather Halsted has abandoned surgery for the dogs and connubial bliss."

That got a laugh from the others. As the measure of how high Halsted's spirits were, he allowed Osler to have the last word.

43

1895, March

Baltimore, Maryland

Dr. Wm. S. Halsted, of the Johns Hopkins Hospital, left Baltimore in company with his wife Saturday night to attend the funeral of his father, Mr. Wm. M. Halsted. The elder Mr. Halsted died at the residence of his son-in-law, Dr. S. O. Vanderpoel. 47 East Twenty-Fifth street, New York city, on Thursday evening. He was sixty-eight years old.

—*The Baltimore Sun, Baltimore,* MD., March 4, 1895

❧

I watched absently as Gretchen, our hound, sniffed every loose brick in the walk as we went up and down Madison Avenue. I was trying to put Aunt Dodie's letter out of mind. Nothing could be done. I had to accept it.

"Caroline!"

I raised my head. William was walking toward me. It was ten o'clock in the morning. On a Friday. My hands balled into fists. *Why wasn't he at the hospital?*

I drew a calming breath. It had been many months since he'd given me any cause to be suspicious. His health was good. His morphine dose was down. So he'd said—I knew better than to challenge him when he offered information. Prying made him grow secretive.

Well, he had called out to me. I hesitated, then waved. "William?"

He drew up close. "Good morning, Gretchen, old girl."

The dog leaped up, pawing his knees, dancing around his feet. He petted her into a frenzy. Then he stopped.

"Caroline, I have something to show you."

"Now? Shouldn't you be in surgery?"

"Bloodgood has it. Another hernia. That's his project now." He took my elbow. "Let's get Gretchen settled, then come with me."

"Where?" I wasn't in the mood for games. But usually neither was William.

"You'll see."

He waited on the stoop while I went inside and transferred Gretchen to Betty's care. "Wipe her feet well," I reminded her. Yesterday the dog had tramped muddy footprints up the stairs.

"Yes, Mrs. Halsted." Betty had a long-suffering demeanor that reminded me of Vera. What would happen to Vera? And Uncle Jeff? Jeff was terribly old.

"Dr. Halsted and I are going out. I'm not sure how long we'll be gone."

"Yes, Mrs. Halsted. Will you still want lunch? For one or two?"

"I'm not sure. I guess you'd better prepare something."

I left Betty and rejoined William, who was pacing impatiently in front of the house. He smiled when he saw me.

"We can walk there. It's close. Wait. You'll see it."

We walked along Laurens Street and turned down Eutaw Place. The houses got larger as we continued on toward Dolphin Street, the nicest part of Bolton Hill. He was bursting with something but would say nothing. It wasn't the time to tell him my sad news.

"There." He stopped at the corner of Dolphin and Eutaw. "Twelve-o-one. Look in the window."

I stepped closer and looked at the notice. The house was for sale. It was enormous. Half again as large as the house we were in. He pulled a key from his pocket.

"The agent showed me about yesterday. I asked if I might bring you to see it before—" He checked himself. "I wanted to see what you thought."

He opened the door. The foyer was bright and open. William toured me about. There were three floors. We walked through the first.

"This would make a fine library. Through here is the dining room. It is hard to get the sense of it empty, but—"

"But our things would look well here."

"In back is the kitchen. A mud room for Gretchen. Servants' rooms. There is a large carriage house too. And I thought this room here," he opened a door off the library, "would make a good office for a secretary."

"If you can keep one."

The first woman he tried could not read his handwriting. I sympathized. The second wore a heavy perfume and William objected. The woman misunderstood and simply changed brands. He let her go as well. I was growing a little tired of serving in that capacity. I enjoyed reading his papers, or listening to him practice them, but he was persnickety about citations and fussed over every detail. It was not a job for a wife.

"Come see the second floor."

There was a very large room for his study with a big open fireplace along the back wall. I saw what attracted him to the house, all that spaciousness. There was also a bedroom and bath. A huge dressing room; he'd like that.

"The third floor is similar in lay-out. There are two smaller closets instead of one large dressing room and the big room is divided into a sitting room with a fireplace and smaller room for what-not."

"What not?"

"Well," he smiled sheepishly, "it is your floor, so you can do what you want with it."

We would each have our own floor? Our bedrooms would be separated by a flight of stairs? He could not simply slip across the hall into mine on nights when we wanted to be together. It would be a whole production.

But he clearly loved the place. He was already setting his furniture in it in his head. And he hated the Madison Avenue house. He'd been searching for five years for the perfect home and nothing he'd seen suited him. This was the first time he'd been excited about one.

"It does seem perfect," I said. It had large windows, good lighting, and the wide wooden plank floors that he liked. The walls needed paint which was just as well because he would have them painted regardless. "I think we should take it."

His face fell. "What's wrong? You don't like it?"

"But I do!"

"Then you would have said it *is* perfect. That we must take it."

"Oh, for heaven's sake. It's perfect. We must take it."

"If you like the house, what is it then?" When I hesitated, he said, "Tell me."

"Oh, William." Sometimes he was oblivious and other times, so very perceptive. I bit my lip. Saying the words might make me cry. "I had a letter this morning from Dodie."

He stepped closer and clasped both my hands. "Bad news?"

"Frank—"

"Frank!" he said, aghast.

"He isn't dead. Good heavens, William." Frank was the only member of the Hampton tribe that William truly liked. We'd gone to Frank's wedding in January and William was exceedingly pleasant about it. "He's dead broke. He can't meet the mortgage on the Woodlands property. He rebuilt the house that was burned so he and Gertrude would have a home and he's been trying to start a sawmill. It was all too ambitious, I'm afraid."

"I'm sorry for that. But he's a smart man. Engineering degree from Virginia? He can find something to do."

William did not have much sympathy for Southern planters who could not make a go of plantations without slaves. He thought they should "work." Thank goodness he never voiced such a theory to the family. I had ceded the point that enslaving people was a bad thing. Well, and I conceded other points too. But he was wrong to imply my folks didn't work.

"He's going to make the sawmill successful," I insisted. "But he needs more capital. He wants...he wants to sell his portion of the Lodge."

"His portion? I thought the Lodge belonged to your aunts."

"It does. Mostly. It's more complicated than that. They all had a share. Kit left his to the aunties, but it's more or less understood it will eventually fall to Frank, Lucy, and me. Uncle Wade has already sold off his share to raise funds."

"What do your aunts say? They're still alive. His share wouldn't come to him yet."

"Oh, you know my aunts. They've deeded Frank half his portion already for collateral on his loans. And now they can't possibly buy him out. They need money too." I was talking too fast, trying not to cry. "And Lucy doesn't care about Cashiers. It's more important that they keep the Columbia house."

If they sold the Columbia house, I would not bat an eyelash. I felt no attachment to the city. Or, frankly, to South Carolina or the fickle South Carolinians. The family would spend their lives fighting the war over and over, but my life was here with William. Baltimore was my home.

Oh, but the Lodge, Cashiers Valley, was my haven.

"Caroline." His voice was very gentle. "They can't sell it. It isn't fair to you when you love it so."

"It isn't fair of me to insist they hold onto it."

"Well, then, we'll buy out their shares."

"Oh, pish-tosh. Be serious."

"Why not?" He frowned. "Would they resent it? If I were to offer?"

"You can't buy out the whole place yourself. It'll cost a fortune."

"I doubt a 'fortune.' And we have savings."

And then I knew what he was doing. What he was offering. I shook my head.

"That is for this house. Our home. We can't spend it on a summer place. That's impractical. We have to live in Baltimore and we both hate the Madison Avenue house."

"I think you should stop arguing with me. I'm not going to let them sell the Lodge to strangers. I'm fond of the place too."

He was so dear. And it would break my heart to lose Cashiers. To strangers.

"I think we shouldn't make any decision right now."

"I'll talk to Dick. Maybe he can finagle a loan. He's good at that sort of thing."

That was even more impractical. But I couldn't think straight. I couldn't let William buy me the Lodge and I was afraid I might. After all, he needed the refuge too.

"Is he?" I said skeptically. "I thought he was something of the family black sheep."

"Dick? No." He scowled. "Gray sheep, perhaps." Then his countenance softened. "No, Dick's all right." He chuckled a little. "Do you know, we were devoted little fellows, but always disagreeing, sometimes to blows. I was an awful bully. It exasperated my mother."

"Fighting is what little boys do."

"Not Halsteds. So she enrolled us in two different schools. With our minders, we would start out and walk to a point mid-way between them, our time together painfully brief, and then part with bitter tears."

I smiled despite my troubled state, appreciating William's effort to soothe me. He didn't often speak of his youth.

"Your mother sounds very clever."

"Oh yes. It brought out all my filial instincts. Dick was only about five and a tiny child. He would look so lost. I was eight, and thought myself quite something. I would urge him to run along, though honestly, my little heart was breaking."

"William! How precious."

"It gets worse. Dick's chin would quiver and his face would turn red. And he'd demand, 'You first.'"

William's voice turned strangely husky. He looked away, as if the memory was a sad one. Perhaps his childhood held secret hurts. Gently, I pressed him. "Was he challenging you to be the braver? Or testing to see if you would abandon him?"

"I never knew." Then, abruptly, his mouth hardened and he stood straighter. "Oh, challenging me, I'm sure. Mother was always telling me to set an example."

The confiding moment was over. I knew better than to dig for more.

"Can you come home for lunch? Betty is making something. Or are you due back?"

"I'll walk back with you. Then I should go do my part in the dispensary."

We didn't talk much on the way back to the house. It appeared even more ill-proportioned in contrast to twelve-o-one. William unlocked the door. We went in and were faced with the cramped entry hall with its dark walls and chipped wood molding. There was an ugly short bench sticking out from the wall for setting packages or umbrellas upon that William always bumped his shin against. I glanced automatically at the foyer table with its bowl for calling cards and mail. It held a telegram.

"That must have come while we were out."

William plucked it out of the bowl. "From Sam."

"Reverend Bushnell?"

"No. Van der Poel. Minnie and Sam in New York."

He opened it. Read it. Then he sat heavily on the bench. His face had gone pale.

"William?"

"My father." He turned his face away and choked. I sat beside him. He started to weep, which I had never seen him do. I put my arms around him and held him.

William and his father had not gotten along. Which I supposed made it all that much worse.

The funeral was horrible, even as funerals went. It seemed the elder Mr. Halsted must have outlived most of his friends—that was the charitable interpretation.

William and I stayed with the Van der Poels. Their New York mansion eclipsed the house on Eutaw Place. I got lost in it more than once. We were put in a single bedroom, which would have been nice except for how loudly William snored. Separate floors sounded more and more attractive.

After the funeral dinner, the others all dispersed to their homes. William and Sam went into the billiard room to play, smoke cigars, and drink brandy. I went with Minnie into the ladies' parlor so that Minnie could exclaim three times during the course of one conversation what a shame it was that there was no new little William to carry on the name. Loud bursts of laughter and ill-defined shouts came from the billiard room. I was miserable. But poor Minnie must have been more so, mourning her father and left to entertain her sister-in-law.

The following day, I visited my New York family so the Halsted siblings could spend time alone together before William returned to Baltimore. He fetched me at Aunt Lu's and dined with a passel of Baxters. He was more at home with them than he was with Hamptons. They were more his kind of people. How different William and I were.

We took an overnight train back. The first-class cabin was not glamorous, but it was plush enough. There were two narrow beds, one above the other; still, William scrunched into mine.

"Just roll me out if I snore," he said, teasing me as he unbuttoned my nightgown.

"You mean when you snore?"

He kissed me. "Thank you for being there with me, Caroline. It would have been unbearable without you."

"Oh, William." How could I not have been there?

We didn't speak for a very good long while. Not real speech.

He didn't leave my bed right away, but lit his cigarette and stayed.

"I spoke to Dick."

"The loan?"

"No." He seemed pensive, then blurted, "I thought my father's money went with the business. I didn't think there was anything left to dole out, but…well, he took care of himself when the company went under."

"Do you realize I have no idea what you're talking about?"

"It doesn't matter." He took a drag, then looked around for a place to flick his ashes. He gave the cigarette a little toss into our sink. "Caroline, you'll probably be horrified but we can afford twelve-o-one and the Lodge, quite easily."

"Horrified?"

"That I'd be happy about that just now."

"Hmmm." I didn't dare tell him I was ecstatic. I was horrified at myself. "It doesn't mean you aren't grieving."

"No." He sighed, long and heavy. "No." He settled back down in the bed and closed his eyes, then murmured, "Put me out when I snore."

"I will," I said, but I wouldn't.

44

1896, May

Baltimore, Maryland

JOHNS HOPKINS HOSPITAL

The trustees of the Johns Hopkins Hospital at a meeting yesterday at the hospital appointed Drs. E. D. Clark, R. E. Garrett and H. W. Cushing as assistant resident surgeons and Drs. L. E. Livingood and Norman Gwyun as assistant resident physicians.

Dr. W. S. Halsted, surgeon in charge of the hospital, will sail Thursday from New York for a six weeks' trip through Europe. He will attend the meeting of the German Surgical Society and will read a paper before the society on "Advanced Surgery."

—*The Baltimore Sun*, Baltimore, Maryland, Wednesday, May 13, 1896

I found William in the dining room, hot iron in hand, pressing the table linen. On the table. The candlesticks and floral centerpiece had been removed to the sideboard.

"What on earth are you doing?"

He glanced up. "There were wrinkles. I told Betty the cloth should be ironed *in situ*."

"I hope you didn't say it like that."

Betty already thought William was a lunatic after he'd insisted that she wipe all the glasses and silver a second time to be sure there were no smudges. We didn't entertain often, but when we did, William showed the same persnickety attention to detail that he did in the operating room. In the O.R., it was an admirable trait. In the dining room, it was strange.

"A wrinkled table linen is simply shoddy, Caroline. It shows a lack of consideration for one's guests."

I shook my head, knowing better than to argue. The guests were Dr. Welch, Mr. and Mrs. James, the Gilmans, and Dr. Bloodgood. I could not imagine any of them caring about microscopic wrinkles in the tablecloth. Especially not with the menu William had planned. We would have several courses: oysters, caviar, terrapin, canvasback, ices, a selection of fruit and cheeses, ending with Madeira and Turkish coffee William brewed himself.

"No one is more considerate of guests than you are," I sighed.

"You look very pretty."

"Hmmm." I wore a navy-blue silk dress instead of my usual more comfortable black broadcloth. My disinterest in fashionable wear clearly perplexed him, but he never criticized. Rather, he encouraged me when I made a special effort. I grumbled, "I believe I have a rather shoddy wrinkle in my stockings."

An eyebrow flicked up. "Well, come on over here and I'll see about straightening it."

"William!" I laughed. How ridiculous he was when he tried to flirt. "You're in an awfully good mood. Are you that excited about this dinner party? Or is it going to Germany next week?"

"Germany," he said, returning to his ironing. "This dinner is only to suit Welch. He ordered me to do something besides rewrite my paper again. He's tired of hearing it."

Welch was not the only one. "They'll love it."

He shrugged, then squatted to scan the tablecloth at eye level. "I hope that boy Cushing comes to the conference. I'd like to talk to him and be sure he intends to show up in October."

"I thought he was eager for the position."

"I did too." He stood and moved the iron to a different spot. "But our letters keep crossing and he never says whether he's accepted. I'm holding the position for him until he gets back from abroad. He'd better take it." Shaking his head, he went on. "I don't know about him. His recommendations are the finest I've ever received. Richardson says he has superb hands."

"But?"

"But he's an arrogant cuss. He seemed disappointed that the position was assistant resident. Seemed to think he should jump right into resident surgeon. Bloodgood is going to have to watch his behind."

"Don't say things like that; you'll make them rivals."

William sniffed. "They're surgeons. I don't have to say anything. If Cushing is as handy as he thinks he is, he'll butt Bloodgood aside. Joe is a smart man, but his eyes and his brain work better than his fingers." He chewed his lip for a moment. "I'll have to think about Joe. He is awfully bright."

"And you're fond of him."

"Yes, I suppose I am. He takes direction. Cushing may be difficult. I've seen what they call asepsis at Mass General. They believe if they cut fast enough, they can outrun the bacteria."

"If he's any good, he'll learn. William, put that iron away and go get dressed. That linen cannot get any smoother."

He set the iron on the sideboard and started moving the candlesticks back.

"Caroline, are you certain you don't mind me going to Lyon after the conference instead of coming straight to High Hampton?"

High Hampton. He bought the Lodge and 450 acres and promptly gave it a lofty name. But, oh, how dear he was. He suggested they knock down some of the falling-down cabins in the back and build a decent cottage for themselves so that they wouldn't be kicking the aunties out of their home.

"I truly don't mind. Go to Lyon and study your French." He was fluent in German but his French was sadly lacking. He must need the break. He seemed more eager for his two weeks away from all things surgical than he was for the conference.

"Your sister won't think I'm avoiding her?"

Lucy would. The aunties too. Because he was. I was going to have a houseful all summer. Even Uncle Wade was likely to show his face for a week or so. Things sometimes got strained between William and my family: uncomfortably polite.

"You did your Hampton duty in January."

In January, Lucy married John Haskell, cousin Sally's widower. Sally was ten years dead and Lucy had practically raised the children. I suspected she married John for their sakes more than for her own.

"The more Hampton weddings I go to, the more I appreciate how well you handled ours," William said. "How did we escape having four hundred Confederates in their cups singing Dixie?"

"I married a Halsted not a Haskell."

He smiled. "I always wondered why you did. Now I know."

"Hmmm." John was one of Uncle Wade's closest friends and most ardent supporters, but he was too old for Lucy. He shouldn't have waited ten years to ask her. "I really don't understand why Lucy didn't marry sooner. She should have had her pick of Southern gentlemen. Daisy too! It makes no sense."

William gave me an odd look, then shrugged. "I'm just glad no Southern gentleman discovered you."

Because he was in such sweet humor I dared ask, "Are you sure you don't mind that I'm going to North Carolina for the whole summer instead of coming with you?"

"I don't mind." He avoided my eyes. He did mind. Or he maybe he was pleased to have time alone with his surgeon friends and didn't want me to know. He looked a bit guilty. "I'll miss you, naturally, but I know there is a lot you want to accomplish at High Hampton."

"Well, yes, but I won't make any major changes without clearing them with you."

"Oh good Lord, please don't ask me. I don't know anything about farm management."

I'd hinted that I wanted to get a few chickens. Maybe a cow. And to grow some things besides flowers. And he hadn't pooh-poohed me.

"I don't either." Not yet, but I'd learn. "And it will cost—"

"Spend what you need to spend. Caroline, make it into what you want it to be. That's why we bought it."

That was why he bought it for me. Without even knowing it, William made my dreams come true.

The Lodge was mine. *High Hampton.* Well, I'd make it his haven too.

45

1896, SEPTEMBER

Baltimore, Maryland

No remedy is so strongly indicated in surgical shock and in collapse as strychnine, but only in very large doses. According to Hare, "not less than 1-20 of a grain should be employed, hypodermically, every half hour."

—*A Therapeutic Guide to Alkaloidal-Dosimetric Medication* by John M. Shaller, Chicago: W.C. Abbott, 1895. p.176.

Within the last few years strychnine has been used somewhat frequently for the purposes both of suicide and homicide...we would remark that while the symptoms of strychnine poisoning are well known, they vary very much according to the surrounding circumstances. When the dose has been large the tetanic spasms will be well marked, but when a minimum fatal dose has been given these will be modified into a species of convulsions which may be regarded as unconnected with the poison...

—"Poisoning by Strychnine," *The Lancet,* Vol 1(3590): p.1375, 1892.

❧

One of Halsted's strictest surgical rules was that one should never violate the integrity of a cancer or one risked spreading it. With careful surgery, complete removal of a carcinoma was not only possible, but critical. He preached this again and again. His residents understood. Other surgeons, skeptical at first, were beginning to accept that disfigurement was preferable to death for most patients; yet few were able to perform the necessary surgery without seeing it done.

Dr. Marsden had come all the way from Cleveland to observe the Hopkins' method for complete mastectomy, which included removal not only of the entire breast but also the underlying pectoral muscles and lymph nodes in the axilla. Marsden brought along his O.R. nurse, so there were more people in the room than necessary, but that was often the case and Halsted's focus was narrow enough to ignore a crowd. Dr. Marsden had the good sense to keep his hands behind his back, but also, annoyingly, leaned in frequently for a better look. The man finally settled into a position that did not obscure Halsted's field, which was fortunate, because the tumor was quite vascular and needed careful attention.

Bloodgood had become proficient at recognizing where best to retract and at placing arterial clamps when and where they were needed. Jim Mitchell, the male nurse Finney had found, was also excellent. The team completed entire cases together scarcely exchanging a word. Marsden had been too chatty the first hour, but Halsted's short answers eventually silenced him. For the next few hours, the room was so quiet they could hear one another breathe.

Halsted did not operate "by the clock." An operation took as long as it took. But he was nearly done now. He raised his head and stretched his neck side to side.

"Dr. Marsden," he said quietly.

"Hmm, yes?" He cleared his throat, probably waking up.

"Would you mind taking a step to the left? You've been standing on my foot for the past half hour."

Marsden jumped. Halsted thought he saw a smirk on Bloodgood's face and Cutler, the assistant resident administering the anesthesia, snorted a laugh.

Ignoring Marsden's embarrassed apology, Halsted lifted the breast to the instrument table and set it into a pan. Sutures of various lengths dangled from several aspects of the tissue where he'd felt the tumor might come close to the margin. Bloodgood would sample those areas particularly well for microscopic work, looking for malignant cells that would bode ill for the patient's recovery. Then Halsted dressed the wound as meticulously as he had caused it.

"All right, then," he said, finally straightening. "Cutler, take the patient back to the ward. I'll be up to see how she's doing after Bloodgood and I take the specimen to pathology." And after he smoked a cigarette or two. "Dr. Marsden, would you like to accompany us? Have you any further questions?"

"To pathology?"

He sounded bewildered. As if pathology was a foreign country that one need never trouble to visit. Halsted said nothing.

"No, no," Marsden said, shaking his head. "This was all a lot to absorb. I'm afraid any questions right now would simply be a jumble. But thank you. This was extremely instructive."

Halsted nodded. "Goodbye, then." He displayed his bloodstained fingers. "I won't shake your hand."

Marsden smiled. "Not necessary. Thank you. Goodbye."

He signaled to his nurse and they ducked from the room.

"What do you think, Bloodgood?"

"I suspect Dr. Marsden has wasted his time today."

Halsted harumphed. "Cutler, is she waking?"

"Not yet."

"Good. It's a rough ride back to the ward. Give her back to Cushing and tell him to—"

"*Tell* Cushing?" Cutler's lip curled.

Harvey Cushing had not been at Hopkins a week, and he was already getting under people's skin. Apparently, every other utterance from the young man's mouth included the words "at the Mass General." But Cushing had admitted this patient and worked her up. He would be caring for her post-operatively. He had made his displeasure at being excluded from the operation very plain. Halsted made it equally plain that junior residents were not allowed in the O.R. for the first two months. He'd said that in front of Bloodgood, who had wisely refrained from commenting. It was a rule Halsted made up on the spot. Scowling, he recognized that if he set an example of hazing poor Cushing, the young surgeons would follow.

"Tell him I'll be up shortly." He turned. "Bloodgood?"

Joe was at the sink, lathering his hands. "Yes, sir?"

Halsted joined him. "Take the specimen over. I need a cigarette." He needed more than that. He had to head home soon. His gut was starting to cramp.

❧

No more than twenty minutes later, Halsted sauntered into the surgical ward. Then balked. To his alarm, his patient lay in her bed in a Trendelenburg position—supine, at a twenty-degree slant, feet elevated above the head. "What is the matter?" he asked, hurrying forward.

"Dr. Halsted." Cushing greeted him with a note of impatience in his voice. "I'm ready to carry out the usual procedure but Cutler"—he jerked his head dismissively toward his colleague—"told me to wait for you."

The usual procedure? For hypotensive shock. Excepting those who entered Halsted's O.R. emergently, already hemorrhaging, no patient ever emerged from his O.R. in shock.

"Is she ill?" he asked.

"She hasn't woken. And you were in there for over four hours! A breast never takes more than thirty minutes at the Mass General."

And there it was. He heard Cutler cough. Cushing turned his head, nettled, chary. Halsted suspected the others were starting to have a little fun with this. Welch would say such behavior should be nipped in the bud. Osler would cough along, delightedly.

"She will wake as the anesthesia wears off. It would be unusual for her to be ill. Let's examine her."

He stepped to the bedside, checked his timepiece, and counted. "Respiration is fifteen. Take her pulse."

Cushing did. "Eighty."

"Does she look pallid? Is her skin cold?"

Cushing shook his head.

Halsted noticed a hypodermic on her bedside table. "What is in that syringe?"

"Strychnine. It will do her good." The assurance was obviously rote.

"What do you think strychnine will do for the patient?" He asked the question calmly, curious how Cushing would respond. Some physicians used it as a stimulant. Swore by it. He suspected physicians were responsible for more poisoning than jilted lovers and inheritance grubbers combined.

Halsted waited until Cushing confessed, "I don't know."

An honest answer.

"Read up on it. If your reading convinces you that strychnine is good for your patients, by all means, use it."

Cushing nodded, but his mouth looked tight.

Halsted said, "Never do anything to a patient unless you know why you are doing it."

"Even if you tell me to do it?" The boy was sharp. Not easily cowed.

Halsted's skin was starting to prickle; it was past time for his dose. He had to go before he broke out in a sweat. He dared not risk the residents starting to notice he was ill. The last thing he needed was a smart, ruthlessly ambitious young surgeon deducing why.

He rolled his eyes and flexed his cowing muscle.

"Lay her flat. *Because* she is not in shock. Trendelenburg may increase her intra-cranial pressure and make her head hurt. Patients forced to stand on their heads also complain more of nausea—in my experience. If, at some future point, you would like to make a more careful study of this, be my guest. I would recommend testing the hypothesis on patients with empty stomachs who don't have abdominal or thoracic sutures likely to tear."

"Yes, sir," Cushing said, a little mulishly.

He slid a glance at Cutler, who looked smug. "Go have lunch." He added pointedly, "*Because* you must be starving."

He looked back at Cushing. "*If* things here are under control, I'm going home."

The young man nodded, red-faced. Good. He was cowed. For now.

46

1897, February

Baltimore, Maryland

Dr. Richard J. Hall, a son of the Rev. Dr. John Hall of the Fifth Avenue Presbyterian Church, died recently of appendicitis at Santa Barbara, Cal. Dr. Hall was forty-one years of age, and was graduated from Princeton College in 1875, and in 1878 from the College of Physicians and Surgeons. After pursuing his professional studies for a time in Vienna, he returned to New York, where he received an appointment to the attending staff of the Presbyterian Hospital, and soon won an enviable reputation as a surgeon of unusual ability. Some years ago, on account of the development of pulmonary trouble, he was obliged to remove to Santa Barbara. As a result of his residence in a more genial climate his health gradually became reestablished, and he was after a time enabled to resume the practice of his profession. He leaves a wife and two young daughters.

—*Boston Medical and Surgical Journal,* Vol. CXXXVI, No. 5, p. 120, February 4, 1897.

Santa Barbara, Sept 2, 1895
My dear Halsted,
It is now quite a long time since I received a long letter from you and a very kind one. I am not sure that I ever answered it for at that time I was only pulling myself together after a long period of misery, the causes of which I do not need to describe. During the last three years I have been slowly working my way into a fairly good surgical practice... Of course, neither my field for work nor my scientific opportunities can ever compare with yours which seem to me the most enviable of any in the United States but probably that is as it should be, for when we worked together in old times I may have thought that in information and perhaps in judgment and diagnostic skill I could pretty nearly equal

you, I always recognized in you an originality which I do not find in any other American surgeon…

—Dr. Richard J. Hall, Santa Barbara, California to Dr. William Stewart Halsted, Baltimore, Maryland

ᔕ

Halsted set the journal down. He'd heard about Hall's death from Welch, who'd heard it from Hartley. Seeing it in print made it all that more real.

From a folder in his file cabinet, he pulled a letter he received two years earlier and tortured himself by reading it through once more. He did send Hall another letter—not right away, but he had written again. He did not allude to the misery they shared. Perhaps he should have. He didn't hear back.

Appendicitis. Ironic. Back in their Roosevelt days, Hall had performed the first successful appendectomy in the United States. He'd been rather jealous of Hall for that.

Hall would have been a phenomenal academic surgeon: scientific-minded and gifted. Gutsy. Too gutsy. They were all too gutsy. A few of the medical students who had helped them dropped out of the program. One died. An accident, so it was said. Halsted wasn't so sure.

He put his head in his hands and rubbed his temples. He hoped it was appendicitis that had taken Hall and not a recurrence of his "pulmonary trouble."

He blamed himself. He shouldn't. They had not known the dangers. They'd been young and enthusiastic and foolish…rushing in where angels feared to tread.

Hall said he was happy. A wife and two little girls. How sad that he'd not been granted more time to enjoy them. At least he'd had a brief while.

Halsted was, perhaps, still jealous. He'd told Caroline he wasn't ready. He couldn't be a father and a morphiomaniac. He'd thought…well, he was right in that, but thought he'd choose fatherhood. It seemed he chose the drug—not even the drug he wanted to choose. His wife was so very understanding. She never reproached him, even though, if she was waiting, it could well be too late.

He should stop. He was comfortably down to two grains. Hardly a noticeable amount, yet if he missed a dose, he noticed. He was supposed to meet Welch and Major Venable at the Maryland Club tonight.

He hadn't been there in a while, and Caroline told him that yes, he should go. She thought the company of close friends would bolster him and, Lord knew, he needed bolstering. But he couldn't show them that. He would have to be pleasant and sociable. Hiding what he felt. So.

He took off his jacket and rolled up his sleeve, double-checked the latch on the door to his study, then unlocked his desk drawer for his morphine and syringe. Morphine would not cure the ache; it simply kept him from caring that he hurt.

He drew up his dose. Then more. Doubling, tripling. How much would it take? To stop this pain once and for all? The entire vial? He could hear Hall's laughing voice. *Fire when ready. Double the dose. No, quadruple the dose. I want this to work.*

He stared at the syringe, aching with regret. With loss.

Then he set it down and took a deep breath. *Caroline.* Another breath. He wouldn't do that to Caroline.

He picked the syringe up and pressed the plunger, spilling the drug onto his desk blotter, until only half a grain's worth remained. He injected that. Then leaned back in his chair and closed his eyes.

47

1898, April

New Orleans, Louisiana

A CLINICAL AND HISTOLOGICAL STUDY OF CERTAIN ADENOCARCINOMATA OF THE BREAST

When our secretary, Dr. Burrell, graciously urged me to introduce the subject of breast cancer for discussion at this meeting, and to tell you something of the results of our experience in the treatment of this disease, it seemed to me that it would be a very simple matter, for our cases have been many and our interest in them great… For the physician, as well as for the layman, a cancer of the breast is a cancer of the breast, and efforts to classify these tumors have not been very successful. But the riches of our cancer storehouse embarrass me, and I prefer in the time allotted to ask your attention to the description of one or two quite rare but definite varieties of breast cancer which we have encountered with sufficient frequency to enable us to recognize them clinically as well as histologically…

—Dr. William S. Halsted, presented before the American Surgical Association, New Orleans, LA, April 21, 1898

After taking questions and comments, Halsted closed with an impassioned speech he had not planned: "I wish it were possible to enlighten the people, as well as the physicians in all parts of this country, on the subject of breast cancer, and make them realize how important it is that the operation should be done as soon as the tumor is discoverable—there are so many physicians who still consider operation for cancer useless, and some who believe that they can dissipate the new growth by nostrums. Patients frequently come to us of their own accord against the will of the doctor."

The applause that erupted embarrassed him, but gratified him all the same.

Caroline had been right, yet again. She said his reticence was silly, that he would warm to the subject as soon as he began to speak. The topic was important and his work—his and Bloodgood's—should be shared. He would have brought Bloodgood along, but Cushing was all too willing to step up and take over. He'd promoted Cushing to chief resident ahead of others who'd been there longer—not winning the young man any friends—because he deserved it. He was almost as good as he believed himself to be. But he also kept Bloodgood on. The two shared the spot: Bloodgood goodnaturedly and Cushing grudgingly. The situation was less than ideal.

Never mind that. It was a good presentation. Halsted believed he had even handled the responses well. He graciously thanked the providers of irrelevant comments and answered inane questions without evident condescension; Welch would have applauded him. And there had been intelligent comments. He would have to speak later with that local surgeon who reported success with his own variation on complete mastectomy. He wanted details.

But not now. He was exhausted. He earned the hour or two to recuperate in his room rather than socializing at the luncheon. He had to conserve himself for the dinner banquet.

He ran the gauntlet of physicians wanting one more word: a question about his presentation, a referral of a patient to Johns Hopkins Hospital, a request for copies of the drawings he'd passed around. One man buttonholed him over a son who sought a position with Osler. He was excessively polite to them all, even that last.

Finally, he emerged onto the street and found a hansom.

"Here for that medical conference?" the driver asked as Halsted named his hotel.

"Surgical. Yes."

The man leaned down and handed him a card. *Willie V. Piazza. 317 N. Basin Street.*

"What is this?"

The driver winked. Winked! "The Countess. Very cultured. Private entrance."

Good Lord. Halsted shoved back the card as if it had bit him. "No."

"I can tour you through Storytown if you'd like a look around." He pointed up the road. "It's right up Canal Street. I know all the—"

"I'm not interested."

He threw open the door and climbed into the hansom, feeling the heat of his embarrassment spread through his face and neck. He'd heard colleagues murmuring about Storytown. Some city leader had hit upon the bright idea of confining all brothels and bawds to a few city blocks. Some of the physicians apparently intended to have a look—as tourists, mind you—not to partake. No doubt there was a good deal of partaking going on.

That particular tourist attraction aside, New Orleans was a fascinating city with much to recommend it: the architecture, the food, the medical college. He had tried to get Caroline to come with him. She would be leaving for Cashiers in two weeks and he would not be able to leave Baltimore to join her until early June. He thought this would be a pleasant time together.

She said no. He would spend his days in conference and his evenings rubbing shoulders and exchanging war stories with his colleagues. Wives were an encumbrance at medical meetings. Caroline was never an encumbrance. If he made her feel so, that was his fault.

He watched the cityscape roll by. It was not a long distance to the hotel. He should have walked it to better dispel his restlessness.

He had packed cocaine, hidden, the last thing tucked in between his socks where Caroline would have no chance of seeing it, even when she slipped one of her little notes into the bag. He'd found the note wrapped around his comb, an encouragement with a little bit of silliness to make him smile, written in her abysmal handwriting as effectively secretive as a code.

If she had come with him, he would not have packed the cocaine, thirty minims of a four percent solution. He'd made the dilution, deciding on injection even while pretending his willpower would prevail. He hadn't used it. His justification for bringing it, that he might be seized with stage fright like poor Tom Sawyer, was absurd. He was experienced at giving lectures and presentations. He hadn't truly thought he'd go knock-kneed and mute.

The carriage rolled to a stop. The driver hopped down and opened his door. As Halsted paid, the man tried once more. "The French House is a little different if you like that sort of thing."

He tried not to shudder, wondering what that sort of thing might be. The only reply he could make was to shake his head and walk away. He would return to Tulane on foot to avoid another such encounter.

The hotel lobby was overdone in the New Orleans style. His wife would have fainted to see so much scarlet upholstery and gilt edging. No, she would have squeezed his hand and warned him not to faint.

He climbed the stairs, walked down the red-carpeted corridor lined by mirrors and portraits of French kings, until he reached his door. His hand shook as he pulled his key from his pocket.

There was never any real doubt. For two days, he had been giving himself plaudits for his restraint, but he had merely been letting the anticipation build. It had been in the back of his mind since the train ride—no, since he'd received the invitation from Dr. Burrell.

Caroline should have come.

He closed the door behind him and turned the key from the inside. His small traveling case was in the wardrobe. He pulled it out and set it on the bed. It had been so long…he would only need half. Another lie. The truth was half now, half later.

He drew fifteen minims into the hypodermic, breathing rapidly, pulse racing before he even injected the drug. But oh, to have a few hours relief from the hunger.

This was the last time. Truly. The last time.

Friday, the third day of the conference, was the most satisfying. Having done his part, he was free to listen to the other presentations, comment when something struck him, ask questions, and hobnob with like-minded men at luncheon. He would have one more day of this on Saturday. However, there was the closing banquet Saturday night and Sunday's breakfast before the train back to Baltimore. Enough was enough. He begged off from dinner, pleading a headache.

Of course, cocaine had gotten him through the day, reliably, in a way that morphine simply could not. He knew the dangers of overindulging but in limited, controlled amounts, cocaine served better. It returned him to himself.

He should have brought another fifteen minims for tomorrow. Or thirty—for tonight and tomorrow. The craving would be unpleasant tonight, even with morphine to calm him. One more day's worth would not have made the suffering worse, and he would have had one more day of feeling alive.

It was a perfect spring evening, so he walked from the college lecture hall toward the hotel. New Orleans had a different odor than Baltimore. The fresh air here was more heavily perfumed, a falsely flowered smell with the occasional whiff of cannabis.

It felt good to stretch his legs after long days of sitting, so he continued along Canal Street past his hotel. He must have a look at Storytown. It was New Orleans, after all. He was curious to see the houses, which were supposed to be remarkably ornate. No doubt he would be able to locate a druggist in the vicinity who would not look too closely at his scribbled prescription.

He strolled along Canal, smoking one cigarette after another, until he reached Basin Street and turned. Bawds solicited him from doorways as he passed. Some were rather pretty in a tawdry way, but the thought of the greasy rooms beyond the doors put him off. Not that he would have considered it even if the rooms were clean.

A shoeshine boy with a dirty rag appeared from nowhere to take a swipe at his foot. Halsted almost tripped over him. Poor child. The boy tried to hand him a card. "Three new octoroons at Florence Mantley's. Number 215."

"No, thank…" He paused. "I'm looking for a druggist's."

"Yeah, I can give you direction." He held out his hand. Halsted gave him two dimes. "Left on Iberville. Right on Franklin. Can I have one of them cigarettes too?"

Halsted pulled the pack from his pocket and put one in the boy's hand. How old could he be? Ten? Twelve?

"If you go to Miss Mantley's, show my card," the child said, trying once again to press it on him. How appalling. He must get some sort of commission for directing men to this Miss Mantley's house. Halsted took the card and stuck it in his pocket before moving on. He would have to remember to throw it away back at the hotel. He'd never be able to explain this to Caroline.

The district was an abominable mix of tacky elegance and disease-ridden slum. He had never seen so many prostitutes plying their trade in such close quarters. And it was not yet night.

The pharmacy belonged to the surroundings. Halsted tried not to touch anything as he entered the building. The transaction was even easier than he'd hoped. The druggist did not ask for a prescription, just handed over the requested amount.

After leaving the store, he didn't bother with the pretense of taking it back to his hotel, but rather stepped into a secluded doorway. He used his pocketknife to scoop out a small mound and carefully lifted it to his nostril. He tucked the rest back inside his vest.

Then he walked back to Basin Street. He would like to see the house of "The Countess." Perhaps he'd even step inside. Caroline would never know.

He felt a flash of resentment. She should have come with him. They could have sneaked out to one of the music halls and gone dancing. She would have enjoyed that. In this anonymous setting, so might he have. And he could have taken *her* back to the hotel to bed.

He reached into his pocket, considering, momentarily, whether to have another snort, but pulled out his cigarettes instead. He lit one and puffed, feeling the effects of the cocaine spread throughout his whole body.

Caroline was more relaxed, more receptive in the mountain hideaway. So was he, for that matter. In Baltimore, even though she didn't turn him away, he felt as though he were imposing upon her if he trooped up the stairs to the third floor after dinner. He wished she would…invite him once in a while.

A whore in a bright red wig grabbed his elbow. "Come inside, sweetheart. Five minutes. One dollar."

He recoiled, shaking his head and wrenching his arm free. She laughed at him, showing cracked, crooked teeth.

"Too rich for your blood? Two minutes for two bits."

He walked quickly away. The hansom driver had said Willie Piazza was cultured. What did that mean in a place like this?

He passed by the French House. Females in little-to-no clothing leaned from the balcony advertising "that sort of thing" with their thumbs and their mouths. His blood stirred even as he gave the house a wide berth. He had decided upon 317 N. Basin for its thin veneer of supposed culture. He suspected that meant expensive but gaudy. Too many mirrors. Too many lamps. Too much glitter. Shapely women in imitation fancy dress that could be easily shed.

He had cocaine to last him the night and knew where to get more. He'd see what the countess had to offer. And then, later, the French House. Why not? As long as he made it back for the conference in the morning, no one would be the wiser. If he was going to reproach himself for New Orleans, he would enjoy himself first.

48

1898, April

Baltimore, Maryland

My dear little Katie,

I am writing with one of the professor's quill pens! Poor Mrs. Halsted is lying in the next room at the house. She was run away with this morning while driving in the park and is very badly hurt but I guess will pull through.

I can't stand these pens and the blotters are worse… I wish you were here. I think you would make a better nurse than the three women here…Mrs. H. is a game soldier. The professor is away but a Special is bringing him across the continent fast enough. It's been a pretty exciting day both at the hospital and here. It seems a year long with some stories we read all cramped into one day. I just had my lunch at 5 p.m. with a cup of the delicious coffee I've told you about and some bread and white unsalted butter. All very Halstedian. What a rambling letter. You will think I am crazy but this is the first time I have had in which to think and I find that I've been somewhat keyed up. Mrs. H. is coming out of anaesthesia and my duties seem chiefly to see sympathizing friends at the door—

—Dr. Harvey Cushing, Surgery Resident at Johns Hopkins Hospital to his fiancée, Miss Kate Crowley, Saturday, April 23, 1898, 5:00 p.m.

❧

Halsted had lost track of time since receiving Finney's telegram:

TAKING MRS. HALSTED TO SURGERY BAD RIDING ACCIDENT.

He left the surgical conference at once, shaking so badly a couple of the attendees chased after him to see what was wrong. One of them, he couldn't remember who, had come with him back to the hotel while he told the management to have his things sent home. Another made all the arrangements with the railway. He insisted, of course, that they needn't leave the meeting, that he could take care of it himself. Thank God they hadn't listened.

The train ride, swift as it was—they'd "cleared the tracks"—had been interminable, even self-sedated with morphine. He kept waking in starts, thinking he'd received a follow-up from Finney. Daytime nightmares.

Why had he gone to New Orleans? *Why?* Why did he ever leave her side? And why did he ever buy her that damn dogcart?

An hour outside of Baltimore, he injected another dose so that he would not break down in front of whomever had drawn the short straw to pick him up at the station. He hoped it would be Finney and not Cushing or Osler. He was not in the mood for Cushing's need for head-patting. Osler would say the right things but he would expect confidences in return and he was not about to weep on the good doctor's shoulder. Welch had chosen a terrible time to go out of town.

And so had he. *Lord, let her be all right and I will never go to another conference.* No, lying to God was about the worst thing he could do right now. If there was a God, He knew by now William Halsted never kept his side of the bargain. A gracious God. Ha!

The train finally reached the Charles Street Union Station. Halsted saw Finney waiting on the platform, looking grim. He tried to keep his gait steady but he felt as if he was in one of those dreams where one walked through air as dense as water. He could barely make his limbs move. Finney came to him.

"Is she dead?"

"No!" Finney's gray face did not reassure. He gripped Halsted's arm, then said again, "No." He took from Halsted the small traveling case he'd snatched up from the hotel to take on the train—necessities: a journal he hadn't even tried to read, morphine, cigarettes, and, if he remembered aright, he'd reflexively thrown in his tooth powder. "I have a carriage waiting. She'll recover, Halsted."

"Thank God." His eyes filled with tears and Finney looked away while he wiped them. He cleared his throat. "What do I need to know?"

"Broken ribs. Fractured pelvis. All closed injuries but we had to evacuate a hematoma. A lot of facial and shoulder bruising. Mild concussion—which she denies."

He managed a "ha," then asked hesitantly, "You operated?"

Finney nodded.

"Thank you."

"Cushing assisted." Finney waited a beat and then said, "Sorry."

Halsted let out a long breath. "Don't be. I could not have wished for a better team."

They climbed into a hired carriage waiting on the sloping driveway in front of the station. Finney gave the direction. They sat across from one another, both looking down at their hands.

"She wanted us to wait for you."

"You were right not to. I couldn't have operated on Caroline." He wouldn't dare. He now understood McBride's caveats about treating loved ones. "Do you know what happened? How?"

"Not in detail. She was riding in the park alone with the dogs. Oh, before I forget. As we were etherizing her, she said, 'Tell Dr. Halsted the dogs are fine.'"

"Pssht."

"That was a great relief to her. Something spooked her horse and it ran away with her. She was very embarrassed by that—that she was unable to bring him back under control."

"Naturally." He couldn't stop shaking his head.

"Apparently the dogs had sense enough to jump from the cart before it overturned." He started to laugh, but stopped himself, ducked his head, and said, "Sorry. I'm not poking fun. We are all a bit overwrought. Cushing needs a dose of chloral hydrate, I think."

Halsted grimaced a smile. He could see the young man bursting with his own self-importance.

"Mrs. Halsted would not let us take her away until someone chased the dogs down and promised to bring them home."

"With broken ribs and a fractured pelvis?"

Finney nodded. "She is also resisting morphine. Says she's not in that much pain."

"Well, that's Mrs. Halsted," he said, and shook his head again.

"We gave her some while she was under ether, but it'll wear off and she'll feel it."

"I will ask you to attend to her. She'll behave better for you than for me."

Finney nodded again, and they said nothing more until they reached 1201 Eutaw Place.

"Go on," Finney said. "I'll get this."

Halsted raced inside while his colleague paid the fare and collected his valise, cane, and gloves. Cushing opened the door.

"Professor!" he exclaimed, as startled as if Halsted had arrived at the young surgeon's own house.

"Don't call me that," he said for the hundredth time, pushing past. He picked up the sarcastic moniker from the medical students because his lectures went over their heads. It didn't matter if Cushing used the term differently. Halsted was not the professor. "Where is she?"

"Second floor."

Good. They put her in his room. Not up alone on the third floor with the dogs. *Oh, Caroline.* He paused on the second step and turned. The young man looked like hell. What a mustering of forces. "Cushing?"

"Yes, sir?"

"Thank you. I would have been twice as frantic if I had not known she would be in such good hands." His voice choked as he realized how much he meant that.

Cushing colored a little and said, "It was an honor."

"All right. Go home. You've had a long day."

He took the stairs two at a time.

He did not spend much time in his bedroom. He worked, read, sometimes even slept in his study. But when he crossed the threshold and saw his wife in his bed, and her eyes opened at his footsteps, and she smiled at him crookedly, he thought he should never have cause to leave it again.

"Caroline," he murmured. "Oh, my dear."

"I'm glad you're back. I told them not to send for you—"

"How absurd of you."

"'Strong wife' theater. I knew Finney would, and I knew you would come."

He sat on the edge of her bed. One should never do that. Not with a patient whose bones had just been set. But she was not his patient.

He leaned over and kissed her, avoiding the bruised tender-appearing cheek and temple.

"I suppose you want me to buy you another dogcart."

"Oh!" Her eyes lit. A little foggily. But her pupils reacted enough that he knew the morphine was wearing off. If she suffered the lack, he was to blame. "Will you?"

"If you let me shoot that horse."

"Pish-tosh. It wasn't Mr. Davis' fault."

"Hmm. Is that a Hampton maxim?"

"Would you kiss me again?"

He did. A little more thoroughly.

She smiled. "Now will you buy me a dogcart *and* forgive Mr. Davis?"

"Oh my God, Caroline. Oh my God. Whatever you want." Tears flooded his eyes, and he laid his head against her shoulder. "I thought I'd lost you."

He felt her hand, stroking his head. So softly. As if he were the injured one. Now he understood what grace truly was.

49

1898, July

Cashiers Valley, North Carolina

High Hampton, July 4th, 1898
Dear William,
I did not intend writing you again but thought of some things that I wanted. (I can hear you swear.) Please read carefully and go about the execution of these requests with this letter before your eyes. I want the paper of Rochester's that you took down last year. It is in the large bottom drawer, left hand side, of my desk. At least, that is where I put it. I also want a little spaghetti. This is in the cupboard with the wire doors where I used to keep the milk in the large back porch or piazza. Just a little…I hope that you will be along soon… I walked to the foot of the falls to see the dam yesterday. It is a little bit of a thing not more than about 18 inches high and about 6 inches in diam. at the largest point. It seems to do the work however…The jersey is apparently a fine beast and I think if the milk were properly attended to that we would be able to make our butter.

Aff.ly

C.H.H.

P.S. Thank you for the candy. Don't send any more.

—Caroline Hampton Halsted to Dr. William S. Halsted, July 4, 1898

I missed old Uncle Jeff sorely. We had Jim for odd jobs, related to Jeff in some way I could not decipher, who was well-meaning but not at all efficient. I hired a manager, who had been doing marvelous work over the winter, but he up and quit because his wife didn't like the seclusion of the mountains. The ridiculous woman claimed she was dying of consumption. Now everything was in disarray.

William wanted me to wait this year, not come down until he could accompany me. He'd been fussily solicitous ever since my carriage accident in the spring. It was sweet at first, but quickly became tiresome. Although I was sore for quite a while, bones healed. It was only my head that still ached now and then, and I told him High Hampton would cure that. The compromise we finally reached was that I would not ride until he came—another reason I hoped he hurried.

As much as I yearned for William's arrival, I did so want to have things in hand before he got here. He'd sent his traveling trunks on down ahead and I tried to unpack them myself. What a mess. I should have left them for him, but he'd want it all aired and pressed.

The silliest thing had fallen out of his jacket pocket: a calling card with a New Orleans address. *Florence Mantley's. Number 215.* My heart seemed to shift inside my chest and I stared at the card a very long time before throwing it away.

A place-marker for whatever he'd been reading, I decided later. Of course, it was. If he was away from his blue slips of paper, he was always sticking trash in his journals. I put it out of my head.

The aunties were staying another month but said they would leave for Columbia in early August. William would be relieved to hear it. I had a few of the cabins torn down, and the new cottage was in the works but far from finished, so when the aunties were here things still felt cramped.

Our new cottage was to be comfortable but small. I didn't want anything like 1201 Eutaw. I wanted rustic and cozy. William would get his large open fireplace. And we would have one bedroom. I meant to beguile him into spending as much time at High Hampton as I could. Family could stay in the Lodge with the aunties. We could fix up one or two of the better-preserved cabins for guest cottages if William thought he would invite colleagues down. He mused about it, but I'd believe that when I saw it.

William did love the place. The tension fell from him when he arrived. He would exchange his London-tailored suits for white flannels and a silk shirt, his Derby hat for a straw boater. He brought down a telescope to study the night sky after marveling at the number of stars. Last year, he purchased an additional four hundred acres from neighbors who wanted to sell and I suspected he was looking for more.

We had plenty of room for "his" dahlias. I'd been ordering a variety of tubers for years now and seeing to their planting before he arrived.

Now he studied catalogues and gardening announcements to order distinctive cultivars on his own.

I grew vegetables too. Not enough to market, but enough to feed us with extra to give away. The jersey cow was a new acquisition that tickled me immensely. And the dam was working very well. I'd worked up plans for a mill that a local man agreed to build. Next summer I would have a chicken coop built and start my flock.

William paid the bills without seeming to notice them. If I had trouble with anyone—some of the locals didn't do business with "little ladies"—he would step in, annoyed with them but never with me. It delighted him, it seemed, to do things for me.

He rode well now, though not as one born to it. And he could drive a carriage rather beautifully, though he did poke along. He even swam JohnBell across a high creek once, or as he claimed, a raging river. Oh! I missed him.

When we wed, I was afraid I would regret leaving his operating room, that my admiration for him might dull if I stopped seeing him in his element. I feared I would miss being a part of what gave his life meaning. Instead, he had worked his way into what gave meaning to mine.

50

March, 1899

Baltimore, Maryland

For thousands of years, probably, goitre has been a familiar malady. An unsightly and frequently fatal disease, it was accepted as an inoperable affliction or dispensation of Providence in communities where it prevailed, and paraded the streets exciting the curiosity of the populace in towns where it was unusual. The sufferers sought relief from suffocation, difficulty in swallowing, failure of the heart and from a distressing disfigurement. Thus this conspicuous tumor of the neck was a perpetual challenge to the physician, and to the surgeon a stigma as well.

—W.S. Halsted, "The Operative Story of Goitre," *Johns Hopkins Hospital Report*, Baltimore, 1920, xix, 71-257

The clock hands had slipped past the quarter hour when William finally stopped grumbling about the caseload. Drs. Bloodgood and Cushing had gone abroad to attend a conference—at William's urging—and now he complained about being flooded with work, left with only one decent but relatively inexperienced assistant.

"Mitchell is a fine young man. He'll be a strong surgeon in a few years, but he's a nervy thing. Never asks for help when he needs it."

Jim Mitchell had been a medical student at Maryland for two years when Dr. Finney hired him to be William's O.R. nurse for a season. The young man idolized William and did everything for him, to the point of stocking William's brand of Bob White tobacco and Cosmolite papers in the O.R. supply room. A little cloying—*I* had never resorted to such tactics. Rather than letting him return to Maryland in the fall, William enrolled him in the first class of students at the Johns Hopkins Medical School. After graduation, William took him on as one of his residents. Dr. Mitchell had Dr. Cushing's confidence without the arrogance. I liked him very much.

"I believe what you are feeling is guilt, William. The poor young man already works twenty hours a day. Now with Joe and Harvey gone, you're asking him to work thirty."

William cleared his throat. "Well, he can handle it. But now, I do feel guilty. I haven't asked about your day. You had an auxiliary meeting, didn't you? How was it?"

The Yale Alumnae Club of Baltimore was sponsoring a play to be performed by the university's traveling theater group. The wives were doing all the work. It had to have meant something to William for him to ask me to take a hand in it, as I didn't generally have much to do with the auxiliary.

"It was lovely. I've told you how much I enjoy the other ladies. Most of them." If I enthused too much, he would think I was sugar-coating the experience. But surprisingly, I was having fun.

"Tell me."

I glanced again at the clock. It was half-past eight. Dinner was over. But I recognized this ploy. He would urge me to talk, then notice the time. Rather than retire to his study, he would suggest finishing the conversation upstairs. My upstairs. He approached it all so obliquely, it used to annoy me until I decided to consider it sweet that he could still be shy.

"Well, I learned something today from Mrs. Tilman. Apparently, you were not just involved with the theater group, you were one of the stars."

"How lowering that you assumed the opposite."

I laughed. "I wish I could have seen you perform. She said you were quite the comic actor. Of course, I said I found that hard to believe."

"You do?" He looked a little put out. He had a fine wit and was vain about it.

"Yes. I see you more as the romantic lead."

He reddened. "Good Lord. I hope you didn't say that."

"No." I smiled at his discomfiture. "Just thought it. But, William, my word! I thought you were an athlete in college. Crew. Football…"

"Yes, yes." He waved a hand. "All of that."

"When did you find time to study?"

"I didn't. I was a terrible student." My face must have registered my skepticism because he went on. "My marks were mediocre at best. If I hadn't stumbled across Gray's book on anatomy and Dalton's *Physiology* my senior year, I can't imagine what would have become of me." His eyes glinted. "Perhaps a life on the stage."

A little boldly, I made the suggestion before he did.

"Betty will want to clear the table. Why don't you come to my sitting room? I'll tell you what else I learned."

He lifted his napkin from his lap, wadded it, and set it on the table. "There's more?"

"The parties. The women."

"Ha. Parties, maybe."

"No women?"

"None worth the time to pursue. Or the risk of humiliation. Not until you."

"I'll take that as a compliment, though I think 'humiliation' reflects more on you than on me."

I stood, feeling a little flushed.

Then the telephone jangled. William scowled.

"I hate that thing. It has turned every twinge into an emergency."

I'd heard that before. After his initial enthusiasm for the device, he regretted ever having it installed. He terrorized the house staff, threatening them with dismissal if they called with "stupid questions" during his supper hour. It was not uncommon for the telephone to ring at 8:35.

A moment later, Betty stepped into the room.

"Dr. Halsted? Dr. Mitchell is calling."

Sighing, he rose from the table. "I'm sorry, Caroline."

"Go take your call."

I followed him. Unless it was a true emergency, I wasn't about to let him forget where we left off.

He put the receiver to his ear. "Halsted here." He listened. "Tomorrow?" His frown grew. "Yes, yes. You'd think they could've given more notice, coming all that way. What have we got in the ward?"

Tomorrow. That was good news. I considered tickling his ear, but that wasn't how we behaved and we'd already been a little silly.

"Mr. Bowling? We'll have to do it under local. The poor man already can barely breathe. I'm not putting him under." He chewed his lip, listening. "How many have we done?" He waited. "Well, that's about what I thought. All right then. Have him prepped for tomorrow. Good night."

"What was that?"

"Oh, the same. Some surgeons from out of town want to watch us operate."

"Want to watch *you* operate."

"From Toronto, of all places. And Boston. We have a thyroid we can do. Apparently, we've done seven all together these ten years. I thought more, but—"

"You were likely counting the dogs."

He smiled at me. "No doubt." He took my hand. "Jim is good. He had all the stats at the ready. I've done six. Cushing did one. Jim watched three. Held a retractor or something. He's raring to go. The patient is a hippopotamus though. And has the biggest goiter I've ever seen. It'll be a challenge."

"Good. You'll like that."

"Hmm."

I didn't like that pensive look. He would give the visiting surgeons a short lecture beforehand. He liked to provide a brief anatomy lesson as well as historical perspective, in case his observers were inadequately informed. Doing so cut down the questions and chatter during the operation. It wasn't only that William preferred a quiet operating theater so he could concentrate, but also, he said he didn't appreciate visitors spraying their oral bacteria all over his surgical field.

He would want to plan his speech. Moreover, with difficult cases, he plotted his strategy in his head in advance. Although every case was different, every case offered up similar pitfalls.

"I suppose you'd like to read through your old operative reports."

"There are one or two things I'd like to double-check. Yes." He blinked and looked at me as if remembering something he'd forgotten. "But it can wait until morning."

His head was already burrowed into Mr. Bowling's neck. He would not be in the right frame of mind to nuzzle mine.

"Nonsense. You'll be the star of the surgical theater tomorrow." I patted his arm. "Best go make sure you know your lines."

William left for the hospital early. I wasn't even up yet to see him off. My day would not be as exciting as his. I had the week's menus to go over with Betty, letters to write, and then I planned to indulge myself with a new novel I'd bought. William would likely telephone to say he would not be home for dinner. Visiting surgeons must be fed, which meant an outing to the Cosmopolitan Restaurant or the Maryland Club. That was all right. In three months, we'd be back at High Hampton and I'd have my husband to myself.

I was a few chapters into a new-ish novel by Henry James, no relation to William's friend, and was just about to toss the nasty thing aside when I heard the front door open then shut with a bang. It was awfully early for William to be home.

I went to my door and called, "William?"

He didn't answer, but I heard his stomping feet in the stairwell, then his office door slam.

My God. Had he lost the patient? It was always a risk, especially with one in Mr. Bowling's poor condition, but William rarely lost one on the table. Even then, it had been years.

I ran down the stairs. There was nothing I could say to ease his frustration. Oh! And he'd had visitors watching.

Dear God, don't let it be that. Don't let William have lost a man on the table.

I knocked on his door.

"William? Is everything all right?" He didn't answer. "William?"

I tried the knob, but he'd locked it.

"Just answer me." I kept my voice calm. "Tell me you are all right and I won't intrude."

"Go the hell away."

"Open the door, William! I'll break it down. You know I will."

"Oh, for the love of God."

I heard him approach. The lock turned. The door opened but he stood in the doorway, preventing my entrance. His jacket was off, one sleeve of his shirt loose at the cuff. I shoved him aside.

"Caroline—"

On one side of his desk was a tidy pile of file folders. A decorative paperweight held down a short stack of papers on the other. A vial and syringe were readily visible in the middle. I brushed past him to the desk. There was fluid in the syringe. He had been moments from injecting himself with cocaine. Damn him!

I picked up the paperweight and smashed the vial, fighting back tears.

"Caroline!"

"Why, William? Why? Explain to me how this makes losing a patient any better."

"Losing—? He isn't lost." He sniffed hard. "Wasn't yet."

"No?" My voice rose, shrill even to my ears. "So you have no excuse whatsoever?"

"I need it." His fury equaled mine.

"That is not true. You merely want it."

"Don't tell me what I need or don't! You haven't the faintest idea what—"

"Then tell me! What does it do for you? What possible attraction can it have for you when you know how this will turn out?"

"I don't care how it will turn out. That is the attraction. That is the truth. I can't paint the picture with words. Unless you have experienced—"

I snatched up the hypodermic and tore open my sleeve.

"Goddamn it, Caroline!"

The horror in his expression terrified me. In the few seconds that I stood frozen, he closed the distance between us, clenched my wrist in his fingers, and wrenched the needle from my hand.

"Ouch, William. You're hurting me."

He threw it across the room. "Don't ever. My God, don't ever!" His fingers still dug into my wrist.

"That hurts."

He pulled me against his chest and buried his face in my hair. I felt the heat of his breath on my scalp. Then he released me, stepping back. He lifted my hand. "I didn't mean to hurt you." He spoke quietly. Then said, alarmed, "You're bleeding. Your fingers."

"You didn't do that." My index finger throbbed. "I have a splinter, I think."

"Hold on." He stepped around the desk, opened the drawer, and pulled out a small forceps. "Let me see."

I held up my finger and he teased out the shard.

"Let me see the rest." He dabbed the other fingers with his handkerchief, rubbing them gently. I didn't feel any more splinters. "Crisis averted," he murmured.

"Are you sure?"

I didn't miss the slight hesitation before he nodded.

"Thank you." He drew a rattling breath. "Promise me, you won't ever."

"You've promised me—"

"A hundred times. I know. I'm sorry. I can't...I can't explain."

"Try."

His mouth bunched and his brow wrinkled with irritation. But he tried. "Think of the moment in your life when you were happiest."

That was difficult. I said the first thing that came to mind. "Our wedding day."

"No. All that stress? Your headache? Laced too tight?"

"I was happy," I insisted.

"Happiest. It must be sometime at High Hampton. A time when you are where you want to be. With whom you wish to be. Or alone, if you prefer. And nothing, *nothing* bothers you. No fatigue. No niggling doubt. No something-I-should-be-doing. No I-wish-I-hadn't-said-that-yesterday. That time."

"I don't think that time exists." It would be impossible to put every little irritation out of one's head.

"That is cocaine."

For a long moment, we were silent.

Then I said, "What happened today?"

He sighed. Long. Deep.

"We were using local anesthesia. Schleich's solution, a combination of cocaine and morphine. Weak solutions, but effective if used adequately. Not just for pain. The cocaine also constricts vessels and limits bleeding. It's very useful, but I...I confess I'm stingy in the application. I use as little as possible."

"That is a reasonable approach. A cautious approach."

"Hmph. Well, I was too cautious. He's a big man. He had the largest, bloodiest goiter I've ever seen. He soaked up Schleich's like a sponge and was still uncomfortable. I'd barely opened the neck and the poor writhing man was weighted down with clamps to catch bleeders."

"So it was a difficult operation. And you didn't have Bloodgood or Cushing to assist."

"I *left the room.*" He turned his head and rubbed a hand across his forehead. "I was standing there, staring at the incision, knowing I had to give more anesthesia, and I got the most horrible headache. I think, my God, my mind had drifted to wishing I was the man on the table. Getting that cocaine. I couldn't think of anything else."

He left surgery to inject himself? My knees quivered. He put a patient at risk. "So you came home?"

"No." He shook his head. "Jim asked the nurse to get me a cup of coffee. I went into the outer room to drink it. Jim and that assistant of his, that new boy, managed to tie off some of the bleeders and remove most of the clamps. I scrubbed back in, gave the patient a little bit more Schleich's, and started again. I didn't even get the muscle divided before the field bloodied up. I couldn't see a damn thing. I worried I might extirpate the parathyroids and put the poor fellow into tetany. Jim was sweating, keeping up with the clamps. I said my headache was worse and left again."

"Oh, William."

"I wasn't lying. My head pounded so hard I felt ill. I truly feared I would vomit. I sat outside and closed my eyes until I felt less nauseated. I tried a third time, but I couldn't see straight. I told Jim to finish the operation. I abandoned him. All I could think…I stole from the supply closet on the way out."

I didn't know what to say. It wasn't the surgical misadventure that had stimulated his craving; it was the mere sight of the drug, the mere thought of another man having it. Was it always like that? Was he always that close to the edge?

So then, I was no help to him. Marrying me, *promising* me, had brought him no closer to a cure. The realization made me feel bereft of purpose. Unbearably bereft.

"Caroline, I am a failure."

"That is untrue. You expect too much of yourself. Is your head still hurting?"

"Yes."

"Why don't you take a cool bath. I'll clean this up. Then we'll telephone the hospital and see how Mr. Bowling is doing."

"My God. I don't know that I can. I don't want to know."

"You can. And you know the moment your head stops pounding, you'll be curious to see how Jim fared. You taught that boy everything. He has spent the last few years glued to your side. I'll bet everything is fine, and you're worried for nothing."

"He's never taken out a thyroid."

"Neither had you. Until you did."

"I broke down in surgery. Everyone saw it."

"You had a migraine. You've had migraines before. You realize Dr. Osler mocks your aversion to red wine? Now he'll say you're a surgeon who can't stand the sight of blood. It would explain why you never let your patients bleed."

"Osler can be an ass." He said it with an embarrassed awareness that Dr. Osler would reluctantly cover for him. Would Jim Mitchell? I thought so. Did I hope so? This was so wrong. And they—we—were all complicit.

"Go take your bath."

❧

Two hours later, after a bath and a nap, he telephoned the hospital. The patient was resting comfortably. The thyroid was in the pathology laboratory. Dr. Mitchell was out to dinner with the visiting surgeons.

William hung up the telephone.

"Better?" I asked.

"Worse. It seems I am entirely unnecessary."

"On the contrary, you are critical. You've taught all those young men how to perform safe, successful surgery, even without you looking over their shoulders."

"All right. Enough, my dear. Let us agree that I bungled it. But thank God I have people to prop me up."

"You thanked me earlier, and God just now. Let me think who you might be forgetting."

"Hmm?" He actually looked confused.

"Come here." I led him back into his study and rolled a piece of paper into his typewriter. "Put this down."

He sat and put his fingers on the keys.

"Dear Mitchell," I dictated. Jim Mitchell might worship William but that made it all the more crucial that William acknowledge him. "I telephoned and found that you finished the operation and that your patient—"

"*His* patient?" His lips pressed together, suppressing a smile.

"—that your patient was all right. Some day you will know what it means to have an assistant in whom you have confidence."

William typed out the words, then added at the bottom: *I hope you will enjoy this bottle of old Madeira.*

He stood. "I'll fetch a good one from the cellar and send this off to the Cosmopolitan. They'll still be there." He pulled the paper from the typewriter, kissed me on the forehead, and said, "My God, Caroline."

51

1902, April

Baltimore, Maryland

WADE HAMPTON DEAD

NOTED FIGURE OF THE CONFEDERACY ENDS A LONG LIFE

Columbia, S.C., April 11.—Gen Wade Hampton died here at 8:50 o'clock this morning from valvular disease of the heart. He had been unconscious several hours.

The general had just passed his 84th birthday. Twice during the winter he had attacks which greatly weakened him, but he rallied wonderfully on both occasions. He was out driving a week ago, but it was evident his strength was deserting him.

No arrangements have yet been made for the funeral, except that it will be, at the general's expressed wish, without pomp of any kind and that it will take place Sunday afternoon…

—*The Baltimore Sun,* Baltimore, Maryland, Saturday, April 12, 1902

William laid the newspaper down on the table. Tomorrow afternoon. That didn't give them much time. He glanced at the wall clock, then back at his breakfast, which had grown cold while he picked at it, waiting to see if Caroline would come down. The telegram arrived late last night. Every single blasted aunt, cousin, sister, brother—they had all been gathered around the dying patriarch's bedside. Except Caroline.

Well, she hadn't known, had she?

Caroline was not as close to her family as she had once been. She'd chosen life in Baltimore over returning to Columbia. Frank and Lucy understood, but the aunties had never quite gotten over it—even though she spent a few months every year in Cashiers. Caroline was no longer the die-hard Confederate she'd once been. Of course, that didn't mean she loved the old folks any less.

He rose from the table, crumpling his napkin as he stood. Then he went and peeked into the kitchen.

"Betty? Any word from Mrs. Halsted? Oh." He cleared his throat. Betty was arranging a tray. "Yes, I see. I–I'll take that up, if that's all right."

He stepped forward and put his hand on the tray, claiming it. A meager offering. Buttered toast and a pot of tea. The napkin didn't even look to be ironed properly. He wished he had a bud vase or something. A magnolia blossom. Though one could hardly stuff a magnolia into a bud vase. Good God.

Poor Caroline. He said all the wrong things last night. Rote words.

He carted the tray up the stairs, unsure whether to tiptoe or to stomp to announce he was coming. He pushed open the door. She was in the sitting room. Not in bed. Rather she was at her writing desk, reading through old letters, wrapped in her dressing gown. Dry-eyed, still. Last night she'd seemed too stunned to take in what had happened. Maybe she still was. One didn't expect old idols to die.

"Good morning, my dear." He cringed. "Not *good.* I didn't mean that."

Caroline let out a long-suffering sigh. "Come in. I'm not angry, William. Just sad. And I wasn't angry with you last night. I'm sorry I was rude."

He had tried to comfort her and she snapped: *Uncle Wade was not one of your patients.* "You weren't rude. I was insufferable. Explaining the prognosis of valvular heart disease—"

"And I know all your patients don't die." Her mouth twisted a little. "I *was* angry." She gestured to the tray. "Did you bring me breakfast? That's very sweet."

"It won't help my case. It doesn't look very appetizing."

"That's fine. I haven't much appetite."

He set the tray down on her desk. The chair she preferred was all sticks and angles. There was no way to embrace her without impaling himself.

"I checked the schedules. There are three trains leaving today that will get to Columbia by tomorrow morning. The first is in two hours."

"You can't be packed in two hours," she scoffed, shifting away from him to pour her tea.

"You can, can't you?"

"Oh." Her voice was flat. She set the pot down. "Yes, I suppose I can."

"I packed last night when I couldn't sleep."

She glanced up at him. Spots of pink appeared on her cheeks. "Oh," she said softly.

Good Lord. She couldn't have thought he was going to send her down there alone. He wasn't that terrible a husband.

"I packed for a week, but we'll stay as long you want. As long as you need. I'll telegram the hotel—"

"There won't be room at the hotel." She sounded a bit exasperated. "I don't think you quite understand what it means when a Confederate war hero says no pomp of any kind." She gave him a faint smile but her brow was knotted. "I'd better get dressed. We should take that first train if we can."

She stood up and stretched. Ah, good. Now he was safe from her chair. He stepped close to pull her into his arms. She stiffened, resisting. She had to get dressed, pack; they had a train to catch. All that. He held on tight.

"I'm sorry, Caroline. I know how much you loved him."

She burrowed her face into his jacket. When she started to cry, he stroked her hair. And kept his mouth shut.

52

1904, June

Baltimore, Maryland

Pain, hemorrhage, infection, the three great evils which had always embittered the practice of surgery and checked its progress, were, in a moment, in a quarter of a century (1846-1873) robbed of their terrors. A new era had dawned; and, in the 30 years which have elapsed since the graduation of the class of 1874 from Yale, probably more has been accomplished to place surgery on a truly scientific basis than in all the centuries which proceeded this wondrous period.

—Dr. W. S. Halsted, "The Training of the Surgeon." The Annual Address in Medicine, delivered at Yale University, New Haven, Conn., June 27, 1904

"Attending the Congress of German surgeons, which each year takes place at Eastertide in Berlin, I heard the topic of hip tuberculosis discussed. One surgeon alone reported on 600 cases, more or less, some of which he had observed twenty years or longer and most of which he had been able to follow. His methods of observation were new to me; his knowledge was inspiring; I—"

"Halsted, slow down," Welch barked. "E-nun-ci-ate. You read like you've never given a paper before. Are you that nervous to talk before this illustrious crowd?"

Halsted gave Welch the quelling glare, the one that would cut a man off at the knees. Unless he was Popsy Welch. Or Willie Osler. Or unless she was Caroline.

"Don't be absurd." Halsted laid his speech on the corner of Welch's desk, pulled a pack of Pall Malls from his pocket, lit the cigarette, and took a deep drag. If it were anyone else, Welch would say he had the fidgets.

At fifty-two, Halsted was in his prime, not past it. Of course, as he was two years older, Welch had a vested interest in believing this.

But while his own course had turned toward administration, toward synthesizing the work of others, his friend Halsted continued breaking new ground. Important new ground. Just recently, he had returned to the aneurysm work that had stymied him years earlier, using X-rays! Using radiation to peer into the human body without having to open it? One might think surgeons would scoff, but Halsted had seized upon the possibilities, even strong-arming the Board to create another subdepartment of surgery and put one of his residents in charge of it. That was his way. Growing his young men and expanding the field. Halsted was as innovative at fifty-two as he'd been at thirty.

Even so, a few gray hairs, a few wrinkles, and people started inviting one to give keynote speeches and annual addresses. Perhaps that was what had Halsted unnerved. And yet—he'd been standing still as he read, not pacing. A nervous speaker paced. Granted, in Welch's cluttered study there was not much room to pace without knocking over a pile of paper, but Halsted was lithe enough.

He picked up his pages and shook them.

"I'm not even halfway through, and the clock on the wall gives me ten minutes."

"So, trim it down." Welch shifted in his chair. He'd been watching the clock too. "You'll be talking after the banquet. Three-quarters of your audience has nodded off already. You're the great surgeon: cut."

"The historical perspective is necessary or the rest won't make sense."

"But must you go on and on about the Germans? This is the United States. Talk about what we're doing here in Baltimore. What you are doing here, training surgeons. Training surgeons to train surgeons. The 'Halsted Model' for surgical education—"

Halsted snorted smoke from his nostrils. "I'm speaking in New Haven. They'll stop up their ears if they hear the word Baltimore."

"Terrapin and madeira." Welch chuckled at the old joke and folded his hands over the bulk of his belly. When Gilman lured him to Johns Hopkins from New York, his colleagues warned him he'd be a connoisseur of those Baltimore delicacies but his best days as a pathologist would be behind him. They'd been half right.

"Our Yale colleagues still have a grudging respect for the German school."

"True enough," Welch acknowledged. "You do need to trim it though. For the address. They'll publish the whole thing in the *Bulletin* and no one will remember you didn't read it all. If they do notice, they'll thank you for it."

Halsted scowled. "You're a great help."

"Go on, then. But skip past the Germans. I know all that. I was there before you."

Halsted grumbled as he skimmed the text, found his place, then started again.

"Conservative surgery was made possible by general anesthesia, as was illustrated particularly well in the exsection of joints and the subperiosteal resection of bone. The discovery of the ophthalmoscope, an invention—"

"Halt!" Welch shook his head. "Half an hour on the Germans, then you give anesthesia half a sentence? What of the importance of local—"

Halsted stiffened. "I'm not going into all that."

The man's hard expression brought Welch up short. Was Halsted afraid the world would crash down around his ears if he publicly pronounced the word cocaine?

"Put it in the manuscript for the *Bulletin*."

"Fine. In a footnote." Halsted tossed the comment off as though to sound casual. A knock on the door interrupted.

"Come," Welch said, more than a mite relieved.

His landlady peeked her head in. "Should I hold dinner?"

"Lord no!" Welch let out a loud laugh. "Thank God. Come along, Halsted. Time's up."

"I should be getting home."

"No, you shouldn't. I know Mrs. Halsted left for High Hampton weeks ago. It's been too long since you've dined here. Mrs. Simmons misses having you at table."

Halsted glanced at the clock again. Welch looked at the papers in his friend's hand, the fingers curled around the cigarette. They were steady enough. Welch waited.

"Yes, yes, all right. Thank you. I can work on this more later tonight."

He laid the speech in a folder, then slipped the folder into his case. Welch rose, sprightly despite his size. Osler used to tease that he could dance for the ballet. And Halsted had once retorted, under his breath but audible to them both, that Osler could clown for the circus. Welch didn't need Halsted defending him when he had taken Osler's jest in the good humor with which it had been intended, but he enjoyed "the professor" taking "the chief" down a notch. Not many men could. Or even wanted to.

Well, they all had egos commensurate with their achievements. If Halsted seemed tetchier than most, he had his reasons. His wit was as sharp as his scalpel and could be just as wounding. He was not, as Osler was, lovable. But oh, how Welch did love him.

"Will Mrs. Halsted be joining you in Connecticut?"

"From North Carolina?" Halsted coughed. "I wouldn't ask her to make that journey for a plate of overcooked beef and a windy address on the history of surgical training."

"You're being honored. She would like that." She deserved a share of the accolades. The only reply was a grunt. "And then you are leaving to join her?"

"Yes. Yes, of course." Welch watched him smile, his mustache twitching. "The dahlias will be blooming. I'll spend a *few* days, naturally, in New Haven. Our old stomping grounds, eh? I still have a couple college chums who haven't scattered. Sam Bushnell is up there preaching and I always promised one day I'd go hear a sermon."

Halsted wouldn't likely be going to hear a sermon. But hopefully he would visit Sam and not sit in his hotel room alone. Halsted had, on very rare occasions, when finding himself alone…slipped. Afterward he would come around moping and finally confess, as if seeking absolution. Welch hated being the keeper of such secrets—secrets that could blacken a man's reputation, wipe away his credibility, destroy an otherwise brilliant career. It was Welch's worst fear that Halsted might be caught out. All they'd worked for, overshadowed…

It was true, he suspected, that Caroline would not have enjoyed Connecticut, but she should have been invited to go. If invited, she would have gone.

A little bicarbonate of soda wouldn't hurt before he tucked into supper. But it wouldn't help. The pit he felt in his stomach had been there for almost twenty years. He once thought it would cure itself, one way or another. But he now understood it would always be there.

53

1905, February

Baltimore, Maryland

DR. OSLER STICKS TO IT

"Telling Work of the World Done by Men Under Forty."

1 West Franklin Street, Baltimore, MD, February 26

Messrs. Editors:

I have been so misquoted by the papers that I would like to make the following statement:

First, I did not say that men at 60 should be chloroformed. That was the point in the novel to which I referred and on which its plot hinged.

Second, nothing in the criticism has shaken my conviction that the telling work of the world has been done and is done by men under 40 years of age. The exceptions which have been given only illustrate the rule.

Thirdly, it would be for the general good if men at 60 were relieved from active work. We should miss the energies of some young old men, but, on the whole, it would be of greatest service to the sexagenerii themselves.

Yours, etc.,

William Osler

—*The Baltimore Sun*, Baltimore, Maryland, Monday, February 27, 1905

❧

William put the newspaper down with a slap. "He put his foot in it this time."

Concerned by his tone, I glanced up from my tea. "More about poor Dr. Osler?"

"Poor Osler," he muttered. "It's his own fault. The speech was going along fine until he got carried away with himself. Cushing says Osler's getting threatening mail now. Reporters won't stop knocking on his door."

"Oh! Grace must be horrified. And Revere?" Dr. Osler's son was only ten and a sensitive boy.

"Cushing offered to hide them, but Osler refused. He believes this will all blow over."

Harvey lived just a few houses away from Dr. Osler. He worshiped the man. I wondered sometimes if it bothered William that his protégé was so enamored of the medical doctor. Probably not. As William himself once said, surgeons competed with one another as a matter of course. Most had better sense than to try to compete with Dr. Halsted. Harvey Cushing, pleasant though he could be when he tried, had an ego that was out of control.

"Will it not?"

"Not if Osler keeps feeding the fire." He sniffed. "Just because he's ready to throw in the towel at fifty-six—"

"Regious professor of medicine at Oxford is hardly 'throwing in the towel.'"

"It's a sinecure."

"Do you think he's not deserving?"

"Of course he's deserving. And overworked and tired. It's the Johns Hopkins' fault. Running him into the ground. But retirement won't be good for him. And moving to England? Absurd."

The Hopkins would have run William into the ground too, if I'd allowed it. He'd received more than one censuring letter from the Board, commanding him to return immediately from his vacation. After the first, I had merely said, "Pish-tosh" and threw the letters into the trash.

"People love a scandal," he grumbled. "After all he's accomplished, it's this bit of stupidity that will attach itself to his name."

"And you'll miss him," I said, getting to the crux while avoiding the parallels.

He was quiet a moment, then said, "Like the very devil. It's the end of an era." He took a cigarette from his case. Pall Malls. Somewhere along the way he chose convenience over affectation. I still hated the habit, but I missed watching him roll his own, the careful quick exercise performed by those marvelous hands.

"Caroline, let's go for a walk, pop in on Osler. Offer condolences. You can cheer Grace."

We had finished our breakfast. William had no pressing matters at the hospital as Cushing and the assistants now did most of the clinical work. William only operated on patients with interesting problems or the occasional luminary. Some might say the surgeon-in-chief position was a sinecure. But they didn't see all that William did behind the scenes, guiding those young men so that they could reach their potential and advance the field.

Performing the surgeries himself would be more efficient and likely less stressful than teaching residents to do it, but he took such pride in his young men—those that learned. If possible, he was prouder of Harvey than the boy was of himself. Likely they butted heads so fiercely because they were so similar.

We gathered up our things, put on our wraps, hats, and gloves, and ventured out into the cold. It was only a mile to the Oslers' home but we seldom visited. I didn't know why the two men gave each other so much space, but they did.

"Should we bring Nip and Tuck?" The dogs would like the walk and Revere enjoyed them.

"Not this time. I might be tempted to sic them on the reporters."

I smiled at the image. The dachshunds were not fierce.

It was one of our quiet walks. William was lost in thought and I didn't want to interrupt. Was he considering that he was nearer to sixty than to forty? He was still productive. His health was good. Better than mine. He carried a few extra pounds better than I did. I worried more when he lost weight.

He took my arm when we reached the Oslers' street corner. There were a few reporters camped out on the grounds who looked up eagerly at our approach. William glared them down and not one pressed for his opinion. He wouldn't have given it. He never spoke to reporters.

He rang the doorbell. No one answered for quite some time. He rang it again, this time in a tuneless rendition of "God Save the Queen." It opened a crack. Then the Oslers' housekeeper let us in.

"Good morning, Dr. Halsted. Mrs. Halsted. They are in the parlor."

The woman took our coats and hats. We entered the Oslers' parlor, homier than our own. Dr. Osler was seated on the floor with Revere, playing with a model ship. Even at leisure, he was dressed as stylishly as William, but with a little more color, a little more flair. Grace was stitching something decorative in her chair by the window. All the curtains were drawn.

Dr. Osler waved.

"Good of you to come, Halsted. Mrs. Halsted. I hope you gave those vultures outside a good setdown."

"You mean those pleasant gentlemen on your lawn? They were very civil to me."

Dr. Osler snorted. He hopped to his feet.

"Very spry," William said approvingly.

"Oh, stop it," Dr. Osler growled. "This is really most annoying. I can't wait to get to England where people have better sense."

"Caroline, would you like some tea?" Grace said, setting aside her work and gesturing for me to come sit closer.

"That would be lovely." I left William's side, grateful to get out of the firing line.

William lit a cigarette. On an exhalation, he said, "Do you want my advice?"

"No."

"It is this. Shut up."

Osler made grumbling sounds.

William said, "When you were a useful young man, you were a superior natterer. Able to extricate yourself from any scrape your tongue got you into."

Osler looked startled. Then he smiled. "Yes, I remember that." He chuckled. "And you still don't get into scrapes."

"I wouldn't say that."

"You never say anything at all. That is your peculiar brand of genius." His head drooped. I pitied him the strain he was under, trying to pretend it was all in good fun when it no longer was. "I suppose there's something to it." He deliberated a moment, then burst out, "Everything I say is taken out of context."

"The context is that America's physician-in-chief is abandoning us for Britain. We can't have that. If you are going, we must boot you out."

"Well, I hope the British are not so humorless."

"We'll see. I understand King Edward is quite popular and he's sixty-three."

"Proves my point! He took the throne at fifty-nine? Sixty? If Victoria hadn't held onto it until she was past doddering, Edward might have had a chance to make something of himself."

William shook his head. "Blasphemy. You're going to end up back in Canada. If they'll even have you."

"Hmph. All I meant to say is old men should step aside to give young men room to grow. Like saplings. They need sunlight, not to stand in the shade of redwoods. And no, I am not talking about you and Cushing. You give him more than enough room."

"It keeps the axe out of his hands."

Osler laughed unconvincingly. He glanced down at his son, who looked worried.

"Revere, shall I shut up as the good surgeon says? Should we all sit down to tea and cakes like your sensible mother and Mrs. Halsted?"

Revere nodded hesitantly.

William rubbed his hands together and gave the boy a huge smile. "By all means. Let's have some cake."

Revere giggled.

William was surprisingly good with children. Frank's brood adored him. And he…well, he blamed himself and I let him. I pushed aside thoughts of what might have been. What was, was enough.

54

1909, January

Baltimore, Maryland

FIRE IN DR. HALSTED'S CHIMNEY

A slight fire about 7 o'clock last night in the chimney at the home of Dr. William S. Halsted, of Johns Hopkins University faculty, 1201 Eutaw Place, caused a passerby to turn in an alarm. No damage was done.

—*The Baltimore Sun*, Baltimore, MD., January 13, 1909

❧

The rule was dinner at seven o'clock, lasting until eight thirty. That was our time. I didn't intrude upon his afternoons, locked in his study, *working,* he said. It was now quarter past, and I sat, straight-backed, in my dining room chair, regarding my waiting soup bowl and the cooling tureen.

William rushed in, looking addled. "I'm sorry, my dear. I lost track of time."

He used the same excuse when he was late to surgery or did not show up for his student lectures, minus the "my dear." I didn't answer, but merely ladled soup into our bowls as he took his seat. He spread his napkin into his lap and raised a spoonful to his mouth.

"It's cold," he said, setting down his spoon, annoyed.

"It was hot at seven."

He grimaced. "It shouldn't cool that quickly."

"Would you like it rewarmed or shall I have the next course brought in?"

He waved a hand at me, which meant nothing. I rang a little bell and Betty came in.

"Please take the soup away and bring the meat."

The housekeeper nodded nervously. She was aware of William's fussiness and probably thought there was something wrong with it. She picked up the tureen and bowls and left the room, to return shortly with sliced pot roast and potatoes. She set it on the table and I served. William began eating.

He had been like this, irritable and short-tempered, since returning from New York. He'd gone up for a few days after Christmas to visit with his family. I had a terrible head cold and stayed home, glad for the excuse. I didn't get along with his sisters, and his brother didn't like me. Apparently, they all thought he would have moved "home" and resumed his New York society life if I hadn't moored him to the South. They had no concept of his accomplishments at Johns Hopkins. Although he was, arguably, the most famous surgeon in the country, they were unimpressed. He didn't make enough money, I supposed.

Still, it wasn't the family visit that bothered me. It was that he stayed two extra days in New York, seeing old friends. He was vague about who, even more vague about what he had done with them. I stopped asking. This was how he was, blue-deviled, when he returned from his summer conferences in Germany or Vienna or France. Not all of them—only those when he stayed a week or two afterwards. He had a few quiet places he liked to go. The weeks following, he gave every indication of tapering morphine again. There was only one reason I could think of why he would increase his morphine after a vacation spent alone.

I took a deep breath, then exhaled.

"William, did you use cocaine in New York?"

His fork stilled. "Why would you ask such a thing?"

"It is a yes or no question."

He pushed away his plate. He didn't speak for a long minute. Maybe two.

"Yes." He stood up, walked away, then came back and sat down. "Very little. Only those last two days. Not since."

"And when you go to Europe?"

"Rarely. Sometimes." He pulled his cigarette box from his pocket. "Caroline, you don't understand."

He lit a cigarette even though he knew I didn't like him to smoke at the table. After poisoning his lungs for a few moments, he set it on his plate.

"It's how I keep myself from succumbing. If the only options were never again or falling into the pit, I would choose the pit. This is a compromise. I can tell myself only to wait. Two years…a year…and then I permit myself a few days. It works for me."

"Not so well that you don't have to increase your morphine afterward."

"But then I cut back. Caroline, I know how to control this."

Control this? My blood chilled. He was making excuses. He was escalating.

"You're going to Bristol for two weeks after your meeting in Bonn this summer. This is not once every couple of years."

He scowled. "This is an exception."

I couldn't do this again. I couldn't. He had no right to put me through this again.

"And what will the next exception be?"

He leaned his elbows on the table. "Then come with me to Europe." It was not an invitation but a challenge. "You would like Bristol. It's quiet. They speak English."

My stomach tightened. I had gone with him once, several years ago, because he was being inducted into the German Congress of Surgeons, an unheard-of honor for an American. I'd been seasick the entire voyage, yet still preferred the boat to the land. Every place we had gone was crowded and loud. I could not understand a word. The sightseeing overwhelmed me. And William knew people everywhere we went. We had not a moment to ourselves.

"All right," I whispered.

"Pssshhtt!" He leaned back, glowering. "I won't ask you to do something you find unpleasant. Even visiting my sisters is too much to ask. Yet you would demand of me that I give up the one thing that—" He gritted his teeth. He would not finish the sentence. The one thing that made him happy? That made his life worth living? How was it he put me in the wrong?

"I will go to Europe. I will visit your sisters. I'll invite them here. I'll invite them to spend the entire summer in Cashiers."

"They wouldn't come." He picked up his cigarette. "What if I were to tell you I was selling High Hampton? That you could never go there again. I would be within my rights."

"Are you threatening me?"

"I am trying to make you understand."

I crumpled my napkin and dropped it to the table. The headache that had been simmering all day now came throbbing to life.

"There is no equivalence between the two."

"Ha!" He sneered. *Sneered!* "Tell me to sell it and I promise I will quit cocaine forever."

I stood up, propping myself by my fists on the table. "The difference, William, is I would not go back on my word. I'm going to bed. My head aches."

"Take a powder," he said. He didn't stand up, but rather sat, smoking and glowering.

A powder would not help. I'd been plagued with occasional violent headaches ever since my carriage accident. Usually William was sympathetic, even solicitous. Tonight, he let me leave the room, relieved to see me go.

I climbed to the third floor and entered my sitting room. I sat by the open window and breathed in the cold air. It didn't help. I shut it all but a crack, undressed, put on my nightgown, stirred the fire, and crawled into bed with a cold compress over my eyes.

I fell asleep and into a nightmare. I couldn't breathe. I was engulfed by smoke. I tried to call for Dodie but my jaw felt wired shut. I tossed about, getting caught in my blankets. *Uncle Kit!* The scream died in my throat. Columbia was on fire. *They'd left me behind. Alone.*

I felt a rush of air. A man darkened my doorway. This time the scream tore from my mouth. He grabbed me from my bed. Carried me from the room. Carried me down two flights of stairs. By the bottom, I stopped fighting. William carried me outside and across the street before setting me down.

"It's all right." He brushed the hair from my cheeks. There was a glimmer of humor in his eyes. "I'm not General Sherman."

He took off his coat and draped me in it. I still shivered. The dream, the memory, still felt real. He put his arms around me.

"You're all right. Take deep breaths."

I clung to the lapels of his jacket, holding him as close as I could. My legs would not stop shaking. I was barefoot, bare-legged, but was not shaking from the cold.

"I'm just going to knock on the Crowes' door and see if they'll send in an alarm."

"No!" I gripped his jacket harder. The shaking wracked my body. "Don't leave me."

"Caroline!" He sounded shocked. But he wrapped his arms tighter. "I'm right here. I'm not going anywhere."

He stood there with me in the road, calmly, patiently. The house would burn to the ground—the house he'd taken such care to find and to fix just so. All his books and papers. The manuscript he'd been working on so diligently. All the antiques he'd so lovingly collected. Oh, Lord! The dachshunds!

"Where are Nip and Tuck?" I asked panicked.

"In the back by the carriage house. I'd taken them for a walk and saw the smoke. I left them outside."

And ran in to save me. I dared turn around to look at the house. Dense black smoke billowed from the chimney. Inferior wood. William insisted we only use dry white hickory, cut to eighteen inches exactly. It was nearly impossible to find in Baltimore in January. I thought it merely another one of his quirks. I would never burn anything else from now on.

"Is everything all right?" Our neighbor yelled to us from her open window.

"Our chimney is on fire," William answered.

"I'll call in an alarm if you haven't yet."

"Much appreciated." William hugged me close again. "The fire brigade will be along shortly. We'll have to send everything out to be cleaned but I don't think we'll lose much."

"I can't lose you," I said. My shaking had eased, but not ceased.

"It's only a small chimney fire," he said, amused.

"I can't lose *you.*"

He was quiet a moment, hearing me, hearing what I was saying. *Don't leave me behind. Alone.*

He squeezed me harder and whispered, "I won't go to Bristol. I don't have to go."

55

1917, September

Baltimore, Maryland

LEADING SURGEONS MAROONED

Among the other Baltimoreans abroad are two members of the faculty of the Johns Hopkins Medical School, Dr. William Stewart Halsted and Dr. Joseph C. Bloodgood, both professors of surgery. They are now thought to be in England.

—*The Baltimore Sun*, Baltimore, MD., August 3, 1914

WERE ON KROONLAND

Dr. Halsted, Richard P. Baer, and Arunah S. A. Brady Land.

Dr. William S. Halsted, professor of surgery at the Johns Hopkins University Medical School, returned from Europe yesterday on the Kroonland, which docked at New York. It was said at the Hopkins that no word had been received from him and that it was expected he would go at once to his summer home at High Hampton, North Carolina.

—*The Evening Sun*, Baltimore, MD., August 12, 1914

PROF OSLER'S SON KILLED

Boy Lieutenant Dies of Wounds Received at the Front

Special to the Inquirer

Baltimore, Md., Sept. 1—Mrs. Thomas Futcher, niece of Sir William Osler, the eminent medical savant, has received a telegram from him telling of his only son, Second Lieutenant Edward Revere Osler, dying of wounds received in action.

Lieutenant Osler was born in Baltimore when Sir William was professor of medicine at Johns Hopkins University. Lieutenant Osler was just about to enter Oxford University when the war began. Not twenty years old then, he joined a Canadian Hospital unit serving at the front but he soon tired of that. It was too "safe" for him, he said. He entered the Royal Artillery, in which branch of the army he was serving when he received the wounds that caused his death…

—*The Philadelphia Inquirer*, Philadelphia, PA., September 2, 1917

ණ

William sat staring at the blank piece of writing paper on his desk. He'd written hundreds of condolence letters in his lifetime. This one, he could not write. What a stupid, wasteful tragedy. This whole war. Pointless. Germans were demonized. He worried about his very good friends in Bonn and Berlin…mail would not go through. And now this. Now he wanted to roll a tank across a battalion of German soldiers himself. Osler must be devastated. What could he possibly say to the man? A soft rap on the door arrested his thoughts.

"Come in. It isn't locked."

"It isn't?" Caroline sounded surprised. His longstanding habit was to lock the door to his study in the afternoons so he would not be interrupted. Not be caught. He had the household well-trained now; he rarely bothered to lock it anymore.

After a time, Caroline had insisted upon a key. In case of an accident. A coronary. An overdose. These days the coronary seemed the more probable. He'd finally lost his taste for cocaine. His tired, old body didn't relish that pounding heart and warm rush to the head. He used less morphine. Time was running out to rid himself of it altogether, to fulfill that promise he made so long ago. It no longer seemed to matter. He had robbed them of the chance for children of their own. Now he thought that was fortunate. He could not imagine sending a son off to war. He could not imagine receiving that telegram.

"William?" Caroline entered slowly, taking in the fact that he was sitting nearly in the dark. The fire was out. He was slouching.

"Come in, my dear. I'm all right. I'm just brooding over this letter to Osler."

She came and draped an arm around his shoulder. "Just say what's in your heart."

"My heart says he's a damn fool for not coming back to Baltimore and dragging the dear boy with him when he had the chance. Why do people fight wars? It's all death and more death. It makes me wonder why I spent my whole life trying to save lives when men are just going to do this to one another."

"You're not telling me anything. I'm a Hampton. A daughter of the Lost Cause."

"I'm glad we didn't have a boy to lose." Then his breath hitched and he coughed a breathless fit before he caught it again. He rasped, "We may lose quite a few."

He had been operating frequently again, teaching medical students too, throwing himself into the work—the antidote for his helpless distress. Hopkins had sent quite a contingent of men, including Drs. Young, Heuer, Finney and Finney's eldest boy who'd just started medical school. They were all in various medical corps. Comparably "safe." But…good Lord.

And Cushing…gone to head the department of surgery at Brigham in Boston two years ago—too self-important to sandwich himself between Halsted at his head and Dandy at his tail—Cushing had gone off with a medical unit to France. By some bizarre quirk of fate, he'd been close by Flanders Fields.

Revere was wounded near Ypres, blown half apart by shrapnel from a German shell. Others managed to drag Revere back into a hole, then send him on a stretcher to the Dozinghem Casualty Clearance Center. American surgeons there, who knew the importance of the name Osler, sent for Cushing. Who rushed to the clearance center in an ambulance in the middle of the night in the pouring rain. This he'd gotten in a letter from Cushing—a letter devoid of any of the usual personality of past letters they'd exchanged. The facts relayed were surreal and needed no embellishment. Revere was in shock, bleeding internally. His colon was rent in multiple places. Blood in the chest. Thigh torn apart. The operation was quite hopeless. Cushing wrote, seemingly without irony: *I don't think even you could have saved him.* They buried Paul Revere's great-great-grandson wrapped in a British flag.

"I hope Osler gets some comfort out of Cushing being there."

"I imagine Revere did," Caroline said. "And that will comfort his parents."

"Caroline," he said, stricken with sorrow and a strange anxiety, "don't ever die. At least, not before me. There is nothing that would comfort me." *Nothing.*

"Oh, I imagine you'd do what all men do. Find yourself a new wife half your age to tuck a blanket over your knees and spend all your money."

"Good Lord," he sniffed, appalled, and hoping she was not serious. "What an embarrassing thought."

56

1922, April

Baltimore, Maryland

DENTISTS HONOR DR. W. S. HALSTED

National Association Presents Medal to Creator of Neuro-Regional Anaesthesia

SPEECHES FULL OF PRAISES

Dr. William S. Halsted, surgeon, scientist, and discoverer, was formally recognized as the creator of the modern method in neuro-regional anaesthesia, was presented with a gold medal by the National Dental Association and, at a dinner and meeting at the Hotel Belvedere lasting until midnight, received the homage and eulogies of men at the top of the medical and dental professions in America, who have studied at his feet and profited by his research.

More than 200 physicians and dentists were present…Throughout all the speechmaking and eulogizing there sounded again and again a note of repression, a constant reminder, expressed at times and implied at other times, that Dr. Halsted, the most modest "great scientist" who ever added a page to scientific history, was quite probably suffering under the heaping up of praise…

—*The Baltimore Sun*, Baltimore, Maryland, April 2, 1922

The Dental Association's announcement and invitation arrived in a gold-embossed envelope, addressed to Dr. and Mrs. William S. Halsted. William made the mistake of opening it in front of me. No doubt he'd rather have disposed of it clandestinely. As it was, he refused to have anything to do with "such a farce, such a load of twaddle." He threw the invitation in the trash. I didn't argue with him, even though he was being ridiculous, because he looked frightened.

He didn't go to the hospital or laboratory the morning after he received the notice, but I didn't think too much of it. Sometimes he didn't. That afternoon, Dr. Welch came to see him. I was upstairs, writing a letter to Lucy, when I heard them arguing. Shouting. William had a temper but it usually made him go very quiet. And Dr. Welch? Surely the man had never shouted before in his life.

The words were muffled, coming through the flooring, but it sounded as though William might be saying things he would certainly regret. I put on my shoes and went down to William's study. Silence had fallen by the time I opened the door. William stood by the barrister bookcase, his hand wrapped in a handkerchief; there was broken glass on the floor.

I gasped. His hands! "Are you bleeding? Let me see."

"No." He sounded furious.

Welch said, "You may punch out every pane of glass in the room. I am not taking no for answer. The arrangements have been made. Invitations sent out. For God's sake. They had a medal cast for you. In gold."

"I don't need a trinket."

"It speaks to your legacy! To the 'Halsted System.' To the supremacy of what has been achieved at the Johns Hopkins. This is emblematic of what we've striven for all these years."

"How can you ask me to do this? How can *you*? You know my reputation is a house of cards. One flick will tumble it down. My God! What if someone cites that mortifying editorial from New York? Or discovers I spent nearly two years hidden away in an asylum? That alone could discredit everything I've done since. This thing they will give me plaudits for doing, this is the thing that nearly destroyed me."

"They will not only be talking about cocaine. I've seen the program. Halsted, your achievements run the gamut—"

"I can't."

"You mean you won't."

"All right. Yes. I won't."

I marched into the room.

"Step away from that broken glass, William. You look very foolish." I put my hand on Dr. Welch's arm. "Who's going to be speaking?"

"Brun from the Dental Association. Barker, Finney, Dandy, a few others." He paused. "Me."

So it had been a long time in the works. Dr. Welch might have warned William. But, of course, that would have given him ample time to refuse.

"Hmm. I can see your concern, William. You've terrorized most of these poor surgeons in the past. Certainly they are plotting to ruin you."

"Caroline—"

"I was invited. I am going, William."

He was silent a moment. Then he unwrapped the bloodstained handkerchief and frowned. "Give me yours, Welch."

Welch handed him a clean handkerchief and William wadded it over his knuckles in a lump. I shook my head, then took it from him to make a proper bandage. Tiny cuts. Nothing serious.

"By all means, then, we must go," William muttered.

I glanced over my shoulder at Dr. Welch, who regarded us with a tender expression.

"I'll see myself out," he said, putting on his hat.

I had never been to a scientific meeting. Dr. Welch, beside us, assured me that the arrangement in the Belvedere's banquet hall was unusual. It looked more like a state dinner. The hall was crowded with tables that were set as elegantly as William would have set them himself. There was, unfortunately, a head table elevated on a dais. We would be on display. I had my arm in the crook of William's elbow, and I swore his knees buckled when we entered the room.

William and I were also elegantly decorated. He had a new suit tailored for the occasion and I wore an evening dress in navy with a splash of white across the chest. I felt like I was wearing a signboard, but William was pleased with it.

Dinner was superb and plentiful. Wine was followed by more champagne toasts than I could count. I felt a little lightheaded by the time the speeches started.

First a few dentists gave talks on the advances made possible by the neuro-regional anesthesia William had pioneered. They referred frequently to "the death of pain." William listened with a rather bilious expression, no doubt thinking of the pain he had endured. However, I, who had had no concept of the importance of William's cocaine work until now, was enthralled. It was a revolutionary contribution.

It almost made the sacrifice seem worthwhile.

Fortunately, the scientific portion of the meeting was over fairly quickly. Then William's colleagues, most of whom had been his trainees, lined up to speak. Nearly to a man, they prefaced their speeches with apologies to their mentor, who they knew must be mortified by the outpouring of praise.

He was an innovator. A brilliant technical operator. One of the most knowledgeable anatomists in the world. He would be forever remembered for his approach to mastectomy, thyroidectomy, wiring of bones, vascular surgery, intestinal surgery…the list went on. Legions of surgeons had been inspired by his insistence upon safe surgery: attention to asepsis, bloodlessness, and careful handling of tissues. Mostly, however, he was being honored as a teacher, mentor, and example to generations of American surgeons. He had a gift for identifying potential, for ferreting out special gifts in his trainees, and for guiding them towards fertile academic careers in newly burgeoning subspecialties. He taught them to teach.

I never dabbed my eyes so often in all my life.

"Young" Dr. Barker, Dr. Osler's successor, lightened the mood with a talk on "Dr. Halsted, the Athlete." He told how they climbed the capitol steps together and Dr. Barker found himself in a race he could not possibly win. When the new country club opened north of the city, Dr. Barker bullied Dr. Halsted into joining, though Halsted harumphed that he had no time for golf. It was a silly game. Then he promptly won one tournament after another.

William's ears were bright red, but he was laughing. Thank goodness.

It was Finney's speech that nearly did everyone in. Some years back, dear Finney had left the Johns Hopkins to enter private practice in Baltimore. He'd always been more of a surgeon than an academician, but so fine a surgeon William did not hold that against him. I, of course, held him in particular regard, and not just because of his care after my carriage accident. He'd also removed my appendix when it needed to come out and William refused to do it.

Dr. Finney titled his talk: "Halsted, the Professor." He began apologetically as well.

"This is what I would say, if I felt he would wish for me to say it. Dr. Halsted is the only man in his class in the world, the greatest scientist, technician, and teacher in this city or any other country."

William cleared his throat quietly. He looked humbled. A little pleased.

Finney went on to give examples of things he had learned from William. He related some funny anecdotes. A few of the stories I'd heard before, from William's point of view, a different, exasperated take. Finney was certainly softening the interactions. Or perhaps he knew William's sarcasm wouldn't translate well in this setting. At one point, Dr. Welch leaned to whisper something to William and the two men chuckled to themselves.

Finney ended with: "As a man, as an inspiring teacher, and as a scientific surgeon, he stands without peer today."

The applause was prolonged and rather deafening.

Dr. Welch concluded the evening with a few remarks about their early days in New York. Nothing that even alluded to cocaine. Only that William's promise had excited an earlier generation of giants, who were looking down now from a medical Mount Olympus, nodding with satisfaction. He closed, pointing out the lateness of the hour, saying they would not permit Dr. Halsted to respond. Anyone who had ever heard him speak at a meeting would know he never stuck to his allotted time. People laughed. I thought it the kindest thing Dr. Welch could have done.

❧

The organizers of the event had provided an automobile to bring us to and from the Belvidere. William would not purchase one of his own, a sticking point between us. He said he didn't wish to learn to drive and I would be a menace behind the wheel.

We climbed into the back seat of the hired automobile.

I sat close beside him, but didn't speak. I was a little tipsy and didn't want him to know. He must have been also, because he pulled me closer and draped his arm around my shoulder, despite the presence of the driver.

Finally, I could not stay silent.

"That was a lovely evening."

"Hmm." He was quiet a moment. Then he said, "Yes, it was."

57

1922, September

Baltimore, Maryland

DR. W.S. HALSTED DANGEROUSLY ILL

Dr. William S. Halsted, surgeon-in-chief of Johns Hopkins Hospital, is seriously ill at the institution whose name he has helped to make world famous. He has a fighting chance for recovery.

Yesterday afternoon, he was operated upon for gallstones by Dr. Mont R. Reid and Dr. George J. Heuer, both distinguished surgeons and Dr. Halsted's former pupils…

—*The Baltimore Sun*, August 26, 1922

❧

We had, neither of us, been feeling well. We had gone to High Hampton to escape the Baltimore heat. I suspected William had gone more for my sake than for his, but he wouldn't hear of sending me alone.

Perhaps we should not have gone.

Cashiers had helped me to feel better, but William lost his appetite and confessed, finally, to being in pain. I knew it was gallstones. The morning I noted a faint yellow hue in his eyes—like Uncle Kit's before he died—I gently suggested we return to Baltimore.

He told me to stay in Cashiers. I would not. He told me there was no cause to worry. I said, "I'm not worried," and sent telegrams to Dr. Heuer and Dr. Reid, commanding them to come to Baltimore at once. Those true good men were waiting at the station when the train pulled in. They did everything they could. I didn't fault them. But if only William could have operated on himself!

He suffered so much the last fortnight, rallying then fading, rallying and fading. The morphine they gave him did not touch his pain. I tried to find the vial he'd been using in High Hampton. He'd had it with him on the train. But what with rushing back and forth between the hospital and 1201 Eutaw, I couldn't find it any of the places I thought it might be. Three days before he died, it appeared at his bedside. William seemed to rest easier. Of course, by then he was near moribund from jaundice and infection. I would have liked to take the incriminating vial away afterward. The dilution marked on the label was almost laughably false. What if it was used on someone else? But I lost track of it and now it was gone.

William had asked me, as he lay dying, if I had regrets.

"None," I said.

I did not believe in deathbed confessions. They came too late and generally caused pain to the hearer. That was not how I wanted to spend our last brief moments alone.

I knew what he regretted. Promises he had not kept. Promises I had not held him to. There was no point in calling one another to task.

He would not have asked about regrets if he didn't have something that he needed to get off his chest, some apology he must feel I needed to hear.

Steeling myself for heartache, I asked, "Have you any?"

If he bemoaned the lack of the next generation of Halsteds, I would point out that children were an unknown quantity, whereas we could predict the success of his surgical heirs.

If it were the other, I could say only this: just as I had never mourned the life I might have had "if not for the war," so I could not mourn the William Halsted I had never known. I thanked God for the one I had.

He answered in a quiet, measured tone, "I regret I did not spend more time in Cashiers."

That, I was not suspecting. My throat and eyes abruptly began to ache.

"You were there every summer," I whispered.

He always claimed it rejuvenated him, that he loved the fresh air, the solitude. But he never missed his train back to Baltimore for the excuse to linger one more day. He never chose another month at High Hampton over attending a conference somewhere abroad.

"I fear I made you feel it was a gift I gave you." He paused to breathe. Labored. His face tense with effort and pain. "The gift of my time."

"It was a gift."

"Yours to me. Every moment—your gift to me."

He had tears in the corner of his eyes. I touched my handkerchief to them.

For a moment, his eyes crinkled. "You haven't lost. . ." He breathed. "That nurse's touch."

This is our calling too. To be there when they go.

He drifted back into the haze of pain and morphine and illness. Before he woke again, Dr. Welch came back into the room. Then William's brother Dick—I left them alone. I never knew if William woke to speak to his brother. Dick did not stay to speak to me. People drifted in and out and in again.

I stayed until he drew his last breath. Our gift to one another, every precious moment.

58

1922, September

Baltimore, Maryland

FUNERAL OF DR. HALSTED SET FOR THIS AFTERNOON

Funeral services for Dr. William S. Halsted, who died Thursday at the Johns Hopkins Hospital, will be held at the home, 1201 Eutaw Place, at 4 o'clock this afternoon. The body will be cremated at Loudon Park Cemetery. The ashes will be sent to New York and placed in the family vault there.

The Rev. Dr. Samuel Bushnell, of New Haven, one of Dr. Halsted's close friends and a Yale classmate, will conduct the services.

The honorary pallbearers will be Dr. William H. Welch, Dr. Howard A. Kelly, Dr. William H. Howell, Dr. John Abel, Dr. William G. MacCallum, Dr. Harvey Cushing, Henry D. Harlan, Dr. Ira Remsen, Dr. J. Whitridge Williams and Dr. Winford Smith.

The active pallbearers will be Dr. John M. T. Finney, Dr. Joseph C. Bloodgood, Dr. Hugh H. Young, Dr. George Heuer, Dr. Samuel J. Crowe, Dr. Walter Dandy, and Dr. Mont R. Reid.

—*The Baltimore Sun*, Baltimore, MD, September 9, 1922

The parlor had been transformed into a morbid crepe-draped gallery with curved rows of mismatched chairs facing a polished mahogany coffin propped on a borrowed table. A small wrinkle in the pall draped over the coffin glared at me accusingly. William would be aghast. I had been fighting an urge since entering the room to go over and straighten the pall.

My whole body ached, starting in intensity with my eyes, then my temples, my heart, and down even to my toes. I believed I could count on one hand all the times in my life that I had wept before August, and now it seemed all I did was cry.

No one would believe that I could miss him so. Were we not accustomed to being apart? No. I had never accustomed myself to his absences but had merely learned to accept them. This, I could not accept: this gathering of solemn, eminent men, faces ashen, murmuring among themselves that they could not believe it. *They* could not believe it? Tomorrow they would return to their lives, their families, their work, and live on.

Reverend Bushnell moved to the front to begin with a prayer. As he slipped past the coffin, he subtly brushed out the pall's wrinkle with his hand. Lord bless him. I thought the mourners gave a collective sigh of relief.

The prayer was beautiful.

Three of William's protegés gave eulogies—not the men I would have chosen. They revered him, of course, but these later residents tended to run together in my mind.

My favorites would always be those two from the early days: Joe and Harvey. They couldn't be more opposite. Dr. Joe Bloodgood was a dear. A quiet, unassuming family man, with a dry sense of humor, Joe worked hard and never complained. Whatever William asked of him, Joe said yes. Dr. Harvey Cushing was, in contrast, conceited, brash, obsequiously charming, and, William said, the most naturally gifted surgeon he had ever seen. Oh! How they had clashed. I'd often thought having Harvey to deal with was what it would have been like if William had had a rebellious son. Maybe that was how William saw him; maybe that was why he was so uncharacteristically patient with Harvey's faults.

I would have liked to listen to Joe reminisce and Harvey pay tribute. But it would more likely have gone the other way around.

Dr. Welch didn't speak, which may have surprised some; was there ever an occasion on which the man did not hold forth? He'd written a memorial for the newspaper, all very professional. I knew the detachment of the memorial and his silence today were hiding a broken heart.

The pallbearers lifted the coffin to take it out to the hearse. There would be no procession to the cemetery. No graveside prayer. I would leave the disposition of the ashes to William's sisters. That might seem cold, but I did not care. William was gone. An urn of ashes meant nothing to me. We had decided, in one rather grim late-night discussion at High Hampton, years ago, that his mortal remains were to reside in the Halsted family plot in New York and mine would go to the cemetery at

Trinity Church in Columbia to be with generations of Hamptons. We had even laughed about it. Much as we disavowed the sentimentality behind rotting married corpses lying together for all eternity, we both admitted to the horror of consigning our own corpse to an eternity with in-laws.

I would find him. We had found each other once, we would again.

I rose stiffly and followed the trailing honorary pallbearers. Old, old men. Giants, of course, a who's who of the world of medicine and science, but old men nevertheless. The world had moved on.

I stood in the doorway of 1201 Eutaw, pressing hands, having my cheek kissed, murmuring thank yous, listening to final words of condolence, last little bits of memory people felt the need to tell me. I thanked them all, wishing it were done.

Some drifted away, down the street, finding cars. Others gathered around the hearse, sharing memories or making plans, or perhaps talking about something else altogether. It didn't matter. The hearse pulled away and more of them dispersed.

Dr. Welch stared after the departing hearse even after it disappeared around the corner. Then he turned, slowly, and came back to the house, where I stood in the doorway. Left behind. All alone.

"A very, very good man," he said. He plunged his hand into the pocket of his coat, fumbling a moment, then pulled out a small, leather-bound book. He held it out. "I found this in my library. I hope it has meaning for you. Or might help in some way."

In Memoriam A.H.H., by Alfred, Lord Tennyson.

I looked up to search his eyes. They were red-rimmed, a bit glazed.

"Thank you." The words were heartfelt, but I could not help grumbling. "William said Osler could be discreet."

Dr. Welch's lips twitched. "He threatened to wring Osler's neck." Then he cupped my hands in his. "William once said you were 'Romance' itself. You saved him. I hope you know that."

He released me to put his hand, once again, into his pocket. He pulled out a vial of morphine and placed it in my palm. "I don't know if you've been looking for this. I didn't want to destroy it if you were. But I will."

I blinked at him, relieved, and handed it back. "Yes. Please." I let out a long, heavy sigh. Even now, our thoughts were centered on this. On hiding this. For William's sake. William's peace. I wondered, with Dr.

Osler gone, if anyone else knew. I supposed Osler had been discreet when it mattered. William's legacy was safe.

"Where was it?"

"In his slippers box. In his study. He sent me to fetch it. He was in pain, but didn't want to ask for the dose he needed."

"I worried that was the case." So high a tolerance would raise eyebrows. The flick that could topple the house of cards. "I looked for it. To bring it to him." I gave him a wry look. "His study? I'm surprised Miss Stokes let you in."

"Ha! So was I."

We were quiet then. Dr. Welch looked to be struggling to find the right words, but he was not a man to leave things unsaid.

"My dear, without you, we would have lost him." His eyes watered. "He would not have survived another stint at Butler. I can't pretend to know what you endured, fighting this alongside him, but I do know this: all that the world owes to him…it owes also to you."

WIDOW OF SURGEON DIES

Mrs. Caroline Hampton Halsted is Victim of Pneumonia.

Mrs. Caroline Hampton Halsted, widow of Dr. William Stewart Halsted, former surgeon-in-chief of Johns Hopkins Hospital, died of pneumonia at noon yesterday in Johns Hopkins Hospital. Her husband died less than three months ago.

Death followed an illness of only a week. Mrs. Halsted is believed to have been so weakened by attendance upon Dr. Halsted during his illness that when she contracted pneumonia she was unable to resist the disease. Before her marriage, she was Miss Caroline Hampton of Columbia, S. C. Later she was a nurse at Johns Hopkins Hospital.

—*The Baltimore Sun*, Baltimore, MD., November 28, 1922

Sir William Osler was the Professor of Medicine in the Universities of McGill, Pennsylvania, Johns Hopkins, and Oxford in brilliant succession. His library of rare books on the history of medicine, collected in Oxford, came to McGill after his death, and Dr. William Francis, Osler's cousin and literary executor, came with them...Among the treasures in his care was a small black book closed with a lock and key of silver. Osler had advised Francis that its contents (he called them the "secret history") should not be disclosed until the 100th anniversary of the Johns Hopkins Hospital in 1989. But Francis, as literary executor, decided otherwise....

—Pennfield, Wilder, "Halsted of Johns Hopkins. The Man and His Problem as Described in the Secret Records of William Osler," *Journal of the American Medical Society*, 210(12): 2214-2218, 1969.

Citations for Archival Material

1. Epigrams for Chapters 1, 16, 19, 20, 34, 41, 49 are from letters found in the William Stewart Halsted Collection at The Alan Mason Chesney Medical Archive, Johns Hopkins at Mount Washington.

2. Epigram for Chapter 12 is a nursing school application for Caroline Hampton from the Medical Center Archives of New York-Presbyterian/Weill Cornell Medicine.

3. Epigram for Chapter 18 is from a letter found in the Sir William Osler Collection at the Osler Library of the History of Medicine, McGill University.

4. Epigram for Chapter 21 is excerpted from a letter quoted in Sabin, Florence R., "Biographical Memoir of Franklin Paine Mall, 1862-1917," *National Academy of Sciences of the United States of America, Vol. XVI – Third Memoir*, 1934, p.84

5. Epigrams for Chapters 35 and 36 are from letters found in the Sally Baxter Hampton papers at the South Caroliniana Library, University of South Carolina.

6. Epigram for Chapter 48 is from a letter found in the Harvey Williams Cushing Papers from the Beinecke Rare Book and Manuscript Library, Yale University.

7. Epigram for Chapter 46 is excerpted from a letter quoted in *William Steward Halsted. Surgeon* by W.G. MacCallum, Baltimore: The Johns Hopkins Press, 1930.

8. Sources for other epigrams are cited within the text.

Acknowledgments

I am grateful to all the kind, knowledgeable librarians and archivists who have helped me pull together the resources needed for this book. Particular thanks go to Andy Harrison at The Alan Mason Chesney Medical Archives of Johns Hopkins; Abby Cole at the South Caroliniana Library, University of South Carolina; Casey Thomas and Lily Szczgiel at the Osler Library of the History of Medicine, McGill University; Elizabeth Shepard and Amanda Garfunkel at the Medical Center Archives at New York-Presbyterian/Weill Cornell Medicine; and Genevieve Coyle and Casey Thomas at the Yale University/Beinecke Library.

This novel has been through many iterations and I would especially like to thank my intrepid family members and a physician/writer friend, David Hudacek, who waded through the first drafts. Invaluable editorial assistance was received from Michele Rubin and Carissa Knickerbocker.

In any work of biographical fiction, there will be liberties taken, but I have striven to stay as close to the historical record as possible. However, in order not to be haunted by Caroline's ghost, I have to confess that although Halsted *was* in New Orleans at a surgical conference when Caroline's riding accident occurred, his foray into Storytown is completely fictional.

Finally, I'd like to thank my husband, Brad Asher, for convincing me not to be intimidated by archival research, for patiently reading every messy manuscript I've asked him to look at, and for supporting me unreservedly. I'd like to promise that I'll start doing my share of the cooking now, but I'd be lying.